Dear reader,

Thank you for joining me again in Rose Hill—the fictional town based on a very real town where I grew up spending my summer vacations.

This time we follow Rhys and Tabby, a couple I can't stop thinking about. Their story touches on so many of my favorite components in a romance book: love, loss, tension, forgiveness, and that soulmate forever kind of connection that makes my chest hurt to read about.

I wrote this story during a rather blue time in my life and in turn feel particularly attached to these people and this place. This book will forever be very special to me.

Basically, I poured a lot of love into this one. I hope you can feel it.

xo,

ALSO BY ELSIE SILVER

Chestnut Springs

Flawless

Heartless

Powerless

Reckless

Hopeless

Gold Rush Ranch

Off to the Races

A Photo Finish

The Front Runner

A False Start

Rose Hill

Wild Love

Wild Eyes

Wild Side

WILD SIDE

ELSIE SILVER

Bloom books

Cover design by Mary at Books and Moods
Cover images © Alx/Adobe Stock, Hermit Crab Designs/Shutterstock, VCoscaron/Shutterstock, Fourseasons/iStock, Leontura/iStock
Map illustration by Laura Boren/Sourcebooks

Published by Bloom Books, an imprint of Sourcebooks
P.O. Box 4410, Naperville, Illinois 60567–4410
(630) 961-3900
sourcebooks.com

Cataloging-in-Publication data is on file with the Library of Congress.

Printed and bound in Canada.
MBP 10 9 8 7 6 5 4 3 2 1

For anyone who has loved someone not because they are perfect but because you manage to find beauty in all their shades of gray.

And for Penny (16) and Twiggy (14). My two sweet canine companions who I basically grew up with. They were there for it all—college, marriage, a baby. They also slept curled at my feet through the writing of eleven whole books and half of this one. They say that your dog is your best friend for a short time but that you are their best friend for their whole life...and I say that makes me pretty damn lucky.

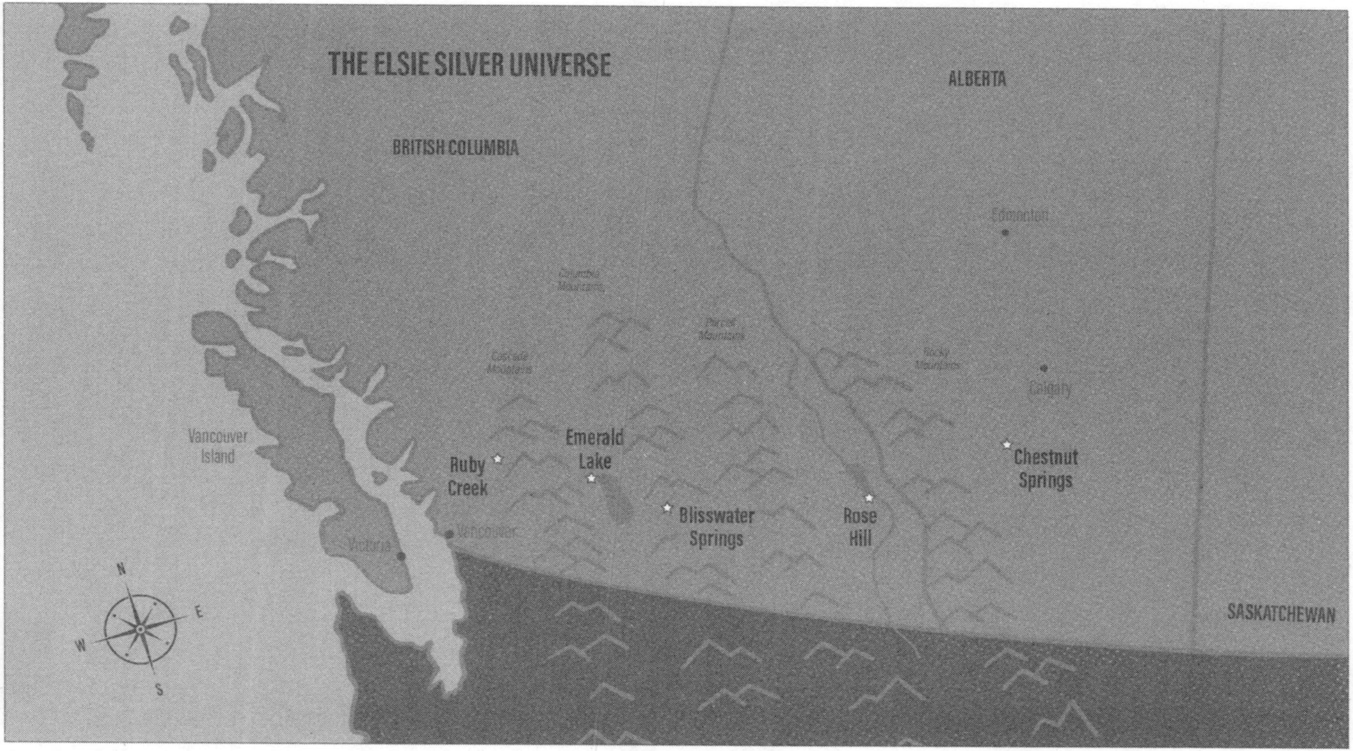
THE ELSIE SILVER UNIVERSE
BRITISH COLUMBIA
ALBERTA
SASKATCHEWAN
Edmonton
Calgary
Columbia Mountains
Purcell Mountains
Cascade Mountains
Rocky Mountains
Vancouver Island
Victoria
Vancouver
Ruby Creek
Emerald Lake
Blisswater Springs
Rose Hill
Chestnut Springs
N
E
S
W

CONTENT WARNING

This book contains references to addiction (discussed), drug use (off-page), death by overdose (off-page), and themes of child welfare, abuse/neglect (off-page). It is my hope that I have handled these topics with the care and attention they deserve.

READER NOTE

I am not a lawyer, but I consulted one on the legalities mentioned in this book. For the sake of the story, some liberties have been taken.

To ensure that the themes in this book have been handled with the care they deserve, a clinical therapist has been hired as an early reader and consultant throughout the writing process.

CHAPTER 1

Rhys

I hear the doorbell. And I ignore it. I don't want whatever they're selling.

So I continue surfing through the options of TV shows to watch next. Nothing appeals to me. *Ted Lasso* left me in a slump, and being too injured to work out has me bored.

Now there's three strong knocks at the door. And I still don't want to answer it. I come to this place to be left alone, so I pretend I don't hear it. Door-to-door people always go away, eventually.

But not this person.

Now they knock five times.

Pissed off now, I push to stand and ignore the sharp twinge in my knee as I march across the open living space.

"Whatever it is, I'm not interested—" I yank the front door open, but I come eye-to-eye with absolutely no one. Just a clear view of the front street.

"Hi. I'm Tabitha." The firm voice comes from below me, and I drop my chin to follow the sound. "Rhys, right?"

There's a woman standing on my front doorstep. She has dark hair, nearly black. The onyx slashes of her eyebrows frame narrowed chocolate eyes that are ringed with a thick fringe of lashes. She's short—next to me, most people are—but there's something about the way she carries herself that feels tall.

She has a presence.

I say nothing, but she sticks her hand out to shake mine anyway. I stare at it, not wanting to be rude, but also wondering what the hell she wants. This place is my haven. No one knows me in Canada.

When I'm in Emerald Lake, no one bugs me.

And that's how I like it.

"Hi? Hello?" She bobs her hand again, calling me out on the fact that I've stood here glaring at her and not made a single move. "If English isn't your first language, I have some passable French. Otherwise, I'll pull my phone out to translate."

My lips flatten, and I reach forward to wrap my hand around her small one. "I speak English," I mutter as I meet her eyes once more. "I just wasn't expecting anyone."

I can feel the calluses on her palms as she grips my hand. Hard. It's a real, proper, honest handshake. "Who doesn't love a surprise, am I right?"

"Me. I don't love surprises." Her eyes don't leave mine, and I get the sense she's sizing me up. Judging my worthiness. For what, I have no clue.

We continue staring and shaking hands tightly, even though at this point, the custom has dragged on for longer than necessary.

"Well, surprise!" she announces suddenly. "I'm your new tenant's sister, and I'm currently helping her move in. I need to have a chat with you while she's out."

I drop her hand and blink. Her tone makes me feel like I'm in trouble. All I wanted was someone unobtrusive to live next door and maintain the place during my stretches away. Now I have some tiny terror on my front step, looking like she's ready to interrogate me.

"Invite me in. We'll cover our bases, and I'll be on my merry way."

She smiles now.

And it's fucking blinding. It's not demure or shy. It's a weapon, and she knows exactly what she's doing by pulling it out on me.

Before, I was quiet because I'm always suspicious of people who randomly show up at my door. Now I'm quiet because my brain is short-circuiting, and my eyes are wandering. Wandering over shiny strands of dark hair, tan skin, and the feminine flare of her hips.

Yeah. Tabitha, sister of my new tenant, is hot, looks like she thinks I might have bodies buried in my basement, and has a mean handshake.

Strangely, I'm into it.

So I step aside and gesture her in.

For a flash, she softens, a relieved smile touching her full lips as she wipes her palms nervously against acid-washed jeans. Her chin dips as she steps into the foyer with a muted, "Thanks."

I muster a nod before closing the door and gesturing her through to the kitchen. The windows on this side of the A-frame face the lake. It's a stunning view, and I can't blame her for stopping to admire it.

"Beautiful."

I watch her for a beat, eyes trailing her profile with a level of interest that I don't bother hiding. She carries her shoulders tall, plush lips slightly parted. "It is."

My gaze stalls out on her mouth. A sly grin twists those lips as she turns to me with a quirked brow. She returns my once-over just as blatantly.

"A man of few words, huh?"

"Guess so," I respond, turning my back as I turn to open the fridge. "Drink?"

"Nah. I won't be that long." I can hear the amusement in her voice as she tugs out a stool at the island.

I take out a can of soda water and crack it, leaning against the counter behind me to face her. She's folded her hands, fingers woven together, and pressed her lips in a tight line.

"So..." The word trails off, and I wait.

And I wait.

I take a casual sip of my bubbly water and set it on the counter beside me.

She continues staring at me, and I'm not oblivious to the way her eyes have shifted, following my arms as I cross them in front of me and take her in.

"So," I say back, with a small twitch of my lips.

She sniffs and straightens, eyes flitting to the side and back. "I'm just going to come out with it. Erika has not had an easy go of it. Her stories are not mine to share. I just need to know that she and her son, Milo, will be safe here."

I shift slightly. "Okay. My home base is out of the country, and I'm only here now and then. There's an alarm system though."

"That's not the kind of safe I mean." Her teeth strum at her bottom lip before she sighs. "Listen, I know I'm overstepping, but my sister is just finally in a good place, and I don't know what she would or wouldn't... Ugh." The woman runs an agitated hand through her hair. "I hate myself for asking this, and she'd fucking kill me, but...if you have any drugs stronger than Tylenol, can you please put them somewhere that no one would suspect?"

My brows drop, and I lean forward. "What?"

"Prescription drugs. I want to make sure she won't have access to them."

"She'll be living next door. Not with me."

Tabitha shrugs and looks away again. "She's charming and beautiful and finally back on track. Never say never."

This woman has no clue how deep my trust issues go if she thinks I have designs on my new tenant. "I'm not planning on pursuing your sister."

She flinches but doesn't hesitate to look me dead in the eye when she says, "Well, that plan might be one-sided."

"Are you..." I trail off, unsure of what to say. I have never had a more bizarre conversation with a perfect stranger in my life.

"I am being a snoopy, overprotective sister who has listened to her gush about you for two days. Just nod your head if you understand me, and we can agree to never talk about this again."

I spent all of maybe thirty minutes around Erika when I first showed her the place. And a few more when I gave her the keys and met her son. She seemed accommodating about managing the mail situation along with the yard and gardens. She was nice. Okay, really nice.

Too nice?

And her kid was cute.

But my head definitely didn't go *there*.

Still, I nod.

Tabitha's palm slaps against the granite countertop, and a triumphant grin emerges on her face. "Excellent. Great. Good talk." She slides off the stool, but not before taking one longing glance back over the space. "This is a nice kitchen. Nothing better than cooking with a view."

"You like to cook?"

A soft smile touches her lips now. "You could say that."

I move past the island, padding across the hardwood floors, drawn to her chaos and unpredictability. But she's already walking toward the door.

Blowing out the way she blew in. Confident and direct but also… tentative.

You could say that.

It makes me wonder what's written between the lines of that response. This entire encounter also makes me wonder about her sister's story.

"Should I be worried about her? Your sister. As a tenant?"

After toeing on her sandals, she straightens and faces me once more. The evening sun filters in from the windows surrounding the front door, casting her features in a warm glow. Her cheeks have a pink tint, like she's embarrassed for barging in here and oversharing. For interfering.

"She's a girl who got injured playing volleyball in high school and was prescribed something she shouldn't have. She's been low. Really low. But she's healthy now. She's gotten help. I swear. She's a good mom. And she'll be a good tenant. I promise."

There's a plea in her eyes. Determination in the set of her jaw. And underneath it all, I'm too fucking soft to push back. If she needs help this desperately, I can give it.

"Okay." I dip my chin and shove my hands into the pockets of my gray sweats. We've all hit rough patches. Far be it from me to hold that over the head of a woman I barely know.

"But…"

I glance back up slowly, not liking the sound of that *but*.

"If—and this is a big *if*—if she ever falls behind on rent, can you please call me? Day, night, whenever. I want her somewhere safe. I want a roof over her head. I want Milo happy and safe. I will pay if it comes to it."

She slips a business card from her back pocket and holds it out to me. I reach for it—a little too eagerly. My fingers pinch the card stock, and I can see *the Bighorn Bistro* printed on it, but when I go to pull, she doesn't let go.

My eyes snap to hers, and I can see the ferocity burning

in them. She holds her opposite hand up, pinky finger extended. "Pinky swear."

"Pinky swear?"

This encounter just keeps getting stranger.

"Yes. Pinky swear to me that you will call me if there's a problem."

I hold my pinky up with a deep chuckle. "You know these aren't legally binding, right?"

Her finger curls around mine as her eyes point like arrows in my direction. "I know, but only a total asshole breaks a pinky promise."

The woman is dead serious. And I'm too off-kilter to deny her.

"I pinky promise," I reply gruffly.

She watches me for a beat, as though assessing the truthfulness of my promise. Then she nods and draws away. Without another word, she pulls the front door open and saunters out of my house. And I just stand there, arm propped on the doorframe, trying to wrap my head around that conversation.

Around that woman.

The one who, farther down the front walkway, turns to peek back over her shoulder.

For a few beats, I catch her looking. Or she catches me looking. To be honest, I don't care which one it is.

I just know that usually I go out of my way to hide from too much attention.

But I don't mind the way she looks at me.

CHAPTER 2

Tabitha

TWO YEARS LATER...

THE YELLOW DOOR BEFORE ME IS ALTOGETHER TOO CHEERful for a day like today.

Scuffs near the keyhole tell a story of full hands and rushed attempts to open the door. There's a pink splatter over the canary gold at the bottom. Likely the only evidence of a grape-juice-box-meets-the-ground type of crime scene.

Milo loves grape juice.

His mom does too.

Did.

Erika loved—past tense—grape juice.

Heat builds behind my lashes, and I blink away the tears. Crying won't see me through this job. Since we got the call last night, everyone around me has been crying. I can't start too.

If I start, I worry I won't know how to stop. Then shit won't get done. And that's my job right now.

Take care of her little boy. Navigate my parents' grief. Run my restaurant. Get shit done.

Numb is preferable. Especially having just left the morgue.

So I push the urge to cry aside, roll from toe to heel a few times, as though I might be able to rock myself forward, into motion.

Toward my dead sister's abandoned home to collect her belongings.

I both need to go in there and dread going in there. My lips twist into a sardonic grimace. Erika would have gotten a real kick out of seeing me wringing my hands on her front step. Too chickenshit to even face what she left behind. I suspect she's somewhere watching me with a grin on her face right now. She'd say something like, *You just identified my body. Vampirism would need more than twenty minutes to take effect.*

I chuckle at my own made-up joke.

She wasn't perfect—hell, I'm not either—but her dark sense of humor was spot-on.

"Okay, Erika, I'm going. I'm going," I mutter in an amused tone, digging out the spare key I've been holding on to for two years.

I had it made when I helped her move in here and haven't needed to use it until now. Mostly because I thought she was doing okay. I've always known addiction is a lifelong battle. I just thought she was holding the line.

I thought wrong.

The key clicks when I slide it in, and the door gives way when I grip the handle and press my thumb onto the lever. Sucking in a deep breath, I wait to see if any strong smells register. Nothing comes.

Judgmental little bitch.

I can hear Erika taunting me, clear as day. Somehow, this imaginary interaction brings me a sense of comfort. As a kid, she'd have killed me for going into her room. Borrowing her clothes or makeup always ended in a cat fight.

But we also always made up.

I chuckle darkly and shake my head. "Okay, sissy." My arm straightens as I push the door open. "I'm here, and I'm going to take your clothes and jewelry, and there's nothing you can do about it this time."

Milo will want her things one day. I want him to have memories of her. Good ones.

With that in my head, my foot finally leaves the ground, and I move to step into the house.

But a deep foreboding voice brings me up short, and I freeze. "What the fuck do you think you're doing?"

My heart rate accelerates as I slowly turn away from the door. And then my eyes land on him.

Rhys.

Her landlord. The one who evicted her without a second fucking thought. One late payment, and he didn't even bother to contact me. Instead, he gave her a week to clear out.

In a mad dash to keep a roof over her head, I swooped in

and took Milo so she could focus on viewing new places in the area. But instead, she spiraled.

It wasn't the first time she'd struggled with housing. When our parents kicked her out, she went on a binge that landed her in the hospital, clinging to life. And it's been something that destabilized her ever since then. The worst was before Milo—she'd hit rock bottom after being kicked out of a house by her roommates.

I spent three sleepless days frantically searching Rose Hill for her. At the hospital. At the local police detachment. In the local shelter. Under the bridge that leads out of town. In that one campground near the river our parents always told us to stay away from. Once, when I found her dirty, and downtrodden, and slumped in a back alley, I promised myself I'd never let her end up there again.

It's an image I've never been able to scrub from my mind.

But this time, I didn't find her at all. Someone else did. She was in the basement of a house owned by people who didn't even know her. There was mention of her arriving with a man that no one was able to identify. How she ended up at their party will always be a mystery to me.

What isn't a mystery to me is that *he's* the one who put her there. Rhys is the one who upended her fragile balance by kicking her out. It's like she hadn't even bothered looking for a place. She'd given up. Given in. And if he'd told me she was struggling like he promised, maybe she'd still be here.

In an instant, my urge to cry evaporates. Instead, the urge to rage on the hulking man standing on the front lawn, staring daggers in my direction, overwhelms me.

If Milo didn't need me, I'd kill this big fucker with my bare hands and march myself to prison, convinced that I'd fulfilled my life's purpose.

For now, I opt to clench my molars and glare back as I bite out as few words as possible. "I won't take long." I have three days to pack up all my big sister's possessions, and then I'll never have to set foot in this godforsaken town again.

The man's head tilts, and a loose piece of dark hair flops over his forehead. It's too long, and he's used a touch too much product in an attempt to slick it back, making it appear almost wet. I focus on how unappealing that one lock of hair is so that my eyes don't look at the rest of him.

The impossibly wide shoulders, the towering height, the dangerously dark eyes, the black tattoos that curl over his forearms, covering him from his wrist all the way up to where his T-shirt sits. It makes you wonder where else they go.

Yes, everything about this man screams sex.

I already knew that he was physically appealing. But now I also know that he's indirectly responsible for Erika's overdose. And I hate him for it.

"You can't go in there." His tone hedges no room for debate.

"Legally, I can go in there."

He crosses his arms, which, with the size of his biceps, looks borderline uncomfortable. "Your name isn't on the lease, and I never gave you a key. I doubt Erika did either." A tendon pulses in his jaw, and the disdain in his gaze intensifies my anger.

"You doubt Erika did?" I repeat the words and nearly

laugh as they leave my lips. "You've got a lot of nerve acting like you speak for her."

"Says the woman who just announced she was going in to steal jewelry. We both know she wouldn't want you in there."

My mouth pops open. How dare he pretend he knows what terms my sister and I were on? "Are you fucking kidding me right now?"

He stands taller, like a sentinel guarding a castle. It infuriates me. Where was this sense of contractual integrity when he booted her without honoring the pinky promise we made?

That agreement may have been childish, but it meant something to me.

The asshole's facial expression gives nothing away. His delivery is perfectly even. "Not a joke in sight. If you want to enter the unit, you'll need Erika's permission."

I bark out a loud, disbelieving laugh and shake my head at him. "Right, well, since you're the Erika expert now, I'll just wait here while you head down to the morgue and ask her permission."

The mountain of a man flinches as though I slapped him, but then he takes a stuttered step forward, eyes searching. "Come again?"

"My sister is dead."

God, saying it out loud is a shot to the heart. My voice cracks, but I forge ahead.

"My emotional bandwidth is shot, and my desire to talk to you is nonexistent. I'm next of kin, so if you want to call the cops and have me removed from the property"—I wave a dramatic hand over the front lawn as if welcoming a crowd to a show—"please be my guest."

With that, I spin and barge into the house. I'm about to slam the door in his face with a flourish when he's suddenly there, crowding me, towering over me, one massive hand gripping the door and keeping it from hitting him in the face.

I can feel the heat of his body, sense the threat in his stance, and smell the cinnamon scent in his hair product.

"And Milo?" His voice is all gravel, and I swear there's a threat in his rough tone. One I don't fucking appreciate.

But I also recognize his concern for the small boy because I feel it too. Acutely.

I let my eyes crash against his, both confused and agitated by his distress.

What I see in his dark irises is an apocalypse of storms. Fire and brimstone. And I'm certain mine are no better. As his gaze traces my face, I let my hatred take center stage on every feature, wanting to show him I'm not standing down, no matter how much he stomps around like he's the fucking man of the house or whatever this territorial show is.

I decide on as little information as possible, but enough to get him to leave. "Milo is happy and safe."

A brief flash of relief touches the man's features as he retreats incrementally.

A soft moment.

A perfect spot for me to strike.

"I pinky promise," I add cynically.

And then I slam the door in his face.

CHAPTER 3

Tabitha

I WAKE UP TO SOMETHING NUDGING MY FOOT, BUT I'M TOO fuzzy-headed to be all that bothered by the sensation. With a groan, I roll to my side. The bed is unusually hard, but I'm more worried about the way my stomach flips over on itself when I move.

A deep "Hey" filters from above as my consciousness finds some semblance of footing. Awareness seeps in slowly.

Boxing up my sister's belongings.

Scotch.

Uncovering photos of us together as kids.

More scotch.

Finding her stash of recovery coins. *Two years clean.*

A lot more scotch.

Mathematically, my body must be at least ten percent scotch right now. The other ninety percent is self-loathing.

It only worsens when I brave opening my eyes and see

the scruffy mountain man looking me over. The dark slashes of his brows only enhance the stony scowl on his face.

I peek to the side, and it turns out I'm not in a bed at all. I am flat on my back on the living room rug, surrounded by partially filled cardboard boxes. I'd held it together through the first day of packing. Day two fucked me though.

I throw an arm over my face as if that will keep him from staring at me. "What the hell are you doing here?"

"We need to talk."

"Hard pass." The smell of my breath bouncing off the crook of my arm makes me want to hurl all over the floor.

This is not my finest moment.

"You can leave now. Thanks. Bye," I add, because Rhys hasn't moved, and I think he might be too big and dumb to pick up on the dismissal.

"No."

From over the ridge of my arm, I watch him take two long strides and plunk himself down on the couch like he owns the place.

Okay. He *does* own the place. But he's…I don't know. He just seems a little too comfortable here. Waltzing in. Lounging on my sister's couch. Waking me up.

It makes me think he spent time here. With her. She spoke of him like she worshipped the ground he walked on, so it only makes sense. And it also makes the betrayal of him kicking her out that much worse.

Pain shoots through my head as I stand, but I ignore it. I refuse to appear weak in his presence. If I can hold my own in a kitchen full of chef-sized egos, I can keep it together around this asshole.

Breathing deep and even, I turn my back on him and walk toward the kitchen where the offending scotch bottle sits—mocking me. I pour myself a water, forcing my hands to be steady, because I can feel Rhys watching me. Analyzing me.

I can tell myself he's big and dumb all I want, but it only takes a few beats of getting lost in his eyes to see the intelligence in their depths.

"Rough night?"

I snort as I stare down at the glass of water. I know I need it, but I also know there's an excellent chance it will come straight back up.

"I'm packing up my dead sister's belongings. Is it supposed to be fun and easy? If I wanted your opinion on how I should cope, I'd ask."

The glass touches my lips, and I take a small sip before turning to face him. His heavy shoulders are pitched forward, elbows slung on his knees, white papers pinched between his massive fingers.

I pop a hip and glare back at him. "Was the part about leaving confusing for you?"

"It was crystal clear. I just don't care."

"Landlords need to give twenty-four hours' notice before entering the property. I checked the rental board website."

His jaw ticks. "You're not my tenant."

My teeth grind. "Oh, fuck off. I'm already down enough. I don't need you here torturing me with your presence. In fact, you've got a lot of gall showing your face to me at all. I'll be done today and out of here before dark. You'll have your place back. Now go."

"*I'm* the one with gall? That's rich coming from you. Haven't visited in two years and *now* you're concerned?"

I recoil the second his words land. He doesn't need to add a single other word for me to read between the lines. Interpret his sentiment. *Blame myself.*

The thought that Erika might still be alive if I'd been a more present sister has tortured me for days. She always told me Rhys valued his privacy and asked me not to come here, and I'd respected that. I tried not to pry, and I wanted so badly for her to feel some modicum of control over her life.

But we still saw each other often. She came to Rose Hill to visit me even though our parents had cut her off. I looked after Milo frequently and worked my schedule at the bistro around being an extra set of hands for her, so she didn't have to care for a toddler all alone. The five-hour drive didn't stop us.

They say it takes a village, and Erika didn't have one even though she needed it. So I became her village, taking on as much as I could. I grew to love that kid like he was my own.

My parents keep telling me I went above and beyond for her...but wondering if I could have done more will haunt me forever.

Those last few times she'd asked me to take Milo, I'd been more exasperated than usual. She'd also been asking for my help more and more frequently.

I was tired. Overworked, overwhelmed, and low on cash.

I'd started to feel taken advantage of, and I began asking a lot of questions about why she needed me quite so often. I think I had an inkling *something* was off…but I hadn't followed up very thoroughly.

My eyes burn, and I hate myself for it. "Get. Out."

Rhys has the good sense to drop his gaze, but I follow his line of vision and watch the tendons in his hands flex as he toys with the sheets of paper that hang from his fingers. "I can't. I have to give you these. And I need to know where Milo is."

I bristle, knowing I'll protect Milo at all costs. Always have. Always will. "You don't need to know shit—"

"This is a copy of Erika's will."

My eyes roll now. I love my sister, but the idea of her having a will is truly absurd. Every time I brought it up to her, she'd tell me she didn't plan on dying. She was a lot of things, but a planner was not one of them. "Bullshit."

What a weird fucking flex. I take another sip of water and shake my head as I set the glass back onto the counter.

The seconds stretch in an awkward silence, and Rhys says nothing.

The less he says, the more anxious I become.

Nausea hits me, but I get the sense that it's not because of the water. It's from whatever is about to come out of his mouth.

"I'm Milo's legal guardian. It's all here in writing. Signed."

He holds the papers out as though they're proof. As though he has some claim over my nephew. The one *I've* helped raise for three years.

It's a cruel joke. It has to be. This guy is toying with me. He's got to be.

A rude scoff tumbles from my lips. "Get fucked."

Rhys's face remains impassive. He just stares at me, and his cool, unaffected demeanor does nothing but fire me up. I storm across the room in my rumpled T-shirt and second-day leggings to go toe-to-toe with him.

In a furious and immature moment, I kick my socked foot against his bare one like he did to wake me up.

But harder.

He doesn't flinch. He just tilts his head back and meets my eyes with his dark ones. They're full of challenge. Hard like stone.

"Listen up, asshole. This is one sick fucking joke. You think this is funny? I'm devastated. I just lost my big sister, and you waltz in here to play inheritance games with me?" I rip the papers from his hand. The sound of the sheets crumpling is the only noise in the room besides my heavy breaths.

"Are you devastated though? Seems quite the one-eighty."

A pained moan lurches from my throat. The sound is like what you'd make after falling from a tree as a child. All the air knocked from your lungs when your bones thud against the hard ground.

The way his words land feels much the same.

"You don't even know her."

"Actually, I do." His gaze bounces between my eyes, searching for a reaction. Like he's hoping to hurt me.

Understanding dawns on me. "Were you...were you together? She never told me." Then fury hits, knowing that he tossed her out. "You fucked her and then fucked her over?"

His brows furrow, and he appears offended. "We weren't—"

"You don't know me." I cut him off, too furious to listen to another word out of his shapely mouth. The thought that I once found him appealing only adds to my nausea. "You don't know me at all. You clearly have no idea how close Erika and I were. Or the things I've done to keep my sister safe. The relationships I've tarnished to take her side. The debt I've put myself in to get her treatment. The sleep I've lost taking care of that little boy so that she could have some reprieve."

I'm shaking from head to toe when I take the sheets of paper and toss them across the room. They float and scatter, but Rhys and I stay locked in on each other. "I *love* my sister, and having to stand here and endure you implying otherwise is, quite frankly, almost worse than the pain of her death. Especially when it's *your* fault. She wouldn't have been out on the street getting back into that shit if you hadn't evicted her."

"I did—"

"No. Shut up. That little boy? He's *mine*. He's all I have left of her. So you can take your bullshit contract and fuck all the way off. Now get out. I never want to see you again."

The tendon in Rhys's jaw flexes, like I've pissed him off by relaying the truth. And when he stands, I don't back down, even though the power dynamic has dramatically shifted. It's hard to look imposing when you barely come up to a man's sternum.

Especially one who exudes the type of raw power this one does.

But I don't care. I stand my ground—arms crossed, eyes narrowed, nostrils flaring.

He steps around me, but he's too broad to avoid contact altogether. His upper arm brushes against my shoulder, and a shiver races down my spine. I tell myself the reaction is utter revulsion. Because being attracted to him would be the ultimate betrayal.

He pads away with stiff movements, head held high, and my eyes wander over his body. His muscular frame shows not a single sign of guilt as he slides his feet into a pair of plain black Vans.

"You still need to read the papers, Tabitha," is what he tosses over his shoulder before leaving.

The minute the door clicks shut, I rush to the pieces of paper and sink to the floor with them. I gather them up, and my eyes race over the lines. Blue ink in the exact shape of my sister's signature flows across a simple, but final, black stripe. I run the pads of my fingers over the indent there, reveling in the connection. Knowing she touched where I'm touching now.

But then the reality of this contract sinks in.

It has me running to the bathroom and throwing myself down in front of the toilet as my stomach turns over.

And it's not because of the scotch.

It's because the will looks awfully authentic.

CHAPTER 4

Rhys

I watched Erika's sister pack boxes of sentimental belongings into a U-Haul with sagging shoulders and a pale face. I saw her open the front door for a local women's shelter and let them take away the furniture that was left behind. Then I listened to her tell herself, "Toughen up, because crying won't solve anything," through the flimsy wall that divides the duplex.

And since she left three days ago, I have felt like a pile of human garbage. And not only because I'm gutted over the shocking news of Erika's death. But because I was a fucking dick to her sister.

When Tabitha Garrison showed up on my front doorstep, I was convinced she was just as problematic as Erika made her out to be.

But now? Having watched her?

The woman is heartbreak personified, and I'm not convinced of anything.

Which is why when my lawyer called me saying that Tabitha requested I come see Milo in Rose Hill, I begrudgingly obliged. Still, I decided to lean into the element of surprise and show up unannounced so that I can get a *real* read on the situation.

I know what it's like to grow up without parents—without family—and I can't in good conscience take a child away from his relatives without seeing the situation with my own two eyes.

But I also know that Erika was clear about wanting Milo with me—even if that meant taking him back to my home base in Florida.

And that's why I'm on the road to a small town called Rose Hill. That's why I'm doing any of this at all.

For Milo.

The little boy with big dark curls and even bigger blue eyes. He reminds me just a little too much of myself—his entire situation altogether too close to my own.

My navigation pipes up with "Your destination is ahead on the right," which has me pressing the brake pedal to slow down. I don't want to roll right up to Tabitha's house. I want a minute to compose myself. To look around and get the lay of the land.

I'd be lying if I said I wasn't here searching for reasons why this is a terrible place for Milo to stay. But the drive wasn't terrible at all. In fact, the town center is downright charming. Quieter, with less glitz and glam than Emerald Lake.

This is a true mountain town, shadowed by jagged,

rocky peaks above, built around the still, dark-blue water of the lake below. It's rugged and wild, and I bet it gets a fuck-ton of snow in the winter. Even now, in June, there's a slight chill in the breeze as I step out of my vehicle.

I open the rear door of my truck and grab my worn denim jacket, weighing whether it's necessary. Eventually, I rationalize that the temperature is just on the edge of needing it.

Deep down, I know that I'm putting off walking the half block up to Tabitha's house to face an uncomfortable situation.

I grumble and shake my head at myself, then press the lock button on my key fob before turning away and beginning my approach. Trees line the street, their fresh leaves a vibrant green. The sidewalk beneath my feet shows the cracks of time, the odd broken piece where a root has breached the surface. The neighborhood isn't new, but it's established. Well-loved.

Every home on the street displays signs of pride and attention, and it makes me wonder if Tabitha's matches the same level of care. Can a woman who works as obsessively as Erika told me she does have time to keep a yard as meticulous as the others?

If she didn't have time for her sister, she couldn't have had time for that kind of thing.

Before I can even see the property, I can hear it. I can hear *him*.

It hits me hard in the chest, my throat clogging with emotion as the sound filters to my ears.

Laughter.

A little boy's *and* a woman's. One deeper and raspier, the other a high-pitched giggle. And it's a giggle I know well.

Because he does it with me too.

The woman's laughter sounds a little too much like Erika on a good day, and the memory has me moving toward the sound without thinking twice.

It only takes me a few tentative steps to have a clear view. Tabitha and Milo are at the base of a large tree, on the lawn of a well-tended yard. Behind them is a quaint craftsman-style home with a sprawling front porch and sizeable windows. White siding and brick pillars that reach from deck to roof add a certain old-world charm to the place. The front door is painted a bright apple-green, which matches the patterned cushions on the patio furniture and the meticulously squared-off hedges that frame the property.

It would appear that Tabitha is perfectly capable of managing her yard.

I turn my attention back to her. She's on her knees at the base of the tree, speaking in low, even tones to her nephew. And when she raises her hand, I see it—a bright yellow-and-black-striped caterpillar inching across her palm.

"Again!" Milo chants with an excited trill to his voice.

"Of course. But you need to be cool. We don't want to scare this little guy. Gentle hands, right?" She looks Milo in the eye and doesn't use some stupid baby voice to relay the information. She talks to him like he understands completely.

And he does. He may only be three, but Milo is an old soul. And with her direction, he goes from wiggling with excitement to taking a deep breath and calmly reaching a steady, chubby hand forward.

"Ready?"

He nods, baby teeth pressing into his bottom lip as though steeling himself. She butts her hand against his, creating a flat expanse where their palms join. The caterpillar inches its way across, and the farther it travels, the bigger Milo's grin grows.

But me? I can't take my eyes off his aunt.

The elegant slope of her neck, the way her bare shoulder peeks from the off-kilter neckline of her navy knit sweater. The tips of her breasts create two clear points in the fabric, but I don't let my eyes linger there. Instead, I move to the silky dark hair that's effortlessly twisted up and clipped at her crown. Loose pieces tumble free and frame her doll-like face.

But the most attractive thing about Tabitha Garrison might be the way she's gazing back at Milo, like he's one of the wonders of the world.

It hurts to watch.

It hurts because I'll take no pleasure in removing Milo from this place.

But it's what I promised Erika I'd do.

CHAPTER 5

Tabitha

I CAN'T TAKE MY EYES OFF MILO. THE LOOK OF PURE WONDER on his sweet face is mesmerizing.

Whoever his father is must have the most beautiful curly hair, because the ringlet dropped in the middle of Milo's forehead right now certainly never came from our side of the family where poker-straight hair abounds.

I never did find out who his biological dad is. Either Erika didn't know, or she chose not to tell me. I never pressed her on it, because the news of Milo came about during a particularly low phase of her life. In fact, he's the reason she focused so hard on healing for those few years. And all I knew was that I was happy to see my sister *trying*.

The fuzzy caterpillar makes its way across his palm, and he's captivated by the experience.

"Good, now move your other hand like this"—I raise his free hand to extend the space—"and you can keep him there for longer."

"Wow." His little cherry lips murmur the word with awe.

"Pretty amazing, right?"

A subtle nod is all I get. It's as though he's entranced. The feeling is mutual, because I see so much of my sister in him. And my heart aches that she won't be here to see him grow.

I haven't broken the devastating news to him yet, though I know I need to. The only saving grace is that spending a few weeks with me or his grandparents isn't out of the ordinary for Milo.

Still, I have my appointment with a highly recommended therapist this afternoon. Because I want to get this right. Say the correct things, support him in the best way possible. Give him what he needs.

I can't even think about losing him to another country right now. If I dwell on that, I'll crumble completely.

So instead, I watch him lift one pudgy finger and swipe gently over the top of the caterpillar. "Wow. Soft," he murmurs. And I can't help but smile.

"He'll grow into a spotted tussock moth, eventually."

Milo's eyes widen. "This becomes a *moth*?"

"Yes. Almost like a butterfly. They're both a sign of a healthy ecosystem. They help pollinate flowers, and you know how important that is."

I grin at him, and he grins back. Because he *knows*. He's been flower picking with me plenty of times. Edible toppers, tea flavoring, a splash of color on the bistro tables. I guess you could say I'm big on flowers.

The rattle of a car driving past draws my attention, but it's not the vehicle that keeps it. It's the scruffy, foreboding mountain of a man standing on the sidewalk at the edge of my property glaring at us.

Rhys Dupris.

The man whose full name has been haunting me since I read it on that will. He looks miserable and delicious all at once. That seems to be his brand. And I hate that I see him that way at all. I just can't seem to help myself.

We stare at each other for a few beats as my stomach sinks down into my toes, dread coursing through my veins. I had planned to make my plea, to use lawyers and tug on some shred of empathy this man might possess to reconsider taking Milo away. Because everything with that will checks out.

But the scowl on his face isn't promising. He looks downright pissed off.

"I had no idea you were coming today," I blurt, still kneeling on the damp ground, completely caught off guard.

"I know," he rumbles in that impossibly low timbre. It's a voice that could make a girl's toes curl, but in this instance, all it does is make me feel intentionally put on the spot. Judged. Like he expected to pop out from behind a bush and catch me doing something untoward.

Nah, all this man does is get my back up.

Which is why my jaw drops when my nephew's body tenses, and his bare feet pitch up onto tippy-toes as he *squeals* in the sweetest, most sugary voice, "Ree!"

I'm so shocked by his familiarity that I almost let him toddle off and take our poor caterpillar along for the ride. "Milo, honey. Let's put the caterpillar back on the tree."

I reach for his arm and guide him back to the trunk. He's vibrating with excitement, and I tell myself that's why my hands shake as I aid him in carefully returning the bug to its home.

But the minute the caterpillar latches itself onto the bark, Milo turns and races across the grass, launching himself at Rhys. He takes a flying fucking leap. As though he knows in his bones that Rhys will catch him. As though he *knows* him.

I find it confusing. I find it hard to watch.

So I clench my jaw and keep my gaze on the lawn as I push to standing, brushing at the knees of my jeans. I sigh in defeat when I realize there are grass stains on the light denim.

Of course I have to look like *this* when he shows up. No bra. Grass-stained knees. Messy hair that smells like cake because it's full of dry shampoo. Dark circles under my eyes that match the old-ass blue sweater I threw on this morning.

I suppose the win is that today I don't reek of scotch.

Small fucking victories.

Still, I refuse to cower in his presence. I shimmy my shoulders and stand taller, crossing my arms and tipping my nose up like I'm the queen of something more than this partially updated craftsman and a semi-successful small-town restaurant.

I watch them. Rhys has Milo in his arms, the small boy nestled against his side with his tiny head resting on a massive shoulder.

It should be cute.

Instead, it makes my stomach clench and pulse as though my heart has dropped right down into the pit of it.

My only hope in hell with this entire shit show was to

make Rhys see that Milo loves me, and his grandparents, and this town. And that we all love him too. Erika may not be here anymore, but Milo is well loved.

And yet, only a fool could witness the tender way this man rests his cheek against Milo's, taking a deep whiff of the little boy's hair before letting his eyes flutter shut, and still think he doesn't love him in some way too.

"Missed you, little man," he grumbles gruffly before lifting his head to meet my watery eyes. Then he nods in my direction. "Tabitha."

"Tabby Cat!" Milo wiggles in Rhys's arms before reaching for me, signaling he wants to be let down. But Rhys looks shaken somehow. His eyes narrow on me, and his nostrils flare and contract. Like a bull about to charge.

"I wanna go down," Milo clarifies. "Show you my caterpillar!"

Rhys gently places him down on the sidewalk, eyes not straying from mine as his powerful body unfurls.

Milo takes him by the hand and tugs him in my direction. My heart rate accelerates as they approach.

"Right here." Milo points at the bug's yellow and black body, and I stand as still as the tree as he regurgitates the information I just shared with him about the species. It's only made more adorable by the confidence with which he mispronounces things.

"Aunty Tabby Cat and I love flowers," he finishes with a thoughtful nod before turning his attention back to the caterpillar.

"Tabby Cat?" Rhys asks.

I shrug nonchalantly. "Long-standing nickname."

His eyes skitter across me, searching my face from beneath his heavy brow as though I'm incredibly suspicious in some way, and I quickly drop his gaze. This guy is one big nerve-wracking mindfuck. My nose prickles and I glance away, skin crawling under the weight of his gaze, heart pounding like it might beat right out of my chest. I don't know why it feels like my worthiness of being around Milo is being assessed right now, but it does.

And I swear Milo must sense my discomfort, because one of his arms reaches back to wrap around my thigh in an absent-minded side hug.

My nephew may find nothing strange about this meeting, but I do. So I steer the conversation back to the issue at hand, keeping things vague. "So what brings you here unexpectedly?" I ask, before dropping my voice and adding in a saccharine tone, "Other than enjoying kicking people while they're down."

The tendon in Rhys's jaw flexes, and he rolls his eyes.

Irritating him feels like success, so I take it as a win and carry on. "I was assuming I'd hear a response to my invite before you showed up."

"I needed to see the situation for myself."

I scoff, threading my fingers through Milo's thick hair as though that will help set my nerves at ease. "The situation is—" I stop short from eviscerating him with my words when Milo turns and presses an absent kiss to my thigh. He's always been snuggly and affectionate, and I've always soaked up that aspect of him.

I peer back up at Rhys, only to see him staring at the spot on my jeans. His eyes linger where pudgy fingers tap happily against denim, as though he can't believe what he's seeing.

"The situation is..." My words come out gently, but my glare expresses how I feel about him. He's an intruder. An interloper. Someone who doesn't know shit about shit when it comes to me and the lengths I'll go to protect the people I love. "That Milo will be heading to my parents' place right away. And then I have a meeting. In fact, it's one you may want to sit in on since you fancy yourself so intrinsic to this entire situation."

Milo turns and looks up at us. "I get to go to Grandma and Grandpa's house?"

Rhys's head flips in his direction, and his body language shows his discomfort. His massive biceps cross, and he seems to rock from side to side.

I force a smile as I ignore him and focus on my nephew. "You know it. Sleep over too, since I work tonight. I'll be there in the morning to get you."

"Will you bring chocolate croissants?" The way he pronounces *croissants* usually cracks me up, but today it just makes me sad.

I'd taken him to the bistro this morning to have them fresh out of the oven. I watched him lick his fingers with such enjoyment and spent the whole time thinking how gutted I'd be to never get to see him gobble up my baking again. The little noises he makes when he's enjoying something. The way his eyes go extra round when he asks for another one.

It had almost moved me to tears, except West Belmont rolled in all smiles and chuckles and talking about his dorky bowling team, which provided the perfect distraction to keep myself together.

"I could—" a deep voice starts.

"Of course! I bet Grandma and Grandpa would love that too. Milo, I packed your bag already." I cut in before Rhys can say something that would undoubtedly be overstepping. Because I swear I can see it written all over him. I'm aware of the legal ramifications of that will, but if he thinks I will roll over, give him my nephew, and send them on their merry way, he's got another thing coming. "Why don't you go grab it from your room?"

Milo's cheeks go round on a wide grin, and he nods excitedly. "Be right back!" He tears off, running a few strides before turning back to face us. "Don't go anywhere. Not you *or* you," he adds, pointing at both Rhys and me in turn.

Then he blasts happily through the front door, oblivious to the tension and heartbreak surrounding him.

"He has a room here?" Rhys's brows furrow when he asks the question.

I hate to give him a single thing, but I can't help but notice he looks genuinely confounded. "Of course. He spends a lot of time with me."

He swallows heavily before straightening, his expression giving nothing away. "And he likes to spend time with your parents?"

Now it's my turn to scrunch my features in confusion.

"I mean, yeah. They spoil the hell out of him. What three-year-old wouldn't love that?"

He gives one firm nod. "I thought they weren't in the picture."

"Seems like you thought a lot of things without knowing a single one."

Rhys shifts in place, cheeks burning, and I can't help but think: *Good. You could stand to be taken down a few pegs.*

"I thought she was...they were..."

"Cut off? Estranged? Yes." I wince without meaning to. It has always killed me that I couldn't help them make peace. And it makes me wonder what other dirty laundry he knows about our family. "Too much water under the bridge, I guess. So I became the bridge to ensure Milo would have grandparents in his life, even if his mother no longer spoke to them. It was a tenuous setup, but it worked. And even when they all agreed on almost nothing, they always agreed on doing what was best for Milo."

Rhys stays quiet, jaw working, eyes laser focused on my mouth as though he's skeptical about the stories that spill from it.

"My meeting is a video chat with a therapist, because I need to tell Milo about his mom, and I don't know how. That's the situation. Seems like you're determined to insert yourself, so"—I reach forward and slap his steely bicep like the old friends that we clearly are not—"welcome to the shit show, big fella."

Before he can respond, Milo comes barreling out the

front door wearing his too-big backpack, his slip-on shoes on the wrong feet, and a wide smile on his sweet face.

"This is the best day ever!" he announces joyously as he trundles in our direction.

And boy, I wish I felt the same.

CHAPTER 6

Rhys

I WATCH TABITHA WALK UP TO HER PARENTS' HOME, HAND IN hand with the little boy I've come to love like he's—I don't know. Not my own, but something awfully close to it.

He reminds me so much of his mom. It's his mannerisms. The way he walks. The way his smile hitches up just a little more on the right side than on the left. Everything he does reminds me of her.

Seeing him here, alone, makes her death feel more real. It makes my chest ache. It makes me miss the woman who became something of a sister to me.

Erika had a perpetual weariness about her, like the drudgery of each day weighed on her. And I couldn't keep myself from offering help while I was off with my recurring injury. It never felt like an inconvenience to lend a hand.

Plus, Milo and I became fast friends, and before long, I looked forward to the stretches she'd be away so that he and

I could do all our favorite things together. Read. Build forts. Play-wrestle.

Now he's walking into the home of two people I've been told nothing but negative things about. He eagerly hugs them; they lovingly hug him back. And it feels a bit like I'm living in the twilight zone.

Because those stories Erika told me made me so sure that Milo needed me. Those stories tapped into a place deep inside me that I'm not sure I ever recognized—or I just didn't want to.

All I know is that I spent my childhood in the system, passed from foster home to foster home, and I won't be letting the same thing happen to Milo.

Over my dead body.

Tabitha glances over her shoulder at me, and I realize her parents have picked up on the guy sitting in her passenger seat. Three sets of eyes land on me, and I try not to squirm under their attention. It's too acute, too pressing. I prefer my solitude. I prefer flying under the radar.

But Tabitha's pursed lips are all radar. Her eyes home in on me with accusation, so I look away, out the window, preparing myself for any pretense of friendliness to fly out her truck window the minute she steps back inside without Milo as a happy, oblivious buffer.

I stare down the curving street. The entire development is just a repeating pattern of the same homes, each in a slightly different color. It's not what I expected. Wide lots. Sidings in all different shades of brown and beige. Not an apple-green door in sight, but still, a safe suburban sort of neighborhood.

The driver's side door opens, and Tabitha fires her truck up without a word.

"Do they know who I am?"

"No. I told them you're a friend, and they squealed like we're getting hitched or something."

"Why did you lie?"

"Because their hearts are already broken. I've decided to pace out the bad news I have to deliver to them like a tasting menu. Right now, they're having a palate cleanser, thinking I might finally settle down."

Her words hit hard, each one a blow I didn't expect to sting quite so badly. Tabitha's concern for everyone else is admirable…and not at all what I expected based on the stories I've been told.

I don't like the way the realization sits, so I change the subject, not wanting to dwell.

"Do they have a car seat?" I ask, realizing Milo's is still in the back.

She's shoulder checking when she snipes back, "No, they just strap him to the roof of their Subaru like he's a canoe."

I sigh. "That's not funny."

She shakes her head, rolling away from her parents' place. Hands at ten and two. Knuckles white like she's pretending the steering wheel is my neck. "It wasn't meant to be."

"Sure seems—"

"Listen, you've done nothing but insult my family and me since I came to get my sister's things. You insinuated I was there to rob her and accused me of not being sad enough. Then, you popped out of the bushes, trying to catch me doing god knows what, like we were on an episode of *Cheaters*. Now you casually suggest I'd leave my nephew somewhere without a car seat as though I don't care about his safety at all. So excuse the fuck out of me for not smiling and nodding at every low blow you lob out."

I settle back in the seat of her truck and cross my arms before grumbling, "You're not very likeable."

And I mean it, even if everything she said is true. I'm suspicious of her and her intentions—how could I not be?—but she's combative and accusatory at every turn.

"Thank you," is her off-the-cuff response before we fall into a beat of silence. And when I look over, a subtle curve lifts her lips. "It must be hard for you."

"What?"

"Not having a woman just fawn all over you. It's like if you have to do more than be a big, broody, poor man's Jason Momoa, you get your panties all twisted."

"Charming," I grumble, forcing my mouth into a frown. I don't want to admit out loud that was humorous.

"I'm not remotely interested in winning over the man who's responsible for my sister's death."

"*I'm* responsible?"

"You pinky promised."

I blink, letting her words sink in as I attempt to piece together where she's coming from without giving too much away. I still don't trust her. And based on the way she continues, she doesn't trust me either.

"You're just lucky Milo likes you. Hard to account for the

taste of a toddler, but he's still the only reason I'm tolerating your presence."

I know I should rise above. Just sit here and let her take her shots.

But I don't.

"That's funny. I thought it was the legal will that was forcing you to tolerate me."

I know she heard me, because the stubborn set to her jaw becomes even more apparent, but that sentence strikes us both silent for the entire ride back to her house.

CHAPTER 7

Tabitha

I'VE BEEN PRETENDING RHYS DOESN'T EXIST EVER SINCE HE reminded me that the law is on his side when it comes to my nephew's future. But he still followed me into my home office. I could feel him glaring at me the entire time, and he's so damn big that I swear the old oak floorboards shook with each of his steps.

When I plunked down in my office chair and went to open the Zoom link, he took it upon himself to retrieve a chair from my dining table. He's now placed it next to me, facing the computer screen in my office.

I can see us side by side on the screen. Close enough for both of our faces to show in the window, but not a single smidge closer.

We both know we have to be here together, but we don't like it.

At all.

We both stare straight ahead, not turning to look at each other. Some sort of Medusan standoff—if that's even a thing. And we definitely don't talk.

I think we both understand that we need to *talk*. Crack this whole mess open and share some cold, hard truths. But I don't think either of us knows where to start.

I'm a confusing mix of furious with my sister for giving my nephew's guardianship to a fucking stranger and devastated that I could even be angry with a woman who's just passed. But putting Rhys in her will has completely blindsided me. It has me questioning her health and state of mind in the last several months. It leaves me feeling…betrayed.

I wish she were here. I wish she were here so that I could ream her out and then hug her so fucking hard that it might even hurt a bit. What kind of person does that make me?

I avoid thinking about it all too much because it makes me so damn anxious, and truthfully, it's all just a little too painful for me to face head-on right now.

Instead, I've been walking on eggshells for the past several days, soaking up every moment with Milo. All the while imagining some awful over-the-top scenario where cop cars pull up to my house and take him away while I cry and am forced into cuffs. It's safe to say I've watched too many soap operas in my life.

The bottom line is, I don't want Rhys here. It all feels like a bad dream each day when I wake up. Every morning, I squeeze my eyes shut again and then spring them open, as though that will reset my life. A true *Have you tried turning it off and back on again?* moment.

Getting lost in the kitchen during summer dinner service makes time pass quickly and brings me a sense of joy and satisfaction that I don't find anywhere else. But what I'd like is to lick my wounds in private. I'd like to cry in the shower where people can't see or hear me, because it feels like no one in the world could be missing Erika as much as I do. Everyone around me would be too quick to judge. They'd turn around and whisper about how they always knew this would happen. And I don't want to hear it.

I *can't* hear it.

Instead, I crave going inward. In the mornings, I'd like to take a cup of coffee to the back side of the mountain and watch Milo pick flowers while I tell him childhood stories about his mom and me. And in the afternoon? I'd kill for a fucking nap.

I am *so tired.*

I want to grieve. And I don't want Rhys watching me while I do.

The tinkle of a digital bell followed by an upbeat whooshing sound from the speakers feels altogether too light for the moment. And yet here I am, bracing myself for whatever this therapist has to tell us.

When her face pops up on the screen, I do that thing I always do. I force a smile onto my face and say, "Hiiiii," in a way that sounds super approachable and sweet. Years in the service industry have trained me well. It's unsettling how fast I can snap a facade into place.

"Hey," is all Rhys can muster from behind a suspicious glare and crossed arms.

"Thank you so much for taking this online call with us, Dr. Bentham. Options for therapists here in Rose Hill are limited," I say sweetly, attempting to make up for the poor first impression Rhys seems determined to make.

"Of course." The woman gives us a genuine smile and claps her hands together. Stacks of bracelets jingle as she makes the motion, and they draw my attention to her general look. Round glasses with thick lenses perch on her dainty nose, and gray curly hair flows down to her shoulders. Behind her is a mess of greenery—plants on stands, vines draped from the ceiling, and crystals hanging in the window just off to the right.

It looks like a hippie haven. And she's the queen. I love her already.

"I do plenty of online consultations, so this isn't out of the ordinary for me. And please, call me Trixie."

Rhys just grunts, like the total asshole that he is, and I can't help but turn and give him a disbelieving look.

"You're a striking couple," Trixie adds with a sly grin.

And we both freeze.

Then we talk at the same time. "Oh hell no," I say, right as Rhys sits forward and says, "Actually, we're not."

The woman's head tilts. "Well then. Why don't you two tell me what the situation is here? We'll see what we can work out to get Milo—it was Milo, right?" She glances down to check what must be notes on the sheets in front of her. "Yes, Milo. We need to come up with a good system to support him through this."

To that, Rhys and I nod. In fact, Milo seems to be the only thing we can agree on.

"So, I know Tabitha is the sister of the deceased. But you, sir, are…" She leaves the question hanging in the air.

Rhys shifts in his chair, and I get the sense it's not just the subject matter that feels uncomfortable for him. It's the entire process of sitting down with a therapist. He looks like he could crawl right out of his skin. "I'm, uh, Rhys."

Trixie smiles and gives a reassuring nod. "Ah yes, the legal guardian. What a nice surprise!"

Rhys tosses me an irritated glance, and I shrug. "What? I explained the situation in my email."

His lips purse, but he carries on. "And I'm…well—I *was*—a friend of Erika's."

I scoff at that, shaking my head, unable to fight back a disbelieving smirk.

The fucking nerve of this guy.

"Oh, a *friend*. Is that what we're calling it now?"

Trixie tries to reroute our tension with, "It's okay to refer to her in present tense. She can still be your—"

But Rhys cuts the woman off by physically turning in his too-small chair to face me, dark eyes boring into my own. "Yes. *Friends*. That's all we ever were. Platonic. Neighbors. Two people who genuinely liked each other. And. That's. It."

I can feel my cheeks blaze as his deep voice scorches the air between us. Humiliation clogs my throat. He seems very adamant, but I also wouldn't put it past him to lie.

Erika was obsessed with him when she first moved in. She carried on talking about him in such a familiar way—in a way that left no doubt in my mind that they were more than just a landlord and his tenant. Which is probably why

I have a tough time believing she was just friends with this man.

But then, I also have a tough time believing she went out and made an honest-to-goodness legal will that left her child to a perfect stranger.

I sniff and look away at the screen, trying to regain my equilibrium, though it's hard under the searing gaze of the giant beside me. "Yikes. Imagine being booted out onto the street by a friend who genuinely likes you."

The growl that rumbles in Rhys's chest is animal-like. I swear I can feel him vibrating beside me. But I don't care. The truth hurts.

And that's why I can't bring myself to look at him either.

"Seems like there's some serious animosity between you two." Trixie sounds borderline amused. "But we should save those issues for another day. We can focus on Milo today if you're interested."

"*Yes*," I say. Talking to someone impartial sounds fucking amazing.

Rhys stiffens and huffs out a curt, "Sure."

"Can you two figure out a way to work together for Milo's well-being?"

"Yes," we both answer instantly. I fight the urge to look over at the man beside me, both relieved and annoyed by his response—and by his dedication to my nephew.

"Well, that's as good a place to start as any. Because the first thing you both need to understand is that this little boy is going to need to know he's safe and loved every single day. He needs community. He needs a *team*."

I nod along, trying to ignore the rigid six-foot-four body beside me.

"At his age, the way he processes the death of his mother will differ from yours as fully functioning adults."

"That's generous," I mutter beneath my breath so only Rhys can hear me. I'm rewarded by his heel bumping against mine in a silent reprimand.

So I place my foot right on top of his and grind my heel into the bridge of his. One dark eye twitches on the screen, but otherwise, he doesn't react.

Childish? Yes.

Satisfying? Also, yes.

"Milo will have three big questions in his mind, and I'll write these down for you in a follow-up email, so just listen for now." She lifts a finger. "One, *how does this affect me?* You will need to be able to tell him that much of his life will stay the same. Two, *am I safe?* We will want to contribute to his sense of safety by not creating any other major changes in his life. So, it will fall to you both to make him feel safe. And question three is *what's happening to me next?*"

She leaves that last question open, suspended in the dead space between us, as though she knows that's the real kicker. I see it as my cue to make a point.

"So uprooting Milo and moving him away from his family would not be in his best interest?"

The woman's cheeks pull back in a knowing grimace, and her eyes flit to Rhys as she answers with a simple "No."

He stares back at the screen blankly.

"Unless you have reason to believe the child is in danger

or is being mistreated in his current setting, I would not move him. Not yet."

Not yet.

Hope and dread crash against each other in my gut.

"I'm not a Canadian citizen," Rhys states. "My home base is in Florida. My work takes me on the road. I can only legally stay here for so long."

Trixie just nods. "That's a shame."

"Yup. You're a Florida Man if I ever saw one," I mutter quietly while trying to brush the grass stain off my knee again, wishing I could be on my best behavior and failing all the same. His indifference makes me too heated.

Did he not hear what this professional just told us? Who gives a flying fuck about where he works? It's not about him.

An awkward silence descends until Trixie speaks again. "I am not the child's guardian. I don't know either of you or your backgrounds. But, generally speaking, children are best served in a familiar setting, surrounded by familiar people."

She's not telling us what to do, but the writing is on the wall. And I can tell by Rhys squirming that he doesn't like the implication. But this seems like something he and I can brawl over later. Because for as much of an asshole as he is, I don't get the sense that he's going to steal Milo away in the middle of the night.

I clear my throat. "Can we touch on the best way to tell him? I just—" My voice breaks, and it takes me a second to regain my composure.

I swallow.

I blink.

I roll my lips together.

And then I feel a big, warm hand on my knee.

One I wasn't expecting. One I have no idea how to feel about. And one I can't look away from.

Tan skin, thick fingers, streaked with veins.

My eyes flit to Rhys, but he's not looking at me. His fingers pulse on my leg, and I'm too confused by his reassuring touch to react.

He doesn't remove his hand, and that works for me, because it leaves me just bewildered enough to take a deep breath and continue. "I just don't know how to explain this to him."

Trixie nods sadly, eyes shining with compassion. "You tell him directly. You will use words like *death*, and *died*, and *dead*. Terms like *passed away* or *isn't with us anymore* will only confuse him. I know these words can be uncomfortable and hard to say, but it will give him the best understanding. He needs to comprehend that he will not be seeing his mother anymore. That when people die, their hearts stop beating. And we won't cover it with talking about her as being"—her knobby fingers come up in air quotes—"'sick.' Because, again, he will relate that back to himself. The next common cold he gets will cause unnecessary stress."

My throat works over and over again as I try to swallow the words. I don't even want to say them out loud in a room by myself, let alone look into Milo's eyes and say them too. The thought makes my breathing go heavy and my stomach churn. And as I attempt to come up with something to say in response, my heart races.

Rhys's hand squeezes again. And I want to punch him for knowing it's exactly what I need. I don't want him to be this attuned to me. I want him to disappear.

But before I can react, he pipes up with a question of his own. "Can you give us an example of how you'd say it?"

Trixie nods, and I let out a heavy sigh, then knock his hand off my knee. I'd rather not be comforted by the man who plans to take my dead sister's child away from me.

"I would take the three-pronged approach again. Answer those questions one by one." She holds three fingers up now and drops one down as she speaks again. "*Your mom has died, and this means you won't be seeing her ever again. It's okay for you to be sad, and it's normal to have a lot of feelings about this.*"

My eyes sting as she drops another finger.

"*You are safe and loved.*"

I wonder if Milo needs to hear this or if I do.

"And last, you'll add something like, *this is who will be taking care of you.*" Trixie's head swivels between us with a knowing, quirked brow, and I feel like I'm in time-out. "*Your mom won't be able to take care of you now, but we will be.*"

The words she emphasizes aren't lost on me. She makes it sound so effortless, so obvious, but I know in practice it will be anything but.

"Then I would tell him that you'll be there for him, and you will talk about his mom with him anytime he wants." She closes with a simple shrug, as though this isn't the worst conversation of my life.

My lips clamp in a tight line, and I nod rapidly as though that makes up for my lack of words. Rhys sits woodenly beside me, and it's hard to make out on the screen, but he looks frozen. Like a statue.

When I glance over at him in the flesh, he looks even worse. Pale and motionless. He looks downright unwell.

And for the first time since life threw us at each other… I feel bad for him.

CHAPTER 8

Rhys

THE MINUTE THE CALL WINDOW DISAPPEARS, TABITHA ROLLS her chair back and flees the room. I swear I see her wipe a hand over her cheek, but it just as easily could have been her flipping me the finger. Either way, I don't move. I sit, the reality of it all settling in.

My hand. Her knee.

Without even thinking it through, I'd reached for her. Tried to throw her a lifeline. And I shouldn't have. I'd taken it too damn far.

The truth is, I made that contact as much for her well-being as my own.

The memory of being told similar things by a social worker at every new home I was taken to as a child bubbled up in me unbidden. At thirty-five years old, it still haunts me.

And so does the knowledge that I would never do

something that isn't in Milo's best interest...but I also promised his mother I'd stand in for her if this day ever came.

I just didn't expect it to come.

The pain of Erika's loss is fresh, still unbelievable in so many ways. Our friendship was easy, and she always seemed healthy. None of this feels real, and everything I do right now is just...on autopilot.

I don't know how much time passes until the sharp clap of Tabitha's hands behind me startles me out of my reverie.

"You can't stay here."

I turn to look at her and come up short when I see her standing in the doorway wearing pin-striped black pants and a white chef's coat. "Why are you dressed like that?"

Her cheeks hollow out, and her expression sours as she examines me with disapproval. She's pulled her hair into a tight bun at the nape of her neck, lending to the severe look.

I miss the messy updo and the grass stains on her knees.

"Because I have to go to work."

"Right now?"

"No. I just love to play dress-up in my free time."

I let out a beleaguered sigh. "We should talk at some point. To Milo. About Milo. All of it."

"About Milo staying here?"

My jaw works. I don't want to lie to her, but I also don't want to give her false hope. "I don't know."

Her lips pop open in disbelief. "Are you fucking kidding me?"

"My life isn't here. My work isn't here. I have a summer home in Emerald Lake. There are laws that require me to leave. Staying for more than six months is frowned upon by immigration. And my time is almost up. I've been off work."

Again.

She rolls her eyes and crosses her arms. "Six months off, huh? Must be nice. What is it you do again?"

Now it's my turn to stiffen. I hate talking about my work. The questions. The assumptions. The way people treat me differently once they find out.

I love being a wrestler with World Professional Wrestling, but I love my privacy more. It's why my character keeps a mask on in the ring. And it's why I don't tell people what I do.

"I work in the entertainment industry."

Her gaze sweeps over me. "Porn?"

"No."

"Okay, suuure." She adds a knowing wink at the end of her already disbelieving sentence.

I don't respond. I don't owe her an explanation. Years of learning to hide things and keep shit to myself in the foster system have become a way of life for me even as an adult.

It's a tough habit to break, and I'm not even sure I want to. Sharing too much always backfires. People always end up wanting something. Namely money.

Maybe even my name in their will.

I can't help but wonder…if Erika hadn't known, would she have asked me to be Milo's guardian?

It's a question that will keep me up at night after seeing the Garrison family in action. If they are perfectly capable of taking care of Milo, why'd she choose me?

Because I'd be good for him? Or because of the number of zeros in my bank account?

The question leaves me unsettled.

"Hello?" Tabitha waves a hand in front of me, pulling me out of my dazed state. I'm not myself, and I know it. I like time to think. Time to process. I like weighing my options carefully, and this feels like such a snap decision.

I don't know what to do, let alone what to say, so I suggest something that backfires spectacularly. "I could let him visit sometimes."

Her face goes red instantly. "You've got some nerve. Rolling in here, a total stranger to his entire family. Acting like you'll be doing me some huge favor by *letting* him visit." She scoffs and wipes a hand over her mouth, agitation lining her every movement. I can see the desperation rising in her body language as she shifts from foot to foot. "You're just some fucking random. You're not his dad."

My molars clamp together.

I have spent many a weekend with Milo. Many a stretch taking care of him so Erika could have a break. I've given up other vacation locales because, after weeks on the road, it turned out that I missed him.

Over the past two years, I have grown attached. There's no point in denying it, so I don't.

"I'm the closest thing he's got to one. And I've been in his life for almost as long as you have."

I didn't think Tabitha could turn any redder than she already was, but she defies the odds.

"Get. Out."

I stand, looming tall over her as I approach, but she's not the least bit intimidated. She's a fucking spitfire. Has been since the first day I laid eyes on her. I'm glad Milo has someone like her in his corner. I wish someone had fought as hard for me as she does for him. I may not like her, but I admire her grit and devotion.

"We still need to hash this all out. And I'm not driving five hours home just to turn around and come back when you decide it's convenient. So where would you have me go?"

She spins away from me, tossing back over her shoulder, "To play in traffic, Daddy." Her voice is heated, and her hand trembles with fury as she swipes her car keys off the table.

Tabitha is hurting. It's written all over her. And hurt people hurt people. That's why I'm not more offended by her jabs. They lack conviction.

She's shoving her feet into black clogs when she scoffs again. "Actually, I have the perfect place for you."

"Is it at the bottom of the lake?" I mumble, toeing my own shoes back on and reaching for my jean jacket.

She jerks at my comment, like she didn't expect me to fire back, but she only misses the one beat. "That's the dream. Except forensics are pretty solid these days. I'd end up in prison, and then Milo would truly be hooped. Get in your car. You can follow me, since that seems to be your new favorite pastime."

I bite down on a chuckle, and it comes out as a displeased grumble.

Tabitha is angry. I don't even know if it's *really* about me, though I'm sure my presence isn't helping. But I know the feeling. The constant niggling thought that you could have done something to prevent this.

It's the kind of consuming, inconsolable anger that comes with grief.

I know because it's been a frequent companion of mine throughout my life.

Tabitha practically shoves me into the roadside pub. I can feel everyone staring at me as we weave through the tables, and I hate it. But I don't stop. I just let my gaze trace the inky strands of Tabitha's bun. The way they twist together and shine when the overhead lights hit them.

Neon signs flash against wood-paneled walls, and it smells like fried food mixed with the stale remnants of cigarette smoke from a time before smoking in bars was outlawed. The carpet sports years' worth of stains, and the older crowd sitting at the bar look as though they've been coming here since the stains didn't exist at all.

This place is a local's haunt if I've ever seen one.

We pass through a low-slung wooden gate. At the back of the building, we go down a few steps to where three bowling lanes are located. Then she marches up to a group of men who look happy and relaxed and nothing like the way I feel inside.

"Tabby!" one of them shouts, lifting his hands like he's excited to see her.

Tabitha's hand clamps tight on my bicep, nails digging in just a little too hard.

"Overheard your phone conversation earlier, West. You need a fourth for your team?"

The man glances back at the other two guys, sitting at a high-top table. One looks embarrassed to be here. The other looks plain annoyed. "Oh yeah, forgot to mention that Crazy Clyde is in the hospital. Kidney issues. He needs regular dialysis. Had to go check on him. Assure him they weren't making up his diagnosis just to harvest his organs."

The grumpy one grumbles and shifts in his seat. "Who the fuck would want Clyde's organs?"

I have no idea what they're talking about, so I just take it all in, completely dumbfounded. But Tabitha doesn't care. She shoves me forward, like she can't wait to get rid of me.

"Right. Well, here. This is Rhys. Take him."

The men eye me with a multitude of questions dancing in their eyes. And I can't blame them one bit. I feel my cheeks burn as they assess me.

The man she called West—the one who was a little *too* excited to see her if you ask me—speaks up first. "You're one big bitch, aren't ya?" he says as he claps me on the shoulder.

"You can say that again," Tabitha snipes from behind me, and my shoulders tense, though I don't turn to face her.

"You ever bowled before?" West carries on, ignoring her snark.

"No," I grit out, trying not to show how annoyed I am by getting marched in here like a naughty child who needs minding.

"You a dad? We can always get you a cat or something if you're not. Then it will still count as dads' night out."

"You're going to make this guy a cat dad?" The stern one is borderline slack-jawed by West's suggestion.

"Not a big cat guy," I bite out, before glancing over my shoulder to glare at Tabitha. "And I'm not really a dad either."

Tabitha barks out a laugh. "*Rich*." Then she turns to West. "He *is* a dad, whether or not he wants to admit it. And for what it's worth, I think you should name your team the Man-Children."

As they laugh, she leans in, her voice dropping low enough so only I can hear her. "Want to waltz in here and play daddy? Here's your crowd. Have fun. Hopefully, they don't find out you're full of shit."

She shoots me a glare with a little smirk, and we both know she's proving a point here. Throw my weight around like I'm a parent, and she's going to call me out on it.

With that, she spins on her heel and marches out of the bowling alley, leaving me alone and completely out of my element.

"You're a real ballbuster, Tabby. I appreciate that about you!" West calls back to her as she leaves.

She flips him the finger over her shoulder.

And it makes me feel a bit better that she's just as mean to him as she is to me.

I watch her leave, hips swaying, head held high, almost regal in the way she carries herself. I should not be this attracted to her. But here I am, unable to look away all the same.

Tabitha winks and pushes out the front door, but not before taking one last glance over her shoulder at me.

It reminds me of the first day she walked away from my house. Our eyes catch for a beat. And then she's gone.

Tabby Cat. I shake my head. More like a black cat.

I turn and zone back in, only to hear West ribbing the tall, lean man beside him about dating his sister. He rolls his eyes and mumbles something, but there's a brand of camaraderie between the two men that I've never let myself indulge in.

Sure, I have friends—like work friends—but those friends come and go. And sometimes the storylines at work start to feel a little too real, and the dynamic becomes strained.

I like my massage therapist, and he seems to like me. But I also pay him, and I would never go bowling with him.

I get waved through with a "Let's go, new guy." And before I know it, I'm faced with an open lane and the prospect of making a complete fool of myself in front of a bunch of strangers.

"You look fucking terrified," the older man, whose scowl puts mine to shame, comments.

I just shrug. "Confused, mostly."

"I'm Bash." He sticks out his hand, and I give mine back, shaking firmly.

"Rhys."

"You're new in town, then?"

I grimace. Tabitha practically dropped me into a small-town pot of boiling water, and we still know nothing about each other. About our situation. About what we're telling people.

And I'm certainly not dumb enough to think she wants me to spill the beans on why I'm really here. So I shrug again. "Sorta."

"Are you a friend of Tabby's?" West asks, now focusing his attention back on Bash and me. "Because any friend of Tabby's is a friend of mine." He flashes his white teeth at me with a charming smile. He's clearly the life of the party with this crew. And even though I had an irrational moment of envy over his familiarity with Tabitha, I suspect he's the type of guy who's impossible to dislike. Even if I wanted to, he wouldn't let me.

"Something like that," is what I settle on as I shake his hand and offer a flat smile.

"Great." West claps my shoulder and then gestures toward the other man. "This here is Ford. My good friend and also the World's Hottest Billionaire, according to *Forbes*."

Ford rolls his eyes and lets out an exhausted sigh. West grins wider. Like a little kid who gets a kick out of prodding a parent.

"Nice to meet you," I say, reaching forward to shake Ford's hand. He's got polish. He's dressed casually, but he screams money. I don't know if the billionaire thing is a joke or not, but I opt not to ask.

"Likewise. Even though it's over *bowling*." His lip curls as he looks around.

"Hey, hey. Don't disparage the charm of Rose Valley Alley."

"By *charm*, he means sticky floors," Bash mumbles from behind the rim of his pint glass.

"Why are they—"

West's arm slices across the space. "Nah. You can't slander the place like that. It's an icon. A relic. An attraction." His finger shoots up triumphantly. "A heritage site!"

"A *heritage site*?" Ford looks appalled.

"When the fuck did you become a thesaurus, West?" Bash stares at him with a tilt to his head.

"I read a lot, Bash. It's good for the vocabulary. Maybe being a fire pilot doesn't require you to know many words."

"Oh, and training horses does?"

Their easy banter is amusing and unfamiliar all at once. I find myself watching them, head flipping from man to man and feeling entirely out of place.

Ford chuckles, shaking his head and taking a sip of his beer. "What about you, Rhys? What do you like to do in your free time?"

"And why is it 'roids?" West quips before covering his mouth with a palm. "Shit, sorry. Mouth is faster than my brain."

Ford groans.

Bash scrubs a hand over his face. "Fuck's sakes."

And I laugh. I can't help it. It feels unfamiliar in my throat. I spend an excessive amount of time alone, and the past week has been impossibly sad. But I still laugh. It was just too good-natured to offend me.

"No 'roids. Just a boring diet, great genetics, and too many hours in the gym."

"Fair. Yeah." West purses his lips and looks me over appraisingly. "Now that I take a closer look, you could definitely be bigger."

Everyone laughs. They laugh even harder when I try my hand at bowling for the very first time.

I stay quiet, appraising. But as bowling progresses, I fall into a comfortable camaraderie with the other three men. For a couple of hours, I don't think about Erika, or Milo.

I wish I could say I don't think about Tabitha.

But that would be a lie. Because much like the very first time I met her, I can't get the woman out of my head.

Haven't been able to for the past two years.

CHAPTER 9

Tabitha

TUESDAY NIGHT DINNER RUSH WAS BUSY. A LARGE PARTY HIT the kitchen hard during an already busy night. It gave me that buzz. That feeling where my mind and body are so focused on the task at hand that every other thought fades away. Being needed is keeping me sane. But the guests have dwindled down to only a few tables, and my mind wanders as I stand at the pass of the open kitchen, looking out over my pride and joy.

The Bighorn Bistro.

Café by morning. Chic communal farm-to-table eatery by night.

Started working in a kitchen at sixteen and never looked back. Worked my way up through the ranks while attending culinary school. And then bought the run-down old building with my own money. Meticulously saved every penny and spent the majority of it remodeling this place.

Now there are thick wood beams spanning the vaulted ceiling, each one wrapped in twinkle lights. Leafy plants hang from above too—they're a pain in the ass to water, but they give the space an outdoor feel. And when the sun streams in from the skylights above, it bathes the entire dining room in a subtle green glow. Tall glass windows line the front, facing the main drag of Rose Hill, just a couple blocks off the lake.

And a mere five-minute walk from where I left Rhys. Tossed him right into the deep end and didn't even ask if he could swim.

Out loud, I'd say I hope he can't. The bitter, petty part of me wants to scare him off and send him running. But then I saw him smell Milo's hair when he lifted him up this afternoon. And the look of relief on his face…it's haunting.

The dirty truth of it is, I wouldn't have left him with those guys if I truly wished him dead. Because if someone were drowning, West would be the first person to leap in after them. Ford comes off aloof, but I think he'd ride into battle for the people he cares about. And for all of Bash's grumbling and scowling, he's got a good heart. You just have to dig for it a bit.

With a heavy sigh, I glance over my shoulder at the two remaining chits. And all at once, I don't have the energy to complete these final dinner orders. As the executive chef, I don't need to—that's what my sous-chef and line cooks are here for. My priorities are the menu, the orders, and the sourcing, and on busy nights, I come in to plate for the dinner rush.

I look back out over the restaurant and freeze. Because like I summoned him out of thin air just by thinking of him, Rhys is sitting at the end of the bar with a big bell of red wine settled between his thick fingers.

Staring at me.

I blink a few times, as though it might make him disappear from the stool he's perched on. Like windshield wipers clearing a splattered fly from the view ahead.

But it doesn't work.

He's still there. Dark hair combed back, one side flopped down, grazing his cheekbone, while the other curves around his ear. Somehow, his stubble looks thicker than it did mere hours ago. His skin is tawnier now that it's bathed in the dim golden light of the bistro.

He looks too big for the stool and too rugged to be sipping a glass of wine.

Yet here he is, doing just that. He's also making me hate myself, because no matter how hard I try, I can't peel my eyes off him. He exudes so much aloof confidence. He's magnetic. Unflappable.

It's like the world is orbiting him rather than the sun.

God, no wonder my sister was so into him.

He doesn't react to my gawking. Instead, he stares back, gaze licking over my skin like flames. It's as though here, in public, with the buzz of the restaurant between us, there's something less scandalous about enjoying the view.

If someone were to ask, I could say I'm staring at the plant beyond him, wondering if it's been watered lately.

Him? No. I hadn't noticed him at all.

But that becomes harder to deny when he tips his chin toward the stool beside him—a clear invite for me to join.

Immediately, I shake my head and hike a thumb over my shoulder to the kitchen.

Rhys smirks, and when I turn to look behind me, all three of my kitchen staff are in a huddle, chitchatting. Laughing. Clearly not working. Selling me out without even trying.

A beleaguered sigh slips from my lips, and I hold up a finger, signaling I need a minute. Then I spin on my staff. "Guys, if you've got your giggles out, one of you can come up here and plate. The rest of you can keep things moving. Sauté. Grill. Clean. I don't care who does what at this point. Just make yourselves useful. Please."

They all freeze and then lurch into action like chickens with their heads cut off. I'm not *that* hard on them, but they also know the reality of an open kitchen like this is that everyone is always watching.

I'm met with a chorus of "Yes, Chef" and guilty grimaces, followed by sheepish smiles.

"Bunch of schoolgirls, the lot of ya," I tease as I walk past them toward the back. They chuckle as I push through the swinging doors. Then I march straight to the staff bathroom where I splash my face with cold water, refasten my bun, and ditch my chef's coat.

I groan when I see the shirt beneath. The saying emblazoned across the front reads, *Holding grudges is my superpower.* Alarmingly, in this case, it's true.

Rhys might as well know what he's up against. That I'm

combative, snarky, and slow to forgive. Character flaws, yes. True? Also, yes.

I drag my tired ass and tacky T-shirt out to the bar to face him, and it's the funniest thing. Every person in the restaurant is staring at him or sneaking peeks, like his energy just fills the space in a way that screams *look at me*.

I spot two of my floor staff making eyes at him from behind the service station at the other end of the bar. They legitimately look like they're sporting those stick-on googly eyes I've used to make crafts with Milo.

The temptation to go over to them and criticize their terrible taste is strong, but I opt to slide onto the stool one down from Rhys without so much as a glance at him.

He grumbles something that sounds an awful lot like, *I don't bite*. It rumbles through the air between us and vibrates over my skin. It's so deep that I feel it more than I hear it.

I snort and volley back with, "I do though."

Rhys goes rigid but doesn't get a chance to respond before my part-time bartender, Scotty, hustles over to me. "Bordeaux?"

I give a weary nod, dropping my cheek into my palm.

"It's good. That's what I'm having," Rhys pipes up from beside me.

"Yeah?" I don't look at him, instead watching Scotty chat up a few women at the end of the bar while he pours my glass. Great bartender, even if his brain is in his dick.

"2015 was a good year for Bordeaux."

I do look at him now, shifting my head so that my ear is propped against my palm. "I know." It's not only annoying that he's drinking wine but also that he has knowledge about it. "I chose it."

His heavy shoulders rise and fall as he mumbles, "Good choice," before taking another sip.

I can't help but watch him. His lips, just a touch too full. His Adam's apple, just a little too pronounced as it bobs in his throat.

When he swallows, I drop my gaze and cross my legs, pressing them together.

Turns out my taste might be just as bad as my servers'.

The worst kind of taste because this man isn't here for me; he's here to *take* something from me. Someone I love. And legally he can, which is why all this hanging around and chatting is feeling an awful lot like a lion playing with its food.

It's the reminder I need to keep my head on a swivel. Rhys Dupris may be easy on the eyes, but he's a fucking nightmare for my heart.

Scotty swaggers back with my wine and slides it across the live-edge bar top. Then he props his palms against his sides and cranks up the wattage on his smile so that his dimples pop. I swear he's practiced this look in a mirror. "Damn, boss, you are looking mighty fine in that tee—"

I cut him off with a raised hand. "No. Go back to hitting on the cougars, Scotty." I take a sip of my wine, letting my eyes close as the liquid hits my tongue, effectively dismissing him like I always do when he pulls this flirty nonsense.

Scotty chuckles as he walks away. "Can't blame a guy for trying."

I'm shaking my head when I open my eyes, and try as I might to look bitchy and dour, my lips quirk up. Fucking Scotty. If it's got a heartbeat, he'll try to have sex with it.

The weight of a heavy gaze on the side of my face has me shifting my eyes in Rhys's direction. "What?"

He shrugs.

"Oh good. *A shrug*. This talk is already going so well."

"You're consistent at least."

"Consistent how?"

"Consistently mean."

I drink and let out an unladylike snort. "You try working in a kitchen with a bunch of dudes your entire life. It's part of my charm." I wink at the giant man beside me.

Rhys scoffs as though he finds nothing charming about me at all.

"Not my fault you aren't man enough to handle me. But look, Scotty is." Rhys glares, but I ignore his sour expression and let out a whistle. "Hey, Scotty," I call down the bar.

The younger man spins on the spot to face me, his enthusiasm palpable.

"You're fired."

Now we get a full-fledged grin and a salute from him. "Ha! Sure thing, Chef." Then he turns around and goes back to work.

Rhys's glare has darkened, and it strangely excites me, so I grin back at him. "See? Scotty can take it. You just need to toughen up a bit." And maybe it's the few sips of wine that have gone straight to my head, but I reach out and punch him on the arm. Casually. Right on the tattoos. Like we're old friends or something.

Except we're not.

He turns his head to look at me. Slowly, methodically. Then his low, dark voice comes. "We need to talk."

I nod as I reach for my wine, hoping it might help clear the sudden lump in my throat. From over the rim of my crystal glass, I watch Rhys shoot Scotty a glare.

"But I don't want to talk with that fucking goof hitting on you the entire night."

My eyes take a turn around my head. The last thing I want is to talk to a complete stranger about such painful personal things. I'd rather stab a fork into my eye. "What are you—"

My words drop off as Rhys tosses a one-hundred-dollar American bill down on the bar and stands in one swift motion. I'm still sitting slack-jawed when he reaches for the back of my stool and drags me away from the bar.

"You don't need to pay for mine." I don't want him buying me drinks. But I'm not comping his either.

"Let's go." His jaw pops, and he reaches out, not hesitating at all to place his massive hand on the small of my back and guide me away from my seat.

The way he takes control is very caveman-like, and it stirs something inside me. I shouldn't like this dominant side of him. I definitely shouldn't let him lead me out of here like we're anything more than adversaries. And I don't want to turn into some simpering, starry-eyed girl over him, so I remind myself why he's so awful as we head to the exit.

He's rude and thinks the worst of me.

He evicted my sister and left her homeless.

He's trying to take away my nephew, who I love more than anything in the world.

All the internal shit talk works beautifully. In fact, it makes me feel like I shouldn't be near him at all. And just like when I shook his hand off earlier, I do so again.

"Where are we going?"

He holds the front glass door open for me, like the gentleman he's not. "I don't know. This town is fucking packed with tourists. I can't get a room anywhere."

"I wouldn't go to your room with you anyway, Rhys. You're trying to fuck me *over*, not fuck me, remember?" I shoot him my best hateful glare as I attempt to walk past him, but he steps out right in front of me before I can escape the restaurant.

His chin drops, eyes now level with mine. "Is that so?" The barely there smirk on his face does nothing but further infuriate me.

Dick.

"Yes, that *is* so." I enunciate the words so that he hears me loud and clear. I'm ready for a fight. It won't be my first, and most likely not my last, but it might be one of the most important of my life. And I'm not about to fuck it up all because he might be the most sinful-looking man I've ever laid eyes on.

His gaze lands on my lips. I'm trapped there for a beat, trying to decipher his expression. Like a deer in the headlights, I stand and stare, wondering if he's going to hit me with his car or kiss me.

The thumping in my ears crescendos with each beat that passes, but it's replaced by flaming cheeks when he claps back with, "I think it might be the opposite." Then he draws back, taking all the air in my lungs with him as he saunters away.

I watch his hulking form make its way down the sidewalk:

Do I follow him? Do I demand he explain himself? Opposite as in…he's trying to fuck me, *not* fuck me over?

What the hell am I supposed to do with that? I feel like I don't know anything anymore.

Except that when he waves a hand over his shoulder and says, "Let's go, Tabby," the first thing my jumbled brain fixates on is that he's never called me *Tabby* before.

And I hate how much I like it.

CHAPTER 10

Rhys

I SHOULD NOT HAVE TOLD TABITHA THAT I'D RATHER FUCK her than fuck her over. It slipped out in a frustrated, cryptic grumble, and now, rather than ragging on me at every turn, she's been dead silent. Well, except to shout at my back, "I have a spare bed in the basement," before turning and walking down the alley beside her bistro.

Then she got in her truck and drove away, leaving me to wonder if she expected me to follow again.

And I did. Because try as I might, I'm drawn to the woman.

Now, parked in front of her house, I try to make heads or tails of this fiasco. Her sister and I forged a friendship—one of my only friendships—and as forlorn as I am over that loss, I'm equally forlorn over the picture that she painted for me.

Erika told me that Tabitha was self-centered and work-obsessed, not cut out to raise a child. But all I've seen so far is a woman who gets grass stains on her knees from playing too hard, who paid a professional to help her do right by said child, and who is accomplished and well-loved by her employees.

A little too well-loved. My thoughts turn to Scotty. His stupid smile and flirty winks.

But my loyalty to Erika draws me up short. I trusted her. She came to feel like the sister I never had. I knew her for two years, whereas I've interacted with Tabitha for all of a few days.

Still, I promised Erika I'd be an advocate for Milo, and it's a promise I don't take lightly. Plenty of my foster families seemed nice enough when they knew someone was checking in on them.

It wasn't until watchful eyes moved elsewhere that the neglect would start. I was always too big and too scrappy to be on the receiving end of anything worse. I mostly got left alone, and I learned to enjoy my solitude.

Which makes this entire situation even more exhausting. I'm not cut out for it. The socializing. The smiling. Even just the noise of being out and around people makes me feel tired on some level.

I sigh raggedly, dragging my palm over my hair, then scrub at my beard. I need to get cleaned up before I head back to work. And the clock is ticking on that too. My knee is solid for the first time in years. They've planned my comeback, and I've been working out like a fiend to get ready. The clock is ticking and I'm due back next week.

Which means I need to face Tabitha. Talk to Tabitha. Assess Tabitha.

And try not to think about ripping Tabitha's clothes off while I do it.

It's going to be fucking torture, but I unfold myself from my vehicle and head to the front door, duffel bag in hand, ready to face her all the same.

I hear her irritated, "Door's open," from inside, and my heartbeat picks up.

Makes me wonder if I get off on being tortured by Tabitha Garrison. Letting her hate me like this is some special brand of self-loathing.

I walk in to see her back heading through a door and down a dark stairwell into the basement. She has a duvet slung over her shoulder and a pile of linens held out on one arm like a serving tray.

"Pull out the wineglasses. Let's get this over with," she says, voice growing more muffled as she goes farther down the stairwell.

I wish I could say that her combativeness makes her less likeable, but it has the opposite effect. I see right through it all. Plus, I get off on a good fight. And the thought of going toe-to-toe with Tabitha makes me hard.

To get my mind off the tightness in my jeans, I head to the kitchen. It's small, but well laid out and functional.

I immediately see a farm-style cabinet with glass doors, shelves of wineglasses within. With two in hand, I turn and take in the kitchen. Gleaming copper pots hang above the massive industrial gas stove top, and an array of Japanese knives are stuck to a magnetic strip on the wall. The butcher-block countertops have stains and divots that tell the story of a kitchen where many a meal has been prepared with love and care.

My stomach growls, and my chest aches in time. It's too easy to remember the days when food was scarce. Not reserved for me. An expense I wasn't worthy of if that "family" was going to make any cash for putting a roof over my head. I'd have to sneak down in the middle of the night and steal unnoticeable pieces just to keep my stomach from aching. Then at school, the gnawing hunger would force me to beat someone up just so I could steal their lunch.

Not because I wanted to. But because I *needed* to.

I was in survival mode.

The angry stomping of Tabitha's feet on the stairs snaps me out of the memory and propels me toward the antique dark-wood dining table with a pedestal in the middle. It's big enough to seat eight people, and as I take a seat in one of the studded leather dining chairs, I wonder if she's ever been able to fill it. Seems unlikely to me.

I place the two glasses in the middle of the table and feel her enter the kitchen, even though I'm not facing her. She's got the energy of a storm. Ominous, electric, unpredictable.

She was softer for a moment at the bar. I felt it—tired enough to let her guard down. Then she'd gone back to pissed off. I'd watched it happen, saw the turmoil in her eyes, the tension in her shoulders as she decided I couldn't be trusted.

Truth be told, I don't blame her. I wouldn't trust me if I were her.

She plunks a bottle of red wine down on the table with all the ceremony of a bull in a china shop and twists the top off, tossing the lid on the table before pouring out two sizable bells. "Great, let's get this over with so I don't have to look at you anymore." She drops into a chair, looking as exhausted as I feel.

It strikes me that she appears gaunt, leaner than I remember her from that first day she sauntered into my house.

Having grieved my fair share in this life, I know this is anger. Grieving something that never was and never will be is a special sort of hell. Tabitha is angry. Deep down, she's even angry with herself—which is a hard fucking pill to swallow.

I can empathize.

That's how I know it's a lot easier for her to make me the target of all her rage. I know because I've done it too. I've needed that release too—it's how I started fighting.

This woman needs a target for her anger. Someone to blame so that she hurts a little less.

And without even thinking it through, I decide I can be that person for her.

I can keep my truths about her sister and her eviction. I can let her hate me if it makes getting through this even a smidge easier for her. She already can't stand me. Knowing the way her sister spoke of her won't change anything. It'll just crush an already broken heart. And I can't stand to see that.

The minute the decision latches on in my brain, a weight lifts from my shoulders. Committing to silently supporting Tabitha through this ordeal gives us breathing room to figure out what the best solution is. It gives me *time*. And it gives her a chance to breathe before everything gets uprooted.

I will move Milo eventually. Maybe just not yet. It's the path of least resistance—even if that's not what Erika would have wanted.

But I know it's what's best for Milo. It's what I wish someone had done for me.

With both our wineglasses filled, we stare at each other from across the table. Staring seems to be our default. I'm pitched forward, both my elbows on the wood, watching her. Most people find my size and appearance—my silence—intimidating, and they end up backing down.

Tabitha does not. She watches me back defiantly, giving nothing away except fuck-you vibes and a few rueful glances that slip down toward my mouth.

Like she's daring me to swipe the glassware off this table and fuck the fight right out of her.

"I know what you're thinking," she says tartly. I cover my chuckle with a grumble that sounds more irritated than I mean for it to.

"Doubt it."

"You're thinking I drink too much."

As someone who enjoys wine and would never judge going on a bender after receiving bad news, she couldn't be more wrong. "No, I was thinking that the wine at your restaurant was better." And that this one would be better served splattered across the floor with my head between—

"Wasn't about to waste my best bottles on you," she replies, smacking her lips for dramatic effect.

My traitorous stomach grumbles in response, and her eyes flit down to my waist. Thankfully, the table covers my lap, or she'd see proof of the persistent boner I can't seem to rid myself of now that we're alone in her house.

Her brows furrow, and I can see her thinking. I haven't eaten dinner, but I don't intend to tell her that information. She'll say she's glad I'm starving, and I'll spend more time wondering why I've been so attracted to her since the very first time I laid eyes on her.

"How was bowling?"

"Fucking awful," I lie. I ended up having a fun time, even though it was embarrassing as hell.

"Good."

Of course she loves that. "I couldn't say much. Didn't know if anyone was in the loop."

She hits me with a droll look. "I've barely had a minute to process my sister's death, let alone"—she waves a hand over my body—"you."

"Have you told anyone?"

She winces. "No. Everyone can find out about Erika when I'm good and ready to tell them. The gossips in town will say mean shit about her, and I'm not ready to hear it whispered when I walk past."

Fuck. She hasn't told *anyone*? It seems as if she might be just as alone as I am. A subject I don't like to dwell on. So I forge ahead, getting down to the nitty-gritty.

"I need to head back to Florida."

Her expressive brows pop up on her forehead. "K."

A single syllable. It annoys me. But only because I don't like carrying conversations.

"In about two days." Her hand flies to her throat, face

contorted in pain, as she rocks back as though I've struck her. Her reaction is visceral. It's hard to watch. And I put her out of her misery quickly. "I won't take Milo with me."

Her shoulders sag as an audible rush of air breezes from her lips, relief personified. "Thank you."

I grimace because she might not be thanking me after what comes next. "For now."

And sure enough, ire flares in her expressive eyes. "What does that mean?"

It means I'm invested in her, though for the life of me, I can't figure out why. I rationalize that Erika—if she could see the way her sister cares for Milo—would want this. I rationalize that if Erika was lying about her sister, then giving this setup time to shake out is the only mature, logical way to handle it.

Milo's well-being comes first. That's my real job as his guardian.

"It means I'll be back in a few weeks."

Her cheeks turn pink, dark eyes dancing. "Oh, so this is a test? Are you going to grade me? Who made you the fucking judge, jury, and ex—"

"Tabitha. I. Don't. Know." That shuts her up. "You were right, okay? I don't know anything."

Her mouth pops open and then closes again.

"All I know is that the stories your sister told me don't fit with what I've seen today. All I know is that Milo's mom is gone, and I want nothing but the absolute best for him. All I know is that he's talked about tabby cats for the past fucking year, and I've told him over and over again that I'm allergic."

Her features go blank at the last part. And it's true. I was wondering why he was more obsessed with tabby cats than dinosaurs. It never made sense. But it does now.

Her lips finally quirk, and she softly asks, "Really?"

"Yes."

"Are you allergic?"

Good lord, this woman will talk about anything but the issue at hand. "Sort of. I'm not a cat guy."

She scoffs and gives me a knowing smirk. I'm tempted to tell her she's reading into that all wrong, but I bite my tongue.

"Listen, this is a tremendous responsibility, one I take seriously and was not prepared for in the least, so can we just lay our swords down for a minute?"

"I don't like you."

I take an absent sip of wine and stare off at the massive industrial fridge. "So I've gathered."

"I love my sister. I don't know what she told you. And I don't mean what I'm about to say cruelly, but she never told me you were involved with Milo either. Just told me how hot you were and that you liked your privacy, so it would be better if I didn't visit her there when you were in town."

My brow furrows. "You visited?"

Tabitha's eyes widen in astonishment. "*Of course*. Dude, are you kidding me? I'm still paying off the debt I have from sending her to the best rehab facility I could find. I swooped in often to take care of Milo so she could have a break. She told me she had a boyfriend but didn't want to bring him around yet. I always assumed it was you."

What the fuck?

My head spins from Tabitha's account. Every time I think I know what I'm doing, Erika blindsides me from beyond the grave. I don't know what game she was playing, but it's starting to look like I got played for a fool by a woman I genuinely cared for. It's hard to accept and even harder to understand.

"It wasn't me. And she told me the same thing about a boyfriend. But *I* took care of Milo when she was with him too."

Tabitha's lips purse and push from side to side as if she doesn't like the taste of what she just heard, but she doesn't address anything.

"Do your parents help out with Milo a lot?" I venture carefully. "I was under the impression they cut her off."

Tabitha sighs and flops back in her chair. She looks as though she might melt and slip right onto the floor. "It's complicated. And I'm the lucky go-between."

I tilt my head in response, wanting more details.

She lets out an annoyed huff before continuing. "They did cut her off, and there's a part of me that doesn't blame them. When she was down, she was…hard to deal with. They were constantly worried. And it went on for a long time. The lying, the mood swings, the disappearing, the stealing. That was the final straw. She stole their wedding rings and pawned them. They were passed down from my grandparents, and I think it just broke my dad's damn heart."

I swallow a lump in my throat, and Tabitha looks away, blinking rapidly.

"There's a part of me that gets it. But there's a bigger part of me that holds it against them. Because I just…I couldn't bring myself to cut ties. I mean, you know"—her voice drops an octave as it thickens—"that's my big sister. My idol. Even though that one fucking injury sent her on a downhill spiral, I couldn't just leave her."

The lump in my throat keeps me from talking. And it's just as well. She seems to be on a roll, and I don't want to cut her off. Truth be told, I hang on every word out of Tabitha Garrison's mouth.

"So, I took over. And when Milo came around, I worked both sides. Basically told them that having a mom *and* grandparents in the picture would be best for Milo. And eventually everyone gave in. And it worked but—"

But she carried a heavy burden.

Her nose wiggles, and she waves the thought off. "Anyway, my mom and dad were great parents, and they are even better grandparents. But I don't know if I'll ever totally forgive them for bailing on Erika." Her gaze drops. "Not that I'd tell them that. But I'm working on letting it go." She lets out a bittersweet chuckle before pointing at her chest. "Hence the shirt."

"I'm sorry," I say simply. And I mean it. It's a sad fucking story. And with the shit I've seen in the foster care system, I also know it's not an uncommon story.

Tabitha presses her lips together and nods in my direction. Her eyes are glassy, but she doesn't cry. She doesn't strike me as a crier. "Thanks. I'm sorry you're caught up in this."

I shrug. I'm used to life throwing me curveballs.

"Are you going to try and take him, eventually?" she asks softly.

I suck in a breath and shift at the table. "I don't know."

She looks me in the eye. "I'll fight this, Rhys. And I won't give up until I'm broke and ruined. I've already been in contact with a lawyer about contesting custody. So just know that I will do *everything* in my power to keep him. I'm not saying this to be difficult. I'm just giving you a heads-up."

"I believe you." And I do. I've faced off in my fair share of brawls, and something tells me Tabitha Garrison would be the fight of my life if I ever decided to go toe-to-toe with her.

Her jaw tightens as her gaze works its way over me, both of us feeling equally distrustful. "So you'll, what? Come back now and then?"

"We can tell Milo about his mom tomorrow—together—if you want. We'll tell him he's staying here, with you. And yeah, it's going to be a couple of weeks before I can get back again. This isn't an easy location for me to pop into, and I don't know what border patrol will say. Gives us time to figure shit out. Talk to our lawyers. Talk out the legalities and the...outcome."

She nods, the stubborn set to her jaw the only clue to what's going on in her head. She's barely touched her wine, but she spins the glass in place by the stem, watching the liquid slosh against the sides and create a wavelike pattern as it streaks back down.

The next question comes out in a barely audible whisper.

"Do you actually want Milo? To raise him and do the whole parent thing? Like, is this just an obligation, or do you actually want this?"

She hits the nail on the head. That's for fucking sure. Because my feelings today are about so much more than distrust.

It's the haunting walk down memory lane. It's knowing how much this woman is struggling with the aftermath of her loss. It's this inexplicable connection to her and to the little boy in this town that keeps me from walking away.

I don't want to tell her those things, but I also don't want to tell more lies than I have to. And the truth is, I do love Milo. And I know Milo loves me.

So I settle on, "I actually want this."

Her eyes stay fixed on the wine, and her lips tip up in the saddest smile. "Okay. We both take some time to cool down and reassess when you come back in a couple of weeks then." She pushes up without another glance. "It's not fancy downstairs, and there isn't a bathroom, so you'll have to come up to the main floor. I didn't make the bed, but there are clean sheets, and you can stay there when you want."

She's leaving when my stomach growls again, and I don't know if she hears it, but I wish I could tell it to just fucking knock it off already. It's borderline embarrassing.

Tabitha doesn't acknowledge me any further though. I can hear her padding up the stairs, probably going to bed, and I'm pretty sure she's dismissed me.

So I drag myself to the front door and grab my things

before trudging to the basement. It's unfinished, with a concrete floor and a lingering damp smell. The walls are framed, but no insulation or drywall has been added. In the corner, a mattress and box spring pass for a bed. Next to it, two sawhorses with a piece of plywood propped across them create a makeshift bedside table that's topped off with an old-fashioned brass lamp.

Like she said, it's not fancy, but I've slept in worse, and I'm too exhausted to care. I put my head down and get to work making the bed, but soon I hear her stomping around on the main floor like a Clydesdale.

She's either still pissed, or just not light on her feet. I'm not sure which, but I hear all the same. And I don't even want to go upstairs to brush my teeth until she's gone.

In fact, I find myself wondering if she's thought through letting a strange man sleep at her house. I should talk to her about that. Along with leaving her front door open.

As I park myself on the end of the bed, I vow to check the locks before I hit the hay once and for all. Then I scroll my phone, ignoring the gnawing hunger in my stomach, and wait for her to finish with whatever she's doing that's taking so damn long.

The creak of the door at the top of the stairs startles me, and my head whips to the corner where the entrance is. Soft light and a delicious smell pour down the stairwell.

And then, so does her voice.

"Hey, asshole. I made you a bowl of carbonara so that I won't have to hear your stomach all the way upstairs. I didn't even poison it. Bon appétit and good night." The door creaks as she closes it, but then it stops. Light spills down the stairs once again as she adds, "Oh, and I sleep with a gun under my pillow, so don't try anything weird."

I drop my chin, and a smile curves my lips. Because I'm pretty sure that—in her own way—Tabitha Garrison was just nice to me.

CHAPTER 11

Rhys

"It's good to see you." Anthony's palm lands on my bare back in a loud slap. The gesture could be friendly, but there's enough force behind it to just make him an asshole.

Not that this is news to me. Anthony Morris has been my boss at World Professional Wrestling since my first day on the job. And he's been a royal dickhead the entire time. Not to me. No, he's always looked at me with dollar signs in his eyes. There's no denying that the man has a vision. And that vision has included me as a key part of the brand since day one.

But I've seen the way he does business, and while I love my job, I don't necessarily love being associated with him. Alas, he signs my paychecks and mostly stays out of my way, so we keep a tenuous sort of peace.

"Thanks," I grumble from where I wait backstage in what we call the Go Position—just behind the curtain.

"You sure took your sweet fuckin' time getting back to us."

There it is—the underhanded jab. Like I chose to be locked up at home recovering from ACL surgery, rather than on the road doing what I love.

For the past decade, being one of the headlining superstars on Monday Night Mayhem has consumed my life. It's taken me all over the world and kept me from slowing down or getting too caught up in my head. The transition from being in a new city every week, surrounded by people, to being stuck on my couch alone was a hard one. It was a lonely one, filled with the nagging worry that I might never return to the one place where I feel most myself.

I force a chuckle, keeping my eyes fixed on the flashing lights trickling in from around the trim of the blackout curtains. "It's almost like ligaments don't heal overnight."

"Ha," Anthony barks. "You can say that again."

It irks me that this is his line of thinking. My knee was an ongoing issue. I had a minor tear that I continued to put off for the sake of the company. I performed night after night and took short breaks—a few weeks here and there—when I needed them. For the better part of a year, I lived on a steady stream of Aleve and regular ice baths, all for the sake of the WPW.

And when my body finally gave out on me, they promptly wrote me off the show. My belt got handed over to my colleague Will—known as Million Dollar Bill in the ring—in a last-minute match. One I completed *with* a blown-out knee.

So it's a huge relief to be back here. Erika's loss may have thrown my personal life into chaos, and a dull ache of sadness over her death might be my constant companion, but being here—doing this—makes everything feel just a little bit better.

I wonder if this is how Tabitha feels when she cooks.

Fuck. I need to focus. Not let my mind wander back to her again. So, I shake my head to clear it, and bounce on the balls of my feet as though skipping on the spot. I let my gaze narrow, and my body give in to the hum of excitement.

"You haven't forgotten what to do out there, have you, Dupris?" Anthony's voice is an unwelcome intrusion to the moment.

I've worked too long and too hard to let Anthony get in my head, and I have every intention of soaking this up. So, I clamp my molars and tug my mask down.

Like always, everything else fades away. Anthony. All the doubt. All the anxiety.

When I become Wild Side, everything falls into place.

Right as the opening notes of my song kick in over the sound system, I grumble, "I haven't forgotten shit."

Then I toss the curtains open and stride into the arena, serenaded by the deafening roar of the crowd.

And I almost smile, because they haven't forgotten me either.

CHAPTER 12

Tabitha

Rhys: Checking in. How's Milo?

Tabby: He's just fine.

Rhys: I'll be away for another week.

Tabby: Great.

Milo is curled beside me in bed. It's Tuesday morning, and I don't have to work until dinner. Rhys has been away for two glorious weeks. The sun has been shining, the birds have been chirping, and I've been pretending that he and his "I don't know" plan to take Milo to a place filled with snakes and crocodiles doesn't exist.

I definitely have not been thinking about his head between my legs. Though, if I was, I could argue that's a great place for it, because at least I wouldn't have to listen to him talk or look at his grumpy fucking face.

Milo stirs, reaching for me in his sleep, and although I had been considering rolling out of bed to make a coffee, his sweetness has now convinced me to stay.

I'm paralyzed by how much I love him. By how much I need him. And by the knowledge that he needs me too.

Ever since we told him about Erika, he's been having nightmares. He wakes up scared, and though they aren't ever about something real, it doesn't take a rocket scientist to know he's processing a lot. Another call with Trixie confirmed as much.

So I've kept him with me in my king-sized bed. We both get more sleep this way, and truth be told, I enjoy watching him sleep. I can lie beside him and pick out all the fragments of my sister. It feels like she's not as gone when I look at him. Like she lives on in him because his earlobe is shaped exactly how I remember hers. Or the way his bottom lip is slightly fuller than the top—she had that too.

Telling him might have been worse than finding out Erika was gone. Rhys looked like a stony-faced ghost. He sounded like the male version of Siri reading a script, and he looked blank—traumatized—as he did it. It might be the first time I've felt a true flicker of empathy for him. I itched to reach out and hold his leg like he'd done mine. But with Milo there, I didn't. Instead, I jumped in and wove softer wording and a few more sentimental lines.

I don't know if it helped Rhys, because, as usual, the man

barely talks to me. But I do think one glare he shot my way might have been appreciative.

Or at least that's what I tell myself.

The conversation was brutal, watching the emotions flicker over Milo's face. He didn't cry. Not then. Instead, he's cried over inconsequential things. His tears have come out in different ways at various times.

And mine? They haven't come at all. Not since the night I was packing things up in Erika's house and dropped a heavy box of journals on my foot. The black bruise on the bridge of my foot has only recently smudged away into my regular skin tone. My nose had stung, and my eyes had welled. It had hurt like hell.

But one thing I know will hurt more is opening those journals. That's the one box left taped shut and pushed into a corner in the basement—formerly called "The Dungeon" and recently renamed "Rhys's bedroom."

Letting him stay here was out of character in every way. And I do my best not to dwell on my decision. I tell myself I'm just doing what needs to be done. Keeping us all afloat—like always.

Which is why I've worked so hard at being present and emotionally available for Milo these past weeks. We've spent our days unpacking his mom's things and incorporating them into the house. Trixie recommended the exercise to weave Erika and conversations about her into our everyday lives. A photo here, a trinket there, a worn Persian rug from her house laid out in the entryway.

Erika's will stated that she didn't want a funeral, so the

urn housing her ashes sits on the mantel, flanked on both sides by small frames we spent the week filling with our favorite photos of her.

In a dark twist, Milo *named* the plant I brought back from her house in Emerald Lake "Erika." Every morning, he gets up and greets her by name. It shouldn't be funny, but it makes us both laugh. And strangely, I find myself smiling over at the plant when something cute happens with Milo, as though I'm looking at my sister and exchanging a look that says *this kid*.

He probably needs a pet, but for now, there's just a corn plant named Erika, with a slightly angled trunk and broad green leaves.

Today our bittersweet bubble is going to be popped though, because the big broody porn star is set to return for a few days. And I'm as nervous as one would be before a major final exam.

I know Rhys says he means well, but I can't help feeling like I'm being tested. And if I'm not up to his standards, I'll have failed. Something I hate to do.

I already feel like I failed Erika.

I can't fail this too.

After a morning spent picking roses for my signature tea blend at the bistro, Milo is napping when Rhys arrives.

He rolls up to the front door and darkens it with his width. From where I sit at the kitchen table flipping through an industry magazine, I feel his shadow snuff out the light.

"Door's open," I call, ignoring the urge to get up and greet him. The way my stomach flips with the eager anticipation of knowing he's about to walk into my house is best left ignored. Shoved down into a dark corner where I hide all my other unpleasant feelings.

When Rhys steps in, I peek up. My eyes have the perfect straight shot down the hallway to see him looking downright murderous and wearing black from head to toe. Jeans, T-shirt, slicked-back hair. *Probably his boxers too.*

It's the way he carries himself. There's something…I don't know, ominous about him? I blame the fact that I've been too busy to have sex for some time now for the way my core clenches. How fucked up do I have to be to get all horny over a man who is here to make my life miserable and looks at me like he wants to kill me?

"You gotta stop leaving your front door open," he grumps, while using his toes to pull off each of his black leather sneakers.

"Why?" I flip through the magazine with a little extra flourish, doing my best to appear completely unaffected by him. He looks like himself, but all tidied up. Hair a bit shorter. Full beard leaning more toward sexy stubble than scruffy mountain man.

Him being so attractive is deeply annoying.

"The gun under your pillow isn't enough."

I laugh. "That was a joke. This is Canada, Rhys. I don't own a gun. Neither does anyone I know." Peeking in his direction provides proof that my empty threat of a gun under my pillow has pissed him off. My body hums as he starts toward me.

"It's not safe."

I roll my eyes with intentional petulance and flip another page. My tone comes out mocking when I ask, "What are you going to do? Punish me?"

His approach has him towering over me. I can feel his gaze, and the way the air shifts around his thickly corded body. "Not in the way you're thinking."

A tug in my pelvis betrays me, and I look up at him, meeting the challenge in his eyes. For a flash, I note how tired he looks, but I brush that aside. "And what way are *you* thinking?" I push the magazine away and sit up tall in my chair, crossing my legs and looking up to give him my best innocent doe-eyed look.

His teeth strum once over his bottom lip as he glowers down at me. And for the first time, I can't tell if the darkness that flashes in his irises is because I piss him off or because he does want to fuck me. All I know is he seems more focused on my mouth than on my eyes.

My head tilts as I consider him. Then I decide to push just a *little* further. Because if nothing else, this situation between us is a power struggle, and I'm not afraid to take my power where I can find it.

If he thought he was squaring off against some timid little girl, he thought wrong.

"Does it involve bending me over this table—"

"Tabitha," he cuts me off, voice hoarse. But I don't miss

the way his eyes flit to the table, his fist clenching around the strap of his bag.

I blink innocently. "What?"

He shifts, hiking his duffel up over his shoulder and moving it to his front. Like it's a shield between us. "You should be worried about an intruder."

My lips press together as I nod my head. This man is out of touch with what it means to live in this small town. "Just think, if I get murdered, you'll be free of me. You and Milo can skip off into the sunset without me holding you back."

He shakes his head as he turns away and saunters toward the basement. And I do mean saunters. His hips sway in a slow and natural motion. His ass...

His. *Ass*.

I give my head a shake too and glance up at the ceiling, asking the sky for a little self-control here. And I remind myself that I do not like Rhys Dupris, no matter what my pussy thinks about him.

CHAPTER 13

Tabitha

MILO KNEW RHYS WAS COMING BACK TODAY. WHEN I TOLD him, he got excited, so I made sure not to rain on his parade. I suppose that's why as soon as he wakes up from his nap, he blasts to the top of the stairs and calls down, "Is Ree here?" in the sweetest voice, brimming with genuine excitement.

"Yeah, buddy. Rhys is here."

Tiny footsteps rush down the stairs, and I try not to wince. But I do hold my breath as I listen. He's pretty coordinated for his age, and he is very clear about not wanting to be carried or helped too much because he's *not a baby anymore*—his words, not mine. I try to respect that, but I still envision him toddling and falling down the stairs like the clumsy, tiny human he is.

Milo's small footsteps summon Rhys's bigger ones, eagerly taking the basement stairs two at a time to get to the little boy.

The sound of them rushing to greet each other on the main floor makes my heart twist uncharacteristically.

Rhys isn't as bad as you make him out to be.

The thought pops up, and it's not welcome. But I also know that, deep down, I have *questions*. I've spent the last two weeks wrestling with the reality that there might be more to this story than I first thought. That Erika may have been lying to me. That Rhys might have had a good reason for kicking her out.

After all, if I've learned anything recently, it's that I'm the only person who thinks pinky promises are binding. Erika and I grew up making them to each other. They became something of a secret handshake between us. We shared first-kiss stories. Confessions about sneaking out. One time, I made her pinky promise not to be mad at me, then divulged that I'd borrowed her mascara, which was why we both had pink eye. I think she'd silently seethed at me for days, though she was never outwardly angry with me.

She'd kept her promises then. But that was before. Most recently, I promised to never give up on her. And she promised not to lie to me again. Then she did anyway.

Still, disliking Rhys is a safe place for me. Holding him responsible for what happened to Erika means I don't have to feel like I failed her entirely. I can shovel some of the responsibility off onto him and save my sanity.

It's not fair, but it's the only way I'm holding it together. The mind works in mysterious ways and all that.

Like now, as it goes all gooey watching them together. Milo launches himself into Rhys's massive arms with a happy squeal. A dagger lodges in my throat as I watch Rhys nuzzle against his mussed curls and breathe him in. *Again.*

I turn my watery eyes out toward the backyard and give them a moment. I feel like an intruder. I feel torn. I feel *guilty*.

How can I hate someone who loves my nephew in a way that makes my chest ache and my teeth hurt? Especially in a world where more people to love him could never be a bad thing.

I actually want this.

The four words I've lost sleep over for the past two weeks. And the proof is right in front of me. Rhys clings to him, and he clings to Rhys.

It makes me question if I'm the bad guy in this equation. But then I think of his nightmares and the way he burrows against me when he's scared. I think of the attention he gets from my parents. And at the very least, I know that this is the best place for him.

When they finally draw away from each other, Milo places one chubby hand on each of Rhys's scruffy cheeks and looks at him. *Really* looks at him. Then he smiles and says, "I missed you."

The grin Rhys gives him back is downright blinding, and I realize I've never seen him smile. Never heard him laugh either.

"Missed you too, little man."

"That's our plant. Erika." Milo points over at the pot with glee, and Rhys stiffens.

"Is that so?"

"It was Mama's."

"It was." Rhys's voice is thick, his eyes never leaving the little boy's profile. "And it is such a nice plant."

Milo grins and nods. "I love it."

Rhys's Adam's apple bobs. "I love it too."

I cough to cover the sad little moan that threatens to escape my throat, and they both turn to look at me.

They're not related. But they sure look like they could be.

"Go swimming now?" I promised Milo a trip to the lake to swim this afternoon, and he never fails to remind me of the promises I've made. He switches gears so easily.

But I'm too agitated to join them, too worried about irritating Rhys and the potential consequence of him taking Milo away just to spite me. I don't want to rain on their parade, and it strikes me that keeping a lower profile might be my best course of action.

I feel emotional, and the beach always reminds me of Erika. Of swimming together as little kids. Of our dad burying us in the sand until only our heads poked out. Of tanning together as teenagers, but ending up looking like lobsters. Of taking Milo for his very first swim and watching his eyes go comically wide when he hit the cold water.

Fond memories pummel me. I cherish all those memories of her, and especially her with Milo. We always had fun together there, and I miss that version of her.

"Why don't the two of you go? Have some time together. I need to…uh…clean the house," I say, nodding with an obnoxiously bright smile on my face.

Rhys's brow furrows as he watches me, but Milo's excited clapping draws his attention away.

Which is good. I find it hard to breathe when Rhys looks at me too closely.

I've gotten pretty adept at avoiding Rhys over the past few days. We don't talk much. In fact, we're a little like ships passing in the night. I'm just biding my time, hoping to fly under the radar until he leaves tomorrow.

And I only know he's leaving because I overheard him telling Milo.

Back out of the country for work, he says. Whatever that means. All I know is he usually comes here on a Tuesday and leaves by Saturday. I also know that he works out a lot, which is great because it leaves Milo and me alone. And then when I'm at the restaurant, Rhys hangs out with Milo. Which keeps him out of my hair. Which is also great. And last night when he went bowling (after grumbling something about how he didn't want to but had made a commitment), I was already up in my room by the time he got home.

Okay, maybe I sprinted up the stairs when I saw his truck pull up.

But I still left dinner out for him. In fact, ever since hearing his stomach that night, I make extra food and leave him a plate. And though we don't talk about it, he always eats it.

Today, I might do something on my own and let Rhys take the morning with Milo, since they clearly enjoy spending time with each other. I hate to admit that having Rhys here makes everything so much easier...but it does.

And it's perfect. We barely see each other, and Milo is happy. Really fucking happy. His nightmares don't seem as bad as they were, but he still sleeps with me every night—something I know Rhys has noticed, though he hasn't commented.

I've started making coffee extra early and retreating to the back deck to enjoy the peace and quiet of a summer morning in the valley.

But today I don't get out of the house early enough. I'm in the kitchen, wearing a baby-blue lounge set—too-short shorts and a skimpy spaghetti-strap top—with the coffeepot in one hand and a mug in the other. Just as I'm mid-pour, a shirtless, chiseled Rhys appears in the doorway, prompting me to gawk and then spill piping hot coffee all over my hand.

"Fuck, fuuuck," I hiss, setting the coffee on the counter. I shake my hand out, sending a smattering of droplets over my clothes.

"Shit, Tabby." His voice is rough and heavy with sleep as he rushes forward and grabs my scalded red hand, turning it over gently for inspection like he's a doctor and not a porn star. "Are you okay?" His tousled hair and the soft heat radiating from his skin speak of a man who just rolled out of bed.

"I'm fine." He's too close, his scent too alluring, like lemongrass with a hint of something smokier. I need to draw away, to create space between us, but his fingers clamp around my forearm, and he grumbles as he marches me over to the deep farm sink.

He flicks on the cold water, testing the temperature with his free hand before giving a terse nod and gently lowering my stinging one beneath the cool stream.

I hiss when the water hits it and try to pull away from him—I'm perfectly capable of tending to my own burn. But his hand has an unyielding grip, not aggressive, but not forgiving either. He doesn't let me go.

It's only when I sigh and surrender to his hold that his thumb brushes against my skin.

Once. Twice. I shiver.

A third time. I soften.

I don't know how long we stand there, him pressed flush against me. My only protection against him is a flimsy layer of fabric.

"There," he says quietly, turning my hand over again to assess the damage, water streaming over the opposite side.

"I've had worse burns," I mutter. And it's true. Burns are a fact of life when you work in a kitchen.

Rhys doesn't seem to care about my thoughts on the matter though. He ignores me and carries on overreacting. "Where's your first aid kit?"

"Under the sink. I can—"

Before I can finish, he drops down at my bare feet and yanks the kitchen cupboard open. I can't help but stare at the way his lips pop open on a breathy sigh as he rifles through the contents.

"Just fucking let me take care of you. Where is it?" He glances up at me, and my stomach bottoms out. All those dark features homed in on *me.* Him on his knees for *me.* Wanting to take care of *me.*

"At...at...uh..." I stutter, and his gaze drops to the hem of my shorts, eyes skirting the curve of my ass. My cheeks flare. *God.* Who knows what he can see from that angle?

"At the back," I say, forcing the words out through a dry throat.

He returns his attention to the task at hand and emerges with the white box. He opens it right there on the floor with a near-violent flick and rummages inside before grumbling something I can't make out, right as his fingers wrap around the burn lotion.

"It's not—" *Necessary* is what I'm about to say, but he stands now, towering over me and stealing my words. He slaps the tap off, and then his hands are on my waist, the contact like an electric current zipping across my skin.

It makes me hiss out a breath that he mistakes for pain.

"*I'm fine,*" he mutters, mimicking me while shaking his head. Then he hoists me up onto the counter like I'm a feather and steps close enough that my knees bump against his steely quads.

He's still inspecting my burn with an expression that makes it seem like it's offended him. When he carefully swipes the lotion over my pink skin, it's too much. Deep down, I feel like I don't deserve the level of doting.

He's too gentle. So handsome that it hurts. I'm forced to look away from the way he tends to me.

Stupidly, I opt to soak in his naked torso instead. A fool's strategy to keep from wanting to climb him.

My eyes trace hard line after hard line, the masculine dark hair leading up from his waist, a bit thicker on his chest.

Then I stop.

Just below his right collarbone is a heavy bruise, its edges fading to yellow. Without thinking, I reach up and run my fingertips over it, as if I can wipe it away. But it does no such thing.

"What is this?"

"A bruise." Leave it to Rhys to give me nothing.

"From what? What the hell kind of porn are you filming?"

"I don't do porn, Tabby." Despite his harsh tone, he continues rubbing my hand gently. "I already told you that."

"You did. But I don't believe you. Are you okay?" I let my genuine worry seep into my words, hoping he'll hear my concern. My fingers move away from the bruise and trail up over his collarbone, as though checking for any further damage of their own accord.

I shift my body to look at him, trying to make eye contact, but he keeps his focus on my hand. I swear I can hear his teeth grind. "I'm fine. And even if I wasn't, it's none of your business."

Rearing back at that, I regard him more coolly now, yanking my hand away with enough force that I finally break free from his hold. Of course, his body still has me caged in where I'm seated.

"The feeling is mutual, and yet you hauled me up here to fix what wasn't your business."

"You need help."

A dry laugh crests my lips. "What?"

Rhys glares down at me and moves his hands to either side of my hips, propping them against the counter, effectively caging me in. "With Milo. I've been here for all of three days, and it's been busy with both of us taking care of him. I can see you're doing too much for one person. You're tired. You've lost weight. You need help."

Now it's my turn to go rigid. Sure, I'm tired a lot. And yes, sometimes I forget to eat more than coffee.

But that's not why I spilled the hot liquid on myself.

They say the days are long, but the years are short. Soon Milo won't need me the way he does right now. And I don't begrudge him this time. I revel in it, especially knowing Rhys could yank it out from under me at any moment.

"Oh, and you think you can do better?"

One firm nod from the mountain man. "I can afford to hire help."

My jaw goes slack. He hit me right where it hurts. In the finances. "Are you kidding me right now? That's your grand plan? Take Milo away from everything he knows and hire help to care for him?"

Rhys maintains an emotionless stare and says nothing.

I lift a hand and give him a push. Right on his bruise. "Are you taking him with you tomorrow?" I ask, not sure I want to hear the answer.

"No."

His one-word answer is enough for me. I hop off the counter and shove past him to pour myself a fresh cup of coffee. Then I march outside like I wanted to do before his naked torso walked into the kitchen and fucked everything up.

But it's not as relaxing as I anticipated. I'm angry and

horny, and I feel like Rhys is watching me through the glass doors. But I refuse to check in case he sees and gets satisfaction out of thinking I care.

The next day, he leaves, and we don't see each other or say goodbye.

The weird part is, I feel guilty about it.

CHAPTER 14

Rhys

Rhys: Checking in. How are you?

Tabby: You're not here. So...poor and happy, I guess?

"Do you guys own guns?"

West, Ford, and Bash stare back at me like I've grown a second head. Okay, not Bash. He looks at me like you look at gum that's stuck to the bottom of your shoe before responding with, "I have a hunting rifle. It stays in a locked cabinet in the basement. Why?"

I shrug. It's been another two weeks since I was last here, and all I did was worry about Tabitha and Milo while I was away. It's fucking insane.

I've been waking up in the middle of the night

questioning if they were safe. Wondering if Tabitha's burned hand is okay. The only saving grace is that she texted me photos of Milo. Never many words though. Which means I know they're alive, but not how they're doing.

Not that I should expect much else after the way I left things.

Flaunting my money and saying shit I shouldn't have while keeping her completely in the dark was a real dick move. But hashing things out is not my forte. I'm well aware that I'm no open book. Sharing things about myself is a quality that people drummed out of me many, many years ago. And the truth is, I don't know what to do about Milo and the guardianship.

It's clear I'm not needed. Yet, I feel contractually bound. And what's worse is that, for some unknown reason, I'm eager to get back to them. As long and inconvenient as the trip to Rose Hill may be, I'm always relieved when I see Tabitha roll her eyes at me and hear Milo's tiny footfalls running my way.

I think deep down I dread the thought of never seeing them again—adding them to the list of families I was never welcome to join.

So I keep coming back. However, this time my relief at walking up to that front door got overshadowed by finding it unlocked. *Again.*

Which turned into another clash between Tabitha and me.

I pride myself on being cool, calm, and collected—even if I have a scrappy streak. But she just…she fires me up.

What are you going to do? Punish me? Bend me over…

I swallow and brush the memory aside.

"Tabitha is always leaving her door open," I say.

"Stupid," Bash mumbles, reaching for his pint while shaking his head.

"See? You get it."

West looks more confused. "Like open-open? Aren't bugs an issue?"

"No, intruders are, you idiot." Bash takes the words right out of my mouth.

"Perhaps an alarm system is a happy medium between an arsenal of guns and an unlocked door?" Ford suggests dryly. His delivery makes it hard to tell if he's mocking me or offering a serious solution.

An alarm system. I don't hate the idea, but before I can ask any further questions about it, all the guys' heads turn to the front of the bowling alley. And I don't just mean our team of four. I mean every head in the house turns to face three women who've entered the building. And leading the charge is none other than Tabitha.

She doesn't spare anyone a single glance except the bartender, Frankie, who she greets with more joy than I've ever seen her give anyone other than Milo. I assume he's with her parents tonight, but I don't know because we don't talk, and I have to fight the urge to rush over and ask her.

What holds me back more than anything is that somehow, tonight, she looks *lighter*. She takes a seat at the bar, and I soak her in.

She's fucking stunning. She always is, but the heavier eye makeup and lively flush on her cheeks, paired with the way her hair falls down her back in a shiny dark curtain, stops me in my tracks.

Usually, I see her looking casual, and that already makes my dick hard. So imagine his excitement when she strolls into Rose Valley Alley wearing leather pants, a cropped Rolling Stones T-shirt, and a pair of strappy black stilettos. The heels are pointy enough that I'm sure she's at least considered attempting to murder me with them later. And it's as I mull this over and try not to gawk that her friends join her at the bar.

One of them has dirty-blond hair and a mischievous twinkle in her eye. The other is Skylar Stone, a famous country-pop star. And based on the way Ford and West immediately migrate in their direction, I quickly figure out who's who.

Tabitha, Rosie, and Skylar are out for drinks. It's not that difficult to identify the women based on Ford and West's constant chatter about them.

But the sly wink Tabitha just sent my way tells me they didn't end up here by accident. From that fuckable mouth to the red tips of her toes peeping out of her heels, she's got *trouble* written all over her.

She looks younger, and it's got me wondering just how young she might be. I wrack my brain, trying to remember Erika's age and figure out the gap between them.

I turn, sit down, and decide to retie my shoes just to keep from engaging with her. Bash is unbothered by the other guys' departure, and he doesn't follow suit, just sips his beer and scrolls through his phone.

The chatter from the bar on the other side of the swinging gate filters my way. I can hear Tabitha giving West hell for something or other. In response, West recounts how the bowling team is named the Ball Busters in honor of Tabitha.

She gives him more hell. He gets a kick out of it, and everything between them is incredibly good-natured.

Once, I thought there was something there. Now all I hear is two people bantering like siblings.

It's nothing like the jabs she and I exchange. Not even close.

With my shoes unnecessarily and meticulously retied, the movement of a tall, lanky form striding past draws my attention. It's the guy all the others call Stretch. He gives off slimy vibes, and it doesn't surprise me that no one likes him. I've known my fair share of guys like him. Hell, I work for a guy like him.

He approaches Tabitha, eyes leering, mouth twisted in a suggestive smirk. Where West is playful, this guy is not.

I don't like it.

I don't like *him*.

I absently start a list of men I want to kill for looking at Tabitha like she's their next meal. It's irrational and out of character.

But here I am, behaving irrationally and out of character.

My steps are quiet and metered as I approach him. Years of training have made me more agile than I have any right to be at my size.

"Strikes me that if you wanted to name the team after Tabitha, you could have called it the Tongue Twisters,"

Stretch says as I get close to hear. "Can you still tie a knot in a cherry stem?"

My teeth clamp and my muscles tense as I measure him from behind. I'm sure he's accustomed to being the biggest guy in the room, but not anymore.

Tabitha looks him over, eyes moving down and then back up like she finds him pathetic, and amusing, and entirely lacking. The way she looks at him hands me back a couple of shreds of my dignity that I threw away when I decided to march over here and interrupt them.

All I know is that I don't want him near her. And she doesn't want him near her either.

"Still dreaming about the only blow job you ever got, Terence? Was that tenth grade? Shame that you peaked so young."

Blow job. She says it with a confident smile. Jealousy licks at my spine. It's both unwelcome and undeniable. I am jealous of every fucker who so much as glances in Tabitha's direction, let alone one who's had his dick in her mouth.

The smarmy loser starts to talk again. "You know—"

But I don't let him get far. With two steps, I'm behind him, and my hand is on his neck. Casually, of course. But I could squeeze and make things a hell of a lot less casual. I use my best stage voice. Speed, clarity, volume, poise, stance—my stance is slightly off to one side. From behind, people might think we're old friends, but everyone facing us knows better when I drop my face down beside his.

"You know what I could tie a knot in? This long fucking neck. And then no one would have to tolerate your presence here." I don't bother keeping my voice quiet. This guy's small-dick shit talk has me riled. "Anyone have any objections?"

Tabitha's eyes flash to mine, wide and alarmed. Then they turn upward as though she's found something especially interesting about the shape of the stain on the ceiling tiles.

The guy ducks and runs, slinking away like the coward he is. Chatter breaks out around us. I register voices saying something about hating that guy and something about girls' night. I don't know, and I don't care. It all falls away, and I only hear generalities, because Tabitha's dark eyes are back on mine. They hold as she wraps her lips around the edge of the cheap rocks glass and takes a swig of pale gold liquor.

She's taunting me. And it works.

So before I do something crazy like drag her out of here and beg her to let me fuck her, I spin on my heel and walk back to our bowling lane.

Bash calls the other guys over, and the game begins, but I'm too agitated to finesse a single thing. Instead of pins, I see Stretch's stupid face, and I throw the ball like I'm taking his head clean off.

"Goddamn, you've got a hell of an arm on ya," West comments, fully amused, right as Bash grumbles, "Calm the fuck down. This isn't a World's Strongest Man contest."

Ford chuckles and shakes his head as he regards me. I think he might be more observant than the others, which means he could be onto me and my wayward crush on Tabitha Garrison.

The one that just fucking blindsided me in the middle of a shitty dive bar. The one I've been ignoring for weeks to avoid all the complications that come with it. The one that's one hundred percent doomed, because crushing on a girl who hates your guts is a recipe for disaster.

No matter what a bad idea it is, it's an idea all the same. One I can't shake. Even bowling can't clear my mind of her. Especially not when I know she's *here*.

It's my turn again, and we're already losing. Our team is fun, but we suck. I can hear the girls taunting us from the bar. I've been trying not to look their way, but it's been impossible to keep my eyes from wandering to Tabitha. Sometimes I catch her looking at me. Sometimes it's the other women. But one thing is clear: they're talking about me.

Seconds later, my hunch is confirmed.

"Your physique is too much like Jason Momoa, Rhys," Skylar calls out, barely audible over the din of heavy balls and falling pins.

I ignore her. Based on the news highlights I've seen, she's had a hard enough time lately without me snapping at her.

"The way you fill out those jeans is criminal, Rhys," Rosie says. I like Ford too much to say anything, so I opt to ignore them even as they continue.

"Your hands don't need to be that big, Rhys."

"How dare you defend Tabby's honor, Rhys? You piece of shit."

Shaking my head in an attempt to clear it, I approach the lane and throw my ball. But there are too many eyes on me. My feelings are too jumbled. And when I release it, I fire it *hard*.

Straight into the gutter.

That's when I hear what I've come to recognize as Rosie's voice calling out the loudest of their jibes so far. "Hey, Rhys," she shouts across the small space. "You're supposed to aim for the pins. Get this man some bumpers, Frankie."

The guys around me fail to hold back their chuckles.

West grins as he takes in the lane with hands propped on his hips. "I thought Tabby was the ball buster. I think Rosie might take the cake tonight though."

It's only Bash who gives me a reassuring slap on the shoulder. "I'm sure you're a natural at something. It's just not this."

That only makes the guys laugh harder.

I turn my head to glare at the women, but all they do is dissolve into a fit of giggles. Tabitha's face is beet red, and she's practically hiding behind a glass of tequila. My lips wiggle, and I turn away to cover a smile. She's having fun. It's good for her. And if mocking me is what brings her joy, then whatever.

I can take it.

I splash water over my face and stare into the cracked mirror of the men's washroom at Rose Valley Alley. My body is sore, and I look tired, but somehow I also look…relaxed. Maybe doing something other than working, performing, training, and holing up alone is good for me.

The Ball Busters lost. Again.

But I had fun. Again.

Even with the feel of Tabitha's gaze hot and heavy on my back, I ended up enjoying myself. But when we wrapped, I felt the need to cool off, to take a moment of reprieve. Even if that reprieve comes by retreating to the run-down men's room at the back of the building. On the mirror, someone has written *For a good time call...* followed by the number in Wite-Out, and there are random stickers plastered around the edges.

As I yank the door open and stroll out into the darkened, narrow back hall to join the guys, I'm pondering who thinks to bring Wite-Out to a dive like this. No man is just wandering around with office supplies shoved in his back pocket.

"Hey, watch—" The voice hits me right as I crash into another body. On instinct, my arms shoot out, and I turn into a roll, taking the person with me as my back hits the wall.

I know I'm holding Tabitha before I look down. It's in the way the pads of my fingers tingle and how she's too short to even show up in my line of vision.

"Sorry," I breathe, looking down into her startled, slightly glassy eyes.

"Are you? Or is this your big plan to take me out?" She makes no move to leave my grip. Instead, she inches closer, the peep of red paint on her toes butting up against my dorky fucking two-tone bowling shoes.

This woman. She never backs down. Every time she pushes me, I just want to push back. Too much pushing and we're going to break something.

I drop one hand to her hip, meeting her challenge as I

tug her closer. "You can stop making jokes about me killing you any time now. They're getting old."

She scoffs. "You know what's getting old? You waltzing in here full of fucking opinions about me and my house and how much money I have and how qualified I am to take care of Milo—like you're the anointed expert on all things ever in the history of the world."

"Tabitha."

She shoves me, hard. Both palms curl into my shirt as she presses my back against the wall with an alarming level of strength.

I wince, and she doesn't miss it.

Before I get another word in, her hands have rushed down the front of my torso, gripped the hem of my gray T-shirt, and ripped it up to expose my stomach.

Her eyes scour me, and her lip curls when her gaze finds the welts on one side of my ribs. A forceful push into the turnbuckle caused the ropes to wrap around my back, leaving visible marks. Usually I'm not this banged up, but getting back into the swing of things after time off means selling it when I get my ass kicked in the ring. I can't waltz straight into a title—I need to earn it.

Her palms stay flat, and warm, and distracting against my abs as she tears into me with renewed ferocity now that she's seen the marks. "I'm done talking about me. Let's talk about *you*, Rhys. Let's talk about the bruises. Let's talk about the secrecy. Let's talk about how the hell you've gotten to a place where you've convinced yourself you'd be such a great guardian for a three-year-old when you have the emotional intelligence of a rock and a penchant for something that is clearly violent. You are one big red flag, my friend. And I don't think being raised by a full-time staff will fix the damage you'll do to Milo by forcing him to grow up in whatever fucked-up porno gangland world you live in."

Good god, this woman is infuriating. I should tell her, just spit it out. But I've had it go south before. First, I had foster parents who made contact, which was borderline heartwarming until they asked for money. And the last time I was brave enough to tell a friend, it became a running joke I had to grin and bear. It niggled at me—embarrassed me. And I don't trust Tabitha not to take this little tidbit and use it to hit me where it hurts.

Not telling her just feels like self-preservation at this point.

So instead, I grip her waist with both my hands and flip us again. Now it's my turn to push her up against a wall. "I don't know why you're so obsessed with me being a porn star. If you want to see me fuck someone, the bathroom is right there. Drag me in there right now, and you can watch in the mirror while I bend you over."

Her plush, pink mouth pops open, but no words come out. We're both panting, our breath mingling between us. Hers smells like lime and tequila, mine adding something sweet from the cola I left at my table.

Her lips fall together, then curve up into a confident smile. She sways a bit, and I can tell she's extra uninhibited right now. Something that becomes clearer when she reaches forward and grabs my rock-hard dick. She squeezes, and I hiss, propping an arm on the wall above us as my head drops down over her.

"I knew it," she whispers, tilting her face up to mine. "It must be exhausting walking around my house with a raging hard-on all the time."

My hips thrust forward into her grip, pressing closer and trapping her hand between us. A shiver races down my spine, and a whimper spills from her mouth. She's too late biting down on it, but that doesn't stop me from watching the way her teeth sink into the pillowy flesh of her bottom lip.

She doesn't miss a beat though. Taking full advantage with her free hand, she trails her fingers over my obliques and around to my back. "Poor little Rhys. I'd feel bad for you, except I take comfort in knowing you want something that you can't have." Her fingers squeeze harder around my cock—almost too hard. "It's like how I want you to just"—squeeze—"go"—squeeze—"away"—squeeze.

Fuck. If she keeps this up, I'm going to blow in my pants.

In a desperate attempt to take back a shred of control, my hand shoots up, wrapping around her dainty throat. Gentle, but firm enough to keep her eyes on me. "That's adorable, Tabby. Especially since we both know you're lying. I've seen the way you stare at me. I bet you're fucking soaked right now."

She stares back at me defiantly, our chests heaving with exertion. Everything about her is ferocious. Commanding. Fucking hot as hell. If she weren't so drunk, I would drag her into the bathroom and follow through.

But she is, so I step away. Only for her to taunt me with a

smug tip of her lips and a parting shot. "Too bad you'll never get a chance to find out."

It's just as well. I have a feeling we'd hate-fuck this entire building to the ground. And truthfully, I don't really want Tabitha to hate me. I wish she didn't.

Plus, my flight out is tomorrow, and I suspect if I go that far with her, I won't want to leave at all.

So instead, I turn around. Go back into the bathroom. Lock the door behind me. And fist my cock while imagining being inside Tabitha Garrison.

Just to take the edge off.

CHAPTER 15

Tabitha

Rhys: Letting you know to expect company today. And a package.

Tabby: Oh? Are you going to pop out of a bush again?

Rhys: No. It's not me.

Rhys: And I didn't pop out of a bush.

Tabby: As long as it's not you, I'm happy.

Life carries on in a hazy blur. Most days blend together in a nonstop rush. And I appreciate that about my current situation. It means I have little time to dwell on Erika. While the lingering sadness is a constant companion, staying busy has kept me from sinking into my heartache. Opening up about her death to Rosie and Skylar over drinks was a relief. It immediately made me feel less alone. Something that I hate to admit Rhys has also accomplished.

He's come and gone a few times over now. Where and who to, I have no idea. Friends? Family? Beats the fuck out of me, and he definitely isn't big on volunteering any information. All I know is his last departure was no less abrupt than the others. We didn't address the elephant in the room. I'm too scared to ask about his plans, and I'm walking on eggshells around the subject. And he's too locked up to share a single fucking thing.

Though that could have had something to do with him offering to fuck me in the bathroom and me squeezing the hell out of his dick.

His really, *really* big dick.

Rhys has always given off big dick energy. But I know now it's not so much energy as big dick knowledge. Big dick surety? Big dick *guarantee*.

I mull over the witty ways to put it as I wait for him to arrive again. Usually, I'd make myself scarce, but all that big dick nerve of his means he took it upon himself to send a company to my house to set up a security system.

Turning them away had been my first instinct. In fact, I had been in the middle of telling them I needed to drop Milo off at my parents' house so that I could go to work. I was even being polite about it. It wasn't their fault that Rhys, Legal Guardian of the Year, is an overbearing asshole.

But then Bash showed up, arms crossed with a no-nonsense look on his face, telling me Rhys knew I was busy and had asked him to stay and supervise. Apparently they text now. I'm not sure about what. It seems like texting grunts and scowls back and forth would be rather anticlimactic.

Bash also told me it was okay to let people take care of me sometimes. And that one sentence struck a nerve I didn't feel like standing around discussing. So I'd offered a watery smile, told him to mind his own damn business, and then taken off.

Turns out having anyone but Rhys show up at my house didn't make me happy at all.

Even the outdoor heater he had delivered for the back deck didn't help. All it did was keep me warm while I sat outside and plotted my revenge.

That was five days ago. Which was the perfect amount of time for me to stew and hatch a plan. Yes, today I'll be presenting Rhys with a surprise of his own. He once told me he doesn't like surprises, so this will be extra special.

The big surprise is why I'm sitting on the front steps waiting for him to arrive. I check my watch and glance at the monitor that's linked to Milo's room, realizing Rhys is later than I anticipated. I'm hoping Milo is still napping when he gets here, so I can enjoy his reaction to the fullest.

By the time he pulls up, I'm painting my toenails a fresh shade of purple out of boredom. The sound of his engine cutting by the curb draws my attention. I expect him to look all ominous and scowly like usual, but instead his mouth is pinched and his eyes drawn. It makes me realize that even though he usually glares at me, there's an element of him that looks...I don't know...relieved to see me.

This face, though? This face looks like dread.

He yanks his usual duffel bag from the back door and tosses it over his shoulder. I watch him. Wondering if he's bruised anywhere. Secretly hoping he's okay.

"Hi…" I venture carefully as he makes his way up the front walkway.

"Hey." Even tentative as he is right now, he commands attention. It's not anything specific he does. It's just him.

My mouth gets drier the closer he gets, and my plan of what to say to him evaporates when he takes a seat beside me on the front step. He lets out a heavy sigh as his body folds down.

"You must be tired. Getting here from Florida has got to be a pain in the ass." I don't know why I say it. He just looks worn out today, and it tugs on my heartstrings. I doubt there's a direct flight to Alberta. And then it's another flight to a small city about an hour away or a three-hour drive across the provincial border from Calgary.

"We need to talk."

I swallow and stare down at my purple toenails, trying not to focus too much on his nearness. "I'm starting to hate that sentence."

"I got hung up at the border today. One of the officers finally called me on overstaying my welcome. Had to call my lawyer and explain the situation at border services."

My stomach drops, and my hands grip my bare knees to keep from shaking, because I don't like where this is going.

"Okay," I say hesitantly.

"Tabitha, he's recommending I take Milo with me when I leave this time. If I leave him here, he has no legal guardian."

"I—"

His large hand falls over mine. And this time, I don't shake it off. I let him steady me.

I'm out of time.

"Listen. I know. I know you are capable. Hell, I even know here is the best place for him. I'm not saying I'm going to keep him from you. But changing the name on that form isn't going to happen overnight. And if something happens to him and I'm not here, then social services will get involved."

My heart beats deep in the pit of my stomach, that sensation of life not being real overtaking all my senses. "You *can't*."

His fingers tighten on mine, and I hear a pained groan rattle around in his chest. "I'm sorry, Tabby. It won't be forever."

It won't be forever.

The idea of being alone with my thoughts, with my guilt, with my grief—it's just too much. And there's something about the word *forever* that sparks an idea in my head.

In this instant, I know that I'm about to make a very, very bad decision. But I figure that after being the sister who carefully thought out every choice in her life, I'm due to make a colossally stupid one. And if nothing else, at least being willing to do anything for my family is consistent.

Which is why I blurt out my totally absurd idea before I can think it through with my usual level of care. "Marry me."

I swear the birds stop chirping. The world stops turning. Rhys stops moving. And I want to dig myself a nice big hole and crawl into it.

"You and me?" is the first thing he says, rearing back to look at me as though checking to see if I've got the vapors.

I grimace and avoid making eye contact. We can pretend I never said that at all. A perfectly forgettable moment of inexplicable hysteria.

"Yeah. No, of course not. That's absurd. We hate each other." I slap my hands together like I'm clearing dust—and all my dignity from them—before I get up, turn away, and take the steps toward the house. "I wouldn't want to marry you," I mumble as I open the screen door and pad inside. "Even if your dick is huge," I add once I clear the doorway.

Rhys doesn't follow me. One look back at him over my shoulder, and I see his hulking form slouched on the front steps, eerily still.

I wonder how he feels about those murder jokes now. Perhaps he's considering the validity of those options. Getting rid of me would make his life a lot easier. I can't imagine a world in which he likes coming all this way to see Milo, or one in which he enjoys spending time around me with how things are between us.

No, I bet a world without Tabitha Garrison to terrorize him and turn his life upside down is mighty appealing right now.

His silence stresses me out, so I decide to wipe down the kitchen cupboards. They aren't dirty—in fact, I did this exact thing two days ago—but it gives me something to do that doesn't involve facing him.

I scrub frantically and act like I'm removing a stubborn spot when he enters the house. He props a shoulder against the rounded entryway, crosses his arms, and stares at me.

I fucking hate when he stares at me. It makes my stomach flop over on itself. The same dropping sensation you get on a thrilling carnival ride. Except those are short-lived. Those end.

Rhys Dupris is the carnival ride that I just can't manage to get off of.

"What are you doing?" he finally asks.

"Cleaning." I reach farther over my head, wiping higher on the gray kitchen cabinets.

"Why?"

"I like a clean house. It soothes me."

Because it's one of the only things I can control right now.

"You need to make sure that Milo grows up understanding that a clean house is important. You can't just send him out into the world thinking that paid staff will clean up after him and that his secret CIA daddy will pay for everything."

"CIA?"

I shake my head, moving to the next cabinet with an irritated huff. "You are secretive and covered in bruises. Porn doesn't make sense anymore. And I'm tired of asking, so whatever. You go ahead and keep your weird secrets. Anyway"—I forge ahead, barely pausing to breathe—"men can't just go out into the world as lazy slobs who don't know how to cook anything. If he's going to be a good partner one day, he should at least have some domestic capabilities. And I don't know what your place is like, so if you don't keep it clean, you better fucking star—"

"I'll marry you, Tabitha."

His words suck all the air out of the room, and I pause

with my back to him. What he said was clear as day, and yet I can't have heard him properly over the pounding in my ears.

"That's not a funny joke," I venture, turning to face him in slow motion.

"No, I agree."

There isn't a stitch of humor in any of his strong features. That nose, just slightly big. His brow, just slightly heavy. Those lips, just slightly pouty. Masculine from head to toe.

And entirely serious.

"But…" My brain searches for the words, but none jump out at me. He's struck me speechless.

Eventually, I come up with, "But why would you do this?"

A shrug. "For Milo."

I swallow the unexpected sting of those words. I'm not under any delusion about what's between Rhys and me.

There's animosity and sexual tension, but not a lot of love. Which is fine. I've never been the girl who dreams about her wedding day with the perfect white dress and Pinterest-worthy decorations. But there's still something hollow about the moment. A pang of longing for something I never knew I wanted.

"Are you sure?"

"Yes. Are you?"

My lips roll together. I know I'm the one who suggested this. But still.

What the fuck am I doing?

My teeth nibble at my bottom lip as I nod over and over

again. "Sure. Yeah. We can hit the courthouse, get our marriage certificate, and then you can do whatever you want. We can stay married just long enough for you to get citizenship and then split. Keep it all very amiable for Milo's sake. I would pinky promise you not to come after half of what's yours when we divorce but..." I trail off with a grimace, deciding now is not the moment to antagonize him over his weak-ass pinky promises.

Still, I don't miss the flash of sadness in his eyes as he looks away.

"Sorry. I just mean—we can get 'er done, high-five, and go our separate ways." I'm talking, but it feels surreal. Like I'm outside myself watching the scene play out on television.

Rhys sighs and lifts a hand to scrub at his stubbled chin. "It's going to have to look a little more real than that, Tabby. We've got Milo in the mix. We can't have people talking about it being fake. I don't know how closely the government will be watching now that I'm on their radar. Immigration will be suspicious as hell."

My stomach drops as I fixate on one thing. *Milo*. How will he take this?

I toss the rag on the kitchen counter and take a few steps closer to him. "Wait. So you're saying we need to have a real wedding? Like with real guests and shit?"

The world around me spins, and my chest goes tight. I know I felt like I was due to make a stupid choice—but not *this* stupid. I must be downright delusional to think that I could pull something like this off.

"With real guests and shit," he deadpans.

"And I have to convince everyone around me that I am madly in love with you and just had to be married this instant?"

Rhys shrugs.

"That's it? A shrug?"

"I mean, is that so unbelievable?"

"Everyone thinks we hate each other, so...yes?"

"Why would they think that? I've never told anyone that I hate you."

"I mean, it's obvious."

His head quirks. "Is it? What have I ever done that makes you think I hate you?"

My breathing goes heavier as I think it over. Sure, there was some distrust at the beginning, but the more I think about it, the more I can't think of a single thing.

"Do people think you hate *me*?" I could swear there's a little teasing in his tone.

Heat suffuses my cheeks and crawls down my throat, flashing across my chest like a big fat *guilty* sign. "Only Rosie and Skylar. I've been vague about our relationship with everyone else. But it's not like we've been"—I wave my hand around frantically—"I don't know, traipsing around town together."

Rhys just lifts one shoulder and drops it. He's so casual. It's impossible to read him. "Then I guess we better sell it."

My pink flush turns red.

Sell it.

I don't know what that means, and I'm too chickenshit

to ask. The thought of Rhys touching me freely sends an unwelcome thrill down my spine.

His hands on my skin. His tongue in my mouth.

I shake my head.

Nah. Even if we have to kiss, there will be no tongue. It's completely unnecessary. We can keep it chaste. Neither one of us is mushy or touchy-feely. No one will think twice about us keeping a cool two feet apart at all times. *Right?*

I want to ask, but don't want him to get annoyed and take the offer back. For Milo, I need this. For me, though? This could be a disaster.

Either way, it's a risk I'm willing to take.

So, for what feels like the billionth time in the past couple of months, I just stand and stare at Rhys while he stares back. His attention is almost suffocating.

Until…

Meow.

Rhys's chin drops slowly, the look in his eye going from reserved to pissed off as his attention lowers.

The tabby cat with four white paws and a little white tip on her tail that Milo and I chose from the shelter waltzes into the kitchen like she's the queen of this house. She weaves herself between Rhys's legs, bunting along his jeans.

I swear she's *purring*.

"Surprise?" I say, feeling less sure of my payback for the alarm system now that Rhys is marrying me as a favor.

"What the fuck is that?"

"A cat. Her name is Cleocatra."

"*Why?*"

Yeah, he's not seeing the humor in this at all. "You can call her Cleo for short."

"No, Tabitha. I meant, why is there a fucking cat in the house?"

I bristle. "Listen, this is still my house. Still my life. If you're expecting me to be a subservient little wife, then I've got news for you, pal. So yeah, if I want a cat, I'll get one. Just like how if you want an alarm system, you'll get one."

His jaw goes tight. "I doubt that anyone in their entire life has used the word *subservient* to describe you."

"Thank you," I preen.

"I'm allergic."

My eyes roam over him speculatively. "How allergic?"

"It's complicated." He can't even look at me. My eyes widen in time with my grin.

"You're not allergic at all, are you? You big fucking drama queen!"

That earns me an eye roll and a grumbled, "I hate cats."

"That's not an allergy. That's a preference."

"I still hate cats," he deadpans.

I smile sweetly in response. "Whatever. Just don't let Milo hear you say that. He's very much in love with Cleocatra."

The rumble in Rhys's chest should be intimidating, but he doesn't scare me at all. So, I walk toward him and pat his shoulder. "You can consider her an engagement gift. You're welcome."

Then I breeze past, going to get my phone so I can make some calls and share our big, exciting, not-at-all-nauseating, happy news.

"Wait." I turn back to the forlorn-looking giant standing in my kitchen, staring at the floor like he's just witnessed some terrible accident. "When's the wedding going to be?"

"Soon."

"How soon?"

His head joggles as he considers. "How long does a marriage certificate take to get?"

"I don't know. A couple of weeks?"

He nods. "Then we do it as soon as possible. I won't be able to get back into the States without it."

"Don't you need time for your family to book flights or something?"

His expression turns stony. "No. We should do it next weekend. I'm due back at work as soon as possible."

I swallow in response, not sure what to make of his chilly reply but not feeling comfortable enough to press him any further. "Next weekend? A week to plan?"

"Sure."

Sure.

God, I could barf. The nonchalance of that response sends my stomach plummeting. Guilt and nerves hit hard along with something else.

Disappointment.

Because, deep down, I wish there were a tiny bit of enthusiasm. I wish there were a spark of...I don't know. Camaraderie?

He doesn't even want his family present, and it stings.

It makes me realize this might not be as easy of a sell as we think. We will have to lie our asses off. But lying to everyone around me shouldn't be too hard. I've been keeping secrets where Rhys is concerned for weeks now.

It's lying to myself that feels like it's going to be a challenge.

CHAPTER 16

Rhys

Rhys: Need to tell Milo in the morning.

Tabby: What a romantic good night text from my fiancé.

Rhys: I'm serious.

Tabby: So am I.

Rhys: You bought me a cat. Romance is dead in this house.

Tabby: Or maybe you don't understand my love language?

Rhys: Is it pettiness?

Tabby: "Pettiness is my love language." I'd wear that shirt!

Rhys: Stop avoiding my question.

Tabby: Fine. Maybe we shouldn't tell him? It seems terrible to lie to a three-year-old. Being oblivious sounds very relaxing to me.

Rhys: Tabitha, he's going to be here with us. At the

wedding. Out in public. He'll hear people talking. He's young, but he isn't stupid.

Tabby: Okay. But I'm not telling him alone.

Rhys: We'll do it together.

"I'm not going to be back in time for the show on Monday."

Anthony groans. "What the hell, Rhys. We just wrote your entire comeback. You're mid-feud." I grimace with my phone still held to my ear. I was already prepared for this to go over poorly. Anthony has always been an entitled asshole, but because of my popularity, I've been spared. "I know. And that's not the worst part."

"Oh good," he replies sarcastically. Anthony is a businessman through and through. The bottom dollar and the viewership rates reign supreme. His wrestlers' mental and physical health come *after* that.

And me spending too much time away from the ring is not good for his business. Especially after my on-and-off returns with ongoing knee issues. The ones I finally got clearance to have surgically repaired rather than continuing to run myself into the fucking ground. "What's the worst part?" he asks.

"I'm going to need a couple of weeks."

"Are you fucking joking?" His disbelief and frustration braid themselves together.

"Nope. Sorry," I mumble, looking around Tabitha's backyard from the lounger I've propped myself on.

I do feel bad. Like my returns, I've been a sporadic employee of late. But this—being here—is more important.

"I'm actually getting married," I say.

That strikes the older man silent for a few beats. "Married?"

"Yup."

"But when I look up *bachelor* in the dictionary, your photo is there."

"Ha-ha." I enunciate the words sarcastically. "I'm not that bad. I just...enjoy my solitude."

"You're right. Maybe it's under *monk*."

I grumble but don't respond.

"Shit. You're not joking, are you?"

"No."

"Well..." He trails off, and I can hear the rasp of his fingers over his beard. "Congratulations. It's great you found someone who doesn't conflict with your solitude, even though it's fucking me over. I'm happy for you."

Oh. She conflicts all right, but for some confounding reason, it doesn't bother me at all.

That's what's new.

"Thanks."

"Could you take the honeymoon later? I could schedule you some time off after the next pay-per-view event."

"No."

"That's all you're gonna give me, huh?"

I palm the back of my neck, feeling a pang of guilt for

letting the coworkers down. Anthony down. They don't deserve this. I know it'll mean rejigging matches and rewriting storylines. There will be grumbling. And while I'm a good coworker and a solid wrestler, I don't think anyone would accuse me of being the sunshine of the crew.

They do me favors because they respect me and need me, not because they enjoy bending over backward for me.

His heavy sigh reeks of disappointment. "I'm going to run this past the writers. Might need you in character filming some promos to keep everything rolling forward. You got a costume on hand?"

"Oh yeah. I take my mask and combat pants with me everywhere I go."

He sighs again. "Spare me the snark, Dupris. I'll have a set sent to you. Emerald Lake?"

"No. I'm in Rose Hill."

"Buttfuck Nowhere. Got it. Text me the address. I couldn't find that on a map if I tried."

"Thanks," I grumble, not loving having to ask him for even more help.

"Don't thank me yet. You owe me for this. And whatever story we come up with, you're gonna do it. No bitching and moaning. You'll come back here, put your head down, and get to work."

My molars clamp. He knows I'm finicky about the shit they do with my character, but I'm not in a position to negotiate right now. "Yup."

"Good."

With that, he hangs up, and I'm left sitting in the sun,

staring at the screen of my phone, feeling more out of control than I have in many, many years.

When I come back inside, I find Tabitha sitting at the kitchen table with Milo. He's focused on coloring, and she's completely absorbed, eyes locked on him. Sometimes I catch her like this—zoned out and staring at specific parts of him. Like his ears or his lips.

I chalk it up to her being tired.

She starts when the patio door clicks shut behind me, but Milo looks up and gives me such a genuine smile that I can't help but smile back at him.

Then my eyes land on his paper, and my smile sours.

He has covered the paper with his most impressive cat drawings. Which is to say that an abundance of deformed cats covers the page.

"Lookin' good, pal."

"Drawing Cleocatra," he says with a pleased smack of his lips.

"She looks…" I glance at Tabitha, who's already glaring at me as though daring me to insult his cat. "Super cool. Love it."

Tabitha relaxes back into her chair now, arms crossed beneath her breasts and a smug smile on her face. She looks—so to speak—like the cat who caught the canary. I take a seat and can tell by the gleam in her eye that she's enjoying watching me struggle.

Still, there's something cozy about all of us sitting at the table together. We've been ships in the night, doing what we need to do but avoiding each other at all costs. Yet, as I sit here with them, I realize I like the simplicity of it. Even if things aren't perfect, there's a sense of closeness that I've always craved.

With that thought in mind, Cleocatra leaps up out of nowhere onto my lap. She does this little purr-meow thing that I'm sure some people would find cute. Me? I start and lift my hands like someone just threw anthrax at me.

Tabitha's lips purse, and her head tilts. Another silent threat.

"She loves you." Milo nods, sneaking a peek up at me and looking extremely satisfied about his cat and me forging what he perceives as a friendship. "Pet her. She's soft."

It's not that I truly *hate* cats. I've just never had pets. Haven't had the time, or the space, or the inclination. More mess, more responsibility. And truthfully, their short life expectancy just seems like you're signing up for guaranteed and unnecessary heartache.

My hand moves closer, and the tawny cat bunts against it, a rumble starting instantly in her throat.

"Aw, look at that, Milo. How sweet. Rhys loves Cleo too." Tabitha's grin is just a little too pleased.

My *fiancée* is pushing her fucking luck with this trick.

I glare.

She smiles sweetly.

Then she hits me with a subtle tip of her chin. I know what she's signaling, and as much as it's a conversation I don't want to have, I know it needs to be done.

I nod and watch her tongue dart out over her lips as though she's nervous too.

"Speaking of love, Milo."

His head shoots up, suspicion dancing in his baby blues. "What's wrong?"

My chest aches for him, and I clear my throat to cover the soft keening sound that lurches into my throat. I know that feeling all too well. Assuming any news is bad news because you've been getting just a little too much of it lately.

"Nothing, nothing." Tabitha rubs a hand on his back. "Right, Rhys?"

"Yeah. No. In fact, buddy, we've got..." Again, I find myself staring at his aunt as I search for the right words for this.

Something to tell you?

An announcement to make?

Nothing quite encapsulates the way I'm feeling about the situation. "Some good news to share."

I don't miss the subtle quirk of Tabitha's one brow.

Good news.

I rationalize that it's good news *for Milo* because it works out best for him.

Milo's rosy lips tip up in my direction as he searches for more information, so I turn, giving him my full attention, one hand gripping the back of his chair for support. "Your aunt Tabby and I...well...we...we're getting married." My voice sounds strained, and Tabitha looks like she's just pulled a precarious piece in Jenga.

Milo's brows furrow for a beat, as though mulling over a problem that confuses him. "Like a mom and a dad?"

Tabitha sucks in a breath, blinking away quickly, as her hand moves on his back again. I swallow thickly, feeling all too kindred with Milo.

"Yeah, kind of like that."

"We be all together?"

Tabitha's eyes catch on mine, and I get lost there for a beat. She's unreadable, save for the soft nod she gives me.

Together with Tabitha. It's a dangerous sentiment, one that has become increasingly appealing with every moment I spend in her vicinity.

"Except when I'm away for work. But I promise you I'll come back in between."

I can feel Tabitha staring at me. Can feel the unspoken questions pelting me from the side. She wants to know more—deserves to know more—but I'm still struggling to feel like I don't have to hide.

It's a tough habit to break. But lately I've become more concerned about what my being in the public eye could mean for her and Milo—for their *privacy*. The last thing this tentative new relationship between us needs is media attention and amateur internet sleuths piecing things together.

Which is why I keep my focus on Milo.

Milo, who rolls his lips together thoughtfully, chubby little fingers twirling a crayon. Finally, he turns his wide, deep-blue eyes on me, then on Tabitha. "This makes me so happy." Then he turns and looks over at the crooked corn plant in the corner. His lips slowly turn up in the softest smile before he delivers the killing blow with his baby voice and fumbled pronunciations. "Erika! Aunty Tabby Cat and Ree are getting married!"

My eyes fill, and my head nods as I watch him go back to drawing like he didn't just eviscerate me with the simplest sentence in the world.

It makes me realize that I'd do anything for him.

Even marry a woman who can't stand me.

One who I can't stop thinking about.

CHAPTER 17

Tabitha

Rhys: What type of flowers do you want for your bouquet?

Tabby: Are there any that you're allergic to?

Rhys: Charming. But no.

Tabby: Maybe I should just carry Cleocatra down the aisle? I don't need a bouquet.

I rub my damp palms together nervously in the small back room of the church.

My dad, Paul, doesn't miss it, but he doesn't jump to conclusions. Instead of assuming I'm antsy and dreading walking down the aisle today, he smiles at me kindly. "Excited, aren't ya, kiddo?"

Since Rhys and I told my parents about the wedding, and they met him for the *very first time*, they haven't shown a single shred of suspicion over the entire thing. Which would seem strange, except it's clear as day to me they need something happy in their lives. They need this wedding to be a joyous, happy occasion. They need it so badly that they can't bear to look any closer.

Yeah, my parents are thrilled I'm getting married to Rhys, even though they don't know him from Adam.

"Yeah, Dad." I smile back. "I'm excited."

Excited to get this over with.

I still tried to bring up a quick trip down to the courthouse, but even as the words left my mouth, I knew it wouldn't work. There's no chance people like Rosie, or Skylar, or West, or Bash would believe that I married Rhys for real if we did that. And I suppose that's why they're all in attendance today.

In the name of keeping things simple, Rosie is my maid of honor, and Bash is Rhys's best man. I don't know how or when, but he and Rhys seem to have hit it off beyond the bowling team. Best man and security system enforcer. Their friendship makes perfect sense and also baffles me.

"You look so beautiful." My father's gaze goes watery as he takes me in, and I fight the urge to squirm.

"Thanks, Dad."

I drop his gaze and adjust the spaghetti straps of my simple, backless, lace sheath dress. They hold it securely, a necessity because my small boobs couldn't support anything strapless. This dress was also easily hemmed to accommodate my vertical challenges as well as our short timeline.

My mom, Lisa, had fussed over me finding exactly what I wanted and had lamented that it was impossible with so little time to plan. I'd said something cheesy like, *Sorry, Mom. The heart wants what the heart wants.*

But the truth is, this dress is what I'd choose on a longer timeline. Feminine, but not too frilly. Hell, I could have this hemmed shorter next week and wear it with a cute pair of cowboy boots for a night out.

"The perfect glowing bride. I'm so proud of you, Tabby Cat. I just wish..."

I nod, my eyes swimming with tears, because I know what he was about to say—*I just wish Erika were here.* And so do I, though I still feel conflicted about how she'd be reacting. I'm not oblivious to the fact that Rhys's and my stories don't match up where my sister is concerned. I just haven't let myself dig into why. It hurts too badly.

Still, the dishonesty of the day sits heavy in my stomach. The deception of it all has kept me up the last few nights, along with the knowledge that my husband-to-be is sleeping down in a dank concrete basement.

He's never once complained. And yet, it bothers me more than it ever has. At first, I felt as though Rhys belonged down there, but now...now I'm not so sure.

Rhys was quiet, agreeable, and steady as a rock as we rushed to plan the wedding. We divided and conquered as though we were a real couple and not solely a business arrangement. I took charge of the food, music, and reception dinner at the bistro, while Rhys handled the ceremony itself and booked the small church just off Main Street. He designed invites, printed them, and handwrote names on the front in the most meticulous cursive.

I had stood at the kitchen counter on hold with the food supplier, phone wedged between my ear and my shoulder. My eyes stayed fixed on him as he made our invites with a level of care I never expected. His hands seemed too big for the pen or for the elegant script that he drew on each envelope. It had looked downright ridiculous when he carefully folded down the flap of the envelope.

But it was the way his eyes flashed to mine as he trailed his tongue over the edge of that flap that had me flushing and leaving the kitchen in a flustered huff.

Marrying Rhys for legal purposes is one thing, but letting myself stare at him like I might enjoy consummating said marriage is a recipe for disaster.

And we both know it. It's an unspoken commitment between us. We're both mature enough to understand that Milo is at the center of this jumbled mess, and we don't need to make it any messier.

Basically, we'd both do anything for him. Including keeping our hands the hell off each other.

That mutual dedication breeds a grudging respect between us. I take solace in reminding myself that marriages have been founded on less.

And when I hear the click of the door and Milo's excited squeal, I take solace in knowing I'm making the right decision for him too.

Rosie is holding his hand as she saunters in, eyes roaming, head nodding. "Yes, girl. You look *stunning*."

"Thank you, thank you." I drop a small curtsy that's received with giggles from everyone.

This morning, *the* Skylar Stone played beauty salon with me, curling my hair and applying my makeup with a level of expertise that I just do not possess. I suppose years in the spotlight have taught her a thing or two about primping. And when I told her she could do it professionally, she didn't laugh me off. Instead, her head tilted, and she met my eyes in the mirror with a soft, *You think so?*

"Here." Rosie holds out a bouquet I don't recognize. Jagged green leaves top long, ribbon-wrapped stems. The white flowers that top those stems are small and delicate, but not as delicate as the slender threadlike petals that shoot out from them.

"Rhys told me to tell you he tracked down your favorite flowers."

I quirk a brow at my friend. "Oh he did, did he?"

"Yeah. Apparently, Cat Whiskers are not a common bridal choice, and he had to have them shipped in by special order."

I blink. "I'm sorry?"

Rosie nods eagerly. "I know. Isn't that sweet? Leave it to you to love something so obscure."

I look down at the bouquet in my hand and bark out a laugh.

Fucking Cat Whiskers. What a man.

I'm grinning like a loon and shaking my head in disbelief when Rosie lays a hand on my arm.

"You ready?" Rosie asks, eyeing me carefully. She wasn't

quite the easy sell that my parents were. *I know the feeling. Sometimes love and hate are two sides of the same coin,* she'd said, and I'd nodded along even though the way she and Ford feel about each other is *nothing* like Rhys and me. She didn't hesitate to accept her role in the wedding party though. And I took that as a win.

Because as much as there's a part of me that wanted to tell her this whole thing is a sham, I felt like I owed it to Rhys not to. It may be a sham. But it's *our* sham. And for better or for worse, we're in this together.

So today I smile shyly, grateful that Rosie is here as my maid of honor and that Skylar is sitting in a pew. Over the past several weeks, they've been the closest things I've had to friends in a long time. We don't work together, and they don't need anything from me—they're just happy to spend time with me. Hell, they make me happy too, and at a time like this, that's special.

Rhys and I don't make each other happy. But I'm here, about to walk down the aisle to him anyway. Because, like always, I do what needs to be done.

"Ready," I respond with a firm nod. "How about you, Milo?" I turn and crouch before him.

"I'll be the best flower boy," he gushes, eyes bright and cheeks flushed.

Even though I can tell he's nervous, his excitement is palpable. I can't help but reach forward and hug him. Seeking comfort in him—in knowing I'm doing the right thing. And when his tiny arms wrap around my neck, all my nerves disappear.

The music starts to play as I straighten, and my stomach flips. Rhys is on the other side of those doors, standing in front of a small group of people he doesn't know at all, like nothing about this entire thing is weird. I casually asked him about inviting some of his friends and family. And in response, I'd gotten a grunt and a "No, that's fine."

I tried not to take it personally. Told myself that it made sense. After all, we're selling this to *my* family. I know we don't need to overcomplicate it with more people and more lies, but it left me wishing my future husband felt some semblance of pride about me.

Dad links my arm through his, pulling me out of my internal pity party. He puffs his chest as we wait, every bit the proud father waiting to walk his daughter down the aisle.

Bash slips out through the double doors, face impassive. His gray suit is immaculate, highlighting the silver flecks in the salt-and-pepper hair near his temples.

"We're up," he says matter-of-factly and ushers a jittery Milo forward. He crouches down to check on him. Bash's son is grown now, so his days of talking to small children have passed, but he still softens for my nephew.

"You ready, pal?" Bash asks him.

Milo nods and takes a deep breath.

"Of course you are. You're gonna fuckin' rock th—" Bash's eyes flash to mine right as Milo gasps and bursts out laughing. Bash grimaces with a grumbled, "Shit, sorry."

Okay, maybe he isn't completely adjusted to three-year-olds. But he's trying.

My lips twitch and then flatten so I don't laugh too.

That's what I focus on as I watch Bash send Milo in first before taking Rosie's arm. In what feels like mere seconds, their backs disappear through the double doors leading into the nave.

And so my wedding begins.

CHAPTER 18

Rhys

Bash: You better be fucking ready. Your bride looks beautiful.

Rhys: I'm ready and waiting.

Bash: I don't just mean the wedding. You better be ready to take care of her. She's been through enough. Everyone wants to see her happy.

Rhys: I'm ready.

WE TURN THROUGH THE DOORWAY AT THE TOP OF THE AISLE. My eyes immediately lock with Tabitha's, and the world stands still.

She's a vision. Shiny dark hair falling in soft, loose curls. Cheeks flushed. The stark white of her dress makes her skin appear more bronze than usual.

I swallow roughly, reminding myself that this day is a farce. A carefully constructed facade meant to fool everyone.

But not me. I'm not meant to be fooled by it.

Yet here I am, heart pounding in my ears, lungs struggling for air, fucking hearts in my eyes as a woman who tolerates my presence glides down the aisle toward me. It niggles at me that she's going through with this thinking I betrayed her, but I push my own discomfort aside.

Bash stands at my back stoically, Rosie across from me, and Milo is on the step below me, staring out at the pews. There are only a handful of people in the crowd, none of whom I know. And I don't even care.

Right now, everything else falls away. My gaze lingers on the subtle up-turn of her lips as she peeks up at her beaming dad. Before I know it, they're standing in front of me, and I am once again reminding myself to act natural. To play my part. If Tabitha can pull it off, then surely I can too. Hell, half my job is acting. This should be a breeze.

"Sir." I nod in Paul's direction as I step down and reach for his hand. We've met once. It was nice, but I'd be lying if I said I'm not a little suspicious of how easily they've accepted the news of our marriage. I know I'm in on the charade and Tabitha doesn't need my pity, but there's this part of me that wants to shake them. Tell them to wake up and notice the burden their daughter has taken on, all for the sake of keeping everyone around her happy.

Over the past weeks, it's become clear that the only person looking out for Tabitha is Tabitha. And fuck if it doesn't make me want to look out for her too.

If there's no one else to take up her cause, it might as well be her husband.

He offers me a firm handshake and a watery smile. "You take good care of my little girl now."

I nod with conviction, staring back at the much shorter man. "I intend to." My voice comes out sure and even, full of determination. Because nothing about the sentiment is fake. I intend to take good care of Tabitha—in any way that she'll let me.

Then her hand is in mine, and I lead her up the low steps to the dais, where I lean toward her and whisper, "You look incredible." Because I can't help myself. And because it's true.

She shivers as she peeks up at me, eyes searching as though to see if I'm telling the truth or not. Then I get a nod along with a quiet and unexpected, "So do you."

And there's no snideness to her voice. In fact, I get the sense she's being entirely genuine. It throws me off, but I don't get much time to fixate. Within seconds, we stand facing each other, in front of a crowd, and it's no longer the time or place to be confused by Tabitha Garrison.

"Tabby girl, congratulations." The officiant smiles at her affectionately, and she gives the same grin back.

I wasn't expecting Doris, who I'm told owns the bar, to be the one marrying us, but Tabitha insisted, and I have a record of sucking at saying no to her. So here I am, getting married by a woman who reeks of cigarettes and looks like she's worn baby oil in the sun for decades. But apparently she's a registered officiant, so whatever.

"Thank you, Doris," Tabitha whispers back.

"I hope he has a huge dick. It makes the dumb shit men do a lot more forgivable."

My face goes blank as I stare back at the woman with no filter. Thank fuck, she's not wearing a mic. Bash groans behind me, and Rosie covers a snort by slapping her hand over her mouth. Tabitha makes a slight choking sound and thumps a fist on her chest.

Doris's eyes slice in my direction. "Don't look at me like that, boy. You get to be my age, and you start telling the truth because you've quit worrying about offending people."

I open my mouth to say… I don't know what I was going to say to that, but I don't need to say anything, because Tabitha reaches her free hand out to cup the woman's elbow. "We thank you for your wisdom, Doris."

Then my fiancée *winks* at her.

My cheeks flame, and I stare at Tabitha, thinking back to that hallway in the shitty bowling alley where she grabbed my dick with all the confidence in the world.

Then I spiral. Thinking about kissing her. Here. In front of all these people.

The past days have been a blur of planning, and the upcoming nuptials have done nothing to lessen the distance between us. Instead of actively disliking each other, the energy between us has shifted into awkward territory. Tolerable, but slightly embarrassed about where we've ended up. No doubt, she's having second thoughts. I'm positive marrying an emotionally stunted, secretive stranger wasn't on her bucket list.

"Okay, let's get started." Doris claps her hands and looks out over the attendees with a slight smirk. "These two lovebirds are so eager to tie the knot that they asked me to keep things simple, but my romantic side got the best of me when I sat down with a gin and tonic to plan this. So the two of you will just have to deal with the vows I've written for you."

Chuckles and drawn-out *awwws* filter in, but I barely hear them over the pounding of my heart. Tabitha's wide eyes focus on mine. I know she told her the simplest vows possible to keep things easy for us, and here we are with a surprise neither of us wanted.

"Without further ado, I ask that you take each other's hands and repeat after me..."

Tabitha and I reach for each other at the same time. Her hands are small in my clammy ones. She gives me a reassuring squeeze, and I give her a subtle nod back. Then we repeat after Doris, making promises neither of us knows if we can truly keep.

"I, Rhys, promise you, Tabitha, to always respect and admire you and to appreciate you for who you are, as well as the person you become."

Her eyes turn glassy.

"I promise that your dreams will be our dreams, and that I will do everything I can to make them a reality for both of us."

My voice grows gravelly. That one rings just a little too true considering the real reason we're both here today.

"I promise to be a spectator to your life, a participant

in your experiences, and your biggest advocate in every moment. I promise to allow you space to be those things in my life too."

A heavy stone settles in my stomach as those words hang in the air between us. We both know I haven't been honest or forthcoming with her. And here we are, promising to be.

"I promise to support and encourage you, laugh with you in times of joy, and comfort you in times of sorrow."

Laugh. I don't know that I've ever laughed with Tabitha. And have I comforted her? Doris's words on marriage slice me like little paper cuts, each one making me feel more guilty than the last.

"I promise to cherish and reinforce the love between us in good times and in bad, when life is simple and when it's complicated—when loving you is easy and when it takes effort."

My shoulders straighten slightly at that one. It doesn't feel like such a blatant lie, more like what we're doing here today. We may not love each other, but this marriage could be called caring for each other when life is not simple. There is nothing simple about Tabitha and me.

I pause before repeating the next line Doris feeds me. It's another thing we haven't discussed. I've always known what type of husband I would be if the day ever came, but what hits me the hardest is that I don't know if this vow will ring true for Tabitha. And that thought turns my stomach. It makes me irrationally jealous.

So I narrow my eyes at her and brush a thumb over the top of her hand before saying, "I promise to be faithful to you and to place you and our family above all else."

Tabitha sucks in an audible breath through parted lips, eyes skittering over my face as though looking for proof that I'm lying.

But I'm not.

With a raspy voice, I carry on, professing things to a woman that I never have before.

"I promise to love you completely and unconditionally, today and every day, and to stand at your side always, wherever life takes us together."

The last line is bittersweet on my tongue. Sweet because in so many ways, this could be us.

Maybe in another lifetime, those things could be true.

CHAPTER 19

Tabitha

I RECITE MY VOWS BACK OVER THE LUMP LODGED IN MY throat. There's something about the way Rhys is looking at me, his dark eyes so intense on mine that everyone else in the room seems to fade away.

It makes saying these vows out loud a little bit easier. And the way his thumb brushes over the top of my hand any time I get hung up makes it a little bit easier to breathe. Somehow, having Rhys here at all makes the pressure of the day more bearable.

And that confuses the hell out of me. I'm torn in a million directions when it comes to him. We clash, but we also work together. My mind constantly contradicts itself with Rhys.

He's trying to take Milo from me.

He's doing everything in his power to keep us together.

He's turned everything upside down.

He keeps showing up and trying to make everything right.

I hate that he's here at all.

Having him here makes my life better.

As I mull this over, I miss the rest of what Doris says. I desperately hope it's not about huge dicks. I chose Doris because she was already a licensed officiant, and I thought she'd keep things blunt and to the point. I didn't expect her to turn into a romance author over our fucking vows.

Bash steps forward and hands Rhys one of the simple gold bands we agreed upon.

Rhys was dead set on being the one to buy the rings, and I was too tired to fight him. I told him to keep it as cheap as possible and that mine needed to be low-profile for the kitchen.

He takes my hand and murmurs Doris's words back to me. "I give you this ring as a sign of my love and devotion." The metal is warm, but I shiver as I watch him slip it over my knuckle and reverently slide it up my finger.

I clear my throat and peek up at him. He looks so fucking handsome. Chin-length hair slicked back, stubble trimmed tight, shoulders impossibly wide. I suppose at the very minimum, we're attracted to each other, and that's not an awful place to start.

When Rosie steps up to hand me Rhys's ring, I startle, shaken from lusting over my almost-husband. She smiles as she passes me the ring, and my hand trembles when it lands in my palm. As I stare down at it, my stomach goes diving off a cliff. That free-fall feeling that wakes you up in a dream before you hit the ground. That bone-deep, what-the-fuck-am-I-doing feeling.

But Rhys is there to steady me. His big, warm palm slides under my wrist, fingers curling gently around my forearm. Without me asking, he's still supporting. I can't even turn my face up to his because I know what I'll see. Furrowed brow, concern, and care. It'll be that day I got the world's mildest burn on my hand all over again. The one when he demanded I let him take care of me.

Sometimes he makes it really hard to hate him.

I take his calloused hand in my trembling grip. "I give you this ring as a sign of my love and devotion," I say in a thick voice, my words brimming with more affection than I intended as I slip the gold band onto his finger.

The sight immobilizes me. The finality of it. The realization that we just went all in on this whole charade. My heart pounds, and I can't look away from Rhys's hands. Big and tan. Strong and gentle. Mine and yet…not mine at all.

For a flash, I wonder how they'd feel elsewhere on my body. In my hair. Running over my back. Between my—

My train of thought comes to a screeching halt as Doris's scratchy voice blasts into my head. "You may now kiss the bride."

My stomach falls again, and sparks shoot through my chest. We haven't talked about this part of the ceremony. We're two grown-ass adults—we don't need to plan out a kiss. It's *just* a kiss. I've kissed plenty of men, so this will be no different. And despite whatever my body is doing right now, it's just for show.

The facts don't stop my cheeks from flushing, and they don't stop us from drawing closer to each other either. He takes one step, and I take one step, neither of us resisting the pull.

My breath stutters when one of his masculine hands slips over my hip with a level of familiarity that doesn't match our situation at all. His palm burns hot and firm against my bare lower back, and suddenly I don't have to imagine what it would feel like for him to touch me there. Now I *know*.

My tongue darts out over my lips as I crane my neck, turning my face up to his. Dark eyes scour my features as though searching for something before his fingers trail through my hair gently as he hooks a loose lock behind my ear with heartrending tenderness. His palm cradles my skull, and my lips part on a shaky breath.

He towers over me. All I can see is him. All I can smell is him. All I can hear is the blood pounding through my veins. And all I can feel is his breath against the shell of my ear as he bends down close and whispers, "Are you still sure?"

A shiver races down my spine. From the corner of my eye, I can see his lips moving. So close and yet so far away. Deep down, I know that if I told him this wasn't okay, he'd put an end to it all immediately.

"Yes," I reply in a hushed whisper, tilting my head to line us up.

And that one word is all it takes for Rhys to close the few inches between us. The first press of our lips borders on chaste, but heat suffuses every limb. The pressure recedes ever so slightly, and then I kiss him back.

Our lips move in perfect synchronicity, with more urgency than I expected and less fervor than I crave. His stubble tickles my face, and I can taste his minty breath. His hands pulse where they hold me, and I hear the deep groan that rumbles in his throat—I feel it in my jaw. It twinges between my shoulders, twists in my hips, and curls my toes.

I can't help but match his vibration with an impulsive whimper of my own. My hands slide up over the lapels of his rented tuxedo, my fingers gripping and pulling him closer.

Just a little bit more.

A loud hoot from the crowd that sounds an awful lot like West draws us back into reality. Our lips part and our foreheads press together for a beat, as though we both need a moment to recover.

There was no tongue, and it didn't last long, but something about the kiss rattles me in a way I can't make sense of.

Doris's simple "I now pronounce you husband and wife" pulls us back a respectable distance from each other. Cheers, whistles, and applause ring out from the small number of attendees.

But I barely notice. I'm too busy staring at my *husband.* The man with dark furrowed brows, rosy cheeks, and a menacing glare.

I'm not sure what's got him looking so surly. Maybe he just realized he's officially stuck with me, and a three-year-old, and a cat I adopted mostly just to piss him off.

Still, I can't help but wonder if he's as confused by this ceremony as I am.

Because yes, I've kissed plenty of men.

But none of them have felt like *that.*

CHAPTER 20

Rhys

Tabby: Still allergic to pussy...cats? The bouquet didn't seem to bother you at all. ;)

Rhys: Exposure therapy. ;)

THIS FUCKING BACKLESS DRESS. THAT FUCKING KISS.

If it wasn't for the fact that I know Tabitha's dress pickings were slim, I'd put money on this being another one of her antics intended to drive me absolutely insane.

Ditching me on a bowling team.

Getting a cat I hate.

Kissing me like she means it.

Choosing a wedding dress that makes it impossible to touch her in even the most casual of ways without feeling her bare skin.

We're at the Bighorn Bistro for the reception, surrounded by friends and family—Ford and Rosie, West and Skylar, and the unlikely pair of Bash and Crazy Clyde.

We kept it simple and casual with our small group. The food is incredible. Farm-to-table, locally sourced, and served up family-style. The wine is French and fucking delicious.

Everything is going great for our big fat fake wedding... except I can't stop resting my hand on my wife's bare back.

Dinner has been cleared, and people have moved into smaller groups. Tabitha and I stand chatting with her parents in the corner. Her dad is telling a story about how one of the first recipes she ever tried to make was a lemon chicken dish.

He's chuckling so hard he can barely get the words out. "It came out so terrible that even our family dog wouldn't eat it."

There's a manic energy to her parents. Like they're so desperate to make today happy that they are ignoring the elephant in the room. Or multiple elephants in the room.

The fact that Erika isn't here. The fact that their daughter married a man who has been around for the blink of an eye. I guess I can't blame them.

"Our Tabby Cat has come a long way since then," he finishes, holding his glass up in a toast.

Tabitha shakes with silent laughter, and the muscles in her back flex beneath my hand, the little dip over her spine becoming more pronounced with the movement. She may be petite, but she's strong. Hours standing, unloading food orders, and doing all the physical labor that comes with running a kitchen show in her build.

Those first weeks, I was concerned about her weight, especially the gauntness in her face, so I love seeing a little color come back to her. I take great satisfaction in knowing what I did today may have played a part in perking her up. And my dick takes too much satisfaction in the way she just stepped closer, her hip bumping against my side as her arm circles my back. The warm weight of her frame pressed against me makes me stiffen. *Everywhere.*

She looks up at me, white teeth on full display, sparkly eyes amused. It's only taken a couple glasses of wine for Tabitha Garrison to get really comfortable faking it in public.

"So, what's the honeymoon plan for you two?" Lisa, her mom, asks with a suggestive brow waggle.

"Not so sure yet," Tabitha replies as I eye her warily. "We've got Milo, and I can't leave the bistro for long. Plus, Rhys needs to get back to work soon."

"That's a shame. Maybe for your one-year wedding anniversary? You know we can always help with taking Milo off your hands."

Tabitha just takes another sip of her drink and offers her mother a thumbs-up. I keep my mouth shut. Usually, I can sidestep work conversations by staying silent.

"What is it you do again?" Paul asks. "It's escaping me right now."

"I'm in the entertainment industry." I force my lips into a casual smile and take a glance around the room, as though ready to change the subject. But Paul doesn't take the bait.

"How interesting. What part specifically?"

I feel my heart rate accelerate. I don't like lying, but

I don't especially like sharing this either. It's not that I'm embarrassed about what I do, I just… My privacy feels like the one part of my life I can control. Something all my own.

"He's a stuntman." Tabitha bullshits with such ease that I do a double take.

"A what?" Her mom looks confused.

"You've probably seen him jumping off a building in a movie or something." Tabitha waves a hand casually. "They always call him when Jason Momoa is too scared to do a scene."

I can hear the amusement in her voice, her barely contained laughter. I shoot her an unimpressed glare and try not to cringe over her parents' *ooh*s and *aah*s.

Then Doris taps Lisa on the shoulder, and the conversation moves away from us, leaving Tabitha and me, backs to the wall, looking out over the restaurant. She sighs contentedly, pride brimming in her eyes.

"I love this place," she says simply.

"A *stuntman*?"

Her lips twitch. "Just supporting my husband the best way I know how. I mean, I could have said porn star."

I grumble and turn my head to give her my most menacing look.

"No, I know. That's gotten old. Touring male stripper was on the tip of my tongue, but if that got back to Doris, she'd be booking you for ladies' night at the Reach."

My molars grind, and her expression turns smug. Her hand drifts down and then up, slipping beneath my tuxedo jacket. Her fingertips poke my side as she walks them along the crisp white shirt near the waistband of my pants.

Then I watch her perfectly painted lips—the ones I can't stop thinking about—as she asks, "What's wrong, husband? You look like you can't decide whether you want to kill me or fuck me."

My eyes bounce between hers. Amusement glitters in their depths, and goddamn. This woman is going to be the death of me.

Call it the wine. Call it the good vibes. Call it the shared insanity that we both signed up for today, but I let my hand slip lower. My fingers breach the dropped hemline at the back of her dress and slide beneath it, rubbing across the thin slip of fabric that lies flat over her hip.

I stay looking out over the room full of people, hand down my wife's dress, doing my best to appear casual as I respond. "Kill you or fuck you, Tabby?" My voice drops lower. "Oh, I've decided."

"Fuck," she mutters, teeth strumming her bottom lip as she glances away.

"Yep. That's the one."

My fingers hook under the side of her underwear and give a teasing tug that makes her breath hitch. I maintain the pressure, twisting the fabric and watching her tongue dart over her bottom lip hungrily.

Should we be playing this game in a room full of wedding guests?

We shouldn't be playing this game at all. But Tabitha and I seem to get a thrill out of going toe-to-toe, and at least we can fall back on newlywed antics if we get caught with our hands down each other's pants.

"Friendly reminder that this marriage is *fake*," she mutters, focusing just a little too hard on the table where our friends sit.

"Nothing fake about how wet you are right now."

A low rumble of a laugh spills from her lips as she offers Rosie a smile from across the room before spinning to face me. Her movement pulls our hands from each other's clothes, and with me now pressed up against the wall, she looks perfectly confident again.

Her hands glide up over my lapels again, just like they did during the ceremony. But where she looked like a deer in the headlights then, she looks like a wolf in the forest now.

"Poor husband." She pouts dramatically. "Obsessed with a pussy he'll never get."

I smirk and arch a brow at her. "Is that so?"

She nods and smiles like the Cheshire cat as her thigh slips between mine. Her hip presses against my erection. "It's okay." She pushes onto tippy-toes and presses a kiss just beside my mouth. A fucking tease. "I promise to give you privacy while you consummate this marriage with your hand later tonight."

With that, she turns and saunters away. And I'm left standing alone at my own wedding reception with a raging hard-on and a brain full of thoughts about my wife that I swear weren't there mere days ago.

CHAPTER 21

Tabitha

I WALK TOWARD MY HOUSE WITH A NEW HUSBAND TRAILING behind me and a ruined pair of panties beneath my dress. Though I'll never give him the satisfaction of admitting it out loud.

Ford gave us a ride back from dinner, and it was so short that no one got a word in edgewise over Rosie raving about the food. Not gonna lie, I live for that kind of praise. Knowing that something I made—a menu I created—brought a friend so much joy brings a deep, satisfied hum to my bones. It's the simple things that get me off.

Plus, all it took was one glance for me to see that while Rhys wasn't battling the full erection he had earlier, the front of his pants was still looking *thick*. He busted me staring at his lap, and I was grateful for the cover of darkness so he couldn't see just how hot my cheeks flushed. Needless to say, I quickly found something *very* interesting out the window.

Oh, I've decided.

Just remembering the way the words came out—full of so much promise—had me crossing my legs to press down on an unwelcome throb.

I hadn't set out to taunt him. He's just so...smug. So sure of himself. So perfectly in control all the time that flustering him has become my new favorite pastime. It's in those moments that I get a glimpse of passion from him.

The low hum of the TV drifts from the living room, a sure sign that Cora, Ford's daughter, is still awake after babysitting Milo for the night.

Reaching down, I hook a finger under each stiletto heel in turn—they've been trying to kill me all night long—and fling them into the front closet with a vengeful toss. When my bare feet hit the floor, I groan and let my eyes flutter shut.

"Sore feet?" Rhys's deep timbre startles me.

"Jesus Christ. You're like a massive ninja sneaking up behind me. It makes no sense."

He's about to respond when a cheerful *prow prow prow* noise draws our attention. And there's Cleocatra, gunning for Rhys like he's her best friend. She presses her forehead against his slacks, her tail curling around his calf as she rubs herself against him like a stripper on a pole.

I giggle. "She loves you."

"The feeling is not mutual," he grumps, standing frozen as he stares down at her.

I bend at the waist and stroke the top of her head, getting a few purrs out of her, though she never stops circling

Rhys. "Cleo, *I'm* the one who rescued you. A little gratitude wouldn't hurt."

"Yeah, cat. Like Tabby instead."

I roll my eyes. Disliking Cleocatra is impossible. Rhys is just…

I blink as I look back at my *husband*. Rhys has a way of shutting everyone out. I'm not sure what it is, but something about the moment makes me wonder if the man I married even knows how to let someone love him.

He's not overt in the ways he shows his affection. It's all sullen acts of service or restrained thumb strokes to show support. And if I think too hard on it, it makes me sad. So, in an effort to escape the big, overwhelming man that I know little about, I pad through the foyer and into the living room.

Cora lounges on the couch with a sketch pad against her legs and a pencil in her hand while professional wrestling plays on the TV.

"Hey," she says quietly, giving me a soft smile from beneath the heavy black fringe of her bangs.

"Hey," I flop down on the couch beside her feet like a dead starfish and let my eyes fall shut before making an exaggerated snoring noise.

"How'd it go?"

A tired smile spreads across my face. "It was perfect." And I'm not lying. It was perfect. The ceremony. The reception. The guests. Aside from the fact that I married a man who shares nothing and mystifies me at every turn—something I try not to fixate on because marrying him was the lesser of two evils—everything was great. "How did it go here? Milo was all right?"

"Yeah. He's awesome. We played with Cleo, and he introduced me to Erika, which was cool."

I snort. Only Cora wouldn't be put off by a plant named after a kid's dead mom. Rosie calls her *little storm cloud*, and I can see why. "Perfect," I mumble.

Rhys walks past with a quiet, "Hi, Cora. Thanks again for your help tonight. Your dad and Rosie are waiting outside."

"No problem," she replies, an unusual hint of shyness in her voice, as she pulls a pencil case off the table and packs her things.

When I can hear Rhys moving around in the kitchen, Cora leans closer and whispers, "Is getting married as exhausting as it looks?"

I snort and roll my head along the back of the couch to look at the teenager. "Girl. Have you met men? Everything about them is exhausting."

She smiles down at her sketch pad with an amused shake of her head. "That's fair."

It occurs to me that I should act more excited. More…I don't know…in love? What will she tell Ford and Rosie when she gets in that car?

"I'm just blissed out. A dream of a day." I'm impressed with how easily I say it. My brain is a twisted fucking place to be, talking about marrying Rhys Dupris like this.

"I mean, yeah. Can't blame you. Have you *seen* your new husband?" Her head tilts as though she could see around the corner and into the kitchen. My lips press together to hold back a chuckle. Then I watch a splotch of red take shape on her cheek as she slowly turns to face me, mortification painting her features as though the words just slipped out. "I'm sorry."

I smile kindly. A watered-down representation of the way I want to just throw my head back and howl.

"Nah"—I wave her off casually—"don't even worry about it." I nod my head toward the television in a desperate attempt to save her from this conversation. "What are we watching?"

She shrugs. "Wrestling. Well, a replay. I'm weeks behind. Had to start from where I left off, so I don't miss out on the storyline."

I try not to laugh. *The storyline.*

My eyes roam over the screen. A full arena. Signs and screaming fans as far as the eye can see. There's a man wearing spandex underwear curled up in the middle of the ring while three other huge wrestlers land blows on him. Punches. Kicks. Something that looks like the bum-drops Erika and I used to do on our trampoline.

I wince at the violence, but as the seconds wear on and the camera angles change, I can see the ways they protect him even as they punish him. A foot stomp to make the blows sound louder, an overacted facial expression to make the pain appear worse than it is.

Suddenly, bright white and lime-green lights flash overhead as the first few notes of a song ring out. The decibels from the crowd spike, and Cora lets out a whispered, "*Yes,*" as a huge man appears at the top of the ramp that leads to the ring in the middle.

Cora's entire frame orients toward the television, her shoulders pitching forward as though naturally drawn to the man.

And then I watch too.

The wrestler who everyone is excited about is wearing a pair of black military-style pants that are just tight enough to trace his muscular thighs, while hanging low enough to show the two hard slashes that rise from his waistband. His abs are defined, but not comically so. He doesn't look like a bodybuilder—he just looks *big*. All man.

Even the wrestlers in the ring stop their assault. It's staged, but I'm still pulled into the drama of it.

The newcomer stands at the entryway, fists clenched at his sides, his head tilted downward as smoke billows out from behind him. His shoulders are broad and round, his pecs a perfectly proportional match. My gaze skims the hard planes of clear tan skin, black tattoos scrolling up one arm, a dusting of hair on his chest.

He tips his head up, and a Batman-like mask on his face comes into view. It's black with lime-green highlights and covers his nose and cheeks before opening below to a pair of shapely lips. Despite the mask, I'm leaning forward to see more of him. I'm pulled in by the mystery of it all, entranced by the inkling of familiarity.

"Oh my god. Yes. Fuck them up, Wild Side." Cora has completely forgotten about the packing up she was doing.

And to be frank, I'm just as invested.

Harsh paintbrush slashes on the screens behind him spell out *Wild Side*. And then the man begins to walk as fucking fireworks shoot off on either side of him.

It's watching him move that has me tilting my head.

It's the way his fingers curl into fists at his sides, the thumbs swiping over his index finger.

It's the way he walks that has my breath freezing in my lungs. The raw power he exudes, the way he holds himself like a king, commanding the thousands of people in that arena to acknowledge him, follow him.

It's the detailed black tattoos that swirl on his right arm that give him away.

Heat suffuses my body. I may barely know the man, and I may have never watched wrestling before, but I identify him instantly.

Recognition pounds me, and all the bits and pieces of him come together. Hours at the gym. Weeks away. The *bruises.*

God. It all makes so much sense.

Now I'm the one turning toward the kitchen as though I can see around a corner. Can he hear us? Does he know? Is he assuming I won't recognize him with that mask?

"Your dad is waiting," I say, bringing my splintered attention back to Cora.

"Yeah. Just hang on. Wild Side is my favorite. This won't take him long."

Her definition of *won't take him long* might be different from mine. Because the wrestler takes his sweet-ass time strolling down the walkway, the crowd growing more excited with each step. He doesn't seem to be in a rush, considering there is a man getting the shit beat out of him by three others.

He stops close to the ring, and the screen switches to a

camera angle with a closer view of his masked face. Those shapely lips quirk up in a cocky smirk, and his tongue presses into the side of his stubbled cheek. He oozes an unbearable amount of confidence.

It does funny things to my ovaries.

"They've done it now, Pete," one of the announcers says with a gleeful flourish. "They haven't had to worry about Wild Side doling out his own special brand of justice for several months. Looks like he's here to remind them who the boss is around these parts."

With that, the man who I'm sure is Rhys takes an absurdly graceful leap onto the ledge of the ring before planting one hand on the top rope and vaulting himself into the melee.

At once, the three men set their sights on him, but it's a feeble attempt.

One goes down with a head butt that makes me wince.

The second meets his match in the form of a booted high kick.

The third lingers back a bit before charging.

"Ohhh, he's gonna take him over the mountain. I just know it." The announcer's gritty voice rings through as Rhys ducks the man's attack, then spins on him as he launches backward off the ropes like a rock from a slingshot.

Rhys picks the large man up like he's nothing and spins him around in some sort of eye-crossing flip before body-slamming him onto the mat with alarming speed and strength. I can't help but flinch.

"Dope, right?" Cora says with a slow nod and hearts in her eyes.

Me? I swallow away the dryness in my throat. "Yeah. Totally dope."

The camera shows Wild Side giving the injured man from before a hand up and leading him out of the ring as he steps over a body he left behind. The fans are feral. There are men, women, children, people of every age and ethnicity. There are signs that read everything from *WILD SIDE IS BACK* to *WILD SIDE, I'LL HAVE YOUR BABIES!* and the frantic announcing only adds to the feeling of pandemonium.

It's honestly a perfect match for what's going on inside my head right now. Chaos, confusion, amusement. They all war together with a heavy serving of red wine as I walk Cora back out to Ford's SUV and bid them good night.

Then I walk back into my house to face Wild Side.

Rhys is in the kitchen, his back to me, a glass of red wine in one hand, the other casually slung into his pocket as he looks out over the darkened backyard.

Like this, in his tuxedo, he looks too refined for the type of brutality I just watched him dole out on TV—*allegedly* dole out—and I could burst at the seams with all the questions perched at the tip of my tongue. I could use another glass of wine, but not before I get this out of my system.

"Hey…"

His head inclines in my direction, but he doesn't turn.

"Can I talk to you in the living room?"

His body stills, but this time, he looks at me. And it makes me suck in a breath as though I've been sucker punched. The harsh lines of his face, that pronounced brow. He does look like he could kill me or fuck me. And with a face like his, I'd say thank you either way.

Thank you, sir. Will you please twist my panties and whisper something dirty in my ear one last time before I go?

I shake my head at myself. No more wine for this gal tonight. Throat too dry to speak, I wave a hand over my shoulder, urging him to follow me. I head straight to the TV and rewind the event Cora was watching right to about when I walked into the living room.

Rhys takes his sweet-ass time following, but when he makes it to me, his face is doing that blank thing he does so well. He avoids looking at the TV like a dog who's made a mess in the corner and thinks if they don't look, their human won't either.

With two sure steps, I reach him, grab his arm, and drag him so that he's standing in front of the TV.

Then I step back from him.

"Tabitha, what are you—"

I hit play.

He winces at the announcer's voice, the thumping of boots, the boos from the crowd. Then those first few notes of a song ring out, and the roar of the crowd almost drowns it out. This time, gooseflesh fans across my arms as I watch the masked man appear at the top of the ramp.

I pause it and draw nearer to him. And then I scrutinize the shape of Rhys's lips. His hand so gentle on the crystal stem of his wineglass. The way his waist tapers in from impossibly broad shoulders.

"That's you."

His dark eyes bore into mine, and his Adam's apple bobs heavily.

"You don't leave for weeks at a time to fuck people. You leave for weeks at a time to fuck people *up*."

His tongue pops into the side of his cheek, and that seals the deal for me. It's *him*.

"Tabitha…"

My lips curve up. "Am I *Mrs. Wild Side*?"

Rhys rolls his eyes and looks away.

"Dude. Are you famous?"

His free hand slides up over his throat before moving around to grip the back of his neck. Then he drops my gaze. His body language is all shy and bashful.

"Whoa, whoa, whoa. What is that?" I step closer again, landing a firm poke in the middle of his hard chest as I come toe-to-toe. "You're looking down? What is that?"

He sighs, and his tan cheeks flare a similar shade to his wine. "I don't usually tell people about this."

"Why? It's fucking *cool*. So much cooler than being a stunt double." His nose wrinkles, and when he finally meets my eyes, he looks… "Are you embarrassed?"

A rough laugh fills the air between us. "No. Maybe. I don't know. I love my job, but people always get so weird about it, so I just don't talk about it."

My head tilts. "Weird how?"

"Usually, I become the butt of their jokes. Or I have to

listen to them talk about how it's all fake. Or it just…it ends up putting a lot of attention on me that I don't want."

My chest twinges at the memory of the bruises on him. It may be scripted, but those were not fake. I shimmy my shoulders. Okay, I'm not Rhys's *biggest* fan, but I'm stuck with him for better or for worse, and that has me feeling a little territorial.

At this moment, I decide that I am the only person allowed to mock him.

"Most things on TV are fake."

One side of his mouth hitches up at that. "The other thing that happens is that people ask for money in a roundabout way. With my background, it's just been…less complicated to fly under the radar. Keep the anonymity. I've learned to enjoy my solitude."

At that, I pale.

Money. I knew he had it. But not like this.

"Oh god."

"What?"

"We didn't sign a prenup. You have stuff. I have…a restaurant."

His smile is grim as he offers me one terse nod. "I know. I would never though."

I'm blaming the wine for the way my heart pitter-patters as he stares down at me. This big, brutal man who holds Milo with such gentleness, who turned his successful life upside down in ways I didn't comprehend until now.

A man I barely know has put it all on the line to keep my nephew with me.

We don't address the enormity of what he's done, and I'm struck by the realization that Rhys is not who I thought he was, in more ways than one. It's not just his job; it's the type of human he is.

His soul—it's a good one. And I don't want to be another leech. I can't promise him that I won't crack some jokes about this, but…

I lift my pinky finger between us as I stare back at him. "I pinky promise that no matter what happens, I will never take anything that's yours."

His eyes bounce between mine, a nervous glint to them. "You know these aren't legally binding, right?"

I swallow, transported back to the day he told me that exact thing. "Yeah, but only a total asshole breaks a pinky promise."

He regards me for several beats, then he lifts his finger and repeats my words back to me. "I pinky promise that no matter what happens, I will never take anything that's yours."

We shake. And his expression is just as sincere as it was when we spoke our wedding vows.

CHAPTER 22

Rhys

I WAKE UP A MARRIED MAN. SLEEPING ALONE IN AN UNFINished basement with a hand wrapped around my dick and the memory of slipping my fingers down my wife's dress playing on an infinite loop in my mind.

I come upstairs feeling on edge about what the day will hold—feeling vulnerable after Tabitha went digging through my life with such ease last night.

But when I step into the kitchen, nothing is different.

Even though fall has started to make its way into the valley and there's a nip in the air, Tabitha sits outside with a blanket wrapped around her shoulders, sipping a cup of coffee. Normally, I'd retreat to the living room with my coffee and scroll my phone, check my emails, or do anything I could to avoid her, but today feels different. Strangely, I don't feel like I need to hide from her this morning.

Whether it's the comforting warmth of the gold wrapped around my ring finger or morbid curiosity about what's going through Tabitha's head after last night, I decide to pour myself a mug of steaming caffeine and join her.

But not before I'm almost tripped by the goddamn cat.

Prow, prow, prow.

She makes that little noise with each step as she comes prancing toward me and practically launches herself at my legs like she's excited to see me. She doesn't even care that the feeling isn't mutual.

"Hi, cat," I grumble, before stepping around her and reaching for the back door. She follows me outside, and I don't stop her.

Tabitha turns. "Rhys! Don't let Cleo out!"

"Why?"

"She could run away."

"That's the dream," I mumble.

My brow furrows as I stomp over to the love seat opposite her. Milo's monitor sits on the table between us, and I can hear the soft sound of his exhales. It makes me want to sneak upstairs and check on him. I've tried to respect Tabitha's space—her boundaries—but I miss the freedom to read him bedtime stories or check on him in the middle of the night just to make sure he was okay.

Alas, what I get is a cat that has no intention of running away. Because the minute I sit down, fucking Cleocatra, the perpetually happy feline, lands in my lap. She makes one agile turn before settling, her front paws pressing gently against my sweats, one after the other.

When I look up, Tabitha is staring at me with a smug expression on her face.

"Is that going to be okay for your *allergies*?" The way she says *allergies* is pure mockery. Okay, I lied about the allergy. Pets just make me nervous. Getting attached makes me nervous.

"Whatever."

"Come ooon. Is she purring? What kind of monster would you have to be to not like that at least a little bit?"

I sip my coffee and look away, doing my best to appear unaffected. Because it *is* nice. "It's fine."

"Wild Side's thoughts on pussy—*it's fine*."

My lips twitch. Tabitha is in fine form this morning. I slice her a withering glare, and she laughs.

"I prefer you when you're being hostile," is my only reply.

"I'm too tired to be hostile today. You get giddy instead."

As she nestles into the cushions of the wicker patio set, I realize she does look more tired than usual.

"Too much wine?"

A snort leaves her as she holds the steaming cup of coffee up to her lips. "I only had a few glasses. I'm fine."

"Yeah, fair. You weren't drunk enough to get handsy or anything like that."

She glowers at me. Between the wedding, the sexual tension, and the secrets she uncovered last night, there's a new level of closeness between us. And despite myself, I like it.

"Well, in that case, what's your excuse?"

God, I should not have been so...bold? Comfortable? There was just something that made me want her more than

I usually do. The dress. The restaurant. The way she pressed closer.

Her.

Everything comes back to her. My head keeps circling back to her. My body keeps moving toward her. And it's instinctual. If I could stop it, I would. I've *tried.*

But nothing works. Even after only meeting her once, she'd pop into my head unannounced. The tiny terror with dark hair and the round ass who marched into my house and told me what to do like I was a grunt in her kitchen.

Now it's worse, because she's here. With me. And she's got me twisted into knots—ones I don't feel especially inclined to untangle.

I shrug. "No excuses."

Her eyes widen, almost comically, but I figure, what's the point in beating around the bush? I meant what I said last night, and given the opportunity, I'd put my hands down Tabitha Garrison's dress over and over again.

The problem is, deep down, I suspect she still hates me. At least a little. She believes I've done something unforgivable, and I've made no move to correct her. When I decided to give her someone to blame for her sister's death, I didn't expect to end up here.

Married to her and feeling like this.

She clears her throat, signaling a change in the conversation, as Cleocatra curls herself up in my lap, like a fuzzy cinnamon bun. "Well, the reason I'm tired is I stayed up all night watching wrestling."

My head snaps up. "Come again?"

She shrugs and tucks her feet under herself. "What? It's entertaining."

I stare blankly at her, figuring out how I feel about this and how I should respond.

Another shrug. "And I was curious."

I search for tones of mockery in her voice, but they don't come. She's not laughing at me. But she stayed up all night watching WPW. I just...

Now her head joggles. "And it's kind of addictive."

Tabitha enjoying wrestling was not on my bingo card.

"You know who fuckin' sucks?" Before I can guess, she continues. "Million Dollar Bill. I can't believe that guy has *your* belt. What an absolute tool."

I blink, dumbfounded. "Tabitha."

She tips her nose up with a light sniffle, as though too proud to look embarrassed by having taken a deep dive into my job. "What? It's true. Brass knuckles? If that clown sends you back bruised again, I'll beat his ass myself."

I bark out an unexpected laugh. I'm not surprised by much anymore, but I am surprised by this.

Her head tilts. "I've never heard you laugh."

I absently pet the cat, just for something to do with my hands. "It's been a heavy couple of months."

Tabitha nods, but there's a soft smile on her face, a flush on her cheeks. "Well, I'm not joking. Watching you lose was infuriating. I'd like to speak to the writers about where the hell they're taking your storyline. I have notes."

I laugh again, and fuck, it feels good. Not just to laugh, but to share. It's a strange sensation, having someone on your team. It's causes an unfamiliar tingling in my chest. "Great, I'll let them know my wife would like to speak to them. They'll love that."

Her lips roll as she struggles to bite down on a laugh. "Good." Then she waves a pointed finger over me. "And don't start smiling like that too much."

I didn't even realize I was smiling. "Why not?"

"Because there are fans flapping posters around in the audience asking you to father their children. Women around the world will combust if you hit them with that."

"Wow, one day of marriage and the rules are already coming out in full force. *Sorry, I can only smile at my wife,*" I joke.

"Okay, well, you can obviously smile at whoever you want. Just not here," she qualifies, voice squeaking ever so slightly. "Like not where people we know would think that..."

"Think what?"

Tabitha sighs, tugging the blanket more tightly around her shoulders. "I'm not stupid." Her voice comes out more hushed now. "I don't expect you to act like we're married when you're away. But if we can keep up appearances in and around town, I'd appreciate it."

Realization dawns on me. "I'm not gonna do that to you."

I get a scoff and an eye roll. "Please, I'm sure I haven't inspired a lot of warm and fuzzy feelings. I know I've been harsh and demanding, but I promise I'm doing my best to move on. I don't *want* things to be like that between us. I just…I don't know how to act around you. And I'm fucking terrible about holding grudges."

It's one of the most vulnerable moments we've ever shared. One of the most honest things she's ever told me. The truth is, I don't know how to act around her either. She makes me nervous in unfamiliar ways. Still, I feel the need to reassure her. To lay it all out in black and white. To wipe the strained expression off her face. I lean forward, propping my elbows on my knees, ducking my chin just low enough to be at eye level with her.

"Tabby, I'm not the kind of guy who fucks around. So you can make up all the rules you want, but I'll be following my own. And that rule is that there won't be anyone else while I'm wearing this ring."

She sucks in a breath and swallows.

I don't know what she's about to say, and I'll never find out because Milo's voice interrupts through the monitor with a dopey, "Hello?" and she fucking dashes for the door.

CHAPTER 23

Tabitha

I FUMBLE THE ROSE HIP BETWEEN MY FINGERS WHEN I HEAR Milo's sugary voice behind me. "Tell me a story," he says to Rhys.

With a day off from the restaurant, I'd told Rhys that Milo and I were going to pick rose hips for my winter tea blend. To my surprise, he hit me with the most earnest puppy dog eyes in the world and asked, "Can I come?"

And I'm not a total monster, so of course I said yes. I thought the fresh mountain air and using Milo as a buffer would help ease the tension. Things have been friendly but awkward after Rhys told me he planned to be faithful, even though our marriage is fake.

But when his deep timbre responds to my nephew with "Are we doing another one about the prince named Milo?" I know the buffer is fucking useless. This man is too much for me.

"Yes!" Milo replies, his voice bursting with energy. "With dinosaurs. And excavators."

My lips twitch as his tongue ties around *excavator*. That one bedtime book has got him calling construction vehicles by their proper names.

"Okay," Rhys says simply, and I can't help but peek back over my shoulder at them.

An old sleeping bag is unzipped and folded out flat on the grass, plaid side facing up. Rhys lies stretched out on his back, one hand propped behind his head, the other ruffling Milo's hair as he sits beside him. They both have rosy cheeks thanks to the chilly air, but warm coats and a thermos of tea have kept us comfortable for the last hour or so.

A huge yawn stretches Milo's pink lips, and I glance down at my watch.

It's nap o'clock, and Rhys must realize it too because he quickly adds, "Why don't you lie back and listen? We can look at the clouds."

I glance up at the perfectly blue sky, complete with big fluffy clouds floating on a leisurely course. When I look back over, I blink away the sting in my eyes as I watch my nephew curl up in the crook of the big man's arm without hesitation. It makes me wonder if they've done this together before.

I turn back to the shrub before me, feeling the most confounding mixture of bliss and heartache. Their wholesome and sweet moment makes me wish Erika were here to see it. I think she'd love this.

Though it's not lost on me that if Erika were here, I wouldn't be. I'd be an interloper. My stomach plummets when I realize it. And then guilt lashes at me for enjoying this moment at all—a moment that should have been hers.

Maybe she wouldn't like this? Maybe it's just me who loves this? My quiet spot on the quiet side of the mountain. With Milo. And, well, my husband.

It's right as Rhys speaks that I realize the only other person I've ever brought here is Milo. We go up the old logging road and through a gate on Crazy Clyde's land. I drop him off tea in exchange for access to this valley. And then Milo and I spend leisurely afternoons picnicking, looking for bugs, and tending to the wild roses. And on the mornings when I can't get the noise of the kitchen out of my head, I'll come here and read.

But today I brought Rhys. And I didn't think twice about it.

I get lost in thought, picking the red fruit and placing it in the bucket wedged beneath my arm. And I listen to Rhys's story, punctuated by Milo's excited giggles and impressed *ooh*s and *aah*s. It's a grand adventure about a small prince who looks identical to Milo. He uses his excavator to go digging for fossils, but what he finds is a portal to another universe where dinosaurs still exist, and he faces many perils.

I wonder the same things I do when Milo watches *Paw Patrol.* How the hell does a child own and operate an excavator, and where the fuck are his parents?

Eventually, the tips of my fingers feel numb, and I turn to peek back at the boys. Milo has stopped interjecting his ideas for the story because he's passed out. He clings to Rhys like a little barnacle on a rock while the bright sun shines down on them.

Bucket in hand, I pad over to the blanket to get a closer look. Rhys is still talking, staring up at the sky and saying something about a Dilophosaurus as his thumb strokes over Milo's shoulder.

He doesn't stop, even when his eyes meet mine. I nod in Milo's direction and hold a palm up to my cheek, miming sleep. Rhys stops talking and lifts his head to peer down at the little boy. And it's the way he smiles at him—the way his eyes soften—that makes my heart skip a beat. He doesn't look at him in a way that people who like children look at any old kid that runs past. He looks at him with pure... adoration. With a tinge of pride.

Rhys looks at Milo like he's as good as his.

I move on instinct, without even thinking. The bucket gets left on the grass as I tiptoe to the edge of the blanket. There's no room beside Milo, which means the only spot for me is on the other side of Rhys.

My tongue darts out over my lips as I consider what I'm about to do. Then I drop to my knees before I can talk myself out of it. I crawl up to the top and roll over onto my back, staring up at the fluffy clouds.

I can feel Rhys watching me, and his body has gone eerily still. He definitely did not expect me to march up and take the spot beside him, but I couldn't help myself. I wanted to be part of the moment in a bone-deep way that I can't even begin to explain.

The weight of his attention almost makes me squirm.

So, I defuse all that pressure with my signature sarcasm when I whisper, "Keep going. I'm dying to hear if Prince

Milo defeats the Dilophosaurus. Actually, no. Tell me one about Princess Tabby."

The ground rumbles with the baritone of his responding chuckle, the vibration of it rolling over my skin and hitting all the most delicious places. Then his arm moves. He lifts it over my head, accidentally bumping me, so I elevate my head and shift, trying to give him space to stretch his arm out. And in the awkward jumble, I somehow end up with my head resting on his bicep.

Wordlessly, he pulls me closer. And I let him.

Neither of us addresses the intimacy of me using his bicep as a pillow. Instead, he just carries on in a quiet voice, like nothing is out of the ordinary about this at all. "Let's be real. She'd be Queen Tabby, who rules the kitchen with an iron fist."

I press my lips together. "And King Rhys, who dresses up in spandex and—"

"I don't wear spandex."

"You should. Those little manties can be part of your new branding."

"Trunks, Tabitha. They call them trunks."

I sigh dramatically. "Weak. That just doesn't have the same ring to it."

Another amused rumble leads us into a pregnant silence. And then I blurt out the thing that has been weighing on me ever since I found out what he does for a living yesterday. "I'm sorry I ruined your life."

He sighs, and his head turns in my direction. "You didn't ruin my life."

I let my cheek fall against the crook of his arm as I meet his gaze. "It feels a little bit like I did. You just seemed like such an asshole. And I just...I love him so much, you know? I couldn't lose him too. But once I'm—I don't know—in a better place, he could go to Florida with y—"

"No."

My eyes widen. "No?"

"He belongs here. With you."

I wrinkle my nose to stem the stinging in my eyes. "But what about you? It seems like he belongs with you too."

He turns back to face the sky now, leaving me to soak in his profile. The strong nose. The heavy brow. A little scar up by his hairline that I never noticed before. I soak him in for several seconds until he breaks the silence with, "I was orphaned too, actually. Milo and I have that in common."

"Rhys," I breathe his name. "I'm so sorry." Any words, beyond the most basic, fail me as my logic rides each wave of understanding. They lap at me one by one.

The way he swooped in instantly. The way he's shown up for Milo, even when I made it miserable for him. The way he's upended his life for this little boy. That he didn't have anyone to invite to the wedding.

God.

He shrugs a shoulder. "It's okay. I'm thirty-five. I've come to terms with it."

"*Thirty-five*?"

"I feel like you just added old jokes to your plan of attack. Did you not read the marriage license?"

Clearly not.

Fuck my life. I must seem like a colossal idiot to this man. "I think I blacked out."

I palm my forehead. My throat is thick with emotion. But my brain? My brain is fogged with embarrassment. I've been toeing the line of flirting with a man who is only here for Milo. He flies back and forth for Milo. He married me for Milo. I'm sure he likes me—in his own way—but he *loves* Milo. And everything he's done for him has come from a place of knowing what it's like to live this story.

My hand slips down over my eyes as I take a few deep breaths.

"Tabitha. Relax. You're twenty-eight. I'm not *that* much older."

"That's not why I'm hiding."

His fingers wrap around my wrist and pull my hand away from my face. "You're not hiding. Even if you can't see me, I can still see you." Amusement laces his typically menacing tone as he pulls my hand to his chest, leaving it covered with his own.

"No, but you seriously have to hate me. You're like Saint Rhys and all I've done is—"

"Take care of your nephew? Go to bat for him? Fight for him with a level of ferocity that makes me wish I'd had someone like you on my team when I was a child?"

All the air leaves my lungs with a choked *oomph.*

"I never knew my parents. What I know is that my mom had me as a teenager and gave me up at the hospital. A couple adopted me immediately, but shortly after my second birthday, they decided parenting was too hard. By Milo's age, I was in foster care."

The words flow from him so easily, and I hang on to every single one. This man I know almost nothing about—partly because he hasn't shared, but also because I haven't asked—is taking me on a walk down memory lane, and I am fully invested.

I want to know so much more about Rhys Dupris. Snuggler of toddlers, master storyteller, professional panty twister, and WPW superstar.

"The longest I ever stayed in one place was a few years."

I blink rapidly, envisioning him. I imagine Rhys like Milo—same chubby, rosy cheeks but with big dark eyes. What I can't imagine is giving him away, turning him over to a system where he'd never have any stability.

"How do you know all this?"

"My file."

I hum, turmoil burbling inside me. No wonder he was worried about Milo ending up there too.

"So you grew up in foster care the entire time? You couldn't stay in one place?"

He shrugs. The gesture is casual, but I don't miss the way his Adam's apple bobs in his throat as he swallows. "I got big. I ate a lot. I was… I don't know. I don't remember what I was like as a small child or any of the families I was with at that time. But I ended up scrappy at school, surly at home. And just not very lovable, I guess."

A battering ram to my chest—that's how those words feel. I glance at Milo, who has his body pressed safely against

Rhys's opposite side. Rhys is giving him all the security no one afforded him as a child. God, I just want to crawl on top of him and hug him, squeeze him tight like I do Milo when he's sad.

I settle for splaying my fingers and pressing my hand against his heart. Then I try his move on for size, letting my thumb rub lazy circles against his jacket. My shoulders feel tight for a moment, as though bracing for him to shake me off or give me a dismissive eye roll and tell me he doesn't need any coddling.

But he just sighs.

"Was it bad?" I pry a little further, not sure if I want to know the answer.

"Hmm. Not all bad. Mostly just unstable. I got juggled around a fair amount, which was tiring. Constantly navigating new household dynamics as a teenager was not ideal. It got better when I found wrestling at a small gym. Had to lie about my age to train, but at my size, it wasn't a hard sell. The only bad part about it was that working out so much made me hungry all the fucking time. Pretty sure all my first paychecks went straight to food, which I'd hide in my room so that none of the other kids would come and swipe it."

He chuckles over the last few words. But I don't. I think back to that night I heard his stomach growling and the carbonara I whipped up for him. Part of what I love about being a chef is feeding people. Providing nourishment is my way of showing I care.

I loved cooking for Erika. She always ate with such gusto. Watching Milo lick his fingers clean after my from-scratch mac 'n' cheese feels like winning Olympic gold for me. And seeing my friends laughing, talking, and savoring a meal made from my recipes at our wedding is a memory I will cherish forever.

It's with those images in my head that I promise myself to never let Rhys go hungry again.

"I'm glad you told me. Milo is lucky to have you in his life."

I hear him swallow and see him nod from the corner of my eye. Something tells me he doesn't open up often and is realizing how much he let out in his valiant attempt to make me feel better. Now it feels like my opportunity to return the favor.

With one hand still holding him, I point up to the sky. "That cloud looks like Cleocatra."

Rhys groans, but I detect humor in the sound.

"And if you squint, that one looks like you petting her."

"Weird. Because I would never pet her."

I snort. *Liar.*

"Plus, that strip of cloud is way too long to be my arm. It looks all stretched out."

"You're right. Maybe that's Terence petting Cleocatra."

His head snaps to the side, and our gazes collide. "Who?"

"Stretch. From bowling."

Violence flashes in Rhys's eyes, and it makes my stomach flip. That he goes from soft to feral so effortlessly shouldn't be this exciting for me. But here I am. *Lusting*. Like the fucking mess I am.

"If that guy pets my cat, I'll tie a knot in his scrawny arm to match the one in his neck."

I grin. "Did you just say *your* cat?"

Now I get an eye roll and a small head shake. "Whatever."

"Are you jealous?" I tease.

"No."

I raise a scrutinizing eyebrow at him as Milo stirs on his opposite side, arm reaching over Rhys's chest.

He doesn't look at me when the next words leave his lips, but they still send my stomach flipping again all the same. "But now you know I *could* tie a knot in his neck, and if he talks to you like that again, I will."

We fall into silence, staring at the sky above us. Minutes later, he breaks it with, "That one looks like Erika. The plant."

"Oooh," Milo's sleepy voice chimes in unexpectedly. "Hi, Mama."

I smile, even though it hurts. It's nice to think that we can see Erika anywhere we choose to look. We pick out shapes in the clouds for I don't know long. And when we go home that afternoon, I get busy cooking the boys what Rhys declares is "one of the best meals he's ever eaten."

And I make way too much.

Just in case he's hungry again later.

CHAPTER 24

Tabitha

Grocery shopping. It's our first mundane outing as a newly married couple. It should feel low pressure, but instead, I feel like everyone in the store is staring at us as we approach the front doors.

Word about Erika's death has officially spread. The whisper network in a small town is both fierce and effective, which means news of our nuptials has also spread. Especially because my parents paid for the announcement to be in the *Rose Hill Gazette.*

They'd told me about it this morning and I'd cringed, but they'd been so happy that I'd done my best to play along at being flattered by the attention.

Rhys had sat in the chair across from me with a knowing smirk on his face that made me want to either kick him or pounce on him.

I start out of the memory when his big, warm palm lands

on my lower back, ushering me into the grocery store ahead of him. Peeking back at him, I see Milo up on his shoulders, bouncing happily with a plastic dinosaur clenched tight in one hand.

"Giddy up, Ree!"

Rhys's lips twitch. "Not in the store, buddy. After."

Undeterred, Milo kicks his legs. The ones that end up gripped in both of Rhys's hands. "Go *neeiiigh* like a pony, Ree!"

Rhys groans and shakes his head, but it's good-natured. "Not right now."

Milo's face scrunches, red splotches forming on his cheeks as his fingers curl into fists before he lets out a shrill, "Right now!"

A heavy sigh rushes from my lungs. *Fucking threenagers, man.* Hearing *no* is currently one of his least favorite pastimes.

I can see the tantrum coming from a mile away. It's the change in his voice, the tension in his tiny limbs. I start to turn, ready to intercept.

"I want—"

But Rhys cuts Milo off, his voice firm but calm as he removes him from his shoulders and crouches down in front of him, coming eye-to-eye with the little boy. "Milo, we're at a grocery store. We need to help Tabby choose food for the week. This isn't the time or place for that game. And honestly, if you talk to me like that, I won't want to play it at all."

I blink. I don't know why I'm surprised by the way Rhys handles him, but I am. Milo's little lips work even as his eyes go glassy. With crossed arms, he tips his nose up and looks away, guilt and pride warring on his face.

"After?" He finally slides his eyes back, one brow quirking at Rhys.

I almost giggle. Erika used to do that too. That exact thing with her eyebrow.

Rhys nods. "If you can shop with us and be polite, then we'll talk. Think you can do that?"

Milo straightens, as though physically rising to the challenge. Then he nods once, firmly. And in that motion, I see Rhys.

It's strange to see and even more strange to think about—this man I barely know really has had an impact on my nephew. Such a profound one that I can pick pieces of him out now that I know what to look for.

Rhys nods back and then takes him by the hand, marching past me with a wink that makes me a little weak in the knees. I watch as Rhys pulls out a cart and lifts Milo into the seat.

Then he turns back to me with an effortless, "You coming, baby?" that makes my cheeks feel warm. And based on the way his eyes trail over my face, I don't think he misses it.

With a thick swallow, I pull myself together and forge ahead into the store while trying not to overthink the show we have to put on for the gazes that linger on us.

We start out in the meat section, and I watch in awe as Rhys basically cleans the place out of all their chicken breasts.

"Breasts, huh?" I joke as he piles them into the cart.

He rolls his eyes, but then they land on me, hot and dark below the heavy slashes of his brow. They trail slowly, intentionally, down over my throat and straight to my chest.

"Yup. They're my favorite," is all he says before turning away and pushing the cart along.

With hotter cheeks than I had before, I hustle after him. I'm grateful for the way Milo chatters away about which snacks he wants so I don't have to make small talk with my husband.

I don't know why I'm all bumbling and nervous around him. I just know that talk we had followed by an afternoon nap in the sun feels like it changed something between us. Like we shared pieces of ourselves and know each other a little better.

In fact, I find myself questioning a lot of the things I know about Rhys. I find myself wondering if there's more to the story with Rhys that Erika may have conveniently left out. Most of all, I find myself questioning if Rhys could possibly be as bad as I made him out to be in my head.

It's starting to seem unlikely, which leaves me feeling… adrift.

But reality comes slamming back when Rhys puts his hand on my back again. I try—and fail—to cover the shiver that races down my spine when he touches me.

This is all for show, I remind myself as I glance around. It's pretend.

"Are you cold?" Rhys's voice is like gravel, the feel of his breath against the shell of my ear a distracting tease as he leans in close.

"A little," I lie.

Which backfires spectacularly when he tucks me against his side, draping one heavily corded arm around my neck. He drops a chaste kiss against my hair and continues sauntering through the grocery store like this is the most natural thing in the world.

Me? My heart is racing like I've just run a marathon. Which is bizarre because I fucking hate running and would never.

Before I know it, our cart is full and we're in line at the checkout. I feel like I just snuggled against Rhys in a blissed-out daze for twenty minutes. I'm not even sure if all the food we got makes sense, but I can get creative and make it work.

Milo is in his own world playing with his dinosaur as I stare at the magazines at the checkout. My eyes catch on one in particular that makes me smile. Skylar's happy face staring back at me with a shiny golden award in her hand. That's when I feel Rhys's body tense and turn next to mine. His fingers dig into my hip and pressure coils in my pelvis before I even realize what's going on.

When I look up, Rhys is glaring at the man one line over. Too Tall, or as the guys have taken to calling him, *Stretch*. My lips twitch. That spin on his chosen nickname probably drives Terence fucking nuts.

I don't know what his deal is, only that he's been a raging dickhead to me ever since I broke up with him as a *teenager*, and that only makes me want to needle him more.

"Ah, Terry. Fancy meeting you here," I say, not missing

the sneer he shoots Rhys's way. The condescending look he gives my husband gets my back up.

But Rhys doesn't take the bait. Instead, he gives him a show of perfect white teeth as he scrubs his left hand over his beard and lets his eyes trail over the other man like he's yesterday's trash. "Right. *Stretch*. I forgot about you."

The dig is clear, but Terence seems the most fixated on the flash of gold on Rhys's finger. His eyes move down to my left hand, which boasts a matching ring.

He scoffs. "Really? I thought you'd remember losing to my team all the time."

Rhys laughs. It comes out deep and makes his broad shoulders shake. "Oh, nah. Hard to think much about bowling when we've been busy celebrating the wedding. Ya know?"

He does that thing where he pops his tongue into his cheek. It's all sass and his eyes are all taunt. Then he turns his gaze down to me. "Isn't that right, baby?"

I swallow and tip my chin up toward him with a subtle nod, feeling the weight of so many eyes on us. The way Rhys is grinning down at me makes my heart pitter-patter in my chest. His free hand cups my jaw, thumb stroking my cheek, and my heartbeat leaps there, right beneath his touch.

I don't answer. But I swear he just *knows*. A satisfied rumble vibrates in his chest as our eyes clash.

"Yeah, that *is* right," he murmurs, before dropping his head and kissing me. Right here, in the grocery store.

I suck in a shocked gasp as his lips turn hungry. His tongue sweeps in, a sultry tease that has my body bowing into his eagerly and does nothing but leave me wanting more. A breathy whimper rushes from me as he pulls away, still staring at my mouth as he bites down on his bottom lip.

"Anyway, it's always a pleasure, Terence. See ya around." He doesn't look away from me as he addresses a guy who hasn't mattered in over a decade. His show of unnecessary territorialism leaves me scrambling, wondering why we needed to fake it right here and now.

I watch in a daze as Rhys manages the checkout, eyes widening when he tosses two copies of the *Rose Hill Gazette* on the conveyor at the last minute.

"Why do you want two copies of that?" I ask in confusion, still reeling from his kiss.

Rhys's fingers tangle absently in my hair and give a gentle tug. "Obviously we have to keep a copy of our marriage announcement for the wedding album," he says, like it's the simplest thing in the world. "And..." He taps his card on the reader, a smug smile on his face while he leaves me hanging, watching, wondering what the hell he was about to say.

Once the machine beeps its approval, I get my answer.

Rhys turns and tosses one paper over the magazine rack, landing it smack-dab in front of Terence, drawing the man's attention once more. "And I thought our good pal Stretch might like a copy for his scrapbook too."

Terence's slender face turns beet red before our eyes, which only makes Rhys grin wider. My lips press together to keep from laughing, only offering the other man a nod as I depart with Rhys's arm slung over me protectively.

"That was so fucking petty," I whisper to him.

But all I get back as we hit the outdoors is a firm squeeze and a gravelly, "I don't know what you're talking about."

It's bullshit, but he clearly doesn't want to talk about it. And before I can press him any further, he's reaching into the cart for Milo. "You rocked that shopping trip, little man. It's officially pony ride time."

His hands wrap around Milo's rib cage as he tosses him up onto his shoulders, eliciting a joyous giggle from the little boy.

"Giddy up, Ree!" he squeals, circling a free hand around his head.

And Rhys does. He gallops through the parking lot in a way that is *entirely* out of character, and Milo hoots and hollers with glee. This big, stoic man we got stuck with, who is constantly tied up tight, goes all soft and gooey for the little boy on his shoulders right before my eyes.

It makes my heart squeeze so hard that it takes my breath away.

But more than that, it makes me feel like we're really fucking lucky to be stuck with Rhys.

CHAPTER 25

Rhys

"Stop judging me, cat."

Cleo has curled herself on the end of my bed, a place she seems to have claimed as her own.

Every night.

She won't leave me alone. And now she's watching me work through my promo lines the writers sent with her paws tucked tightly in front of her and a judgmental fucking look on her kind-of-cute face.

"We don't even like each other," I add for good measure.

She just purrs. This cat is always purring. Wakes me up purring at 3 a.m., kneading my chest like she's rolling dough.

Annoying.

I tug my mask down over my face and step away from the world's worst sidekick, taking my place in front of where I've propped my laptop. The backdrop of a plain concrete wall makes it look like I'm living in a bunker, but that's fine.

It's unidentifiable, and more than anything, I want to keep Tabitha and Milo clear of any media attention.

This is their safe space, and I will not fuck it up by tipping off my more unhinged fans. Not when this place has started to feel like home over the past weeks. Life has become busy in the days since the wedding, but we've fallen into a rhythm. Morning coffee under blankets on the porch across from Tabitha. She works, I take Milo. I work out at the local rec center or hit up my new favorite yoga class, she takes Milo. We grocery shop together and hold hands in public.

I think we both find it easier to talk to each other all the time—just not about the hand-holding. Or the kissing. Or how irrationally jealous her stupid high school boyfriend makes me.

Tabitha cooks the best fucking meals I've ever had in my life, and I eat so much that I worry I might need to cut down hard and fast when I get back to work. We go our separate ways at night, and I fist my cock in the shower, thinking about my wife. Then I fall asleep, forcing myself to list all the reasons crossing that line with her is a terrible idea for what is already a tenuous setup. Milo is—and needs to remain—our number one priority.

I check the mail daily, but the marriage certificate has yet to arrive. I know it's my ticket out of here. And I try not to overanalyze the way I feel disappointed and relieved all at once. Because I love my work, but I'm starting to love being here too.

I tip my wrist up to check my watch and realize I need to get this promo squared away quickly. It won't take Tabitha long to drop Milo with her parents, and I need to get to bowling sooner rather than later.

A quick click of the mouse gives me a three-second countdown to get in position. I've slicked my hair back, and the black T-shirt I'm wearing clings to my skin. Intimidating is the vibe, and this works. Anthony's email said to send a threatening message to Million Dollar Bill, otherwise known as Will. I need to challenge him to a matchup next month at Pure Pandemonium—the biggest professional wrestling event of the year.

When the tone sounds, I leave Rhys behind and become Wild Side. It's part of what I love about this job. I get to be someone else for a brief time. Someone tough, strong, and commanding—not an insecurity or worry as far as the eye can see.

Being Wild Side was my ticket out of a tough upbringing, and slipping into character always feels like tugging on a favorite old hoodie. It feels like peace.

I heave my shoulders once and stare down straight into the camera, curling my lip in a subtle sneer. "I may not be there in person, but I've got a special message for Little Willy, as I like to call him."

A quiet snicker sounds from behind me, and my eyes close. I don't even need to turn around to know that Tabitha is somewhere near the top of the stairs, watching me.

I sigh heavily. "Tabby."

"Wild Side."

"*Tabitha*."

"Sorry," she squeaks back. "Little Willy broke me."

Tugging my mask off, I turn to face her. She's huddled at the top of the stairs, peeking through the railings, one piece of unfinished lumber in each hand, face visible through the gap. Like a little kid caught spying.

"I need ten minutes."

"You really expect me to go upstairs and pretend you aren't doing this down here? You overestimate my maturity, Dupris. If I'm not sitting here, I'll be holding an empty can up to the door to eavesdrop."

I say nothing, opting to glare at her and cross my arms. It's getting harder and harder to keep this unaffected front up around Tabitha. Between the wedding, the odd outburst of sexual tension, the constant touching in public, and me spilling my guts to her at the rose field, we're feeling a lot more like friends who want to fuck than enemies who want to fuck.

We're feeling complicated and inevitable all at once.

"Let me help you," she says, surprising me with her offer. Then, without an invitation, she marches down the stairs and heads straight for my laptop.

Anxiety swirls in my gut. I have never merged these personal and professional worlds in any major way. But Tabitha waltzes across the divide with such ease and eagerness that I don't have it in me to stop her.

Instead, I stand back and watch her approach the screen and start the video over from the beginning. My cheeks go hot as it plays back. It's one thing to know she's watched me on TV and another thing to stand here and experience it.

"Do you like this background? It looks like you're being held hostage."

My lips twitch. "That's fine. It's unidentifiable and all one color."

"You look fucking jacked in this T-shirt."

I scrub a hand over my mouth. "Thanks?"

"Yeah. But the lighting is all wrong. We need you to *pop*. We need..." She tilts her head, her body doing this shimmy thing which does absolutely nothing except draw my attention to her perfectly round ass. The faded black Levi's she's wearing just add to the shape, and I have to think about something gross to stave off the hardness in my boxers.

A long piece of hair that you can feel but can't get off.

The liquid on top of sour cream when you open the container.

Band-Aids in a public pool.

"I'm just going to..." She moves around the unfinished basement, flicking lights on and placing the bedside lamp into a strategic spot. Then she goes to stand where I was and peers back at the screen. "Okay, the lighting is better, but the camera on this thing sucks. Let's do it on your phone."

"What?"

"I'll record you. That way, I can zoom in and shit. I do aesthetic food videos for the bistro all the time."

She holds a palm out in my direction, and I stare down at it. "No."

"Yes. As your wife, I refuse to let you turn in a shitty mouth-running video."

"It's a promo," I correct petulantly.

"Whatever. As Mrs. Wild Side, I demand they only portray you in the best light possible. Literally and figuratively."

Her fingers curl in a hand-it-over motion. My brows furrow, and I don't know why I feel shy. I've taken my fair share of acting classes. I film these in front of people all the time.

But Tabitha isn't just people.

"Chop, chop, big man." She taps at her bare wrist impatiently. "We're child-free, and I've got a girls' night to get to."

With unfamiliar butterflies in my stomach, I approach the spot with the words *we're child-free* swirling in my head. It's how she said *we*. The familial term slipped from her tongue so naturally.

I have never been part of a *we*.

That's why I hand her my phone.

She holds it up, examining it with a speculative gaze. "Okay, you know what you're going to say? I don't want my arm to shake. I already fucked up one take."

It's funny. I've spent all these years hiding what I do, avoiding conversations about it, feeling wounded when people have something to say about it. *Oh, it's so fake. Steroids aren't good for you. That's trash TV.* And here I am, married to a woman who is—I don't even know. Invested? Supportive? Even excited?

I'm not sure what to make of it.

But I like it.

"Hello?" She waves. "Earth to Rhys? Put that mask on. Let's go. It's time to shit talk Little Willy." Her lips clamp together, but she doesn't let the laugh out. She just looks… *happy*.

I hesitate to put my mask on. I've only worn it in front

of work people. Doing it here, in a quiet basement with Tabitha, feels fucking weird.

But I can't deny her shit. So with an irritated eye roll, I pull the mask over my face, securing the straps over the back of my head so it stays in place. Then I force myself to look her in the eye. I expect to see a tinge of mockery in her gaze, but I don't. Her dark eyes are sparkling like the lake at night as her tongue darts out over her plump pink lips in concentration.

"You've got..." She trails off, and I quirk my head in question. Her finger points up toward my head. "You've got—you know what? *Here.*"

She steps forward, and the scent of her citrusy perfume hits me as she pulls in close. It suits her perfectly. It stops me in my tracks.

Her arm lifts, and her fingers slide into my hair. Gentle and a touch tentative. And fuck if my heart rate doesn't ratchet straight up.

"Is this okay?" she whispers, gaze moving back down to meet mine. "You had hair sticking out. Hard to look like a badass with messy hair."

All I can do is nod.

And think about kissing her.

And I don't mean the polite, nothing kisses we exchange in public for appearances' sake. Or the ones I pretend are just for show.

Because there's nothing polite about the things I want to do to Tabitha Garrison. Even just knowing she's walking around with my ring on her finger makes me hard.

Soon her fingers flatten and smooth my hair. "There."

Her head tilts as if inspecting her handiwork. "That's better."

It's just cool enough that I can feel the warm dampness of her breath against the side of my neck. She's too fucking close.

Her eyes drop to my mouth. And god, I want to do it. I want to kiss her. But my fear of fucking it all up tugs me back. One step away and her magnetic pull lessens. A second step and I can breathe again.

With a firm dip of my chin, I grumble, "Okay, let's do this."

"Okay," she replies breathlessly. I could swear her cheeks are more flushed than they were before, lips a little glossier. "Just say when."

I get into position, close my eyes for a beat, and straighten up. When my lids open back up, I'm Wild Side. Tabitha counts down on her fingers and then points at me.

And without overthinking the fact that I'm doing *this* with *her*, I point at the camera with authority, and talk. "I've got a special message for Little Willy. And it's that he better be ready to lose at Pure Pandemonium. He'll be wiping his tears with all the money he never earned. Because that belt is going to be back where it belongs"—I gesture to my waist—"and that's with me: a real champion.

"Yeah, I'll let him borrow my belt just long enough to make a fool of himself. He can traipse around in his fancy suit, running his mouth, relying on cheap shots and brass knuckles—as every loser in this company needs to when they try to beat me. But none of that is going to work, because

I'll be ready. I'll be training where he and his goons can't find me."

I pause for dramatic effect before continuing. "In fact, I'll be the one to find *him.* And when I do, you better believe I'm gonna drag that pathetic trust-fund baby to the Wild Side, take his ass over the mountain, and show him how real men settle the score."

I wait several seconds and then nod. Tabitha is grinning like a total loon when she nods back and lowers the phone.

I tug my mask back instantly and glare at her. "What?"

Her cheeks twitch. "Nothing."

"You're smiling like the Joker. That's not nothing."

She shrugs, staring down at the phone. "I just didn't have you being an overgrown drama nerd on my bingo card."

Hands on my hips, I look away to cover a smile.

"*Gonna drag that pathetic trust-fund baby to the Wild Side*," she imitates with gusto. My first reaction is to go on the defensive, but then she adds, "God, that was amazing. Do you make that shit up on the fly? I could never."

I watch her smile down at the screen as my gravelly voice filters from the device. With only a few long strides, I stand beside her, looking down at the recording. And she wasn't wrong. The lighting *is* better. She even zoomed in slowly so that you get a good close-up as I deliver my parting words.

I put an arm over her shoulder, mask dangling from my hand, and pull her in for a side hug. Partly a weird attempt at being friendly but casual, and partly because I itch to touch her. I want to tell her how special it is to me that she jumped in and helped with this.

But where Wild Side is just fine with expressing himself, Rhys is more like squeezing blood from rocks where emotions are concerned.

"Thank you, Tabby," is what I settle on. It's simple, but it gets the job done.

She turns her smile up at me. And fuck, it's blinding. "Mrs. Wild Side to the rescue. Do we get to do more?"

My brows jump in surprise. "More?"

"Yeah. Like…again? Will I get to see my clip on TV?"

"*Your* clip?"

"Oh yeah." She scoffs and mimes brushing dirt off her shoulder. All it does is draw my eyes down the front of her soft black sweater—the one with the plunging neckline and layered gold necklaces. From here, I can see a peek of a red bra, and I swallow the groan that surges up in my throat at the sight. "I'm your official camerawoman now. In fact…"

I'm so busy gawking at her that my reaction time is slow.

She grabs my mask and spins out of my hold, hiking it over her face in one fluid motion. "I think I need a headshot and video credit."

"Absolutely not." I reach for her, but she turns away again.

"Never mind this wedding band. I need a matching mask," she calls over her shoulder as she hustles away, laughter floating through the chilled basement.

I go after her, covering the ground in long strides. I don't know why I'm doing this. It's one of several masks. Nothing special, really. Maybe I'm just looking for an excuse to follow her around. "Tabitha."

She turns and strikes a pose with a hand beneath her chin at the base of the stairs. The lime-green lines on the mask pop against her dark hair. "Admit it. I look cute like this."

"That's not the word I'd use," I grumble, reaching forward with a chuckle as I make a feeble attempt at unmasking her.

Her sweater slips between my fingers as she jogs up a few steps before taunting me. "How are you going to catch Little Willy, Rhys? You can't even catch me."

And then my wife, wearing my mask, holds her fingers up in a peace sign, sticks her tongue out, and snaps a selfie on my phone.

I take two steps with one stride, and this time, I do catch her. My hands snag on her waist, and I drag her down onto my lap as I turn. And then I'm seated on the stairs, back pressed to the steps behind me, with Tabitha straddling me.

I peel the mask back and toss it over my shoulder, gaze burning across her features.

My plan ends there.

I'm met with flushed cheeks, wide eyes, and parted lips. Her mouth. God. I can't stop staring at her mouth. The light from upstairs shines down on us, illuminating her in the most enticing glow. What started out playfully suddenly feels serious.

"Caught you," I rumble. "Now what?"

"Now…" she breathes, but doesn't finish the sentence. Instead, her head drops closer, body arching toward mine. Then she fists the front of my shirt and kisses me.

CHAPTER 26

Tabitha

My husband has no fucking business looking this good. That's how I'm justifying pouncing on him. Because Rhys and I are far too complicated for this to be a good idea.

Grief is still my constant companion, and a feeling I've become numb to carrying with me. I should be too sad—too angry—to maul this man.

But right now, I don't feel any of those things. No, I feel electric. With Rhys holding me, I feel no sadness. And I want more of that feeling. Straddling his lap, with his hands on my waist, and that fucking mask tossed a few stairs up—I want *him*.

My hands cup his bristled jawline as I move my mouth, savoring this sensation.

He stills.

But then his fingers flex on my waist in a way that sends a current straight to my core. He makes no other move, so

I take the lead, firm and demanding from the first swipe of my tongue. Leaving no sliver of doubt in his mind about what I'm after.

A quick nip at his bottom lip gets me a groan and a whispered, "Fuck, I've dreamed of this," against my damp lips.

Then he grabs the back of my head and sears me with a kiss of his own. Like everything he does, there's a raw power to each motion. The way his tongue lays claim. The way his opposite hand roams my hip, as though he's touched me a million times before this moment.

His hand slips beneath my sweater to splay over my back. Having his hands on my body does nothing but drive me wild. It makes me want so much more, and that desperate feeling coursing through my veins gives me pause.

My fingers flutter over his cheeks. I cling to him, and he clings back. We fall into a rhythm. Give and take. Hard and soft. There's no fumbling, no rushing, no clanking of teeth. We are perfectly in sync.

My heart thuds with a heavy, undeniable certainty as I kiss Rhys. I roll my hips and grind myself down, the hardness of him responding immediately. And when I startle back up, his hand lands on my shoulder, pushing me back onto him.

"Rhys," I whisper, dragging the tip of my nose over his cheek while my fingers tangle in his mussed hair. "We should..."

He peppers kisses over the column of my throat with a reverence that makes my chest ache and my hips swivel. Pressure coils behind my hip bones as a familiar heat races up my spine.

"What should we do, Tabby?"

Tabby.

God, I almost purr at the way my name rumbles in his throat.

"We should... You should—"

His fingers slide down the column of my spine with firm, even pressure, and my ability to form words evaporates.

"Make you come before you leave for girls' night?" I hear the taunt in his tone and feel the rasp of his stubbled cheek, no doubt hitching up into a smirk against my chest. "Tell me you're on birth control so I can dream about fucking you bare, Tabby."

"I am. Yesss." I hiss the word, eyes fluttering shut as I imagine how it would feel to have him slide between my legs. To ride him. To have him fill me the way I'm sure only he can.

God, it would be heaven.

I grind down on him, lost to the fantasy.

"Fuck yes," he groans, lifting his hips to match my fervor. He sends me into a delirious haze, dry fucking me while he sears me with another kiss that promises so damn much.

We claw at each other frantically. I'm drunk on him, and I want more. I want it all. His big hands. His deep moans. The smell of his skin all around me. Him moving inside of me, pushing me higher with every thrust.

My skin sizzles, and I feel ready to rip my clothes off just to feel more of him.

I can barely breathe. One sharp breath in and one slow exhale. My complicated feelings about Rhys and where we began have me twisted up beyond comprehension.

That's why I don't want to let this fantasy become reality.

But I don't want him to stop either. I want this to go on forever.

His palm roams over the curve of my ass, fingers edging lower. When I drop my gaze to meet his, I'm met with pure heat, and what looks an awful lot like…vulnerability.

Like he can read my mind, he says, "Tell me I should stop, Tabby. Tell me I should stop, and I will."

His thumb circles against my jeans as he waits.

I breathe him in, and he breathes me out, both of us toeing the edge of what could be a disastrous fall.

And I realize it might not just be disastrous for Milo. It could be disastrous for me *and* for Rhys. Because kissing him to make myself feel better when he's looking at me like I hung the moon feels dangerous.

Dangerous, because when he looks at me like that, my heart beats harder and my brain starts asking questions that I don't especially know how to cope with. Questions like…

You're sure you want this marriage to be fake?

All at once, I'm struck by the gravity of the situation. We aren't just two people anymore. There's a legal element, a co-parenting element. His fortune. My restaurant. The ways this could go bad are…*bad.*

So I pull back. For his protection and for mine.

I fumble around like an awkward mess as I try to extricate myself from him while avoiding falling down the stairs. "Listen," I mutter as I look over my shoulder to place my foot safely. "I don't really want you to stop. But that's why we should."

When I sneak a peek back down at him, his features have twisted into an expression that is the perfect blend of amused and confused. "It's a bad idea."

His lips quirk, and he regards me calmly—save for the massive ridge in his pants. There's nothing calm about the way his dick is standing at attention right now. "Is that so?"

My eyes roll. *Is that so*? He says that all the time. "Yeah. Milo."

His head tilts in question. Like Milo isn't a good enough reason for me to back out of whatever just happened.

"And you. And me. Just…complicated."

He nods, lips twitching with amusement but never breaking into a smile. "Making my wife come is a bad idea because…*complicated*. Did I get that right?"

I prop my hands on my hips. "Listen, I can tell you're mocking me, but you know I'm right. If you were thinking with your head and not your massive dick, you'd agree."

Fuck my life. Why did I have to compliment the size of his dick again? He's never going to let me live this down. I'm practically spoon-feeding him.

I need to get away, so I head up the stairs, stepping over his shoulder and focusing on making it to the door. If I don't, his adorable fucking smirk may annoy me enough that I drop down and enjoy his offer.

"Sorry," I say. "I lost my head there for a second. If it's any consolation, in another lifetime, I'd climb you like a tree, and not think twice."

He lets out a beleaguered sigh as I reach the top of the stairs, and his voice comes out more tortured than I expected, his parting words hitting me right in the chest. "That's no consolation at all, Tabby."

"Why are your cheeks all flushed?" Rosie eyes me suspiciously over the rim of her drink.

I swallow and look away, pretending to take in the decor here at the Reach. "They're not. I was in a rush and put on too much blush. It's very grade ten of me." It's a lie. All my blush rubbed off on Rhys's stubble, and my cheeks are flushed because I can't stop thinking about how it felt when he held me down on his dick.

A suspicious, "Hmm," is all I get back.

From the corner of my eye, I see Skylar give Rosie a firm elbow from her side of the booth. "Ease off. They're *newlyweds*."

The word drips with innuendo, and I can't help but scoff. *If you only knew*.

Luckily, Doris cuts off the conversation as she storms up to the table with a pretty blond girl in tow. "Girls," she barks in her signature smoker's voice, and we all straighten immediately. Doris has never been anything but sweet to us, but there is an authoritative vibe about her that doesn't seem to fade, no matter how old I get.

"Doris, we're women," Rosie corrects playfully, only for Doris to roll her eyes.

"Funny, I didn't overhear you calling it *women's night* when you walked in giggling like a bunch of schoolgirls."

I snort and take a sip of my red wine.

"See? The emo one knows when to keep her mouth shut."

Skylar almost sprays her drink across the table but covers by dabbing daintily at the sides of her mouth.

My brows shoot up, and I lower the wineglass. "Wait. Am I the emo one?"

"Am I the only one who remembers the phase with all the black makeup and clothes? Even the elastics on your braces were black."

I smirk. Fucking Doris. Been around long enough that she's practically a town encyclopedia.

"Which one am I?" Rosie asks with a shit-eating grin on her face.

"The bratty one," Doris responds, and we all laugh. Then she points at Skylar with an affectionate glimmer in her eye. "And that's the smart one."

Skylar's reaction to the compliment seems almost bashful. After years in the spotlight, where compliments focused on everything except her intelligence, I think Doris's praise hits differently for Skylar. It's special—and more sentimental than she'd ever let on.

"Anyway, *girls*. This is Gwen." She shoves the blond woman forward and smiles brightly. "She's new in town, working at the yoga studio I go to. Helps me stay limber for the bedroom. But she's been sitting up at the bar like I'm her only friend, and she doesn't realize how old I am, which is just sad. So I'm pawning her off on you."

Gwen palms Doris's shoulder with a light laugh. "Doris, please, I'm fine—"

"She's fine all right. All the regulars are eyeing up her tits like they're available to order off the menu or something. Guess she's the busty one."

My eyes drop and bulge a bit. I can't blame them. Gwen has all the right curves in all the right places. Soft and feminine in every way while I feel like a scrawny, flat board. Except when Rhys's hands are on me, asking me what he should do.

God, I really need to stop thinking about the stairs.

Gwen's cheeks blaze in time with mine, but her eyes twinkle with mirth. I can't help but jump in and save her from the roll that Doris is on right now.

I scootch over on the banquette and pat the vinyl seat. "Gwen, get in before shit gets any worse."

She smiles at me with a mix of surprise and gratitude and swiftly takes a seat.

Doris brushes her hands together like she's just finished building something, and who knows, maybe she has. "Good. A team of four for our first trivia night."

"Wait, what?"

"Thursdays. Trivia night. Bet the smart one read the sign on her way in and knew this already."

Skylar sips her drink and shrugs. "I mean...maybe."

"Told ya." Doris turns to leave. "Lucky y'all have her to carry your asses through this."

I shoot a bemused look at Gwen, who is laughing into her clenched fist, and then Rosie, who is watching Doris walk away with a look of awe on her face.

It's Skylar's sugary voice that brings all of our attention back to the table. "Trivia might be fun, no?" Her grin widens as she leans back in her seat. "Don't worry. I'll carry your asses."

We all laugh, then Rosie looks across the table and salutes our newest addition. "Gwen, welcome to women's night."

Gwen raises her beer in a toast. "Thank you all for having me. Do we have names? Or should I stick with Emo, Bratty, and Smart?"

I glance over at the woman with a subtle shake of my head. "I like you, Gwen. My name is Tabby."

She brightens. "Oh! Chef Tabby?"

I regard her with a casual shrug. "That's me."

"Rhys talks about you all the time."

Now my head tilts at her, piecing together how they know each other while ignoring the sharp jab of unfounded jealousy that just cropped up in my gut. "Does he?"

"Oh yeah. He's been coming to my classes, and he's quiet, ya know? So I've tried to get him talking a bit, and he's always all"—she puffs up and drops her voice in imitation of him—"*My wife this, my wife that. Did you know my wife owns that restaurant?*"

My jaw goes slack, and she sighs dreamily. "He's so proud of you, you know? God, it's adorable." She grins at me. "So, at any rate, it's nice to meet you."

I'm not sure what I was expecting her to say, but it sure as shit wasn't *that*. I don't even know how to respond. All I know is my tummy feels warm, my chest tingles, and my fingers itch to run through Rhys's hair again.

But Rosie's snark doesn't miss a beat.

"Oh weird. It's like you're putting on too much blush right before our eyes."

CHAPTER 27

Rhys

We walk into the Reach after winning our very first bowling match. Ford, West, Bash, and I are here to celebrate.

After weeks and weeks of losing, the competitor in me is preening. I only wish we'd beaten Stretch and his team, because I fucking hate that guy and will never forgive him for how he spoke to Tabitha.

In fact, sometimes in the ring, I imagine his face just to help with emoting for the crowd. Works every time.

But tonight, it's Tabitha's face that stops me in my tracks. Her head is thrown back in laughter, her eyes are bright, and her cheeks are warm. She's surrounded by friends, and she's *glowing*.

She looks happy, and god, I love to see it.

I'm not oblivious to the fact that she's been feeling low since Erika's death, but sometimes her stoicism makes it easy to forget how deep her grief must run. So the stark contrast of seeing her happy now hits me with a hard pang in the center of my chest.

It only makes me wish I could make her look like that. Instead, I've mostly succeeded at making her scowl, look confused, or look like she wants to rip my clothes off—which was great until she followed that up with awkward reasons she needed to leave. Most likely brought on by the reminder that I'm me...and she thinks I evicted her sister.

"What the fuck is going on in here?" Bash grumbles, looking around at multiple tables, each one scattered with small pencils and squares of paper.

West shrugs as he assesses the bar. "Beats the fuck outta me."

Doris yells out over the tables from behind the bar, "Last question. It could be a tiebreaker since we have two teams with the same number of points right now. What is a group of unicorns called? A herd, a flock, a blessing, or a rainbow?"

Ford's brows knit together as he whispers, "What the fuck?"

"Oh, a blessing. Duh," West says with an eye roll. Bash shoots him a scornful glare, which only makes him laugh. "You're just mad you were thinking *rainbow*, aren't you?"

"You're an idiot."

"A happy one," West volleys with a wink.

I turn my attention back to Tabitha's table, watching the heads of four women drawn together, all different shades of hair, but it's the shiny black strands that I watch closely. Just her hair makes me think of how it felt to fist it, to have her climb on top of me, kissing me like nothing else in the world mattered.

My cock thickens as I recall our moment on the stairs. The thrill of chasing her across the basement. The *almost* that will provide shower fodder for the rest of my life.

West bounces on the spot, peeking across the space at the sheet. "I swear Skylar knows this one. She's got this. When did they start a trivia night? And why does it have to conflict with bowling? This would be so fun."

Bash crosses his arms. "This would not be fun."

"Rosie would kill me if we started crashing girls' night," Ford adds. And he's got a point. Between him, West, and me, our significant others are all here tonight. Plus, one more who I have yet to meet.

"Time's up," Doris calls out. "Please drop your answers in the pitcher in front of me, and make sure your team's name is on there, or I'm not giving you any points. This isn't kindergarten. You should all know how to identify yourselves."

My lips twitch at the older woman.

West just looks amused. "God. Doris is such a legend."

I nod my agreement as I watch a person from each table stand up and head toward the bar with their answer in hand. And I now recognize the fourth team member who was sitting with Tabitha.

"Who's that?" Ford asks, tipping his chin toward her as she makes her way to the front, wearing a long flowy skirt and bracelets on each arm.

"That's my yoga instructor. Gwen."

"You do *yoga*?" West turns and looks at me like I just said I can walk on water.

I shrug. "Yeah. I like it."

"Like for inner peace and shit?"

I scoff. "Something like that."

"You should take Bash with you. He looks like he needs some inner peace."

I glance over at Bash, expecting his usual level of resting bitch face. He's grumpy, sure, but it's part of his charm at this point. I like to think of him as honest and direct. He says what he means and means what he says, but he's also reliable. He helped me out with the alarm system and is always forthcoming with bowling tips.

Deep down, Bash is a pretty nice guy.

Which is why it's hard to make heads or tails of his expression right now. Cut from stone and devoid of all color.

I nudge him. "You okay?"

One sharp nod.

Doris starts going over the answers, but Bash's eyes stay trained on Gwen. He's tracking her every movement across the floor, jaw flexing when she slides back into the booth next to Tabitha.

"Okay, enough loitering," Ford says. "Let's go find a table." He strides away with authority.

"Near the girls!" West calls as he heads after him.

Bash and I follow, and where I feel a stirring of excitement at the prospect of seeing Tabitha, Bash looks like he's heading to a funeral.

When the women realize we're here and look up, my eyes go to Tabitha. I don't know what to expect after earlier.

But the blinding smile she hits me with is not it.

It stops me in my tracks.

All my wishing I could make her happy, and here she is. Looking at me. *Happy*.

Here she is, getting up and heading straight for me.

Here she is, greeting me with a bashful, "Hi," before pushing up on her tiptoes and pulling my face down to hers.

Her plush lips stay on mine for just a beat or two longer than is appropriate for the setting, and her tongue dances across mine, just like mine had at the grocery store.

And fuck, it feels good.

My pulse races as I sigh against her mouth. "What was that for?" I whisper, eyes bounding between hers.

"That was…" She licks her lips, gaze drifting to my mouth.

"See?" Rosie's amused voice filters in from behind us, cutting her off. "She takes one look at him, and her cheeks are all red."

"Shut up, Rosie," Tabitha calls back without looking away. Then she changes the subject entirely and starts introductions. "Gwen, this is Bash," she says, gesturing to my teammate.

He scowls at Gwen, and she pushes her blond hair behind her ears. "Yeah, actually…we've met."

Rosie's eyes widen, and her head rears back a bit. "You have?"

"Yup." Bash's voice is brusque. "Good to see you again. I'm going to head out. You kids have fun."

Kids? Bash is maybe five years older than me. He's never called us kids before.

Before I can call him on it, he spins on his heel and is gone. All of us look confused, except for Gwen, who can't take her eyes off him as he leaves.

"Do you know him from yoga?" I ask.

Gwen smiles sadly, only responding with a hushed, "No," and zero other information.

The group falls silent for a moment, and then, in his usual manner, West shifts everyone into chatter and cheer.

Except for me. I feel off-kilter. I want to know what Tabitha was going to say.

I watch her as she turns away and heads to the bar for another drink. She bends over and props her forearms against the edge and waits for Doris, who is busy talking to someone at the other end.

And I can't resist the pull to her. Not after that kiss. Not after the stairs. I follow and approach from behind, caging her in as I prop a hand on either side of her and step in close.

She doesn't turn to check; she knows it's me, and she doesn't draw away. In fact, I hear her suck in a breath, feel a tremor race down her spine, and watch her stiffen when my thighs press against her ass.

My lips graze the lobe of her ear as I drop my head to speak quietly. "You really think you're gonna run away without telling me what that was?"

"Hmm," she muses, leaning into me and pressing her back flush with my chest. Her ass rubs against my dick like the tease I know she can be. "That was…how real newlyweds would say hi."

I lean in farther, covering her, pushing her against the bar and not really caring who's watching. We're fucking married. "Real, huh?"

She nods briskly, and I can hear her swallow. "Yeah. That."

I hum thoughtfully, feeling her heat, the way she melts—the way her back arches against me. "You telling me I'm just imagining you grinding that ass on me right now?"

"Yeah," she breathes. "All in your head."

I tilt my head to take a look at her profile. The flush on her cheeks. The way she's nibbling at her bottom lip.

"Tabby, baby, are you sick of playing this game?"

Her eyes slice over to mine, all wide and intentionally clueless. "What game?"

Guess I'm playing it too.

I drop my lips to the spot just beneath her ear. Then the side of her neck. The top of her shoulder, where I let my tongue dart out for a taste as my hips drive slowly against her jeans.

"The game where you pretend you weren't about to tell me what that fucking kiss was about."

Her chest is heaving. I can see it moving. I know exactly what I'm doing to her, and I could not care less.

"Okay, I was going to say—"

"Oh look! The emo one has become the horny one," Doris announces, fists propped on her hips.

Tabitha straightens instantly, pushing me back like she's a teenager who just got caught sneaking a boy through her window.

"Very funny, Doris." Tabitha laughs to cover the tremor in her voice.

I scowl at Doris as I draw up straight and watch her take Tabitha's drink order. Then I'm forced to stand around making small talk when what I really want is to be at home.

Alone.

With my wife.

At the end of the night, we both take our respective rides home, me with the guys, and Tabitha with the girls. And when West drops me off, she's already there, sitting out on the front steps. She has her jacket collar pulled high around her neck to keep the chill out, turning over a white envelope in her hands.

I wave goodbye without taking my attention off her and saunter toward the stairs with a growing sense of dread. Because I'm pretty sure I know what that envelope holds.

It's the only thing that's kept me here rather than on the road.

"Marriage certificate is here," she says with forced enthusiasm, holding it up to me.

"Oh." I stop and stare at it. I should be happy, because we were waiting for this. It makes everything easier. I go on the road, and Tabitha keeps Milo at home. We eventually only meet up for… I don't know. Christmas? Easter?

Suddenly, I'm relieved that Tabitha didn't tell me to keep going earlier. Bad as it stung, having to pull away from her after taking that turn would be worse. No, this is better. We can part ways as two...friendly acquaintances. Sharing nothing but brief moments of insanity to laugh about when Milo is older.

Yes, this is much better. So long as I ignore the nausea building in the pit of my stomach over leaving them, this is just fine.

My feet carry me forward, and I take a tentative seat beside her. I reach for the envelope, and her gaze stays on me as I peel it open. My hand shakes when I pull out the contents, and I know she notices, because she slides a comforting palm over my knee.

Then, under the porch light, I analyze the marriage certificate. *Our* marriage certificate. Tabitha Lynn Garrison. Rhys Malcolm Dupris. I run my fingers over her name and then mine. Her name proudly chosen by her parents, the same middle name as her mom. My name...a mystery. I'll never get to know why they chose my name, only that people who gave me up assigned it to me along the way. A thread of shame tightens in me.

"You don't have to take my last name, you know," I say, keeping my gaze on the certificate. "I'm not a fan of it either."

She rests a shoulder against mine. "I love your last name. It's strong. It suits you. I like the way it sounds with your first name. I just..."

"I know. We're not—"

"No, it's not you. It's Milo. He's a Garrison. I feel like matching that will just be easier for school and stuff as he gets older. And I feel tied to my sister with our last name in a way. I'm actually not sure I'll ever change it."

I nod. "Smart. That makes sense."

And it is. And it does. But something about it hurts. I'm still on the outside. Still on my own. I've got a pretend family—but not a real one.

I bump my shoulder against hers. "I'm gonna have to hit the road now, you know."

"I know." It grows so quiet that I can hear her swallow. "How long will you be gone?"

"I don't know. I need to make up for some lost time. Anthony is far too excited about the creative liberties they can take while I'm not there." I scrub a hand over my mouth, somehow dreading saying this out loud. "Weeks? The lead-up to Pure Pandemonium will be busy."

"Weeks," she repeats the word back to me as though it's new to her. "Okay."

"I'll…uh…" I clear my throat, feeling emotional about leaving them for *weeks*. This woman and this little boy who I've grown to…care for. "I'll make sure I pick Milo up in the morning, say goodbye to your parents and him. Maybe I'll take him to the park for a bit. Then I should drive to the city and start heading back."

"Okay. Yeah, of course. Sounds good."

Her thumb moves in a circle on my knee, and my lips quirk up.

That's my move.

"I'm going to hit the hay," she says, pushing to stand.

I nod, but don't look up. Then her fingers glide into my hair, combing through tentatively. Nothing like earlier today. When the tips of her fingers slip from my scalp, I miss the pressure of them. The heat of her nearness.

God. I'm so fucked.

The door creaks as she departs, and I don't look back until the sounds of her moving stop altogether.

"Hey, Rhys?"

I glance over my shoulder, and her beauty steals the air from my lungs. All done up, the porch light shining down on her like a spotlight screaming, *She's the one!*

I clear my throat. "Yeah?"

"Gwen seems sweet. What I meant to tell you earlier is that she told me you talk about me all the time. And the restaurant."

I shrug. Gwen *is* sweet. But clearly, she got to me with her chatter about opening your love chakras and creating space for your heart to heal from past bruises or whatever other hippie shit she spouts. Her salt-of-the-earth ramblings though…

They made me loose-lipped.

They made me think of Tabitha.

And on the off chance my new yoga teacher was getting the wrong idea about me and my reasons for attending her class, I raved about my wife.

"She said she can tell that you're proud of me." Tabitha's voice comes out thin, and she covers the vulnerability of the sentence with a sarcastic scoff. Always covering with dry humor and cutting one-liners, as though she expects me to roll my eyes and play it off. As though she's spent a lifetime being overlooked and expects the same from me. I look her dead in the eye and tell her the truth.

"I am proud of you, Tabitha."

"Thanks. I…" Her voice fades out, and she looks away shyly. "You're a good man, Rhys. I hope you know that. I think Milo moving in next to you was meant to be. I'm glad he has you."

My nose stings, and I nod again as I watch her turn and retreat into the house. I desperately want to say something, to call her back out here. But I just…*can't*.

Conversations like this are out of my wheelhouse. A lifetime spent keeping people at arm's length means this thing with Tabitha has me feeling like a deer in the headlights—wide-eyed and frozen. My chest aches as if the unspoken words are burning from the inside, trying to make their way out.

But by the time I think of what to say, she's gone.

CHAPTER 28

Tabitha

Tabby: Give Little Willy hell.

Rhys: Yes, wife.

WATCHING RHYS DRIVE AWAY THE NEXT MORNING ROLLED over me as an overwhelming wave of dread. Milo waved goodbye with a big smile, chattering away about how much fun they had at the park, and all I could think was, *I don't want him to go*.

What worked between Rhys and me in the beginning was a mutual distaste for each other and a shared love for Milo. Our arrangement had nothing to do with us, and everything to do with one little boy.

But after months spent together and seeing all the subtle

ways he supports us, I... Well, I'm not sure what our arrangement is founded on now. He told me he was proud of me, and my chest swelled. I'm not sure he even understands how badly I needed that praise.

All my hard work, all my sacrifice, it always ends up coming along with implications about Erika. There is an unintentional tendency among the people in this small town to compare us. Like anything I do is great because it's more than what Erika did.

My accolades have always been attached to her in some way. Which not only makes me feel like shit, but it makes me feel angry on my sister's behalf. Her mental health was a constant uphill battle, and she struggled, but she had a soft heart. It kills me that no one sees her the way I do.

Except for Rhys. I suppose we're kindred that way.

So now the distaste is gone, and in its wake? Mutual respect.

With just a drop of obsession.

Because I have not been able to stop thinking about Rhys all day.

Is he safe?

Is he hungry?

Is everything at the border okay?

Is he thinking about me too?

Dinner rush at the restaurant was the only thing that stilled my spiraling mind.

But that was short-lived, because now I'm back home. Luckily, my mom already had Milo peacefully tucked into my bed upstairs, and I'm...watching fucking wrestling.

It's not even Rhys's night—his show is on Mondays—but with a cup of tea in hand and a brain too wired to fall asleep, curiosity got the best of me. I find myself fascinated, from the costumes to the names to the way they throw themselves around with reckless abandon.

It's riveting. The drama is full tilt, the women are badass, and the men are more varied than I remember from my childhood. They're not all fake tanner, blasted-out pupils, and so muscle-bound it looks painful. They look more like Rhys. Big, built, and *fit*, but not like they chew steroids for breakfast.

The camera zooms in on the man wearing the manties that Rhys doesn't, and I lean closer, gauging if he shaves his legs or if he's just so oiled up that I can't see the hair. Even his arms are smoother than mine. Perhaps it's a strategy thing? I think back to touching Rhys's forearms—there was definitely hair. I'd have noticed smooth skin or scratchy stubble.

I stroke Cleo, who is curled beside me, and then slide my hand down my own leg. Yes, like *that*. Stubble—because I took one look at my razor in the shower and decided shaving my legs seemed like way too much work.

I reach for my phone, the question burning in my mind and not at all just an excuse to contact Rhys.

Tabby: Do you shave your legs?

I hit send and immediately consider deleting it. We left things on such a tender note last night, and here I am, asking if he shaves his legs like the awkward weirdo I am.

He responds within seconds.

Rhys: What?

Rhys: Also, did you put that sandwich in my bag? I ate it on the plane. I hope you didn't poison it.

Tabby: Your legs. For wrestling. Is there a benefit to having them look like a Ken doll? Because I'm watching tonight's matches, and this dude is smooth and glazed like a doughnut.

Tabby: And yes, I made it. No, I didn't poison it. I've given up on killing you off. I just wanted you to have something in case your connections were tight.

Rhys: Sorry. You're watching wrestling?

Tabby: I'm a very supportive wife. I mean, come on. I made you a sandwich.

Rhys: Yeah, looking so close at my coworkers that she has questions about their body hair.

Tabby: Well, I haven't seen your legs! Inquiring minds and all that. I promise not to make fun.

My head joggles as I read the words back, realizing that's a bald-faced lie. My thumbs move again, to clarify.

Tabby: Much.

Rhys: Maybe I like to maintain a little mystery.

I grin maniacally, because that seems a bit like flirting. I didn't know what to expect when I sent that first text. But this? This feels good.

Tabby: No shit. You let me call you a porn star for weeks. Now tell me about the state of your leg hair!

Rhys: No, I think I'll let it be a surprise. Something to look forward to in the spring when I don a pair of shorts.

Tabby: I'll just sneak down and check when you're sleeping.

Tabby: You know...when you're here next. So maybe spring. Whenever.

I lob it out there, thinking he might give some indication as to when he'll come back. But he doesn't correct the assumption, which makes a pit form in my gut.

Rhys: The cat would protect me.

Tabby: She wouldn't know. I'm sneaky like that.

Rhys: You'd have to move her to get under the covers.

I bark out a laugh, head shaking in disbelief at the screen in my palm.

Tabby: RHYS DID YOU JUST ADMIT TO SLEEPING WITH CLEOCATRA?

Tabby: THE CAT YOU ARE "ALLERGIC" TO AND DO NOT LIKE?

Rhys: I'm not allergic to her.

Tabby: Clearly.

Rhys: Listen, I'm not a cat person. But as far as cats go...that one is fine.

Tabby: That one? Fine?

Rhys: How is she?

He ignores my jabs, so I send him a picture of Cleo coiled up with white paws tucked tight.

Tabby: Good. But now that you mention it, I caught her meowing by the basement door before I brought her on the couch.

Rhys: She can sleep down there while I'm gone.

I actually laugh. This big, tough, emotions-locked-up-tight man for whom I adopted a cat solely to piss off is now worried about her coping while he's gone.

Tabby: Adorable.

Rhys: The two of you are like a fungus. I can't get rid of you, so I've just learned to like you.

My head tilts. As far as Rhys goes, that's pretty expressive. And kind of…sweet?

Good lord, this guy has really fucked with my head.

Tabby: I wish you had put that in the wedding vows. It's very romantic.

The dots swirl as he types, and I glance up at the TV to see what I'm missing. In the center ring stands his current nemesis, Million Dollar Bill. He's wearing a tailored suit and a cocky smirk, one hand on his championship belt and the other wrapped around a mic.

And he's shit-talking my husband.

I know it's loosely scripted and they're following a storyline, but my brows furrow and my molars clamp down on each other all the same.

Tabby: I hate Little Willy and his stupid, smug face.

The dots stop and start up again.

Rhys: You're supposed to. Everyone loves to hate him. If it helps, he's a nice kid. Young and eager, but a natural. I like wrestling with him.

Tabby: It doesn't help.

Rhys: Lol. I will let him know.

The opening notes of loud music cut off his tirade about how Wild Side is old and past his prime. Out walks a gorgeous blond woman with a belt slung over her shoulder. She smiles at the crowd, waving like a pageant queen. Her silky hair is poker straight, and her bike shorts and crop top do her nothing but favors.

Tabby: Damn. Who is she? She's so hot.

The woman struts down the ramp to the ring, taking the mic that's handed to her from someone on the side. "Will, Will, Will. You sure have a lot to say for someone who hasn't beat a world champion without the help of all his little goon friends."

"Elle, how lovely to see you. Looking good, as usual. Did you come to beg for me back?" Will's gaze roams up and down her body like she's a piece of meat, and he licks his lips for extra dramatic effect.

"Careful, trust-fund baby. I've traded in and traded up. If my man, Wild Side, catches you looking at me like that, he might beat your ass harder than he's already going to."

I go still. *My man?*

The crowd's response is a mix of surprised gasps and *oohs*. Will's face goes slack as he does his best to look terrified by this revelation. I'm assuming it's a revelation. Rhys's character having a love interest is news to me. Or maybe I'm out of the loop. It's not like we are in the habit of telling each other lots of things.

I make a mental note to google it later. Or bring it up casually with Cora next time she babysits.

My phone vibrates in my hand.

Rhys: I didn't know about this. I haven't been back to HQ yet to talk with the writers.

My brows furrow. I *know* it's not real. Nothing about it matters, but it still feels like a bucket of icy water down my back, and obviously it's caught Rhys off guard too.

"Oh, don't look so scared, Little Willy." Elle pouts at the suit-clad wrestler across from her as she circles him. "You had to know this was coming. Wild Side just needed a little nursing back to health." She gives him a suggestive wink. "And I was the perfect girl to get him back on his feet."

Hoots and hollers sound from the audience as my cheeks heat.

"That's right. I've been keeping him locked up safe with me. Working out *hard* to get ready for that championship match. In fact, we have a little message for you."

Then she points up at the Jumbotron. It crackles to life, and on the screen, playing to tens of thousands of people, is the promo *I* filmed. The one that led to teasing, and chasing, and a hot and heavy make-out session that is burned into my brain. Seeing it on TV hits me with a thrill I didn't expect. And the screaming of the crowd hits me with a realization that Rhys is a much bigger deal than I've been giving him credit for.

Tabby: That's ours! We did that! I filmed that!

Rhys: Tabby, I swear I didn't know about this storyline. No matter what, it's fake.

I swallow. He seems very fixated on that point, whereas I was trying desperately to move on. And while he may not have been entirely honest with me in the past, I get the sense that he's an earnest and thoughtful person.

So, I opt to cut him the slack he needs, playing it off like hearing some hot-as-hell chick talk about working out *hard* with him doesn't make sparks of jealousy flash in my chest *at all*.

Tabby: Of course it's fake. I've had you locked in *my*

basement. How on earth could she have you locked up safe with her? That's absurd.

Tabby: Unless you have a twin brother?

Okay, now I'm just filling the space with weird jokes again.

Rhys: No twin brother.

Tabby: Damn.

Rhys: Sorry to disappoint.

That last text makes me feel kind of bad. Like I took it one joke too far. So I change the subject to asking him about wrestling, how it all started, when he knew this was what he wanted to do.

He starts from the beginning, recounting his days on the high school wrestling team, then training at a pro wrestling gym and trying his hand at it professionally. He shares more about himself than he ever has before, and I gobble up every crumb like a woman starved.

Rhys: Then I went and trained in Mexico. Even did some time on a circuit in Japan.

Tabby: Ugh. Now you're just making me hungry. I'd kill for a good mole or ramen right about now. Midnight sushi? Yes, please.

Rhys: Lol. My girl has food on the brain *always*.

My girl. The term shouldn't make me feel all warm and

fuzzy inside, but it's late, and no one is here to judge me. I don't think I've ever been in a relationship long enough for a man to call me his girl. So I bask in being on the receiving end of that kind of endearment from this man of few words.

Tabby: Is that where the mask inspiration came from? You really never take it off?

Rhys: Yeah, wrestling with the luchadores in Mexico was like an alternate universe. Honestly, some of the best wrestlers in the world. They taught me so much. Inspired me hugely. And I never take it off. Not even for in-person events. Now and then, another wrestler will try to unmask me as part of a storyline. But they never succeed. The anticipation is addictive. They try. I kick their ass. The crowd goes wild. I like to maintain my privacy. I like being able to slip on that mask and become someone else.

I like to maintain my privacy. It hits me then that Rhys isn't in the habit of sharing these things with anyone. He's built an entire career on keeping a front of complete anonymity. Of becoming another person when that camera turns on.

And yet, here he is blurring all those lines. With *me*.

In his own quiet way, it feels like Rhys has given me a gift. Given me a peek behind the mask. Given me his *trust*.

I spend so long trying to fit the pieces of the Rhys puzzle together—to come up with how best to respond—that I zone out entirely. By the time I pick my phone back up, I figure he's gone to bed.

Still, I send him one final thought.

Tabby: I feel very special that I get to know both Rhys *and* Wild Side.

Then I doze off with my phone in my hand.

And when I wake up to drag myself upstairs, I see one final text from Rhys.

Rhys: You are.

CHAPTER 29

Rhys

"WHAT THE *FUCK* WAS THAT?" I SPIT THE WORDS ACROSS Anthony's office before the door has even clicked shut behind me. On my way in, I walked past several colleagues, and though they offered polite hellos, they stayed far away thanks to the massive storm cloud hanging over my head.

Anthony looks up at me over the rims of his wire-framed glasses. He's wearing a suit like always, and his head looks freshly shaved. "Nice to see you too, Rhys."

I don't bother sitting down. I'm too agitated.

Instead, I toss my phone down, grip the back of the chair, and lean over his desk. "I've been trying to call you." I nod at my phone. "The weird I-stole-your-girlfriend storyline full of over-the-top sexual innuendos needs to die a fiery death. I'm not playing that fucking game, Anthony. I'm a wrestler, not a soap opera actor."

"Yeah, but you look like you could be on one." His hands spread wide as though he's envisioning a headline. "*He stole his girl, and now he'll steal his championship belt*," he quips, clearly not concerned about the fury rolling from me.

"This has always been a no. End it." I've always maintained that I don't want one of these storylines and have threatened to quit if they wrote me one. And I've been in demand enough to get away with it.

The older man leans back in his swivel chair, peering at me over steepled fingers. "You agreed to this when you took unexpected time off to get married. Plus, the internet is buzzing about you popping up for that promo with a shiny new wedding ring on your finger."

Fuck, I should have taken that off. That's Tabby's ring. Not a prop.

But he's not above using my personal life for his show.

My teeth gnash as protectiveness surges through me. I've always known Anthony is not my friend. He's a businessman, a shark with dollar signs in his eyes, and I've only been able to keep him at a heel because he's needed me more than I've needed him.

Until that one call. And I'd make that call again, but it doesn't stop me from wanting to rip his fucking head off.

"Nice wedding gift, Tony," I grit out.

The asshole just smiles. "Relax. It's not like you need to fuck her. We're talking a kiss when the timing is ri—"

"Absofuckinglutely not." My knuckles go white as I grip the chair.

"And an unmasking, but you'll get your championship

back. It will push you into full baby-face territory and give Will that full heel turn we want for him."

Shock renders me speechless. *Baby face* means he wants to make me the "good guy," and *turning Will heel* means "full bad guy." Personally, I prefer to straddle the middle line, but it's not looking like I'm being given that option. My body coils tight as I glare back at my boss. "I'm not doing this."

He shrugs. "You're under contract, and you gave verbal agreement. You're too honest to say you didn't."

A feeling of helplessness surges through me. It takes me back to my childhood. Moved around. Assigned to new families. Choices being made about my life when I had no say in them. My power stripped.

Words fail me as my throat constricts. Years spent working for this company. The travel, the lost sleep, the injuries, the exhaustion, the loneliness. And this is where it gets me.

"Elle had no problem with the creative direction, so it's time for you to swallow your pride and get on board."

I scoff. "Of course she didn't."

I've been beating off her advances behind the scenes for the better part of the last two years. She's a prime example of someone who knows exactly what she wants from me—a partner in the company to create a wrestling legacy with. To be attached to the highest paid and arguably most popular wrestler on the roster. Maybe we're a match that way. But I could not be less attracted to her.

Most of all, I don't trust her, which might be the biggest turnoff of all. She knows *nothing* about me, so I can't for the life of me understand why she pursues me beyond superficial reasons.

It's shit like this that's kept me single.

It's shit like this that makes me think of Tabitha. Strange as it may seem, I trust her. And this entire situation makes my chest ache with missing her.

She'd have an earful to give Anthony right about now. She'd go to bat for me.

Where Elle knows I'm going to hate this and is eager to do it anyway.

"Monday night, you'll open the show, and while you're talking, Jake and Axel will jump you from behind. You'll start off strong, and then it will go downhill quickly. Elle is going to come out with a chair and save the day. At the end, you'll do something affectionate and let her lead you back out. Do you need to get your wife's permission or something?" He sneers the last line.

My jaw works. If I wasn't so angry, I'd laugh. Because this is laughably stupid. They've never given me a romance storyline, and I have been abundantly clear that I don't want one. For personal reasons *and* because it makes little sense with my reclusive mountain man character.

It's then that my phone lights up and my new background, the selfie that Tabitha snapped wearing my mask, glows back at me. A text notification from her sits just beneath.

The light draws Anthony's attention. "Tabby? She's cute."

Something inside me snarls at him for using her

nickname. It feels too personal, and I don't like it one bit. "Her name is Tabitha, not that you need to know. Because you? You're going to keep my wife's name out of your fucking mouth."

My boss raises his eyebrows at me, as though both amused and surprised to be on the receiving end of my fury.

"I'm weeks away from reclaiming my title at the biggest event of the year, and you want me to get rescued by my fake girlfriend after two B-list goons attack me?" The word *fake* feels more accurate on my lips than it ever felt when referring to Tabitha.

"We're going with *wife*. You guys eloped. A secret love. A rush to the altar before Will could stop it. That's the story. So remember to wear the ring."

The knife he lodged in my gut twists. "That's fucking ridiculous! The audience will never buy that." My temper flares, and so does Anthony's.

He shoots to standing, fist slamming on his desk. He's known to be an asshole and a yeller, but I've been spared his fits. Until now.

"You listen to me, boy! And you listen good. You're going to make them buy it! I've given you free rein and far too much say. That ends now. You're going to fall in line, just like every other wrestler in this company. Get that god complex under control, and stop referring to this as *your* title." My tongue presses into my cheek, and I glance away from his beady blue eyes. I'm too furious to even look at him.

His fist slams again. "Look at me, Rhys! This title is *mine*! Everything in this building is *mine*! I built this company.

This business. And you are *lucky* I take your ass along on the ride with me. Now get out of here, and go find some fucking gratitude."

My mouth is dry, and my throat feels like it might turn inside out. I've never considered Anthony a friend, but I've respected him in my own way. We've worked well together.

But this? Today? It makes my stomach turn. It's tossed me back in time in an unexpected way—having to be grateful for whatever scraps I've been given. Maybe I've overstepped, but having my control stripped like this?

He's gone too far.

I have nothing left to say, so I turn rigidly and stride out of the asshole's office.

Will waits outside, his handsome face twisted in a chagrined grimace, blond curls sweat-slicked against his forehead after a hard workout. "Boss... Fuck, man, I'm sorry."

Clearly, he heard the conversation. Will might come off as an airheaded tool in the ring, but he's not that guy. He knows he's about to lose his belt, and no matter how fake this gig might be, it easily starts to feel real. Losing a fake championship doesn't *feel* fake at all. It hurts and comes with a heavy dose of humility.

I clap his shoulder, not wanting him to stress, even though I'm spiraling. This isn't his problem. It's mine. "Not on you, pal. Meet you in the ring this afternoon for practice. We're gonna give them a hell of a show."

He nods, eyes scanning me as I move past him, continuing down the hallway, wanting nothing more than to get the fuck out of this building.

"Rhys!" Elle's too-sweet voice grates down the back of my neck like nails on a chalkboard.

"Not now," I growl without turning.

"We need to plan what we're—"

I pivot toward her. "Elle, do not push me on this. I am not in the mood. And I do not like this."

She smiles gently, still moving in my direction. "We're going to make this fun. Don't worry."

I hold a hand up to stop her approach. "Elle, if someone tells you they don't like something, you fucking stop."

Her eyes widen like I've hurt her feelings rather than just told her the truth, and with a shake of my head, I leave. The training center headquarters, like an arena made for wrestling, has several exits, and I take the closest I can find, not especially caring where I end up. I'm planning on taking a few laps around the building to help calm myself down, so it doesn't matter.

The minute I hit the warm, humid Tampa air outside, I suck in a breath. It tastes bad, nothing like the crisp mountain air in Rose Hill. It tastes like salt and smog rather than rose petals and sunshine.

I've always loved wrestling—the training, the conditioning, the drama, everything about it. But today, for the first time, I wish I were lying on a blanket with Tabitha and Milo, picking out shapes in the clouds.

I look up, and the sky is a uniform shade of gray, rain threatening at any moment.

My fingers pulse around my phone. I'm both desperate to open Tabitha's text and nervous to see what it says.

She didn't respond to my final message last night, and it left me wondering if I took it too far by telling her she's special. I didn't know whether to message her again. Didn't know if it would come off too…eager. And then I figured, we're married, so what's the worst that could happen? She ends up thinking I'm a huge sap? Oh well.

But there isn't a shred of awkwardness in her message.

Tabby: Did you know that if you trace Dupris back to its French origins, it means "from the meadow"?

My brows lift. Of all the messages I expected from her, that was not it.

Rhys: I did not. Are you looking me up?

She responds right away.

Tabby: Seeing the marriage certificate got me thinking about last names. Gwen was talking about feeling grounded in the universe by exploring your roots, and I thought I'd dig around a little for mine too. Garrison has a few meanings, so I'm choosing my favorite, which is "fortified stronghold."

I swallow. That sounds like something Gwen would talk about, but my feelings around my family name are complicated. I haven't spent much time looking into my background. Instead, I've focused on looking ahead.

Tabby: And you know, actually, most Dupris families lived in Canada. So maybe you really were meant to end up here. Part-time. Or whatever.

Rhys: Maybe.

I do not know where she's going with this, but even though it's a subject I hate, I want her to keep talking. I like the idea of being meant to end up in Rose Hill. That would mean grasping control is futile because this life is just rolling along—beyond my power.

Tabby: There's even one search result that says newer variations of Dupree (with an accent, because, French) might mean "special family." The website doesn't look very legit. But who cares? Maybe you like that one better.

I wince. I'm not sure that definition is better at all. Seems a little tongue-in-cheek if you ask the kid who was passed from family to family.

Rhys: Special, all right.

Tabby: Our family *is* special. Unique circumstances. Chosen rather than born into. All tied together in an unusual way.

Rhys: Tabby. Our marriage is one big extenuating circumstance. I'm not sure you could call us a family.

Tabby: Rhys. I'll call us a family if I want to.

Family.

I swallow hard. It's difficult to read intonation over text, but I don't get the sense she's joking even though that's the first place my head goes. After the dressing-down Anthony just gave me, having Tabitha call us a family is equal parts shocking and soothing.

Rhys: What are you up to today?

Tabby: When Milo wakes up, we're going to prep some frozen meals. Any requests?

Rhys: I don't know when I'll be back.

Tabby: That's okay. We'll be ready for when you are.

I sigh, walking as my thumbs fly, and my chest goes tight. I love eating anything she makes for me. Her meals aren't just delicious—it feels like she cares about me.

Rhys: Okay. I loved that first pasta you made me. The one with the bacon.

Tabby: Carbonara! Will do. But it's touchy to reheat, so I'll have to show you how.

I love the domesticity of this conversation. I love it when she's soft like this. Her walls become a little less opaque as she gives me a glimpse into what it's like being part of a family. It makes me wonder if she's found a way to forgive me for Erika and the role she thinks I've played. She hasn't mentioned that lately, which is both a relief and a problem.

Because when it comes out… I don't know. I didn't plan

for the white lie to matter. She hated me anyway, so I didn't care. Why not let her hate me a little more if it made the death of her sister a lighter burden?

But now it feels like a lie that sits between us, growing larger and more cumbersome by the day. Especially since I find myself wanting to talk to her more and more.

I want to tell her about the shit show here at HQ so badly. My first inclination is to think she won't care to get involved. But the subtle way she's been reaching out gives me a flicker of hope that she'll have some ridiculous spin on the situation.

Deep down, I want to trust her enough to bring this up, no matter how embarrassing it might feel. I won't bring up the unmasking, because truthfully, I'd rather take my mask off than kiss Elle on national television. So I spit it out with zero tact before I can talk myself out of it.

Rhys: Work is shit. They're making me pretend Elle and I eloped.

Tabby: Juicy. I love the drama.

Rhys: There's internet chatter about me wearing a wedding ring in that promo we filmed.

Tabby: Oh shit. I noticed it and didn't even think about that. I should have told you to take it off.

I bristle as I start my second lap around the massive building. I don't want to take it off.

Rhys: Tabby, I'm not taking my ring off and pretending to be single just because I'm working.

Tabby: Okay. Then let them all think what they want. You and I know the truth, so who cares if millions of people think you're married to a mega-hot blond? It could be worse.

Rhys: That is the worst.

Tabby: Nah. Millions of people are wrong. You're actually married to a short, flat-chested, prickly chef from Buttfuck Nowhere, Canada. HAHA. Joke's on them.

Rhys: No. I'm married to a mega-hot brunette who makes the best carbonara in the world.

Tabby: Oh, Wild Side, you're so romantic.

A smile curves my lips. Leave it to Tabitha to make me almost laugh at a time like this.

Rhys: What if I have to kiss her?

It seems like a juvenile question, but if Tabitha tells me no, then I won't. I'll violate my contract—I just need an excuse that isn't my ego.

Dots roll and then stop. Roll and then stop. Seconds pass with nothing. Then…

Tabby: Just pretend it's me. ;)

Rhys: I'm serious.

Tabby: So am I.

Rhys: I don't like this.

Tabby: I'm sorry, Rhys. I hate that you're in this position.

I really do. But if it's any consolation, I don't always like work either. I hate chopping onions during prep, but some days I get stuck doing it because I can't pawn it off on the kitchen staff every time. But it's part of the gig. If this is part of the gig, so be it. Don't shoot yourself in the foot on my behalf. I'll be fine. Maybe pretend she's onions?

Rhys: Are you sure?

Tabby: Strangely, I think I'd rather not watch it. So give me a heads-up. But yes, of course—work is work. Like you said, we've got a lot of extenuating circumstances. Don't worry about me.

And that's all the answer I need to know this is never going to fly. Because I do worry about Tabitha—a lot more than I expected to.

CHAPTER 30

Tabitha

"Don't forget to use bug spray. I swear they like him extra because he's so cute, and then he gets these super-sized lumps all over his arms and legs, and it's so sad."

My mom nods calmly, her eyes reflecting reassurance. "I don't know that bugs will be a problem this time of year, hon. It is fall after all."

I shift on my parents' front porch, hearing Milo's giggles filter back as he and my dad chase each other around the house. Milo is thrilled about going camping in the trailer with his grandparents.

But I'm a nervous wreck.

"That's true, but it's better safe than sorry. And if there's a super sunny day, just toss a little sunscreen on for good measure."

My mom laughs now, shaking her head as though I'm ridiculous. "We're going to be fine, Tabby. What's gotten into you? We look after him all the time. We've raised two..."

She trails off with a flash of pain on her features. The sentiment flowed so easily, and then she caught herself. It's like because they cut Erika off, they still don't want to reminisce. Or can't? I'm not sure which, but I think that's what I've found in Rhys. Someone I can talk to about my sister who also has fond memories of her.

I don't have to be the one who came out on top. I just get to be the girl who lost her sister.

"You raised two wonderful women, Mom. Both of us imperfect in our own ways." *God, I'm so tired of being treated like the perfect one.* I look her dead in the eye. "And if Milo wants to talk about his mom, you're going to need to engage with him. Forget the bug spray. Just please don't pretend she never existed."

Her eyes water. "It hurts."

I nod, gritting my molars so I don't cry. Partly because it angers me that their way of coping is pretending that she never existed. Like they could just...erase her from their life. It's fucking bizarre and shitty, but I'm not about to tell them how to grieve when—like I said—I'm not perfect either. I still haven't cried about Erika. I don't know if I ever will, but at least I pay her homage where I can. I mean, hell, I'm going to therapy, *and* I have a plant named after her that I talk to sometimes.

If that's not healthy, I don't know what is.

"Yup. It hurts."

She nods.

"Promise me. Don't make it weird for him."

"I promise, Tabby. I promise."

With that, I give my mom a tight hug and make my departure with a lighthearted, "Have fun!" over my shoulder to ease any lingering tensions from our interaction. Years spent smoothing things over have made me an expert, but it wouldn't take a rocket scientist to see that I'm on edge today.

And so, I indulge in a little retail therapy to quell my nerves. After a quick stop at the antique shop in town, I have a bed frame and two nightstands set for delivery this afternoon. Another stop, and I have fresh bedding and a plush set of new towels. And once I get home, I really get crazy—I pull out my old sewing machine and whip up some curtains from a pretty fabric I bought for a project at the restaurant.

My basement may not have drywall, but goddammit, the next time Rhys is here, he will not sleep on a mattress on the floor in a place I assigned him just because I was angry.

It's my way of saying I'm sorry for being so combative. Or maybe with Milo gone and two days off looking me dead in the eyes, I'm just fucking lonely. Or maybe, just maybe, I miss Rhys and want to see him smile when he eventually comes back.

Whatever it is, making the "guest room" feel like more than a dank dungeon eats up several hours of my day. It keeps me from being still, because if I'm too still, my mind will wander down paths I'd rather avoid.

At this stage of my life, busy is good. Busy hurts less.

I step back when the sun has set and dinnertime has passed, hands on my hips as I admire my handiwork in the basement. The concrete walls still give it a shabby-chic vibe, but I dug out a rug to cover the matching floor, leaned a tall mirror against the wall, and placed knickknacks and photos on the framing boards. There's one of Milo, there's one of Cleo, and there's even one from our wedding day of us walking down the front steps of the church, looking suspiciously happy.

The space has warmth now, and the mismatched aesthetic adds charm, in my opinion.

It takes me back to the day he said he's slept in worse conditions, and my heart clenches just thinking about it. I get the sense he's not used to someone taking care of him, and he's a grown-ass man, so I know he doesn't require it. But now that he's opened up to me, his backstory has the "acts of service" part of me in its grip.

Maybe our marriage wasn't born from being madly in love, but I don't think caring about him will hurt anything at this point.

My stomach grumbles, pulling me back to reality. Without Milo here, I'm terrible at remembering to eat, which—for a chef—is hilarious.

Upstairs, I make myself a ham sandwich and toss a couple of mini cucumbers on the side for some color. Very gourmet. Then I take my plate to the living room and waffle on whether I should watch Rhys tonight. The curiosity is killing me, and I'd be a big fat liar if I said watching him in character didn't do something to me. The confidence, the swagger, the way he commands the emotions of an entire arena full of people—it's thrilling.

But I also don't want to watch him kiss another woman.

I click the program on and take an aggressive bite of my cucumber, ready to be entertained...or hurt. Depending on what happens tonight.

The show opens with Rhys's entrance music. The heavy bass and ominous tones blare through the stadium as the lights go black. A bright white strobe light illuminates the crowd in pulsing flashes. Rhys's hulking silhouette appears at the top of the ramp, the crowd screams, and butterflies erupt in my stomach.

I scoot closer to the edge of my couch as I watch him take a leisurely stroll down the ramp. Electricity sizzles around him, every step almost lazy in its confidence. His sleeve of swirling black tattoos shine on his tan skin, and his dark hair has a wet look to it where it frames his face.

He trails his fingers over fans' outstretched hands as they scream and reach for him. Signs in the stands boast his name. Shirts on their chests proudly display his logo.

It chokes me up. I watch in awe, shaking my head with a soft smile on my lips. I wonder if he realizes how loved he is. I wonder if he knows that *this* might be a part of his family—his roots.

I'm not sure he does. I don't know if Rhys has the confidence Wild Side possesses. It seems like he might hold the two versions of himself in such different regard that he doesn't recognize they're just two parts of one complex, perfectly lovable whole.

With practiced fluidity, he leaps into the ring, sliding under the ropes before popping up with ease. He steps up in the corner, holding a fist in the air as the beat to his music changes. The attendees hold their fists up too, mirroring his pose while singing along to his music so loudly that I almost can't hear the original. Every corner follows suit.

Goose bumps roam up my arms. It's magic.

Finally, someone hands him a mic, and the lights brighten as his music wanes.

"Minneapolis!" His voice is all gravel over the speakers. "Welcome to the Wild Siiide."

The cheers are downright deafening, and the absurdity of the entire thing makes me laugh out loud in the privacy of my own living room.

A fucking professional wrestler.

He chuckles into the mic. His black-and-green mask conceals his face, but I can see his eyes, and the way his tongue pops into his cheek. For me, it's obvious it's *him*. I wonder how no one else sees it. His lips curve seductively, and it sends a zing of awareness down my spine that lands right in my core. I cross my legs and settle in to watch.

"I've been away for a few weeks, and I've missed you. But I've been busy." The odd hoot sounds out, but Rhys carries on. "Busy preparing to take back what that spoiled goof in a suit has been playing with. What I've let a lesser man—if you can even call him that—borrow while I've been recovering. He may have knocked me down…but not. Hard. Enough."

He turns to look into the main camera and points, my eyes snagging on the flash of his wedding ring. "That's right, Will. You should have hit me so hard that I couldn't get back up. You should have finished the goddamn job. That was your first mistake, because now I'm back—in my house, with my people—where you've been living comfortably for far too long. If you'd finished the job, I wouldn't be here. Back for blood. Because everything you thought was yours? By the time Pure Pandemonium rolls around, it's going to be *mine*."

The crowd surges again, partly due to the message, and partly due to the two men who've popped up behind him.

One takes a cheap shot while the other one circles. Rhys folds under the blow, hitting the mat with a heavy thud as the mic goes flying. But he's not down for long. He pops back up in an agile kip-up that a man his size should not be able to execute so gracefully.

He turns to the man who kicked him without missing a beat, lifting him into a chokeslam. The move takes the man high and curves him into a rainbow shape over Rhys's body, his signature move that has everyone chanting, "Over! The! Mountain!"

When the guy hits the mat, he rolls from the ring, writhing and holding his neck.

The second goon has the good sense to look concerned. He's overacting his response, but that doesn't bother me one bit. It adds a dose of humor, a dose of drama that has me internally cheering even harder for Wild Side.

Rhys doesn't hesitate like him though. He turns fluidly into a high kick aimed at the other man's head that drops him on the spot.

I lean closer, trying to see where he holds back. He's masterful. Where some wrestlers are obvious with the space they leave to prevent injuring their opponent, Rhys is not.

He's a technician. It's seamless, believable, and I'd say he's so good that he makes the other two guys look a hell of a lot better than they are.

One is on all fours outside of the ring, pretending to cough and crawl away, while the other lies prone on the mat. Rhys climbs the ropes at the turnbuckle, and with his back to the man he just kicked, he circles a finger over his head in a *let's fucking go* motion. Then he does a massive backflip off the top rope that has me shooting to standing, sandwich and cucumbers flying across the floor.

"Oh shit!" My hand flies to my chest as he lands on the man, lifting his hips ever so slightly, letting his elbows and knees take the brunt while the announcer screams about him having the best moonsault in the company.

But the celebration is short-lived when guy number two pops back up and kicks Rhys right in his very sizable penis. He doubles over with great theatrics, and I have to remind myself that he's *probably* okay.

The guy is readying his attack when a flash of blond hair flies into the ring with a metal chair in her hand. She winds up and slams it into the face of Rhys's attacker. I know I'm not supposed to like this storyline with Elle, but the anxious part of me is relieved someone came to help him. Because watching him throw himself around and take hits doesn't feel fake at all. In fact, I'm more stressed by it than ever before.

The two of them make quick work of their foes, and once they're both sprawled on the mat, she turns to grin at Rhys. He doesn't return the gesture. Instead, he scowls, failing spectacularly at acting like she's his partner.

And because I know him well enough to recognize the glare, I find it oddly…amusing? Reassuring?

But she doesn't back down. She reaches for his hand and hefts it high in the air, pointing at him and mouthing, "*That's my man*," over and over again.

I twist my wedding band on my finger, relieved he's leaving the ring unscathed.

And jealous because she's holding his hand.

But I refuse to indulge that emotion. I'm not the jealous type, and I don't want to start now. Plus, I truly have no reason to be jealous. What he's doing in the arena is for show. *Fake*.

However, my budding feelings for him are not. Which is why I fire off a text message that even two weeks ago I would never have sent. Rhys and I are similar in a lot of ways, and I know what he needs to hear tonight.

Tabby: I'm proud of you.

Then I go to bed without eating. My appetite is gone anyway.

CHAPTER 31

Tabitha

I BOOKED MYSELF TODAY OFF. MY PLAN WAS TO UNPLUG AND relax, try to enjoy having a clean, quiet house all to myself. But I went into the restaurant anyway. My staff mocked me mercilessly and called me a workaholic, so I hid in my office. I did some paperwork—that was in no way pressing—and flipped them all the finger on the way out.

Then I came home and cleaned my house from top to bottom like I planned. Not having Milo here to make an instant mess in my wake seemed like too good of an opportunity to pass up.

Then I went to Gwen's yoga class—something Trixie thought might be good for *stilling my mind.* It was lovely, but I'm not so sure it worked, since I'm sitting in the cool backyard with my mind spinning.

The gas heater Rhys bought pumps out warm air as I watch the sunset wrapped in a blanket, having an early evening cup of coffee. I know it will keep me up later than necessary, but it doesn't matter. Plus, I figure it's better than wine, considering how blue I've felt for the past twenty-four hours.

I thought Milo being away was bringing me down. But I'm starting to think I might miss my big, broody wrestler too.

Either way, jittery is better than depressed.

And when I finish my coffee, the jitters kick in big time. I pad back into the house, wash my mug, and put it back in the cupboard, not wanting to make a mess after the cleaning I did earlier.

"I know, I know," I mutter to Erika the plant. "I'm being weird and neurotic. Trust me, I know."

I swear she continues to glare at me judgmentally. She'd have dropped her mug on the counter and sauntered into the living room, flopped down on the couch, and put her feet up on the edge. A smile tugs at my lips as memories flood me of her lying on the couch and putting her feet on me. They were usually stinky after volleyball, and I'd squeal and plug my nose as she locked me between her legs and tried to rub a foot in my face.

I'd hated it then.

And I'd give anything for her to do it to me now.

With that thought in mind, I decide not to sit in the living room. Feels too raw in there.

Instead, I find myself in front of the storage closet with the door swung open, staring at the box of her recovery journals. My fingers ache to reach for them.

And I do.

I take the box down and make my way back out to the patio—the spot where Rhys and I had been meeting every morning. A spot that makes me feel less alone, even though he's not here.

Wrapped back up, I reach into the box and pull out the black leather-bound books. All the same style—not fancy, but not your basic scribbler either.

Flicking through a couple, I force myself not to read ahead as I search for the one dated furthest back. And when I find it, I settle in and read.

Dear Universe,

Apparently, it will be good for me to get this journey down on paper. I'm not sure I buy it. But my parents have disowned me, and my fucking angel of a sister just emptied her bank account to put me through the best rehab program money can buy. So it seems like the least I can do is follow the professionals' suggestions.

This is rock bottom. Well, I'm thirty days clean, so maybe that's one step above rock bottom? But I'm also pregnant, so that might knock me back down...or move me up another notch? I'm not sure how I feel about it yet. Especially since I can't for the life of me remember who the dad might be.

I haven't exactly been on my best behavior.

What I do know is that I'm not going to fuck up a human who didn't ask for any of this. I can stay sober for nine months. For them.

I'll reassess after that. But for now, I feel responsible for something a lot bigger than me.

I suppose this is as good a place as any to start.

How the hell do people sign off from a journal entry? This feels very juvenile.

Whatever,
Erika

I snort at the *Whatever* sign-off. It's pure Erika, holding two middle fingers up to the universe. There's a sadness in the entry, but also…hope. She's hooked me, and maybe I shouldn't be reading these, but I can't stop myself. It's not like she can come back from the dead and kick my ass for going through her diaries like she would have when we were kids.

So I carry on.

The first journal details her pregnancy, her internal battles throughout, the *demons in her head* that just never quite let up. It makes me realize that using was never buried at the back of her mind. It was an urge that sat right on her shoulder, and she battled it so fucking hard.

My eye sockets feel full reading about it, and my nose tingles when she recalls wanting painkillers during her labor but refused to ask. Even in childbirth, she fought.

The second journal chronicles her life with a newborn, the way Milo gave her a new lease on life. She still addresses the universe and signs off with *Whatever*, but there's a brightness in these entries—which she writes with perfect dedication and regularity. I can see right before my eyes that motherhood has made her a more reflective person.

> *There's something about becoming a parent that has given me a new and profound understanding of my own parents. Suddenly, I appreciate the things they've done for me. The sacrifices they've made for me seem a lot bigger than they did before Milo.*
>
> *I hate to admit it, but I can understand why they cut contact with me. I think I've broken their hearts irreparably (over and over again), and now I carry a guilt that I never did before.*
>
> *One day, I hope I can repair what I broke, but as it stands, I'm too embarrassed to face them. Instead, Tabby does it for me. I can tell she's fucking pissed at our parents, but she still faces them on my behalf, acting as the go-between so that Milo can have grandparents in his life.*
>
> *As a mom, I feel bad for her too. It makes me realize she's played this role in our lives for years now. The carrier pigeon. The eternal sunshine—even though I know she's a scrappy little bitch at heart.*

Tabby is loyal as hell. I don't think there's anything I could do that would make her abandon me. And that knowledge is both reassuring and...infuriating? I don't know if I deserve that kind of dedication. She's just so damn good—so reliable—that I almost feel small next to her, even when she's helping me. It's that I look even worse in her shadow. Shiny versus tarnished.

Maybe I'm jealous.

I wish I could have been more like Tabby.

I feel like I've swallowed something sharp as my throat works to digest her words. This is what I get for reading her journals—the knowledge that she both admired and appreciated me while simultaneously begrudging and envying me. And what's more hilarious is that I don't think anyone would accuse me of being *sunshine.* I'm matter-of-fact, and I get shit done.

But I never considered that she may have felt as though I was marching in some superiority parade by helping her. I just did what needed to be done to support her.

I did what needed to be done to keep her alive.

I wanted her to live as if my own life depended on it.

And I still failed.

I ignore the twisting sensation in my gut and the thickness in my throat as I read ahead. She recounts sleepless nights and exhausted days when she knew one hit would give her a high she desperately needed. But then she talks about

Milo's button nose and the way he smiles at her, and how it would give her the boost she needed.

She talks about me, and it makes me smile.

> *Tabby is a godsend—even if she is a bit of a micromanager. I think without her I'd die from exhaustion rather than addiction. I don't think many people know the love of a sister the way that I do. One day, I'll work up the nerve to tell her how much I appreciate her.*

I sniffle as I read the passages. Happy sniffles, but no tears. In this phase, it seems like she has more good days than bad. Somehow, even her handwriting looks cleaner—stronger.

When I flip open the third journal, my eyes home in on Rhys's name, and I slam it shut as I shimmy in my seat. A nervous flutter in my stomach has me pulling my feet up to sit cross-legged as I tug the blanket tighter around my shoulders. Rhys has sworn there was nothing between them, but there's always a voice of doubt in my head that constantly questions if trusting him is smart. One I've been ignoring.

Anticipation and dread braid together and wrap around my throat as I open the journal once again to read something I may not want to know.

> *Dear Universe,*
>
> *Excited to report that I have found a beautiful new place to live. Emerald Lake, technically a*

> *small city. It's big enough to feel different from home, and still tiny enough to be cozy. It's clean, and safe, and unlike anywhere I could have imagined for myself. For the first time in a long time, I feel proud of myself. I feel like all my hard work and all the right choices I've made are finally paying off.*

My heart soars. Knowing my sister felt this moment brings me a level of peace that I've needed.

> *I've got a salaried job at a car dealership and a townhome with a view of the water in Emerald Lake...and my hot-ass neighbor.*

Oh. I suck in a breath and forge ahead.

> *Tall, dark, and handsome personified. Gruff but friendly. No wedding ring. And used an adorable baby voice when he talked to Milo and reached for his hand to shake. Needless to say, I'm pretty sure I'm in love with my landlord. Did I mention he also owns the whole building? LOL.*

LOL? She hasn't used *LOL* in a single diary entry. It's like I can feel her giddiness leaping off the page.

I skip ahead to the next entry.

Tabby helped me move in, and as much as I needed her help, I was ready for her to leave. Not because she did anything wrong. Just because...this place feels like a fresh start, like something that's finally mine. And I can't handle the constant nervous glances and the "You're all good, then?" questions.

It's like she's taken on a mothering role and is scared to watch me fly from the nest. There's something embarrassing about having her all up in my business when everything is going so well.

It also annoyed me that my hot-ass landlord popped his painfully handsome head over the fence and asked how long my sister was going to be in town.

That's how I knew it was time for her to leave.

I blink at the page. Rhys asked how long I was going to be in town? Based on the date at the top of the entry, this must have been a day or two after I marched into his house and laid out some ground rules for being my sister's landlord.

Guilt licks at my subconscious. It makes me wonder if I fucked up a relationship that might have kept her alive. If she and Rhys had happened, would she still be here? With her perfect sister crushing on her partner?

My head shakes as I brush the thoughts away. I'm taking serious leaps of logic to get to that point.

So instead of playing the "what-if" game, I keep reading through the book under a darkened sky, pages lit only by the soft glow of the back porch light. The night is peaceful, but my brain is a raging storm.

> *I baked cookies and brought them next door as a thank you to my landlord for letting us rent the other side of his duplex.*

The attempts at making contact with Rhys just keep coming with each entry.

> *Left my car door open and drained the battery. Watching Rhys give me a boost was a fantasy I didn't know I had.*

> *Sometimes I get Rhys's mail in my mailbox by accident. Hand delivering it is always a highlight. Now and then, he even opens the door shirtless.*

> *Usually, my attempts at making contact with my hot-ass landlord are half-hearted, but today*

he came through for me. The woman who runs the daycare that I take Milo to called saying she was sick, and I was too nervous to take a day off work—I really need this job. Rhys heard me on the phone in the backyard, and this time, when he popped his head over the fence, he didn't ask about my sister.

He offered to watch Milo.

I have no idea what the man does for a living, but he's often home. He seems nice enough, and I was desperate, so I took him up on the offer.

My stomach was in knots all day. The mom guilt was real. Leaving your child with a man you barely know probably isn't recommended. It gave me another dose of guilt for all the times I disappeared to god knows where on my parents.

Needless to say, when I rushed home, Milo was happy as could be. Fed. Changed. And asleep in Rhys's arms while they waited for me on the front porch.

With no dad in his life, it was the first time I'd seen a man hold him. It was a sight I could get used to.

Talk about butterflies.

I swallow, eyes scanning the entry again as my fingers trail over my sister's pen strokes. Touching the proof that Rhys has been in Milo's life for a long time.

As I make my way through the journals, the familiarity between the three of them only grows.

We had Rhys over for dinner to thank him for bailing us out.

Rhys joined us at the town fair. He won Milo a stuffed panda bear so big that it almost looks real. Watching them together is…something I didn't know I needed.

Today Rhys asked about my sister, and it fucking pissed me off. All the time we've spent together, and he saw her out the front window a year ago and still thinks about her?

It was petty of me, but I told him she doesn't come around often, even though I'd let her visit last time he was out of town. Made it sound as though she's so focused on her own life that she's practically forgotten about Milo and me. May not have cast her in the kindest light.

But she's gotten so much in life. She can't have this too. I don't want her to come here, bringing up old Erika where new Erika is making her fresh start. It's easier to have Emerald Lake be free of all that shit.

At any rate, I ended up telling Rhys about my addiction issues to help explain the situation. He listened and let me talk it out without interjecting at all. I think it was therapeutic to get it off my chest. There's something so steady about him. So compassionate. He thanked me for sharing with him and hugged me when I got it all off my chest.

Today was a good reminder that I can't have Tabitha visit when he's in town.

It's a view into her head that isn't mine to take. And yet… a part of me gets it. I just never saw my presence that way. I did the best I knew how with a situation I wasn't properly prepared to navigate.

It also shows me the turning point when Erika came to visit more often, the time when she started saying her landlord didn't like her having visitors. In retrospect, she became secretive, and I interpreted it as busy and happy and just…thriving.

And maybe she was, but her fixation on Rhys takes a different turn. And as the year passes, so does her tone. She's agitated. Cutting in her words.

Still, I read on.

Rhys bailed me out AGAIN with a childcare mishap. Today I worked late, so he had to do bedtime. I wasn't sure how it would go, but when I came home, the house was quiet. I tiptoed upstairs, eager to see Milo and worried I might wake him.

That's when I saw Rhys, standing over his crib, big hand laid over his tiny chest, singing him "Twinkle, Twinkle, Little Star."

Watching them brought on tears, so I snuck back downstairs and locked myself in the bathroom to hide. I don't know what it was specifically. It was just sweet. Got me right in the feels.

They were happy tears. They made me want that nuclear family for Milo. But when I asked Rhys to stay for a drink, he politely declined. The look on his face said it all.

It made me realize he only comes around when Milo is here.

It made me realize this may not be going where I hoped it would.

Which is fine.

Whatever,
Erika

That entry makes me wince. The *whatever* hits differently on the heels of her realization. That *whatever* is a turning point.

Today Rhys overheard me on the phone telling Tabitha that I was exhausted and feeling down. Not an hour later, he showed up at the front door with a bottle of glycerin bubbles in hand and his signature harmless scowl perfectly in place. He played bubbles with Milo in the backyard, so I could take a nap.

I'm mature enough to keep things in friend territory, and I needed a break. Toddlers are no joke.

When I woke up, we chatted. I don't know if he was feeling bad about the way he quietly turned me down the other night, but he ended up telling me that he's a professional wrestler. Like orange tans, greasy muscles, fake fights, and cringe interviews.

I burst out laughing when he told me, and I'm still giggling as I write this. He'd mentioned before he worked in the entertainment industry, and I didn't press because, well, he's my landlord. Didn't particularly want him digging into my past.

But I guess we were exchanging secrets, and this was his. Now I get why he wouldn't want to tell people.

Maybe this will be less funny tomorrow.

I bristle, feeling defensive. He told her outright, whereas I had to pry it from him. And sure, it's entertainment, but the bruises on his body are not fake. If nothing else, I feel relieved that I've never mocked him for what he does. It's probably why he didn't want to tell me in the first place.

If Erika were here, I'd kick her in the box. This is the side of her that was "too cool" for so many things. Too cool for school. Too cool for volleyball. Too cool for family events. This is the underlying attitude that got so much worse when the drugs came into play. I vividly remember the eye rolls and the cutting mockery that became almost constant. Those were the precursors that led to distance before she pulled away completely.

> *I decided that the best way to get over Rhys was to get under someone else. And I did. One town over, I met Tyson. He's lanky in that Tommy Lee way and hung like him too. He's raw and edgy. He's exciting. I had the time of my life.*
>
> *Rhys watched Milo for me, and when I came home looking mussed, all he did was smile and say he was glad I had fun.*
>
> *I think deep down I was hoping to make him jealous.*
>
> *It didn't work.*

A sense of dread surges inside me, slow and steady. Each entry is like a big breath into a balloon. The feeling presses against me as I flip the pages hungrily. It's as though I can feel the impact coming but can't take my foot off the gas.

She mentions Tyson more and more. Going out is mentioned more and more. Rhys taking care of Milo becomes a given, an afterthought—an expectation. And the dates on the entries match up with when she started leaving him with me more often too.

Nights out turn into weekends away.

A social beer becomes *a few too many highballs.*

The highballs are a gateway, and though she never puts it in writing, I know in my gut what she and Tyson were doing when either Rhys or I were taking care of her son.

Her reflective tone shifts, and suddenly she's casting blame on everyone else.

I'm both furious and fucking devastated as the change in her persona unfurls.

She was *so close.*

I blink at the page beneath me. A wet dot bleeds out into the paper, the pen stroke becoming slightly blurred.

It can't be.

One furious swipe at my cheek, and I stare back at wet fingers, my lips popping open into a silent *O* shape.

Then I decide not to fixate but to keep reading.

> *Tyson has run into some trouble. All the nights out and extra-special treatment he's given me have caught up with him. I didn't realize he was treating me so extravagantly. He wanted everything to be top of the line, but he couldn't afford it.*
>
> *The least I could do was help him out. But it's not enough. I gave him so much that I couldn't make rent. Luckily, Rhys was understanding. I promised him I'd pay it back, and I fully intend to. I wish everyone had as much faith in me as he does.*

> *The dealership is giving me fewer shifts, and when I asked why, they said they had to hire another receptionist because I was taking so much time off. Which is bullshit. It's only been a weekend here and there. I know I can't ask Tabby for help again, or she'll be all fucking over me.*
>
> *But this time is different. It's not because I'm in trouble. I'm just taking care of Tyson—my family. It's exactly what she'd do in this situation.*

Alarm bells sound. I want to reach into the pages and shake her. I want to scream at her, *This guy is not your family! He's your downfall!* But she's not here for me to make her see reason.

Another tear tumbles from my lashes as I watch my sister's life crumble right before my eyes.

> *When I told Rhys my shifts were slow, he didn't hesitate to offer a rent break. And the way he's been so overly helpful financially got me thinking. I finally looked him up, and my eyes about popped out of my head when I saw his reported salary.*
>
> *That's why I asked Rhys to be Milo's guardian in the will I finally got around to doing. He seemed taken aback at first, but said yes.*

> *It was an immediate relief. At least if something happens to me, Milo will land somewhere with a good security net. Plus, Tabby has been so fucking nosy with her questions lately, pushing back when I ask if she can take Milo for another weekend, and it ticked me off.*
>
> *She's been on my ass about a will for years, so when I drop Milo off in Rose Hill, I'll let her know she finally got her wish.*

She chose Rhys to spite me. And for his money. My stomach turns hard and fast. *Fuck.*

Fuck, fuck, fuck.

Tears fall with each curse that flies through my head as I piece it all together.

It's only when I read through the final entry that everything finally clicks.

> *Things have been extremely stressful, so I lied and told Tabby that Rhys evicted me, and I needed to go look at new places to move into so that Tyson and I could take a much-deserved weekend together. Naturally, she swooped in to help—zero questions asked.*

My head throbs, and my heart shatters.

The grudge I've been carrying against Rhys this entire time evaporates on the spot. The one he's been letting me throw in his face, even knowing it was unfounded.

And all that's left in its wake is an all-consuming agony. I should have noticed the subtle changes in her. I should have swept in sooner. I should have known better.

The heavy weight of realizing *I'm* the one who failed her is unbearable.

For the first time since my sister's death, I cry.

CHAPTER 32

Rhys

I'M NOT SURE WHEN I DECIDED TO GO FROM PINING FOR Tabitha silently to pining for her out loud. But here I am, exhausting myself and traveling for almost twenty-four hours straight just to surprise her for the few days I have off.

I should be practicing. Training. *Working*.

But I'm not myself right now. Anxiety about the tension with Anthony and his demands have me seeking comfort. And that leaves me thinking about only one person.

Tabitha.

I'm not who I used to be. Something has shifted, and I can't ignore it.

I cut the engine, tug my bag from the back seat, and duck out of the small rental car—the only one left at the last minute from the airport. I slam the door before heading up to our house. Well, Tabitha's house.

It's dark already. The sun has long disappeared behind

the jagged peaks that tower over Rose Hill. It's cold out, the grass stiff with frost as I head toward the front door. My strides cover more ground than usual, but I refuse to admit that I'm rushing to see her. I know she had today off, so there's a chance she fell asleep with Milo already. Even just peeking in on them might make me feel better.

When I reach the front door, it's unlocked. "For fuck's sake, Tabby," I mutter, entering the house and kicking off my boots. Lights are on in each room, giving the house a cozy glow that my place in Florida couldn't achieve on its best day.

That house is sterile. This house feels like a home.

"Tabby?" I whisper-shout, not wanting to wake Milo, as I wander through the living room toward the kitchen at the back of the house. When Cleo comes running for me, weaving herself through my legs and purring, I crouch down to give her a scratch under her chin—her favorite spot. "Go downstairs. I'll be there soon."

She doesn't listen, but I continue through the house, searching for Tabitha anyway. It smells like the citronella cleaning spray she likes to use, and the entire place is *spotless*. I hope she hasn't spent her day off cleaning.

I pop my head up the stairwell but decide against taking that direction when it's black at the top. She's not in the kitchen, but I catch sight of her form on the back porch, sitting on her usual love seat beneath the patio lanterns.

My lips tug at the sight of her, and my feet carry me in her direction.

I start explaining my presence before I've even fully opened the door. "Okay, just hear me out—"

But I draw up short when her head snaps to attention and I'm met with blotchy cheeks, red-rimmed eyes, and wet lashes.

"Tabby, what's wrong?" My eyes search the space for the cause of her distress. She's seated cross-legged, with a heavy blanket wrapped around her shoulders. There are leather-bound notepads scattered around her and a plain cardboard box at her feet. "Is Milo okay?"

Tears glisten on the apples of her cheeks, and her dark irises are flat—devoid of her usual sparkle. Her hands sit limply over her knees, left ring finger wrapped in my gold metal band.

The ever-present instinctual pull to her yanks on me, hard, and I'm out the door and across the deck in mere seconds. I drop to my knees at her feet. "Tell me what's going on," I murmur as I reach for her.

She flinches and draws away, looking stricken. Her gaze falls to my hands when I hold them up to either side as a show of backing off. "He's camping with my parents. What are you doing here? You said *weeks*." Her voice cracks on the last word, and a jagged line splinters through my chest as I watch another three tears roll from her lashes, each one a shot of pain to my heart.

I've been through some shit in my life.

But having to watch Tabitha cry might be the worst of it.

I don't hesitate to tell her the truth this time. Hands up in surrender, I confess what I never thought I'd be able to let myself admit out loud. "I missed you."

Beats of silence pass between us, her eyes searching my

face as my hands lower slowly, dropping to grip the edge of the couch mere inches from her knees.

She stares at me, silent tears slipping over her full lips. "You lied to me."

Fuck. I suck in a harsh breath and freeze, lungs full to bursting as I watch her.

"You didn't evict Erika."

My eyes fall shut, fingers digging into the rough canvas of the cushion as the air rushes from my lungs, leaving behind a heavy ache. "No," I whisper, still unable to look at her.

"You were so *good* to her."

My nose scrunches as her words crumble into a heavy sob. All I can offer is a nod as I let my lids lift and my eyes take in what I now recognize as journals strewn all around her.

Erika's journals. I'd see her writing on the porch sometimes, but they hadn't crossed my mind beyond that.

Tabitha's hands clench into tight fists, the sound of her hollow whimpers like death by a thousand shards of glass. "You let me believe..." Her lips smack, a disbelieving huff leaping from them. "I was awful to you."

I face her now, her dark eyes boring into mine. "You weren't."

"I *was*. I was awful to you. I accused you of—my god." She slaps a palm over her mouth, shoulders heaving as another sob wracks her tiny body.

My fingers itch to touch her, but this time when I reach for her, she slaps my hand away. "Why the hell would you lie about that?" Her hair dangles beside her cheeks as her head shakes, mouth popped open in disbelief. "*Why?*"

I swallow thickly. "I just…" I wipe a hand over my mouth and look away, searching for the right words, the best way to explain things to her. "Tensions were high between us, and I didn't know if I could trust you. And then I came here and got this whole new perspective, and I—fuck, Tabby, I don't know. You were so broken, and I couldn't handle it. I couldn't tell you anything to make you feel better, but my silence could ease your burden, so…" I let out a frustrated growl and look up at the clear night sky, not sure what I'm saying makes sense.

Then I drop my gaze back to hers. "You needed someone to be angry with, and I figured I could be that person for you."

"Rhys. It hurt *you*. I hurt *you*. You didn't deserve that!" Her frustration sparks, hands slapping at the cushions beneath her. "And me?" She laughs, but there's no humor. "That was my cross to bear—not yours. I've been walking around like I'm all fucking holier than thou, and I just…*I'm* responsible—"

"Tabitha." I grip her leg, urging her to hear what I tell her. "Listen to me. You are *not* responsible."

She shakes me off, breaths coming more quickly, eyes going from dead to frantic. "Don't touch me, Rhys. I…I need…I don't know what I need. But don't fucking touch me right now."

She pushes to stand, blanket falling from her shoulders as she walks stiffly into the house. Still kneeling on the wooden deck, I drop my face into my palms, trying to figure out how to make this better.

I realize that I don't know, but I stood in a church, in front of a lot of people who care about her, and promised to comfort her. To nurture this relationship when life is simple and when it's not.

Right now, things are not simple. But the way I've come to feel about her is.

I follow her into the house. Up the stairs where I can hear the shower running. I enter the bathroom without knocking, just in time to watch her step into the shower fully clothed. She stands there woodenly, face to the spray, water mingling with her tears and drenching her.

Her body lurches on a sob, and watching her hurt like this almost brings me back to my knees.

This. This is why I didn't tell her.

She slams back against the tiled wall and slides down it until she's sitting, knees bent, elbows propped, head hung.

"Fuck it," I mutter as I rip the glass door open and step in with her. The shocking spray of ice-cold water sluices over my clothes, soaking through to my skin and forcing me to suck in a quick breath.

I drop down beside her, maintaining a few inches between us in a pathetic attempt to respect her wishes.

I'm not sure how long we sit there with the white noise of rushing water making it feel like we're living in our own private, frigid water world.

It's fucking freezing, but I barely feel it. All I can think about is Tabitha and how I'd give anything for her to let me comfort her right now. Hell, I'd kill just for her to talk to me right now.

I've spent a lifetime thinking I don't like talking. It turns out I just needed the right person to talk to.

"You should leave," she says, her voice tinny as it echoes around us.

"No."

Her face whips in my direction, eyes flashing, chin held high and defiant. "I said get out!"

I match her glare. "Tabitha. You're my wife. I'm not leaving you."

Something flickers across her face at that, and instead of responding, she stares at me. Really stares at me. To the point where it's unnerving. I lick my lips and swallow, then with a resigned sigh, her eyes flutter shut, and she tips her head back against the tiles. Seconds stretch as I watch her carefully.

"I wish you weren't seeing me like this."

My brow furrows. "Like what?"

"At my worst."

I tip my head toward her. "Then it's all uphill from here, baby. It's going to make seeing you at your best so damn special."

A sad smile wobbles through another strangled sob, and I watch a droplet leak from her eye as she sucks in a few breaths through her parted lips.

"Rhys, what are you doing? I mean, this is… What are you even *doing*?"

I know she means the question on a much bigger scale. The wedding, the flying back to her unannounced, the way she's always on my mind even when I'm doing something else. And the truth is, I don't know. I can't explain it. It just *is*.

But I know what I'm doing here in a freezing cold shower with her.

"Trying really hard not to touch you, Tabby."

She whimpers, hand covering her closed eyes as though that extra layer will help her hide from me.

I expect her to tell me to leave again, but with no preamble, she turns and crawls into my lap, wrapping her arms around my neck and dropping her head on my shoulder.

Then she sobs.

And I hold her.

CHAPTER 33

Rhys

We sit under the freezing spray, wrapped together, for I don't know how long. All I know is that eventually her sobs abate and all the tension in her body melts away until she's slumped, limp in my arms.

My thumb hurts from rubbing circles on her temple, my tailbone is sore from sitting on hard tiles, and I'm cold to the bone, but I'll hold her for hours more if she needs me to.

Except a shiver races down her spine, and her jaw quivers.

"Okay, Tabby Cat." I swipe her wet hair back, gently urging her up. "Let's get you warmed up now."

She nods and lets me lift her. I take her from the shower and step onto the bath mat, easing her down to her feet. Water drips heavily from both of us. When I reach back in to crank the handle to off, a hush falls over the space. What felt loud now feels unbearably quiet, save for the odd chatter of her teeth.

My lips flatten, and I shake my head, irritated that I let her get so cold.

I cup her shoulders with my hands, rubbing up and down briskly. "You need to get the wet clothes off, honey. You're freezing."

She nods again, but I don't get the sense she's absorbing much of what I've said. Her eyes are far away, and her typical perfect posture has slumped down into something deeply sad.

I set my jaw for what I'm about to offer. "Do you want me to help you?"

Now her eyes meet mine, red and devastated.

She nods, and I nod back. Then I reach for the hem of her sweatshirt. I don't let my hands linger—I make quick, respectful work of peeling the wet fabric from her body. Her arms lift, and I tug it over her head.

And fuck me, she isn't wearing a bra.

I drop the sweatshirt to the floor in a sopping pile and take Tabitha's naked body in for the first time. My throat goes dry as my eyes snag on her breasts, and then I follow her shirt and drop to the floor in front of her, trying to focus on the task at hand, desperately trying to ignore the voice in my head. The one reminding me that this isn't the way I've imagined kneeling in front of Tabitha's naked body.

I start with each woolen sock, gently gripping her behind her knees and tugging the heavy fabric away.

"Pants next, okay?" I look up at her, searching her face for some sign of consent.

I get another nod, though her mouth doesn't move.

Her hair and her arms hang limp at her sides. She looks so defeated, and it fucking kills me.

I look away, focusing on the button on her jeans. When my fingers pop the metal open, her hand moves to my head, and she sucks in a sharp breath.

I'm not brave enough to look up at her, so I stay focused, even though the tips of her fingers trail through the strands of my hair.

My digits curl over the waistband, and I tug.

Her other hand falls to my hair as I peel the sopping denim from her hips. A plain black thong has never looked so appealing, but I ignore the stirring beneath my waist—and the way her hand slips down my neck to grip my shoulder. I tap her inner thigh when I get the pants low enough, and she lifts her foot for me to pull the jeans clear. We repeat the motions on the opposite side, her hands roaming more freely as I do.

I swallow before finally looking back up at her. Now her dark eyes are swirling, and there's a light flush on her previously pale cheeks. Her palms slide back, cupping my head as her fingers continue twisting in my hair.

I don't know how long we stare at each other, but it's just vulnerable enough to make my heart race.

Eventually, she breaks the silence with a thin sounding "Thank you."

It's my turn to only offer her a nod. I don't trust myself to speak at the moment, so I just press a quick kiss to her hip, right where the strap of her panties hugs the bone. Then I move on quickly, reaching for a towel, drying every inch of her. Her skin, her hair, all the way down her legs. I move over the top of her underwear, not willing to cross that line at a moment like this.

Once she's dry, I push to standing and lift her small frame into my arms before striding from the bathroom.

I need to get her tucked in before I do something stupid. Like look too closely at the swirling heat in her eyes, kiss her, or peel her flimsy underwear off her body. This isn't the time or the place—hell, there might never be the right time or place. But I'd rather live with knowing that than thinking I took advantage of a fragile moment.

Her bedroom door is open and the bed perfectly made. I hold her flush with one arm as I reach forward and turn down the sheets. When I place her down on the mattress, she sighs and her eyes go heavy. I lift the down-filled duvet over her, trying not to gawk at how fucking beautiful she looks in the warm glow of the small bedside lamp.

Unable to resist, I run a palm over her hair. She stares at me with that same look from the bathroom, and I can't quite put my finger on what it means.

All I know is no one has ever looked at me the way Tabitha Garrison does.

I clear my throat as I pull away, towering over her. "You rest. I'm going to go clean up. I'll let you get rid of the underwear."

Her lashes flutter in a languid sweep, fingers wrapped around the duvet as she tugs it up beneath her chin. Her lips pop open, and my brain can't fucking handle it. Sordid images crash through my mind. Me crawling in with her.

Making quick work of those flimsy panties. Sliding down her body.

I spin away from her, giving my head a hard shake as I leave. I go straight for the bathroom. With a click, I lock the door and strip the wet clothes from my body, each piece landing with a sopping sound. My dick is at half-mast when I ditch my boxers.

"You've got the self-control of a gnat, Dupris," I mutter to myself as I bend to lift our soaked clothes from the floor. After I make a big wet ball of them, I march out into the hallway and make my way to the basement where I can start the laundry.

Agitation lines every motion, my feet landing on the floors harder than usual. I open the door at the top of the stairs with a forceful yank, my hand flicking at the light switch like it's done something to offend me.

I'm grumbling under my breath as I stomp down the wood steps into the concrete-covered basement. But when I turn to face the space, I freeze in my tracks. Water from the clothes held against my naked body drips onto the bridge of my left foot as I stare.

My room is...not the same. New bedside tables flank a matching bed frame, with deep maroon sheets and perfectly plump pillows. A large rug softens the floor. There appear to be photos propped on the framing. There's... I don't know. It's cozy and warm and full of love.

Someone who cares put together this room, and it makes my heart fall hard on a heavy stutter step. No one has ever put a room together for me.

But Tabitha did.

CHAPTER 34

Tabitha

I DIDN'T WANT TO GET OUT OF BED, BUT I ALSO DIDN'T WANT to lie there in wet underwear. The discomfort had me kicking back the covers and leaving the bed behind.

And the view down the hallway kept me from returning to it.

Because when I walked to the hamper near my open bedroom door, I got an eyeful of Rhys.

Naked Rhys.

Firm ass, trim waist, hair on his legs, tattoo-covered Rhys.

Walking down my hallway—away from me. The urge to follow him hits me the way he throws a bowling ball. Hard as hell.

But instead of following him, I just watch from the doorway, heart racing, feeling flayed open. Like each of Erika's journal entries peeled back a strip of skin until I was left raw and messy, the air stinging me all over. Like scraped knees, but so much worse.

Then Rhys came. And when he held me, it eased the pain. He wrapped himself around me like a bandage and made all the worst parts of my night feel better.

I knew I missed him.

I just didn't realize until now that I *needed* him.

My eyes clamp shut, and I turn away when I hear his footfalls hit the bottom of the stairs. My reasoning for any major decision is severely compromised tonight.

He kept the truth from me.

He came back for me.

He's sacrificed for me repeatedly, and I can't for the life of me see what I've done to deserve that loyalty from him.

He tells me almost nothing with his words, but everything with his actions.

I slip off my underwear and toss them into the basket before I crawl back into bed naked. I'm feeling both ashamed of myself and desperate to seek him out. I'm a little angry with him, but in a strange turn of events, I also understand his choice.

I understand it because it's what I would have done. It's what I've been doing for my family for years.

I've just never had anyone twist a situation to spare *my* feelings. It's a strange sensation to be on the receiving end of that kind of selflessness. That kind of loyalty. It's especially a mindfuck to wonder if I deserve it.

The turmoil in my mind wipes out my exhaustion. I'm well past tired—I'm delirious.

Naked in bed, I think in circles. Erika's manipulation of me—and him—should be at the forefront, but in the shower, the realization hit me: what's done is done. No matter how much I want to go back in time and smooth this over, it's impossible.

I felt my hold on my idealized version of Erika slip through my fingers as I cried in Rhys's arms. I'd been so keen to grip it hard, to make her story into something more palatable than it was. Did she hurt people? Or was she wonderful? I'd realized she could be both things at once and that my memories of her didn't have to be all sunshine and rainbows for me to still love her.

The rush of profound relief as I accepted the situation for what it was—beyond my control—soothed me.

And I let it go.

Then all I was left with was Rhys. Undressing me. Drying me. Every touch brimming with respect and dedication that I'm not so sure I deserve from him, but crave all the same.

It's that craving that pulls me out of bed and leads me down the darkened stairs. It stirs in my core and pebbles my nipples. But it's more than that. I crave his heat, his bulk, just...his company.

Tonight, I would settle for just drifting off beside him.

The basement door creaks, and I stare down, remembering how I'd just finished redoing this room for him. I didn't expect him to see it so soon.

I can hear the washing machine humming as it spins, and I can see the outline of his hulking form in the bed when I peek through the banisters below the railing. The same spot where I spied on him as he attempted to film that promo.

Light filters from behind me, just enough that I can tell he's facing away. But he holds his shoulders just a little too rigidly to be asleep.

I don't bother asking if I can come in, because I don't think my heart can handle him turning me away. And in my bones, I know that he won't.

I pad down the stairs, strumming my bottom lip between my teeth. When my feet hit the Persian rug beneath the bed, his head shifts. But I don't stop. I follow that draw to him that I've felt since the first time I laid eyes on him. The one that had me glancing back over my shoulder at him as I left his house in Emerald Lake.

I couldn't help myself then, and I can't help myself now.

So I go straight for the bed, softly slip in behind him, wrap an arm around his bare ribs, and press my forehead to his back.

He says nothing, but he covers my arm with his own as he links his fingers with mine.

"Hi, Tabby," he whispers in the darkened room. And I find myself wishing he'd call me baby or honey again instead. The familiarity of those names in such a vulnerable moment soothed me.

"Hi, Rhys." I trail a fingertip over his shoulder, tracing the swirls and patterns of the tattoos that wrap around his entire arm.

He shivers but doesn't turn toward me.

"I love my room. Thank you."

I nod, cheek brushing against his bare skin. His body carries the faint scent of cinnamon, and that makes me feel warm inside, like apple pie and cozy Christmas baking.

"I should have done it sooner. I'm sorry."

"You have nothing to apologize for."

Maybe not, but it doesn't stop me from feeling like I've been too damn hard on him for no good reason. Like we've been holding ourselves back. And right now, I can't think of a single reason to hold back anymore. Sure, he could hurt me. But after everything, something tells me Rhys would do anything in his power to keep me from feeling any pain.

It's a heady realization. To trust someone like that.

With one palm flat on his shoulder, I press a kiss to his back. He stills.

"What are you doing, Tabitha?" His voice is rough, the words strangled.

I breathe him in and exhale. Once. Twice. And on the third time—"Something I've been wanting to do since I first laid eyes on you."

My chest aches with needing him, with wanting him to say something, wanting him to turn and face me. "Rhys, please. *I missed you.*"

That confession has him turning toward me, his heavy features coming to the same level as mine. I feel his breath against my lips and his heat seeping into my body, ridding me of the chill I couldn't shake. His hand lies possessively on my bare hip, and need stirs inside me as I slide my palm up his bare chest. My feet tangle with his calves beneath the blankets.

"You told me you missed me, and I missed you too. I was… I don't know. I don't know anything, except that I missed you."

He nods firmly, eyes searching my face as though he can't believe what I'm telling him.

"And I need you to forgive me."

Sadness sweeps across his features, and his fingers tighten on my hip. "There is nothing to forgive, Tabby. I got it all tangled up. I promised to comfort you, and I didn't do it quite right, but I was trying the best I knew how."

My eyes sting, and if I wasn't out of tears to shed, maybe one would fall. Instead, I'm stuck staring into the earnest eyes of the world's most beautiful, tender, complicated man, and…I want him.

I lick my lips and drop my gaze to his sinful mouth. "Show me."

"What?"

"Comfort me. I need you to touch me right now, Rhys."

His hand slips around my waist, splaying at my lower back as his tongue darts out and questions dance in his eyes.

I hook a leg over his, pulling us flush. "Please."

"Jesus, Tabby. Are you begging?"

"Please," I repeat with a desperate little moan, dusting my lips over his stubbled cheek.

"Because you don't need to," he says. Then he seals his mouth over mine and crushes me against him, giving me everything I wanted in one harsh exhale.

His tongue seeks mine, and his hands grip me like I'm integral to him in some way.

We've kissed in anger. We've kissed to taunt. We've kissed for show.

But we've never kissed like *this*. Like we need each other to breathe and don't care if the other one knows it.

His hands roam my body, and stopping him doesn't cross my mind a single time. We pull closer, tighter, like we could swallow each other whole.

He groans when my leg tightens around him, my wet core sliding against his firm quad. And, god, it feels good.

"Tabby, fuck." His fingers grip my damp hair, forcing my head back as he drags his mouth over the length of my throat.

I swivel my hips again, rubbing myself on him, getting off on the feel, and the desperate snarl he lets out against my neck.

"You're fucking soaked." His free hand cups the curve of my ass, grinding me into him again as his leg stays firm. "Just like I said you would be."

I pant out a breath, remembering when he'd told me he bet I was soaked. I couldn't even look him in the eye and lie about it, so I'd said nothing.

Today, I come clean, tired of lying about this thing between us. "I told you," I whisper. "I need you."

He kisses me again, pouring himself into me, and I give it back. My hand slides down over a heavily roped torso to a blissfully naked abdomen. This time, when I wrap my palm around his cock, there's no denim in my way and no taunt on my lips.

Just smooth, hot skin. His steely length and a breathless

sigh. I revel in the feel, the weight, the rough gasp he lets out when I twist my hand over the head.

"Tabby."

Fuck, I love the sound of my name on his lips. Full of hunger and desperation, like he's been waiting for me to catch up and stop pushing him away. He's wanted me and let me loathe him anyway.

How fucking selfless. How fucking *stupid*.

A flash of frustration burns bright as I think about it. All the time and energy I wasted being mad at him when everything was beyond my control from the start.

I grip him harder, pumping as I pull away to glare at him in the shadowy light. "Rhys, never hide shit from me again. No secrets. I hate it."

I don't know what I even mean by that. It sounds permanent, and I have no idea where we stand. All I know is that I want him. God, I want him so badly. And now there's nothing stopping me from having him.

He stares back at me, giving one sure dip of his chin as his thumb moves in his signature slow, gentle circles. His voice is thick when he responds with, "I'm sorry."

I release his dick and plant my palms on his shoulders as I crawl over his body and straddle him. "I don't need you to be sorry. I need you to fuck me."

"Jesus, baby," he mutters, right as his broad palms slip over my ass and up around my waist. He presses me down and glides me back, my clit rasping over the length of his cock, which lies flat on his stomach.

Baby.

My head tips back as I revel in all the sensations of him. The term of endearment. So much has hurt lately, but everything with Rhys feels warm and safe and delicious.

Everything with Rhys feels so *right*.

"Again." The word is a breathless plea, and he doesn't hesitate. His hands maneuver me, and my hips move of their own accord, following his lead as my pussy spreads and slips down his length. That final little twist hits my clit and sends electric shocks through my entire body.

"Fuck," I whisper when one of his hands roams up my stomach to cup my breast. He groans, and a look of satisfaction transforms his face as he plucks at the nipple before moving to the other.

My skin sizzles as he explores. Every movement feels desperate, but there's nothing rushed or fumbled about the way Rhys handles me. He savors me. Every inch, every second. His eyes trace the curves of my body as though he's memorizing each angle.

I fucking love the way he looks at me.

My hand wraps around his forearm, and I follow his every motion, wanting to be part of whatever is running through his head. He moves from my breasts up over my collarbones to my neck.

His thumb brushes against my lips, and our eyes lock as he presses it into my mouth. I moan and hold his gaze as I slide myself up the length of his cock once more, making a mess all over him. At the top of the motion, his thick, blunt head catches at my entrance, and I suck harder on his thumb.

God, he's big. Just the anticipation of taking him inside of me is a thrill.

"What are you gonna do, Tabby?" He slides his thumb between my lips and pushes back in. "You think you can take it?"

That smug fucking twist to his lips that I know all too well pushes me over the edge. I match his expression, eyes igniting as I reach down between us to fist his dick.

And then I drop my hips and take him in one swift motion, gasping for air as his thumb pulls away and my body works to adjust to his width. My thighs shake, and my back bows.

"Tabby. Tabby. *Fuck*." His hands slip to my waist and grip me in place.

My gaze trails over his face. Lips parted, dark lashes dropped low.

He's fucking *beautiful*. And infuriating. And mine.

My core pulses around his hardness, and I smirk as I bend over his body, fingers trailing over his. I press a kiss to his sternum, his heady scent swirling around me.

"Was that a challenge?" I murmur against his golden skin as I slowly drag my hips up and glide them back down again. Pleasure radiates through every limb, a delicious ache unfurling behind each joint. I'm smiling when I move again, licking my way up his neck.

"Because I love a challenge." My teeth snap at his ear, hips riding him as his fingers grip me harder. Hard enough to leave marks. God, I hope he leaves marks.

Suddenly, I'm feral for him.

I slam down on him harder and hiss at the slight sting.

"Jesus," he grits out as he sits up, one hand pushing us into a new position where I'm still straddling him, but upright. Somehow, even more intimate, because now I'm not on top and in control. We're face-to-face with nothing between us.

His hot, minty breath fans against my lips, and when I move again, he grips me in place. "Baby, hold up. I need a second."

I clench at the term of endearment, hands draped over his shoulders as I watch him. Adam's apple bobbing, tongue darting out over that full bottom lip.

No wonder it was so hard to hate him. Especially now, looking so undone, so vulnerable—all for me. It's like my body knew all along and was just waiting for my mind to catch up.

My fingers rake over the back of his neck, and I search his eyes. Irises so dark, yet sparkling so brightly.

He shakes his head softly, disbelief flashing over his features, and then he drops his mouth to mine. His palm is flat and firm, moving up the column of my spine before his fingers tangle in my hair.

And then he's kissing me. Holding me. Pumping into me. That sting from earlier transforms into the most delicious ache as we join.

We take our time, all those protective walls we put up crumbling down between us as my hips roll and his hands roam. My chest aches from the tenderness of it, the reverent exploration freeing in so many ways.

His stubble against my neck tips my head back as I give him space to keep going. "Goddamn, you feel so good. So tight. So wet."

My hips drop harder as I ride him.

"So fucking eager."

The frenzy inside me builds. His praise feels too good to keep going slow. It makes me hungrier. "More, Rhys. Give me more."

He chuckles, low and sensual, in my ear. "So fucking demanding too. Downright desperate—"

"I'm not—"

He cuts me off when he turns us so that he's seated on the edge of the bed. Then he flips me like I'm a doll, manhandling me into position so that I'm still straddling him but facing away.

Facing the mirror that I so lovingly propped against the wall for him.

And I can't look away. The dim light from the stairs lights the space enough to give me a clear view of what he's doing to me. With both hands on my waist, he lifts me, lines us up, and slowly impales me on his cock.

He watches from over my shoulder, both of us panting and unable to look away as he fills me. The way his hands look on my body, the way his tattoos look even darker in the shadows—it all makes me wetter. My chest blazes with heat, and my nipples tingle so intensely that I reach for them, twisting gently between my thumb and fingers.

"See? Look at you. You gonna tell me you're not desperate for it?"

"Maybe you're the one who's desperate for it."

Our eyes meet in the mirror. Dark on dark.

He lifts me and drops me down again. I whimper, refusing to admit it out loud to him. That one last shred of power is just too fucking hard to relinquish.

He hums a low chuckle at my silence and bites my shoulder before smoothing away the sharpness with a delicious swipe of his tongue. "Desperate to fill my wife's tight little cunt once and for all?"

I suck in a breath as he moves again. Pulling out. Pushing in.

"Why would I ever bother denying that? Especially since I promised you no more secrets?" The pace between us ratchets up a notch. His thrusts come more quickly. The pads of my fingers pinch harder. His soft lips and bristly stubble at the crook of my neck make me squirm in his lap to the point where I'm practically bouncing on him.

"Been dreaming about bending you over since that first day you waltzed into my house, Tabby. So yeah, I'd say I'm desperate for it."

"*Fuck.*" From a man who went from telling me nothing at all, that confession hits like a wrecking ball. Warmth spreads throughout my body, and my hamstrings tighten.

His palm slips around my front, fingers finding my clit with mind-numbing accuracy. He circles there as we rock together.

"But I think what I'm most desperate for is seeing you come. Right here, riding my cock, where I can watch you."

One glance up at the mirror, and his intense glare pierces

me. I look downright wanton. Wild in his arms. His fingers work my clit. His cock fills me. And his words undo me.

I come hard and fast and on a breathless shout that pitches me forward. Heat suffuses every limb, and my entire body pulses. A sheen of sweat breaks out across my skin as my heart beats in time with his.

Too far gone to keep my eyes open, I don't watch in the mirror. But he does.

I hear his raspy, "Fucking beautiful," right before his grip goes rougher. He fucks me with reckless abandon as my pussy continues to spasm around him.

Within seconds, he joins me. His release rushes into me as I take it all and revel in every throb of his cock.

He lifts me without pulling out, hugging my back to his front as his forehead rests on the top of my shoulder while we both attempt to catch our breath.

And all I can think is that I am desperate for it. Because I definitely want to do that again.

CHAPTER 35

Rhys

I WAKE UP IN THE SAME BASEMENT THAT I'VE WOKEN UP IN many times over the past couple of months, but nothing about this morning feels the same.

I'm surrounded by color and texture and thoughtful touches.

Cleo is curled between my feet.

And Tabitha is tucked against my side—naked—with her hand laid over my chest.

I'm not sure I've ever opened my eyes and felt so instantly happy. So at home. Like I could just lie here all day soaking it up.

Even in the wake of all the sadness and truths we shared last night, it feels like a pressure has lifted from my shoulders. The weight of the world isn't so heavy today.

I've always kept myself locked up tight. But I've never had a Tabitha. Someone so fierce and loyal on my side. I've watched the way she is since first meeting her. Protective and always looking out for her family. It seemed so foreign to me, like something I could witness from afar but never have for myself.

This morning, I'm not so sure I was right about that. This morning, it feels like I might have it already and am just realizing that I do.

I see now that my fumbled attempt at shielding her from the truth could have backfired spectacularly. But it didn't, because she's *her*. All fight and no quit when it comes to the people she loves.

Love.

I glance down at her and wonder if that's what this is. This warm, cheerful feeling when I lay eyes on her that turns to cold, despondent dread when I have to leave.

I've felt it with Milo, but not like this. Not where it hurts to breathe, and I can't focus on anything because all I see is her.

Tabitha would like this show.

Tabitha would make a better version of this dish.

Hell, I see another woman in a nice jacket, and think *I should get that for Tabby. She'd look fine as hell in that coat.*

I can't even step inside the ring without wondering if she's watching.

Does love start off as obsession? Because that's what I am.

Obsessed with my wife.

She stirs, nuzzling against my side, and I glance down at her. Eyes still puffy from crying, but lips at ease, lightly parted as she rests.

I can't help myself. I crane my neck and drop my lips to her hair, dusting kisses against her silky strands, only to note the tangles in them. Proof of a trip straight out of a cold shower and into my bed. To *me*.

Slowly, I trail my fingers over her hair, gently working the knots out until I can easily run my digits through the section. Then I settle for stroking her, watching the morning light highlight all the different shades of brown in her full head of hair.

Eventually, her lips curve into a soft smile, but she doesn't open her eyes. She snuggles closer and hums contentedly. "Are you petting me, Dupris?"

There's humor in her voice, and my lips quirk up at the tone. "Are you purring, Tabitha?"

She laughs, and I can feel her wide smile against my side. "Maybe. It feels nice. No wonder Cleo loves you so much. You pet a girl like that, and she can't help but fall."

My heart stutters, but she doesn't seem to notice. No, the mention of love doesn't terrify Tabitha in the least. It comes so naturally to her. It's what captured my attention about her in the first place.

I can't help but notice the change in her voice when she speaks next. "Rhys, I think…I think you need to read Erika's journals. I don't feel like I can relay it all to you, and I think there are things written on those pages that you need to know."

I nod, still stroking her hair. "It doesn't matter to me, Tabby. Her reasons, her inner thoughts. I have a lot of fond memories of Erika and…" I swallow roughly. "You know,

I've been grieving her in my own way too. I think about her often. Impossible not to with Milo around."

She props herself up on my chest, so comfortable draped over me. I feel like I should pinch myself and make sure I'm here, and this is all real.

Big doe eyes latch on to mine. "I'm sorry. I never thought of it that way. She speaks fondly of you, you know."

I swallow again. "Yeah?"

"Yeah. But I…I feel like only I've learned things that we both need to know. It's like…if we're not going to keep secrets, we need to move forward knowing the same things. I realize she didn't portray me in the best light to you, and I—"

"I already figured out that wasn't true. I think I subconsciously always knew."

Tabitha blinks at me, eyes going shrink-wrapped again. And I can't fucking handle it. I don't especially want to read those journals, but I want to see my wife cry even less.

"I'll read them," I clarify. "Let's make some coffee, and then I'll go read them."

And that's what we do. We snuggle up on the patio, frigid air biting until I turn on the patio heater. Tabitha moves into the same position—tucked under my arm—as I sit and go through the journals.

For hours, we drink coffee and stick close to each other, always touching in some way. I read through Erika's highs and her lows. With every page, I feel more like a rubbernecker who is watching a train wreck that's about to hit. There's no way to stop it though. I just have to sit and endure.

Fury hits me when I get to the part about why Erika

asked me to be Milo's guardian. For my money. To spite her sister.

I must be breathing harder, because Tabitha's arms slip around me from where she's been reading over my shoulder. "Don't forget all the entries when she saw what a good man you are. Don't let this one erase those. She's angry in this entry, but if you take that away…"

I turn my head to look down at her. She smiles sadly. "If you take that away, I still think she made a sound choice."

Nodding, I stare back down at the page. I can see the smudged ink where one of Tabitha's tears fell last night. My thumb traces it, my throat thick with emotion as I confess, "I think if she'd made any other choice, we might not be sitting here together at all."

It makes me wish I could tell her *thank you* for bringing me Tabitha.

CHAPTER 36

Tabitha

THE ENERGY BETWEEN US IS...WEIRD. LIKE WE DON'T KNOW how to act around each other with all the bullshit stripped away. It's a mix of shocked, affectionate, sad, awkward, and horny. All made worse by the fact that Rhys is always so in his head that I can't tell what he's thinking. All I know is that he seems *very* introspective.

It's as though we got married and knew fuck all about each other.

I smother a smile as I stare down at my empty bowl. Maybe it's just quiet between us because it was hard for Rhys to speak as he shoveled carbonara into his mouth.

"You know what I think we should do?"

His head snaps up from scraping his fork along the bottom of the bowl to get any last remnants of the sauce. Sometimes watching him eat makes me happy, and sometimes it makes my heart hurt. Imagining him hungry and alone kills me.

I tip my chin at him. "I can make you more, you know."

He leans back, giving me a sheepish grin as though I've busted him licking the plate. "What do you think we should do?"

"Go to yoga. I was planning to go to Gwen's class today."

His arms cross and he regards me. "Together?"

I bristle, sitting up taller. "You can pretend you don't know me when we get there if you want. It's not like we need to link fingers during downward dog or someth—"

"Tabby, that's not what I meant. I just didn't know if you wanted to be alone and were only inviting me because I showed up unannounced."

I cross my arms, mimicking his position, and scrunch my nose as I stare back at him. *Be alone*. The way I practically recoiled at the words catches me off guard.

I usually enjoy being alone. I've never been the girl who does everything with her boyfriend. Typically, I've always felt a separation of "mine" and "yours," so it hits me hard, as I sit here staring back at my big, burly husband, that I don't feel that way with Rhys.

And I don't think it's the wedding ring that sits warm and heavy on my ring finger. It's *him*.

For the first time in my life, I don't want to do a single thing without him there with me.

"I don't want to be alone," I tell him simply.

He blinks more than once and swallows, as though digesting the sentiment. Then he gives the firm dip of his chin that makes me smile.

My man of few words and many feelings.

A quick glance at my watch tells me we have limited time to get out the door. "Meet you back here in thirty?" I ask, pushing to stand.

"Done."

I expect him to go change or clean up or whatever he needs to do, but he lingers and silently helps me tidy the kitchen.

I bite my lip when his hand trails over my lower back as he passes to the sink. I swallow a moan when his hand presses against my hip to move me out of striking distance of the dishwasher door. And I find myself obsessing over his nearness and what it all means—where it all goes.

It's like we've had the rug pulled out from under us and are both surprised that we like the floor beneath. Or maybe that's just me. The girl who feels sad watching Rhys retreat to the basement to change rather than up to the room where I stay.

Thirty minutes later, we are out the door and walking down the street side by side. I'm in a puffer coat with a yoga mat slung over my shoulder, wishing I'd focused more on bundling up instead of Rhys and his massive dick and even more massive heart.

I blow into cupped hands and rub them together to chase the chill away, only to hear an exasperated grunt from beside me. Rhys's big hand clasps mine.

"Put the other one in your pocket," he grumbles, checking both ways before leading me across the street with hearts in my eyes.

I clear my throat and try to unjumble my orgasm-riddled brain. "Do you do a lot of yoga?" I ask blandly.

He shrugs. "Yeah. In conjunction with everything else. Keeps me limber. I like what it does for my brain too."

"So you can do your crazy flips and maintain some semblance of inner peace?"

"Basically. Therapist said it'd be good for me, and he wasn't wrong."

"Wait. You have a therapist?"

A nod.

"Good."

He barks out a laugh and scrubs his free hand over his face.

"I didn't mean—"

"You crack me up. Sometimes, I wonder what it would be like to say the things in my head so freely, without agonizing over every word or second-guessing every sentiment before I say it."

I smile. At least he's self-aware enough to know he's like that. "Well, I can tell you that sometimes saying the first thing to pop into your head backfires spectacularly."

We walk into the yoga studio holding hands, and neither of us pulls away. When Gwen sees us, her eyes light up, and she clasps her hands to her full chest. She looks genuinely thrilled to see us.

She's like…painfully bright and happy sometimes. It makes me wonder what that must be like. As a woman of many constantly changing moods, she seems like some sort of unicorn.

"Ah, look at you two! You've got that newlywed glow. The sacral chakras are *flowing.*"

My head tilts in question, and Rhys groans. I feel like I missed something, but his firm grip keeps pulling me toward the room at the back.

"What's the sacral chakra?" I whisper-shout to his back.

"According to Gwen, it's the energy center responsible for emotional well-being and sexuality. Apparently, mine was blocked."

I snort as I toe off my boots. "Don't say I never did anything nice for you."

"What?" He reaches for my coat, lifting it to remove it from each of my arms as though I'm a child. But he does it without hesitation, without even asking. Then I watch him remove his and hang it beside mine. The simplicity of our coats hanging beside each other gives me the most smitten thrill.

"You're welcome," I say, for clarity.

Confusion rolls off him as he follows me into the sunny room. "For what?"

"Unblocking your sacral chakra." I brush imaginary dirt off my shoulder as I glance back and wink at him.

He steps closer, his heat pressing into my back as he moves my ponytail from one side, draping it over my opposite shoulder and dropping his lips near my ear. "Careful teasing me like that, Tabby. I already admitted to being desperate. Means I'm not above dragging you out of here just to get back into that pretty little pussy."

Fuck. A shiver races down my spine right as my teeth sink into my bottom lip. Suddenly I care a lot less about yoga, and a lot more about getting home.

Rhys doesn't miss a beat though. Instead, he slaps my ass soundly enough to draw looks from other people already at their mats.

I flush and head for an open spot, peeking at Rhys beside me as I lay my mat on the floor. His lips are upturned, and when he finally looks my way, he *winks*.

My jaw drops a bit, and I stare at him, slightly taken aback by his playfulness. A side of him I didn't see coming.

Maybe that chakra shit is real, and I healed him with the magic of my pussy.

"Babe, you okay?" he asks, all innocent, pulling out those acting skills he hides away. "You're *staring*."

I huff out a laugh and shake my head, imagining all the ways I will get back at him for this Dr. Jekyll and Mr. Hyde display here.

Gwen enters, and we begin, but I find my eyes wandering. His hands. His arms. The way his sweats hug his ass in warrior pose. He might as well be naked, because all I can see in my head is him fucking me in that mirror. The way his legs flexed and his throat bobbed.

As the class progresses, it becomes clear that I am not the only one staring at him. Rhys keeps his head down and stays focused, channeling his inner athlete.

I have the focus of a gnat. I keep watching the way everyone else's eyes roam. The way the women in here—which is almost everyone—let their gazes linger a little too long. Or the way one woman makes eyes at the girlfriend beside her before discreetly tipping their heads in his direction.

Maybe it should make me jealous, but I find it…

exciting? It taps into my competitive side. I take a secret satisfaction in knowing I've got what they want.

Sort of. Technically. Fuck. I don't know. Rhys and I are married, but I don't know where that leaves us.

Complicated. Rhys and I are complicated.

But that doesn't stop me from committing to jumping his bones the second we get home.

CHAPTER 37

Rhys

We leave the studio, and the conversation between us is pretty much nonexistent. We've been walking for at least four minutes without exchanging a single word. I would say Tabitha's zenned out, but I catch her chewing on the inside of her cheek, her face still flushed the same shade of pink as before class.

"That was nice," she finally says, clearly desperate to fill the silence.

I keep walking and sneaking glances at her, contemplating the best words to say. Things between us went from fucked up to...confusing.

The only part that I'm not confused about is knowing that those skintight leggings won't last long once we get home.

I also know that small talk isn't my strong suit, so I offer her a flat look that portrays all my are-you-kidding-me feelings.

She snorts as we turn into the house, reading me so clearly.

"Okay, no awkward small talk. Got it." She unlocks the door while adding, "Let's talk about something more interesting then."

"Knowing you, this ought to be good." I'm talking, but all I can think about is tackling her the minute that door closes.

I watch her toe off her fur-trimmed boot, her voice taking on that singsong teasing tone I so enjoy. "Do you know how many of those women were gawking at you?" She goes for the second one, keys still looped over her finger. "Like does being so sexy ever get tiring for you?"

She turns, and I pounce.

I wipe that mocking grin right off her pretty fucking mouth when I cup the back of her head and slam her back against the door.

"The only thing that was tiring for me was having to suffer through that class dreaming about peeling these tight fucking leggings off of you."

Her responding throaty laugh only makes me harder. I nip at her jaw as I unzip her coat and let it fall to the floor. "You think that's funny?"

"Hilarious," she breathes out, pressing her chest toward me. And it's all the invitation I need to drop to my knees in front of her. My hands slip to the waistline of her leggings, and I yank, finding beautiful bare skin.

I groan and drop my forehead against her thigh. "Tabby, are you trying to kill me?"

Another chuckle. "Panties aren't comfortable at yoga. They ride up."

"Fuck." I nip at her thigh this time before pulling the stretchy fabric down lower. Then I take a taste of her right here at the front door, running my tongue over her clit and reveling in the feel of her nails raking across my scalp.

I circle the sensitive bud, using my thumb to spread her, to taste her.

She moans my name, so I do it again, alternating between swiping my thumb and sucking her into my mouth, watching her wetness as I paint her pussy lips with it.

Her breathing grows more rapid, her hands gripping and tugging at my hair as I work her.

I chuckle against her core when her hips wiggle and her feet shuffle. "Are these flimsy pants getting in the way of you spreading your legs for me, Tabby? It's like you're *desperate* for it."

Her eyes flash down at me, the corners of her lips tipping up, but she doesn't give in. "No."

I fucking love this game.

I lick my lips, and she watches me raptly with a rosy stain on her cheeks. I spread her again. "Good. I'll just leave them there around your ankles while I enjoy myself."

She's about to bite out a retort, but it dies on her tongue when I slip a finger inside her.

"Did you have something to say, Tabby?"

"Yeah, it was—"

I add a second finger and twist into her, thumb grazing her sensitive clit. I can't look away as she writhes above me.

Last night only proved that I get off on watching her, and this is no different.

"Let me guess, you hate me? And that's why you're fucking soaked for me." I'm smiling when I say it, but the sincerity in her voice wipes that smile away.

"No, I don't hate you at all. And *that's* why I'm fucking soaked for you."

My head snaps up, and there isn't a single touch of teasing on her features. She means it. And it stirs something inside me. To know she sees me. To know she doesn't hold a grudge.

This woman's capacity for forgiveness is staggering. It's what first pulled on my heartstrings, and it's what has me hook, line, and sinker for her now.

It's why I drop my head and go back to worshipping her right here and now. My fingers twist as I work her with my mouth.

"Rhys. Rhys. Rhys," she chants as her legs strain and shake. And then I feel it. Her entire body goes rigid on a strangled yell. She pulls my hair hard but comes harder.

She sags against the door, tremors wracking her body, but I don't let up. I keep going, steady and even, making sure it lasts.

Only when I hear her sigh and let out a soft, "Good god," do I pull away. But it's momentary. I spring to my feet and scoop her into my arms, carrying her only a few strides away to the living room.

"Not done with you yet, baby," I murmur, placing her on her feet and bending her over the back of the couch with one firm palm between her shoulder blades. "Hold on tight. I don't have the patience to go slow right now."

Her fingertips sink into the soft leather, and I'm untying the waistband of my sweats when she looks over her shoulder to watch me. Eyes glassy, lips damp, ponytail all fucked up, pussy on display. She looks downright wild as she eyes me up and responds with a breathless, "I'm waiting."

"Fuck," I mutter as I yank on my pants, patience shot. "You know how fucking hot you are like this? How fucking perfect you look? How fucking distracted you make me? I should be working, and all I can think about is *you.*" Her tongue darts out as I make quick work of my boxers. My cock springs free, and her gaze latches on to it immediately. I wrap my hand around it and pump once.

"And *this*. Been imagining this view while I fuck my hand for months now." I run the tip through her wetness, smirking when I see her clench and shiver at the contact.

And as promised, I don't make her wait. Gripped at the base with my opposite hand on her lower back, I feed my cock into her dripping pussy. Her forehead drops to the top of the leather cushion as she moans, and my mind goes blank at the snug, hot feel of her wrapped tightly around my cock.

"Yeah, just like that, baby." Fully seated, I palm her ass cheeks and spread, watching as I draw back out, her pussy gripping me and leaving a wet sheen behind. "All tight, and wet, and bent over, moaning for me. That's the dream, right there."

A throaty, "Again," followed by tipping her ass up, is the

only response I get. And since I would give her anything she wants right now, I flex my hips and slide back in with a deep groan.

Her panting filters back as I fill her, fingers flexing and slipping against the leather. "This position is…" Her head shakes, and her muscles contract around my width.

"Is it too much?" I draw out and push in again, harder this time, drawing the sexiest fucking noises from her.

"No, it's just *deep*. I can take it."

"Of course you can. Fucking look at you. You take it like you were made for me." Again, I thrust into her, drawing a deep hum from her lips along with another shake of her head. "Let me hear you work for it, Tabby."

"Holy shit," she curses as I pick up the pace, hands sliding to her hips for purchase.

As if that was the permission she needed to get loud, the curses come more quickly, more breathlessly. Her whimpers turn to shouts. Her screaming, "Fuck," turns to, "Fuck me harder, Rhys!" The sound of my hips slapping against her ass sets the pace as we meet each other stroke for stroke.

When she shatters, I feel it. I hear it. It's harder and louder than the first orgasm, and my vision blurs as I follow her over the edge, pulsing in the vise grip she's giving me. Even as I draw back, cum spills from my cock. It slips out of her pussy, and I don't miss the opportunity to fist myself, swipe the white mess off her puffy lips, and push it back in on a long, slow stroke.

"Fuck, Tabby. Fuck." My palm slides up the column of her spine as my eyes close and my head drops.

"Yeah," is all she says as she goes soft over the back of the couch. "Tell me and my sacral chakra all about it."

I chuckle, folding over her to press a kiss at the back of her neck. She smells like the laundry soap on the tank top she's still wearing and the lavender essential oil Gwen dotted on us all at the end of class.

When I stand and pull away, I watch a line of my cum trickle down her inner thigh and like the sight of it a lot more than I should.

She turns to look at me with a quirked brow. "Enjoying the view of the mess you made?"

"Promised I wouldn't keep any more secrets from you, so..." I shrug. "Yeah, I am."

A shy smile graces her lips, and she shakes her head at me.

But her expression turns hungry again when I add, "Think I'm gonna throw you over my shoulder and enjoy the view in the shower next."

And I do.

CHAPTER 38

Tabitha

I'm pretty sure I walk bowlegged into Ford and Rosie's house. It's like someone flipped a switch between Rhys and me, and now we're fucking like rabbits.

Or newlyweds, I guess.

All I need to do is look at him, and he's on me. All he needs to do is that thing where he pops his tongue into his cheek, and I'm on him. I don't think I've slept, and somehow, I feel incredible.

Must be all that energy in my chakras.

"Come on in! Ford's out at the barbecue." Rosie waves us along, and I reach back for Rhys, not wanting to be far from him even if he's ruined my vagina with his massive dick. Doris always says her husband's big dick makes her happy, and I have to confess I can see why.

When Rosie invited us over for dinner, I didn't want to go, but I was also hungry, and we both agreed we didn't feel like cooking.

Rhys's warm hand slips over mine, and I lead him into their house. It's an old farmhouse in the area that Ford had stripped down to the studs. It's all exposed wood beams and floor-to-ceiling windows. Open concept, modern, yet cozy as hell.

West and Skylar are already seated at the kitchen island and turn to greet us.

"Hello, Duprises!" West says with his signature shit-eating grin. "Or wait. Are we Garrisons? I'm a modern kind of guy. I can see the merits of either."

Rhys's fingers tighten on my hip. It sends a zing of excitement through me. I love when he grips me hard, but in this instance, I get the sense this is pressing on a sore spot. So I move to cut in. "We're actually—"

But West keeps going, a stream of consciousness that nothing can stop. "Oooh! You could also hyphenate. Garrison-Dupris has a nice ring to it."

"We're undecided," Rhys says with an easy smile, though it's the tension in the lines beside his eyes that gives him away. "All great options."

I press closer to his side, slinging my hand into his back pocket and giving his ass a firm squeeze. An amused snort draws my attention back over my shoulder to the huge sectional facing the fireplace. Ford's daughter, Cora, is seated there, sketch pad in hand, smirking at me.

When Rhys sees that a child has busted me groping him, he groans and starts toward the counter to take a seat. He's a shy boy at heart. It's part of his charm. It's part of what makes his filthy mouth in bed hot as hell too.

I turn and point at Cora. "Beat it, kid," I tease with a wink, and she just shakes her head before going back to drawing with a big grin on her face.

With only a few steps forward, I swoop in to give Skylar a hug before holding her out with a hand on each shoulder and looking her over. "You look good. Really good."

And she does. She looks rested and happy and healthy and so unlike the woman who showed up in town earlier this year.

"Tabby Cat, you hitting on my woman?" West teases as he takes a sip of his beer.

Skylar rolls her eyes at him before glancing back at me. "You do too." She taps her undereye. "You look like you've finally been getting some sleep."

And okay, I've looked pretty bedraggled the few times we've spent time together. Tired, sad, and too skinny. But mourning is hard, and some days feel worse than others.

Today feels good, even though the comment about sleeping almost makes me snort. I definitely have not been sleeping. But what I've been doing has been rather restorative.

"Or just getting *some*!" West teases like the absolute menace that he is.

I roll my eyes at him and then turn my attention back to Skylar. "Thank you," I say and slip onto the stool next to Rhys. He pulls it closer to him before draping his hand possessively over my thigh.

"We're just doing a variety of apps, keeping it casual," Rosie says as she slides us both a glass of red wine.

"That's perfect," I say, but it comes out dreamy and

absent-minded because I'm watching Rhys test the wine. The tendons in his hand flex as he swirls it, his square jaw looking defined as he tips it toward his nose and smells it.

"Good god," Rosie laughs the words out as she gawks at me.

"What?" I feel my cheeks heat instantly as West and Skylar look my way. Rhys turns, and I feel his gaze lick down my side profile.

"You two are like..." Rosie waves both hands over us with a flustered expression on her face. "I don't know. An energy."

West giggles, and from the corner of my eye, I see Skylar subtly elbow him. Rhys's full lips twitch, and I slice him a glare before turning back to Rosie. "What is with everyone and energy right now?"

"Gwen," she says, lifting her wineglass and pointing my way.

Of course.

I deflect the conversation with, "Is she coming tonight?"

"I invited her, but apparently she's helping Clyde up at his cabin?"

Ford walks in with a scrunched brow and carrying a plate of grilled skewers. "Hi, everyone. A show of hands if you think we should go rescue Gwen after dinner."

West's hand shoots up, and Rhys just laughs, but Skylar is curious. "What is she doing up there? Isn't it kind of remote?"

Rosie shrugs. "I don't know. It sounds like he's having some health issues, and she's helping around his place. Bash might know more."

My lips flatten. Based on Bash's reaction to her recently, I somehow doubt that. But hey, what do I know?

From there, conversation flows freely, and I relax into the evening. Rhys is never far, and even while he eats, there's contact. It ranges from knees tipped together beneath the counter to his big hand massaging my shoulder.

Which should feel good, except it makes me uncomfortably horny.

The food is delicious, the setting is homey, and the company can't be beat. And for the first time since Erika's death, I'm happy.

The guys talk about bowling, and I settle into a happy, relaxed buzz. Only when Rhys says he won't be able to meet them for an extra practice on the weekend do I pay closer attention.

Partly because, deep down, I don't want him to leave again. And partly because West asks, "Are you ever gonna tell us what your job is? It keeps me awake at night."

I jump in, ready to keep the story the same as what I told my parents. It seems simple. "He's a stunt—"

"I'm a professional wrestler."

My head shoots in my husband's direction, and my jaw drops open.

"Whoa. Whoa. Whoa." West holds up both hands with a look of astonished excitement on his face. "Like a WPW type of thing?"

Rhys takes a sip of his wine, eyes darting to mine. "Yeah, actually WPW."

"Holy fuck, that's so cool."

Skylar nods with wide eyes. "Agreed. And I can totally see it!"

I'm still in shock that he said it out loud when West adds, "What's your wrestler name? I'm going to watch now. Cora, you watch, right?"

One glance at Ford, and I see him zeroed in on the couch behind us. Rhys turns to look—just in time for Cora to turn the color of the world's ripest cherry.

She stares at Rhys, her gaze dropping to the sleeve of black tattoos that scroll up one arm. Then she mutters, "Fuck my life," and leaves the living room without looking up from the floor.

"Is she okay?" Rhys sounds genuinely concerned.

"You don't happen to be Wild Side, do you?" Ford asks from where he's leaned against the counter with crossed arms.

"I…" There's a nervousness in Rhys's gaze as he glances at me. "Am?"

Rosie winces and covers her mouth with her palm, shoulders shaking as she laughs and looks back at Ford. "What are the fucking chances?"

Ford tips his head back and groans. "Fuck my life."

And I'm already piecing it together. I didn't even think about that night when Cora showed me his entrance. Or the fact that she seemed so excited about him being back.

"Is someone going to tell me what's going on?" Rhys is still bewildered.

"Cora is a huge WPW fan," Rosie says carefully.

"Okay and?" West asks, also confused. Because…men.

His sister glares back at him. "More specifically, a huge Wild Side fan."

"And?"

Skylar lets out a little snort before turning to him. "Seriously? You, of all people? My number one fan doesn't recognize someone who has a crush on someone famous?"

West's mouth turns into a round *O* shape as realization dawns on him, and Rhys sits up straight, staring back at our friends and looking like he's in trouble. "But I'm...old?"

"You do wear a mask, so it's hard to tell," Rosie says with a light laugh. "Honestly, who hasn't had a crush on an older man in their life, ya know? Totally normal. This too shall pass. I'll go find my little storm cloud and show her some other good options for crushes, so it doesn't have to be on our friend's husband."

"Rosalie." Ford sighs.

But she's already walking away. "Don't *Rosalie* me, bossman. We're not at work."

She's almost to the stairs when he shouts, "Can you at least give her some age-appropriate options?"

That sends Skylar and me into a fit of giggles.

"Anyway." Ford reaches forward to toast Rhys. "A fucking wrestler, man—that's pretty cool."

West lifts his glass, but then pauses. "Wait, so are you just a cat dad?"

Rhys shrugs, looking almost bashful. "I'm a cat dad. And I was friends with Erika, so I've done my best to fill that role for Milo. Like where I can. I love him like he's my own. Even though I know it's not the same—"

"Nah." West waves him off. "Don't qualify that. Parenthood isn't black and white. It sneaks up on us where we least expect it. If it walks like a duck and all that."

Rhys gives him a grateful smile. And like West can tell he's struck an emotional chord, he pivots to lighten the mood. "I mean, look at Rosie. Who ever knew she'd be a mouse mom one day?"

Skylar laughs. "Hey, don't pick on Scotty. He is a well-loved—and fed—mouse!"

West chuckles and lifts his drink once more. "To parenthood, in all its iterations."

With that, we all toast. And I watch my husband smile as a visible weight lifts from his shoulders before settling in to enjoy a night with friends. One less secret weighs him down, but a brand new one pops into existence for me.

My newest secret is that I'm happy.

Being married to Rhys makes me happy. Really, truly happy.

So when we get home and he turns like he's going to go to the basement, I stop him.

I take him by the hand and lead him up to my room instead.

CHAPTER 39

Rhys

I WAKE UP EARLY TO BURN OFF SOME STEAM. AND I DECIDE to do that with my jump rope out back, even though it's fucking freezing.

But it doesn't deter me. The concrete pad out back is the perfect spot for me to squeeze in a quick workout.

And think. Because between the looming possibility of having to show my face on national television and all the newness with Tabitha, I can feel the familiar heaviness of anxiety in my chest. One that pulls tighter and tighter the more my mind spins.

I pull my hoodie up to cover my ears, knowing that I'll warm up once I get going. Earbuds in, I start by swinging the rope at a gentle pace to warm up. At first, my mind is scattered, but with time, I find my focus. My shirtsleeves get rolled up, and the hood comes back down. My breath comes out in white puffs, and sweat trickles down my back.

I take breaks, but they're short, because I relish the feeling of pushing myself to the limit. Double jumps and skip steps get worked into the rhythm of the song.

And it's not until I stop to check my watch that I see Tabitha, wrapped in her favorite blanket, sitting on the back steps, observing me. She smiles as I turn, and my heart stutters in my chest.

I feel like I should pinch myself when she looks at me like that.

Things between us moved at a snail's pace at first. Then we both gave in, and everything happened so quickly—so easily. But sleeping next to her, in her bed, like we're a true married couple, hit me with a new level of intimacy I wasn't expecting. It felt real, and not like a secret we were hiding away in the basement.

"Why are you looking at me like I terrify you? Can't a woman enjoy watching her hot-ass husband jump rope in the morning?"

"Because you do," I tell her honestly.

"Fair. It's part of my charm though."

I prop my hands on my hips and drop my eyes, chest heaving as I struggle to catch my breath. "What are we doing, Tabitha? Not knowing is stressing me out."

She takes a sip of her steaming coffee as her eyes narrow on me. "That's vague. Can you clarify?"

"Us." My finger flips between her and me. "This. Sleeping in your room together."

I know she's toying with me by how dramatically her brows furrow. "Wait. What's wrong with my room?"

I tip my head back now, struggling to find the words. Communication and relationships are not my strong suit, but for Tabitha, I want to be better. No secrets. "I'm not used to sleeping with another person. The basement felt like one thing, but upstairs in your room feels like another."

"Sorry. Wait. I'm still stuck on the part where you're not used to sleeping with another person. Like…ever? Or just not lately?"

"Ever."

Her jaw drops. "Why?"

I groan and scrub a hand over my stubble. "I don't know. It just feels very personal. I grew up hiding my favorite things between my wall and my bed and wondering if someone who wasn't my family was going to come into my room at night to take them. I never wanted anyone in my space, felt like it needed preserving and protecting. I'm sure that contributed to my complete lack of long-term relationships. Or whatever—that's what my therapist would say, and he'd probably be right."

I watch her throat bob as she gives me a small nod. "So you slept in my room with me because?"

The answer is right there—it comes to me naturally. "Because I wanted to."

She blinks once, hard, and a few times more rapidly, never looking away from me with those big, glowing eyes. "Well, I guess we're…" She clears her throat and looks away, thinking. "I guess what we're doing is being married."

"For how long?"

"I don't know that people usually plan that type of thing."

I swallow. "Right. But this marriage…it's fake."

Her head tilts as she regards me with a tight smile and narrowed gaze. "That's funny. It doesn't feel very fake to me."

Air rushes from my lungs. It's like I didn't even realize how badly I needed to hear that from her. But there's an echo of hurt in her eyes that makes me feel guilty for calling this thing between us fake. Because I know better.

So I face her head-on and tell her the secret I've been keeping for weeks now.

"It doesn't feel very fake to me either."

"Well, this is such a treat to have you all here." Tabitha's mom claps her hands together and looks at us over the table.

She and Paul have returned from their camping trip, and when they found out I was in town, they insisted on having us over. Their house is comfortable and cozy, if not totally generic.

They've ordered in Chinese food, have each cracked a beer, and seem so elated to have us here that I almost feel uncomfortable.

The things making me feel better are Milo on one side of me—chair pushed extra close—and Tabitha on the other.

"It's so nice that you two had a few days together. How romantic of you, Rhys, to surprise Tabitha like that. I'm just thrilled that you two are happy."

Tabitha and I turn to look at each other at the same time. She offers me a wink, and I swear I blush. Ever since we cleared the air about where we stand, things have felt extremely relaxed between us. It makes me want to tell her more things, to talk them out, resolve them, and feel this kind of contentment and closeness on the other side of it.

I've never felt so rewarded by being open with another person.

"Thanks, Mom."

"How did you two meet again? Landlord, right?" her dad asks as he scoops a serving of black bean chicken onto his plate.

I clear my throat, preparing to continue with my total honesty policy. "Actually, I wasn't just Erika's landlord. We were good friends."

Both their heads snap up, wide eyes on mine. It's as though in their cloud of grief, they were so happy to see Tabitha ticking marriage off the list they forgot to ask any details about us.

"Really?" Paul clarifies.

"Yeah, I lived next door to her. We got to know each other and became fast friends. She was wonderful, and Milo was the cherry on top."

Both her parents look shell-shocked by this development.

"Ree's my babysitter," Milo oversimplifies, around a mouthful of thick noodles.

I lean close, nudging him. "My man, I don't babysit you. We just hang out."

With that, we fist-bump, and he throws his head back in a manic giggle. One that sounds overtired based on what I know of him.

"Best friends forever!" he shouts before going back to shoveling food into his mouth.

When I look up, the table still looks stunned.

"We met when I helped Erika move in, and..." Tabitha looks at me, as though gauging how much she should say. "The rest is history."

Her mom looks tearful, and so does Paul, but not so much so that he can't find any words. "That's a hell of a love story if I've ever heard one. I know your last name is Dupris, but I'm sure proud to consider you a son. An honorary Garrison. You've got the heart of one."

Tabitha's hand lands on my leg, like she just *knew* that sentiment would hit me square in the chest. And it does. I swallow and roll my lips together before offering this man a smile.

"You know." I clear my throat before continuing. "On that note, there's something I should tell you guys."

Tabitha shoots me a questioning look, like she's not sure what I'll say next. But I'm on a roll now, and I need to get it all off my chest. Telling our friends freed me, and it was an overwhelming relief to no longer keep hidden a huge part of who I am. And I don't want that hanging over my relationship with Tabitha's family.

"I know Tabitha and I told you I was a stuntman." I rub a hand over the back of my neck. "What I do is actually sort of stuntman adjacent?"

Tabitha snorts at that, and I can see her grinning at me from the corner of my eye.

"I'm a professional wrestler, so that's what keeps me on the road so much."

Her mom nods and grins, recovered from the last bombshell I dropped. "Well, that explains all the muscles, doesn't it, Tabby Cat?"

Tabitha slumps back and laughs. "Yeah, Mom. I suppose it does."

Paul's brow furrows. "Like on TV?"

I nod.

"What channel?"

Now it's my turn to laugh. "Why? Are you gonna watch it?"

He scoffs and shakes his head like I'm an idiot. "You're family. Of course I'm going to watch it."

And just like that, I *feel* like I'm part of the family—not a single one of us perfect, but supporting each other anyway.

When we leave, I have a passed-out Milo laid against my shoulder as Tabitha jokes, "You survived your first family dinner! Congrats!"

I smile down at her. She looks so fucking happy compared to where she started. And then I shrug, because it didn't feel hard to survive at all. I loved it. So all I say back is, "When can we do it again?"

CHAPTER 40

Tabitha

THE KITCHEN'S BUZZ ON A FRIDAY NIGHT INVIGORATES ME. I walked into work feeling a little blue, but it wasn't due to any of the usual suspects. It was because Rhys is leaving in the morning. I considered calling off and spending the night at home with him and Milo, but being a responsible adult and business owner won out.

And now that I'm out the door, I'm glad I'm here, doing the things that make me, well, me. It would be easy to get swept up in this euphoric feeling I have with Rhys, but there's still this part of me that knows I need to protect myself and everything I've built.

This part knows that it's all fast and new and we have a long way to go. I know relationships aren't easy—I've watched my parents struggle through some of the hardest shit two people can face. And I don't want to take it lightly and wander around with stars in my eyes.

I want to do it right. For Milo. For Rhys. But most of all, for myself. I owe it to myself to make a go of this thing, and that means still working and not turning into a lovesick sapfest.

"Kev!" I push the plate back toward the line. One look at the arctic char and I can tell it's overdone. "Rush a new char, and this time, don't overcook it."

"On it, Chef," he calls back. "Sorry."

I shrug. Whatever. Shit happens in a busy kitchen. But this is why it's good that I'm here, plating, quality checking, looking out over my baby. My baby who is still busy even though it's no longer tourist season. My chest swells with pride.

And then it fills with warmth as a tall figure draws my gaze to the front door. A tall, dark man I'd know anywhere, holding a little boy I've loved all his life. He speaks politely to the hostess but gestures toward the bar and meets my gaze from across the restaurant.

He turns heads as he walks through, but I don't care. The gold of his matching wedding band catches the light, and I take deep satisfaction in knowing he hasn't gone anywhere without it since the day we said our vows.

"Tabby Cat!" Milo calls, reaching for me from across the room.

"Be right back!" I call to the kitchen staff before rounding the corner out into the dining room. I head straight for them, taking Milo in my arms, though he feels heavier than usual.

"Sir, have you been growing while you were away camping? You need to knock that off. I don't like it."

He laughs like I'm ridiculous and leans in to rub his nose against mine—our signature greeting.

"Hi, baby," Rhys whispers, wrapping an arm around us and dropping a kiss on the top of my head.

I turn into him, letting him fold both arms around us in a bear hug before looking up at him with a smile. "What are you guys doing here?"

He stares down at me, eyes searching my face, before he shrugs. "Milo said he missed you. Figured we'd come in for dinner."

Milo points a chubby, accusatory finger at Rhys. "You said you miss her too."

"Oh, did he now?" I ask.

Milo nods solemnly, and Rhys rolls his eyes, trying to play it cool.

And my heart thuds at the sweetness of it.

My boys.

Here I was, missing him, though he hadn't even left town yet, thinking I was being bizarre about it, but he was feeling the same.

I pop up on my toes and press a quick kiss to his shapely mouth, not caring about the audience one bit. Rhys slips his tongue against mine, sending a shiver down my spine. He's always had this effect on me, and it hasn't lessened at all. In fact, it's getting more intense the better I get to know him.

I pull away, giving him a scolding look even as I lick my lips. He smirks, like he knows what he does to me.

With a shake of my head, I step over to the bar. "You boys, sit. What are you having tonight, Mi?"

"Crème brûlée," he exclaims, though it sounds more like *cram boolay* with his toddler pronunciation.

"Healthy food first, little man," Rhys laughs. Rhys who has been eating copious amounts of chicken and rice since he came back. I swear he eats nonstop.

"I'll surprise you guys," is what I settle on before dropping a kiss on Milo's head and giving the back of Rhys's hair a flirty little tug.

Then I'm back in the kitchen. Back in the flow. Though my eyes never stray from them. Rhys engages with Milo the entire time, and I watch him teaching Milo how to play tic-tac-toe. His large frame leans in toward the little boy while his huge hand holds the crayon so delicately. Him cutting up Milo's chicken and blowing on it to cool it down almost puts me over the edge.

They are a gift. And Erika, in her own complicated way, gave them to me. And I love her for it. In all her complex glory, I love her.

I will forever be grateful to her. In fact, I think I understand her better than ever. And my parents too. Things with them have been a tangled mess, but I think I've found my way. I've made peace with their choices.

And I've made peace with mine. I chose Milo and Rhys. And now I can't get enough of seeing them together. Listening to Rhys read him a bedtime story. Witnessing the way Milo's entire face lights up when Rhys walks into the room.

Even now, I could watch them together all night.

Milo speaks in toddler, and Rhys makes eye contact

with him as he listens. In fact, the kid doesn't stop talking the entire time, and Rhys can barely get a word in edgewise. It's like he lights up around Rhys, thrives on his attention.

And when I send them out a crème brûlée to *share*, I swear Rhys only takes a bite, letting Milo finish the rest. He shoots me a guilty look, and I quirk a brow at him. It sends his attention back to Milo but leaves him smiling.

Smiling.

It makes me realize how much more of that he's been doing. Like, although no one would believe our story, he somehow ended up happy about it.

I think he's craved this. Friends. Family. A home. But he never knew how to go about getting it, and somehow being forced into it worked out.

And that night, when we get home with an overtired, over-sugared Milo, who is on the verge of a meltdown, we do another thing Rhys has never done before.

We all crawl into my king-sized bed together.

In the dark, quiet room Rhys whispers, "Night, Mi. Love you, buddy."

Milo yawns and I can hear the smile in his words when he responds easily with, "Love you too, Ree."

I brush away the dampness on my lashes as my eyes adjust and the silhouette of them cuddled together takes shape before me. I swear I can feel the love between them.

Then my gaze meets Rhys's and it just...stays.

I'm not sure how long we lie staring at each other in the dark with a sleeping Milo between us. All I know is that I fall asleep with the warm weight of his eyes on me…and wake up under the same loving gaze.

And when I ask him if he slept at all, he shrugs and says, "Best sleep of my life."

When the doorbell rings, I expect West is on the other side, so I swing it open, only to come face-to-face with my parents.

"I brought beers, and I want my own chair," Dad says.

"What are you guys doing here?"

My mom rolls up onto her toes, shrugging her purse higher on her shoulder like she can't contain her excitement. "We ran into West, and he said you were having people over to watch Rhys on TV."

"Oh." Yes. I received a text from West this morning informing me I should host a watch party tonight since I don't work on Mondays. He invited himself over, and my parents too, apparently.

"Really, Tabby?" My dad rolls his eyes. "You didn't think to invite us?"

I snort and open the door wider, inviting them in. "You guys know West. He's like an excited border collie, herding us all together. I didn't even know I was hosting this until today."

My parents chatter away happily as more people arrive.

Bash comes first. Gwen comes second. And they are

like the same sides of a magnet—they stay as far away from each other as possible. Each takes one of my parents and clearly works hard to engage so they can avoid each other. If I wasn't so damn nosy, it might be funny. But all it does is make me want to ask what the fuck is the story between them.

Skylar, West, and his two kids, Ollie and Emmy, arrive, and West greets me with his usual enthusiastic "Tabby Cat!"

My lips twitch. He's impossible not to like, and I love seeing him so happy with Skylar. I hug them both and gesture toward the living room where people are gathering.

"I'm so glad you planned this." He pushes his shoulder against mine and grins playfully.

"Oh, is that what I did? *I* planned this? You are like the head of the town social committee or something."

"West." Skylar shoots him a look. "Whose idea was this?"

He shrugs. "What? Emmy always says that no just means try harder, and it seems to work for her. Plus, we're talking about our boy. He's bad at bowling, but it sounds like he might be good at this. It's our job to cheer him on."

My annoyance evaporates, and I'm struck by how much I love this for Rhys. I wish he could see it. "Don't worry about it. It's gonna be fun."

The living room continues to fill, and Milo is thriving with all the attention and the thrill of having other kids around. Cleo makes herself at home on Skylar's lap, and then more people join the mix. Ford, Rosie, and a chagrined-looking Cora stand at the door.

"Hi!" Rosie says brightly, holding up a bottle of wine. "I brought booze! I know it's a Monday, but, as they say, it's Friday somewhere."

Ford rolls his eyes, but I don't miss the way his lips twitch. "That's not possible, Rosie. The saying is—"

"Whatever. Come on, buzzkill. This will be like sports with a bit of drama. Almost literary in nature. You'll love it." She yanks him by the hand, winking at me as she passes, and I can't help but laugh.

Ford would do anything for Rosie and—as I've learned with Skylar and the way he helped her through a career nightmare—for his friends. He might come off as prickly, but he's a big softie underneath, and I get a kick out of watching my friend keep him on his toes.

I'm left staring at Cora, and we both say, "I'm sorry—" before stopping and laughing.

Her cheeks glow as she says, "Listen, I'm sorry for crushing on your husband. I'm over it now that I know he's so old."

I school my features so I don't burst out laughing. Thirty-five isn't old, but I don't tell her that.

"I'm still a fan of him as a wrestler, though, okay? Like I can't just pick a new fav. So I'm still gonna wear this shirt and shit." She's dressed in head-to-toe black with a pink scrunchie in her hair, but her shirt sports the Wild Side logo in lime green.

"It's a sweet shirt, and Wild Side is pretty cool, so this all makes perfect sense to me. But you don't need to apologize. I'm sorry I didn't tell you it was him. He..." I trail off, again analyzing how much I should or should not say. "He's been very private about his identity, and I was trying to respect that." It's not a lie, but it doesn't give anything away.

Cora gives me a firm nod. "Good. I'm glad he's with you and not that chick they're playing off as his girlfriend. I fucking hate that storyline."

I resist a wince. Deep down, I fucking hate that storyline too, and I'm trying not to let it get to me. I trust Rhys though, and I know it's just part of the gig. But I'm seriously hoping it doesn't go too far with everyone here watching.

"Well, get in there." I hike a thumb over my shoulder. "It'll be starting soon, and I've got snacks and hot appetizers galore."

Cora's head tips back, and she groans. "Oh, fuck yeah. I love your cooking." Her eyes widen like she shouldn't have sworn in front of me. "Don't tell my dad." And with that, she darts into the kitchen and dives into the plates of food set out on the counter.

I prop a shoulder against the spot near the entryway and watch everyone together. Laughing, eating, conversing.

This. This is what I love. It's why I opened the bistro. It's why I've got a freezer full of meals for Rhys and Milo.

Rhys.

A searing ache hits my chest just thinking about him. I know he's away doing what he loves, and that makes me happy. But I know this would blow his mind. A room full of people, waiting to watch him do something that he's hidden for so long.

So I pull my phone out and fire him off a text.

Tabby: You already in show mode?

Rhys: Not yet. What's wrong?

I chuckle down at my screen. Such a worrier.

Then I snap a photo of the living room and send it off to him.

Tabby: Watch party.

Rhys: Funny.

Tabby: What is? I'm serious. Everyone is so excited.

Rhys: This is actually happening right now?

Yup. It's blowing his mind. I go out on a limb and send him a video call request. When his face pops up on the screen, I sigh.

"Wild Side. Nice to see you."

His eyes roll, but it doesn't stop him from coming back with, "You too, Mrs. Wild Side."

I'm grinning when I turn the camera around and show him the living room just beyond me. "See? This is actually happening right now."

His eyes move through, as though soaking up every person crammed into my small house, and all he comes back with is a rough, "Your parents are there?"

"Oh yeah. I think my dad is a little pissed I didn't think to invite him. Showed up unannounced because he heard about it from West."

His Adam's apple bobs. "Wow."

"An entire enthusiastic cheering section for you up in

Canada. Cora even said you're too old for her to crush on now, but that she's still a fan, so that was nice."

"Tell her I'll get her tickets. But everyone else...they know it's just a regular Monday night? Like not a special event?"

He sounds so confused.

"I don't think they care. They just wanna watch you. So win tonight. Or do I need to talk to the writers?"

That draws a gravelly chuckle from him. "Well, I can't officially say anything, but I don't think they'll be disappointed."

"Excellent. Okay, go kick some ass out there. I just wanted to show you what was going down at home."

His shoulders heave as he lets out a huge sigh and hits me with a heartfelt, "Thank you, Tabby."

I smile, trying not to let it turn watery. "Always." He told me that it may be a few weeks before he comes back, depending on his schedule, and of course, I was fine with it. Just like I need my work, he needs his. That he has a passion for something—that drive, that focus—it's one of the most attractive things about him.

"We miss you. Please tell Little Willy that I hate his guts."

Rhys laughs now. "He will certainly get a kick out of that."

"Okay, bye."

"Bye."

I'm about to hang up, but his voice mere seconds later stops me.

"Oh, and, Tabitha? I—"

He pauses, and my heart seizes, and I wonder if he's about to say something that will change the game between us. I don't think I'd even hesitate to say it back.

The silent beat has me on the edge of my seat, but he takes it in another direction. "I miss you guys too."

CHAPTER 41

Rhys

Rhys: I have a confession to make. It's been stressing me out and I could use your input.

Tabby: No. I have not been faking the orgasms.

Rhys: Funny.

Tabby: If you send an ominous text like that then you should 100% expect me to get weird.

Rhys: Okay, but it's not about you. Well, not directly. Anthony wants to unmask me at Pure Pandemonium. He brought it up a while ago and isn't letting it go. Now he wants Elle to remove it.

Tabby: Fuck Anthony.

Rhys: I've always known this storyline might come. It's been done before. It's always kind of exciting.

Tabby: Still fuck Anthony.

Rhys: I'm more worried about the circus it will turn into with the fans. Right now, that separation feels like it keeps you and Milo safe.

Tabby: Wait. Do you *want* to take your mask off?

Rhys: I don't know.

Tabby: Listen, I appreciate you worrying about us, but we'll be fine. This is about you. Your privacy. Your identity. Your career. If you want to do this, then do it. But do it on your terms. Don't let that asshole control you. You can take that mask off AND fuck Anthony at the same time.

Rhys: I do not enjoy that mental image.

Tabby: YOU KNOW WHAT I MEAN.

I lift Will by the scruff of his neck after tossing him from the ring. "You good?" I mumble close to his ear, hoping he can hear me over the loud chants from the crowd.

"Yep," he grits out. But I have no doubt the landing stung. It always does.

I was meant to face one of his sidekicks, but then the storyline changed—as it often does—and the producers opted to have Will and the other member of their group run out to rescue their friend after the match. I delivered a hell of a beatdown to my opponent, pinned him for a full three seconds, and now his boys are here looking for payback.

Or that's the story.

Elle ran out to back me up. A ringer in a case like this, because none of the men would hit her, so they just let her unload on them. And for all the things I don't like about Elle, I could never deny that the woman is a good wrestler.

"My wife says she hates your guts," I whisper into Will's ear as I turn him into a headlock.

"She sounds sweet like you," he whispers back, grinning like the cocky little maniac he is before I toss him through the table he'd set up for me beside the ring.

We were supposed to be done by now. The ref has been giving us our time markers, but I'm too busy feeding off the audience. I know I'm a fan favorite, and I have been down for too long. They're ready to see me back on top.

The energy is electric. They fall back on the classic chant of *this is awesome* over and over again as Will and I beat the hell out of each other. And the younger wrestler is a fantastic showman. This was his idea, or at least I think that's what he meant when earlier in our showdown, he whispered, "Daddy, put me through the table. They'll love it. Let's bring it home."

I'd put him through the table for calling me "Daddy" alone. Goofy little fucker that he is.

I stand over him, watching, still wanting to make sure that he's okay. He moves his middle finger and flips me the bird subtly, the signal we worked out to communicate *all good.*

Whereas if we tap our pinky finger three times, it means *red alert, let's wrap this match up.* But that's never happened because neither one of us is going to call a match. Short of getting knocked out, the show must go on, and the adrenaline keeps you going anyway. When I'd been injured before,

I didn't even realize that I had torn my ACL until I felt a pain in my leg backstage.

Either way, Will and I look out for each other. We may have an on-screen rivalry, but behind the scenes, we're cool with each other. He's a solid worker. He sells the story, and though he's new, he's just enough of a perfectionist that I can trust him to wrestle safely.

So that middle finger sends me stepping back, cameraman following my motion as I stare down over my fallen enemy, who is moaning and gripping his ribs in the shambles of the table.

I hop into the ring, grabbing a mic as I go, and as I saunter to the center, I take a long look at the belt he carelessly dropped in the corner before attacking me. I can hear the shouts of people telling me to pick it up.

But I shake my head. "Nah," I growl into the mic. "Bad luck. I'll win it at Pure Pandemonium." I drop the mic and turn to leave, but not before Elle slips under my arm and wraps herself around my waist.

She gazes up at me, grinning like we're some happy couple celebrating a win, and I fucking hate it. "Do it. Sell it." I read her lips, because the thunderous crowd makes it difficult to hear.

But I can't.

So I do something I know Anthony will give me an earful for later—partly because it's not kissing her and partly because I look awkward as hell doing it.

In front of thousands of screaming fans…I pat her on the head.

"Like a dog, Rhys! Your stage wife was looking at you like she wanted to jump your bones, and you fucking patted her on the head! What in the actual fuck were you thinking?"

Anthony has been monologuing his anger at me for at least three minutes straight, but I'm already most of the way to Rose Hill. The sun is setting, and I don't give a shit if he's mad. His words roll off me like raindrops down a window.

"Well, I don't want to kiss her. The story doesn't need it, and I don't think I'm contractually obligated to do it."

"This is all for the show! And at Pandemonium, you *will* follow through, and you will be unmasked because the storyline calls for it, and at the heart of it all—you. Are. An. Actor. So fucking suck it up and *act*."

"No." The single word comes out even and calm, like second nature now. Without guilt. It's as though I've figured out who I am and who I want to be. And it isn't someone who compromises on their morals. Sure, I'm an actor, but it's still my life. And while I signed a contract, my lawyer, who I checked with earlier on the drive, assured me it doesn't mean I have to follow every demand they make.

"*No* isn't an option! Follow through. You will win—you're welcome for that—and Elle will present you with the belt. You will kiss, and then you will let her peel your mask off."

"I don't want to do that."

"I don't care what you want! This isn't about—"

I glance down at my phone, lips twitching as my eyes

land on the total lack of reception bars. I can imagine Anthony losing his shit now, thinking I hung up on him. It's satisfying, actually.

I run through the match in my head for the rest of the drive, determining if I'd do anything differently. Trying to decide if I'm being unprofessional somehow. I may not be a man of many words, but I am a man of my word, and I told Anthony I'd do whatever storyline he wanted when I asked for the extra time off.

I just didn't think he'd do this one. And it's not like I didn't express my concern before stepping into the ring. He knew damn well how I felt, and he tried to force it anyway.

No, I feel comfortable with my choice. Elle and Anthony can do whatever they want, and they'll get head pats from me.

I pull up in front of Tabitha's house about an hour after my call with Anthony dropped. Light glows from the windows. I know she worked tonight, and Milo is staying at her parents' house. The thought of removing him from this place now, after all these months, twists something deep inside me. His family, his entire support network—I could never.

No, Milo belongs here in Rose Hill.

And so do I.

That's why I'm back. Unannounced. *Again.*

I couldn't stay away. The travel is long and grueling and worth every second. I've never been in love, but I've also never felt like this. So it seems reasonable to assume I just might be in love with my wife.

Bag over my shoulder, I stride up to the cozy craftsman and enter through the *unlocked* front door. I lock it behind me.

"Tabby?" I call, not wanting to waste time looking around.

Footsteps rush across the floor upstairs, and her head pops down from the top landing. "Rhys?" She hurries toward me, eyes bright, hair damp.

She's wearing the same tiny shorts and tank top pajama combo she wore the day I treated her burn. It had been a herculean effort not to look up her shorts. Today, I don't worry about that. They won't be on for long.

"What are you doing here?"

"Surprise?" I reply, watching her spring down the stairs before launching herself at me.

I lift her up, hands on her ass as she wraps her arms around my neck. "The best surprise," she says. "Careful. I'm going to expect that you come home every week."

"I'll do my best."

She grins, dropping her mouth close to mine. "On the weeks you can't, I'll watch you on TV and slip a hand down my shorts. Pretend you're here."

"Fuck, Tabby," I growl out before she presses her mouth to mine. My fingers grip her tighter, pulsing against the globes of her ass.

"That's what I did last night after everyone left." Her lips drag over my cheek, nipping at my ear. "Went to bed. Pulled your entrance up on my phone and fucked my fingers until I came. Thinking about riding your cock."

I'm hard now, cock rearing up toward her. I don't even kick my shoes off before I carry my wife straight down the hallway like a caveman and plunk her on the kitchen table. I shrug off my duffel bag, shoving it across the smooth expanse next to her.

She watches me, looking amused by how frayed my patience has become at the drop of a hat. Her lips quirk, and she bats her eyelashes, taunting me. It reminds me of the smile she'd hit me with the first day I met her. She'd used her looks like a weapon then, and today nothing has changed. She knows exactly what she's doing to me.

"Are you feeling okay? You seem very *distressed*."

"Tabitha, wipe that smirk from your mouth, or I'll fuck it off."

She smiles wider, reaching out to trail a finger over the waistband of my jeans. "Maybe you're just tired?"

I push her back gently, so she lands on her elbows. She looks pleased about the development. "Tired of listening to you talk when I'd rather hear you choke on my cock." I hook my fingers in her shorts and roughly tug them down, groaning when I see the smooth expanse of skin down her stomach to her perfect little cunt.

She smells like jasmine and looks like dinner. I toss her flimsy shorts over my shoulder.

"Maybe you need a snack?" God, she's not deterred at all. She just keeps pushing back, and I fucking love it.

"Tabitha, what the fuck does it look like I'm trying to do? Now quit running your mouth, and get on your back."

A knowing giggle slips from her lips as she crosses her legs to keep me out. "Hmm. I have terms." Her eyes slice to the side. "Mask on, Wild Side."

"What?"

She reaches out and hooks a finger into the mesh side pocket of my bag, where I carelessly shoved my mask in my rush to the nearest airport. I blink at it. That was fucking reckless of me. Anyone could have seen it. Could have recognized me. I always travel in a hoodie to cover my tattoos, but the mask would be a dead giveaway. It didn't even cross my mind though. All I could think about was getting home to Tabitha.

She tugs it out and swipes her thumb across the leather. "You ever fucked someone with this on?"

I swallow. I've never merged my two lives. Until her. "No."

The grin she gives me is pure sex, her tongue sliding out over her bottom lip sensually. It's one of the hottest things about being with Tabitha. She loves sex and has no shame about coming for it.

"Good. I can be the first." She holds it out to me, anticipation dancing in her dark irises.

"You always had a mask fetish, Tabby?"

Her tongue slips out over her bottom lip. "Not until you."

I regard the mask, this part of me that I've always hidden away. With a gruff shake of my head, I take it and tug it over my face. I lick my lips as I look back at Tabitha, her teeth biting down on that pillowy bottom lip.

"First *and* last, baby," I rasp out. "Because I have no plans to fuck anyone other than my wife for the rest of my life."

She swallows, looking less cocky than a moment ago. Fisting her tank top, I draw her toward me, sitting her upright on the kitchen table before dropping my face close to hers.

Eyes latched together, her breaths fan across my jaw.

"On your knees, Tabby. I changed my mind. I'll fuck your face first. Eat your pussy after."

"Fuck," she mutters, slipping off the table and dropping to the floor eagerly as I rip my shirt off and toss it behind me.

She grabs the waistband of my jeans, popping the button and tugging hard to get the denim out of her way. It's frantic and clumsy, only because she can't stop staring up at me. Her eyes flit over my mask as I stand above her, letting her work my pants down all on her own.

When they're past my knees, she abandons them and makes quick work of my boxers. My cock is at full mast, bobbing near her lips as she licks them, attention finally drawn down.

Her fingers press into my thighs. "Fuck. It's been like a week, and I forgot how big you are."

I press closer, watching my head nudge against her mouth. "You can take it."

Her tongue darts out and licks away the pearl of precum beading on the head. My molars clamp as I watch her savor it and strum her teeth over her bottom lip.

One side of her mouth quirks up as she turns her sultry gaze my way and taunts me again. "Too big. I'll choke."

I chuckle darkly as my cock hardens at this game she's playing. I fist her hair. "Then choke on it, Tabby."

Her mouth pops open as I thrust forward. Only a few inches fill her mouth, but it feels like heaven. I press farther on the next thrust, reveling in the suction of her mouth and the way she hums when she takes me. It sends a sizzle of heat down my spine.

"Yeah, baby." I smooth a hand over her head, drawing her eyes to mine. The black of the mask frames my vision. "Just like that."

Her cheeks hollow as she sucks me back farther. Her tongue swirls and her lips suction so hard that my vision blurs. She looks disheveled and hungry and hot as hell. I push the flimsy spaghetti straps off her shoulders and watch the tank top fall to her waist. She doesn't let up, taking me deeper each time, even as her eyes water.

My fingers slip through her silky hair again as I praise her. "So fucking pretty like this. Sucking my dick like your life depends on it."

Her lashes flutter and her gaze heats as she pulls off with a wet popping sound and whispers a deep, "Yes," before lifting my cock and taking my balls into her mouth. I watch her press her legs together, seeking relief. Because if I know Tabitha at all, she gets off on this too. The same way I get off on spending time with my head between her legs.

I gasp as she sucks me in, hand twisting over my length. "Good god, Tabby." My hands turn to fists in her hair, tugging her head closer, feeling the vibrations of her moans in every limb.

She works me and I groan as she pulls away and trails her tongue over the root of my cock. She hits me with the widest doe eyes before sucking me back in against her tongue.

And it's my undoing.

"Baby, play with your tits and hold on," I grit out, keeping her head in place. "Tap my leg if it's too much."

I push in, watching for any signs of distress, but all I see are glassy eyes, rosy cheeks, and the drugged expression that takes over her face just before she comes.

My hips pump into the heat of her mouth, and I hit the back of her throat. She makes a strangled noise, but her chin juts forward, seeking my next stroke right as her fingers twist and tug at her nipples.

"Fuck yeah, baby. You take it so good." I thrust again, watching the way she struggles to take it all but comes back trying for more every time.

The heated way her gaze lands on my mask gets me off. And the desperate little whimper she gives when I withdraw pushes me over the edge. I come hard and fast, filling her mouth and watching her throat work eagerly to keep up.

My head tips back, and my hands soften in her hair as she goes from sucking to licking, cleaning me up like I'm her favorite flavor. When I look back down at her, her mascara is slightly smudged, and her lips are red and puffy.

"Thank you, Wild Side," she says demurely, hitting me with a wink.

Without another word, I lift her to the table and look her over. She's disheveled and panting, her shirt scrunched up like a belt around her waist.

"Spread your legs, Tabitha. I want to see how wet gagging on my cock made you."

Her lips tip up, but she doesn't move. "Make me."

Fuck. Me.

A growl lets loose in my throat, and I don't hold back. If this is what she wants, I can deliver.

One palm on each knee, I pry her legs open and spread her over the dining table just like I wanted to all those weeks ago.

Her pink pussy glistens, and my cock fills again at the sight of my wife spread on the table for me.

"Look at that." I swipe my fingers through her wetness before stepping up close and pressing them into her ravaged mouth. "A fucking mess."

She hums and sucks my fingers into her mouth, not backing down in the least.

"You need it here." I press my cock at her entrance, running it over her.

She nods, tongue swirling around my fingers, and I wonder how far I should take this game she started. I lean in and whisper, "You've been watching me on TV, dreaming about taking my cock like the hungry little slut you are. Is that right?"

Her eyes flutter shut, and my fingers pop from her mouth as her head tips back on a moan. Yeah, my girl likes it.

I press in an inch and watch her writhe, head flipping back and forth, pussy gripping me hard. I pull out and fist my cock, feeding in that same inch. Teasing her with the tip.

"Use your words, Tabby. Is that what you want? My cock?"

Her tongue darts out over her lips as she pants, eyes latching on to mine. "Yes. I need your cock."

Now it's my turn to smirk at her. "Too fucking bad. I told you I was hungry."

I pull out and drop to my knees between her spread thighs, pressing a palm to the inside of each leg and latching my mouth on to her pussy.

She shouts my name, part pleasure, part frustration, as she yanks at my hair.

All that does is make me double my efforts, alternating between penetrating her with my tongue and sucking hard on her clit. She's close. I know by the way she thrashes and chants my name. By the way she clamps down on my tongue.

So I don't let up. I hit a steady rhythm and let her fall apart with my name on her lips.

"Rhys!" Her back arches up off the table, and her legs wrap around my shoulders as she shatters.

It's satisfying as hell. I let her ride the wave, slowing only as she softens around me. Her gasps turn to panting as she slings a palm over her chest, and I pull away to admire her.

The flush on her chest. The wetness leaking between her legs.

My handiwork.

Ready to go again and needing more of her, I run myself over her slick cunt. "You still need me to fill you up, baby?"

She peeks at me from beneath heavy, sated eyelids. Defiance and eager lust spark in her irises. "I don't know. I'm probably good—"

I grip her hip and shove myself into her with one long stroke. Her head falls back, exposing her elegant neck, and a smile curves across her lips as I give her what we both know she wanted.

"You're probably good at what, Tabby? Taking it like a champ? Spreading your legs for me?"

"Yes. Yes. I love being good at that for you."

Pumping into her, I lick my lips, thriving on the little *ahh*s that spill from her lips. I hike her left leg over my shoulder while the other stays hooked over my elbow, and draw her closer to the edge of the table. As I slam into her, I go even deeper than before.

I can't help but look down, breaths coming in harsh spurts as I watch her pussy stretch around my girth. Leaking on me and making a mess of us both.

"Play with your cunt, Tabby. I want to watch you come on my dick like this."

Her hand flies to her clit, the other going flat on the top of the table, fingers spread wide in a desperate attempt at getting some purchase. It doesn't matter. I fuck her so hard that the table makes a screeching sound every time I hit her with a forward thrust.

Her fingers rub rapidly over her swollen clit, and her breathless murmurs turn to breathless chants of "yes" and "just like that." Her sounds of satisfaction drive me wilder and push me toward release for the second time.

"Tabby, Tabby," I breathe. "Come for me, baby. Let me see it."

Moments later, she does, gaze on mine as I slam into her, mouth popped open on a silent scream as her body arches off the table, legs shaking against me.

Watching her ecstasy is all it takes for me. Everything goes tight, and I topple off the same cliff as her. Coming hard. Filling her like I promised I would and whispering her name like a prayer.

When the sensation fades, I release her legs and rip my mask off. As she lies sated on the table, I drape myself over her damp body, dropping my face to the crook of her neck and breathing her in. One kiss to the top of her shoulder has her nails trailing up my spine as we lie together.

"Hey, Tabitha?" Her hands don't stop moving when I talk.

"Yeah?"

"I might be in love with you."

I can hear the smile in her voice when she responds. "Oh wow. You *might* be? How special. Let me know when you decide."

That smart fucking mouth. I smile against her skin, letting a warm wash of adoration blanket me. "No, not *might be*. I am. I have been for a while now."

Tabitha sighs contentedly. "That's good. Because I've been in love with you for a while now too."

She loves me.

It feels like a piece of my puzzle finally slips into place, the satisfaction of completion making me feel more whole than I could have imagined.

CHAPTER 42

Tabitha

We turn Pure Pandemonium into a girls' trip, despite the bitching and moaning from West and my dad—both of whom, basically overnight, have transformed into Wild Side fans. But work and a highly active grandson kept them both home, though I'm certain they plan to watch together.

So it's me, Skylar, Gwen, Rosie, and even Cora, who make a trip to Los Angeles for the event. We arrive the night before to give ourselves enough time for dinner. Rhys is busy with prep, but it doesn't stop him from showing up late and spending the night with me at my hotel. He's so tired that all he does is crawl into bed and hold me. For once, he falls asleep before I do, and I take my turn watching him sleep while I savor the feel of his arms wrapped around me.

In the morning, Rosie treats us all to the spa and puts it on Ford's business card. She assures us it's a "write-off" with a little giggle, but as a business owner myself, I'm not so sure that's true.

Regardless, considering Ford has been featured in *Forbes*, where they dubbed him the World's Hottest Billionaire, I'm not too worried about it.

I gratefully accept the gift and bask in a hot stone massage, cold plunge, and hot tub, followed by a facial and pedicure. After years of running myself ragged to care for everyone else, it feels both foreign and deeply satisfying to take care of myself for a few hours.

In the hazy mist of the steam room, I think about Erika, wishing she were here. She'd have acted too cool for a girls' spa day, but deep down, she'd have enjoyed it. What I'm less certain about is how she'd feel about seeing Rhys and me together. I suspect it would have tapped into those feelings of me getting everything good while she was left with nothing.

Especially knowing now how she felt about Rhys. It's something I've wrestled with since reading her journal entries, but it's not a sentiment I feel obligated to honor. She was into Rhys for his looks, then for what he could do for her, and in the end, she liked him for his bank account. All of which I find unpalatable.

She may have loved the way he was with Milo. But there's no mention of his voice, or his hands, or how he's really vulnerable under that surly exterior. There's no mention of loving him as Rhys Dupris *and* as Wild Side.

No, Erika didn't love Rhys. Not in the way I do. I've let go of the guilt and decided I'm not taking anything that was hers or could have been hers. I'm taking one thing for myself after years of giving to everyone else. And I'm not letting him go.

I leave the steam room feeling clearheaded and ready to get dolled up to go watch my husband win his belt back.

I settled on a pair of leather pants and a Wild Side T-shirt that I ordered off the WPW website—though Cora insisted I crop it just enough to show a hint of midriff. Neon green heels to match Rhys's mask complete the look. Skylar works her magic on my hair, giving me big, blown-out curls I could never achieve on my own. And when I apply a touch more makeup than usual, I feel full-on glam vixen.

We walk to the arena and grab a drink at a high-top table, taking a breather because the merch line Cora wanted to wait in was absurdly long. Plus, the people-watching is downright epic. All ages and all ethnicities. Some people are fully in character, while others are in casual street clothes, accompanying kids wearing tiny plastic versions of the different championship belts.

The amount of Wild Side merch that passes us by is staggering.

Rosie nudges me. "Dude. I used to think Skylar was famous, but I feel like we've stepped through a portal into a world where Rhys is a king or something."

Cora snorts. "He is."

Gwen peers around with an expression of amused awe

painted over every feature. "The energy in this place is fucking *wild*."

That makes me laugh, and I shake my head as I take a sip of my criminally priced arena beer.

Skylar nods, looking around with wide eyes. "Agreed." Her sheltered, fancy-pants upbringing is shining through right now. She looks floored by her surroundings. It's adorable. "Usually, I get recognized and approached, and I just… Like, I've gotten a few looks or waves, but it's freeing, you know? I was worried."

She's been through the wringer with the media and her fans, so she was hesitant to come with us. But West's idea of going a little incognito, surrounded by friends, seemed to allay her fears.

I reach over and rub her shoulder. "It's that Wild Side cap you're wearing. The Skylar Stone everyone thinks they know wouldn't be caught dead in that."

She rolls her eyes and inclines her head toward me. "Well, new Skylar is a huge fan of this cap. I'll start wearing it more often. Green is so in right now."

"Sky," Rosie starts in, looking around with a slight smirk on her lips as she lifts both hands. "I think what's happening here is that the Venn diagram of people who listen to Skylar Stone"—she shakes her left hand—"and the wrestling fans who love it enough to attend live events"—she shakes her right hand—"do not cross over very much."

We all laugh now because Rosie might not be wrong.

Cora lifts her soda, and we all follow suit as she leads us in a toast. I grin, loving that she's here, joining in with us.

"To Skylar finding her new people and Rhys—uh, *Wild Side* taking back his championship!"

"Hear, hear!" Skylar says, more loudly than I anticipated. And to that, we all cheers, and then roll out to find our seats.

Rhys: Expect the unexpected.

Tabby: What does that mean?!

He never texts me back, which makes waiting for Rhys's match fucking torture. The arena is electric. Only the best wrestlers are out for tonight's event, but nothing holds my attention. Nervous butterflies erupt in my stomach, and I twist my wedding ring as each match progresses.

Eventually Million Dollar Bill makes his entrance, strutting out like he owns the place, all blond curls and defined muscle paired with cocky smirks and finger guns. I know Rhys has told me he's not so bad, but I can't see it.

He must be a hell of an actor, because he *screams* douchebag to me. He's wearing black tights and boots lined with gold trim, and one of those loose-fitting robes that boxers wear, also printed in a garish gold pattern.

I suppose that's part of the character, but it's interesting to watch. The crowd is booing him, but it might as well be a cheer. It's like they're all in on the joke. They love to hate him, and he thrives on their reaction. He hops up onto the ropes and holds a hand up to his ear, which makes the boos intensify.

His response is a grin. Then he brings his fingers to his lips in a kiss, and extends the gesture to the audience, pressing his fingers to his thumb in a chef's kiss motion.

It's theater at its core, and being here in person feels so different from watching it on TV. I find myself swept up in it, and looking down the row of chairs beside me, it would appear that the girls are too. All of them have their hands cupped around their mouths and are booing, except Cora. She looks sullen, glaring at him as though looks could kill, holding up two thumbs down.

When the music changes, the arena goes absolutely insane. Everyone, including me, shoots up to their feet. My front row chair shakes with the noise, and I suspect my ears will ring for at least a full twenty-four hours after this, but I don't care. I'm consumed. I'm all in. I'm having so much fun.

My stomach flips when Rhys's hulking form appears at the top of the ramp. Strobes flash and smoke fills the entryway as the first chords of "Killjoy" by Rob Sonic and Aesop Rock blare from every speaker. At the pause in the music, a barrage of fireworks explodes, marking the moment he makes his way down the ramp. Elle appears behind him, as some type of escort, but he doesn't pay her any mind, even as she lifts her arms, urging the crowd to be louder.

He takes his sweet time, and it's such a power move. It's like he knows everyone will wait for him. Like just watching him walk in will satisfy people. He's so significant that waiting for him to get to the ring builds the anticipation until the air vibrates with it.

Or maybe it's just me who's vibrating. My chest rattles from the heavy thud of my heart, and my hands tremble with a heady blend of excitement and nerves.

He turns at the ring and heads in our direction. Although he has walked toward me countless times—passing in the house, heading to the back patio, hand in hand with Milo—I never felt like I might have a fit and faint.

It must be a widespread psychosis that I'm not immune to. Women and men alike stretch their arms over the barrier, hands reaching for him. He glides his fingers over theirs without sparing them a glance, like a benevolent king.

Me? I keep my fingers gripped on the edge, not wanting to stand out or make a show of anything while he's in character.

I know his hands will be all over me later, so I let his fans have their moment. But it doesn't stop me from licking my lips as he approaches. I think he's looking at me—no, staring at me—but it's hard to tell with the mask on and his wet-looking hair dangling over his cheeks.

Still, just the illusion of his attention makes my mouth go dry.

Cora, the first seat in our row, sticks her hand out when he nears. And it pays off. She gets a casual high five and a wink from a mask-framed eye.

The other girls follow suit.

And I freeze like a lovesick teenager. I just stare at him with slightly parted lips and white knuckles. But bless him, he doesn't make a show of me locking up. Instead, he hits me with a panty-melting smirk and trails a finger over the tops of my knuckles, initiating contact in a way that people around us don't fail to notice.

Elle's eyes land on mine, a flash of venom there that I don't bother feeding into.

I've already won, and we both know it, so I turn my attention back to the man commanding a crowd of seventy thousand like a puppet master. It takes me a minute to catch my breath, and by the time I do, he's almost finished standing up on every corner of the square ring, drawing enthusiastic cheers from each side as he goes.

Before I know it, the announcer has introduced both him and Will, held up the belt that's on the line tonight, and sent them to their respective corners.

The bell rings, and all bets are off.

Both men launch at one each other in a blur of limbs. Punches and kicks land, and it reminds me of what Rhys told me this morning. Yes, much of it is fake, but when you're in character, it becomes difficult to remember that. Even though losing a belt is part of the plan, it can still feel like a gut punch. And winning can feel more real than it is.

The match goes on and I can see the men growing more tired. The sweat. The heavy breathing. It's grueling, but they forge ahead. I watch him own the ring with a new appreciation—and a new level of anxiety. Suddenly, everything he's doing looks much more dangerous. When he flies from the top ropes, everyone cheers, but I press a palm to my chest and watch with bated breath. When he goes down and falls to the stomps of his opponent, my teeth clench.

Again, the crowd starts their chants of *this is awesome* as both men pull out every trick in their bag. Strength, agility, and cardiovascular fitness blend to put on a hell of a show.

I can see why he skips rope. I understand why he does yoga. Because he's not just all muscle. He moves like a wildcat. He can kip-up from flat on his back and kick higher than his head.

They pin each other several times over, always kicking out on the two count.

It's all absurd and completely entertaining.

When Rhys tosses Will from the ring, I startle and rear back. Will crawls away and grips the divider, slumping over it right in front of me.

"Oh my god," he huffs. At first, I'm concerned that he's injured, but then he peeks up at me. "Rhys told me you hate me." His words are hushed, but I hear them all the same. He takes a break, dramatically resting his forehead on the black padded wall, thumping his fist like he's working through the pain before gritting out, "Still nice to meet you."

I bark out a laugh, but my amusement fades when Rhys's shadow looms over us. He bends over Will, gripping his hair and holding his back, and he whispers into his ear with an unhinged grin. "Did I say you could talk to my wife?"

"Oh, hot," Rosie exclaims, which makes me let out a manic giggle.

I cannot believe this is my life.

What I can believe is the way the crowd goes wild as Rhys

lays Will out with one high kick and lifts his bulky body in preparation for his finishing move. Over the mountain.

Chants of *Wild Side, Wild Side, Wild Side* thunder through the arena as he lifts Will in the opening choke hold. Then Will pushes off in a dramatic arc over Rhys's six-foot-five frame. His body goes limp and bows over the structure of the ring as he lands. Rhys, sweaty and out of breath, drops to the mat and lies over him, one leg hitched up under Will's arm.

The ref drops too, fist held high before beating it down on the ground.

One.

Two.

Three.

Pandemonium.

That's the only way to explain it. Absolute mayhem that makes me giddy and unhinged. I'm screaming at the top of my lungs as I watch Rhys hold his hands up in victory and turn in a slow circle, soaking up the pure chaos of his win.

He looks so happy. Tears spring to my eyes, and I bounce on the spot, screaming even louder.

Elle leaps into the ring with the championship belt, holding it out to him with a wide smile. Rhys pauses only for a beat before taking the hardware.

She says something to him I can't make out before stretching her arms toward him, one toned leg stepping forward in a sultry stride—all hip sway and sass and just exaggerated enough to be slow.

Too slow.

Because Rhys has turned and slid out of the ring toward *me*.

With the massive gold belt slung over his shoulder, he stalks toward me, making my stomach plummet and my heart thunder. The weight of all the eyes in the arena combined with every camera at ringside swiveling in my direction freezes me.

"What are you doing?" I whisper-shout as he draws close to our front-row seats.

But he doesn't answer. Instead, he just reaches for me. One strong hand grips the back of my neck as he drags me toward him and kisses me soundly for everyone to see. My hands land on his slicked pecs and slide up to his shoulders as whistles and cheers break out around us. I feel the roughness of his stubble against my mouth and the smoothness of his mask against my cheek. He slips his tongue into my mouth in one teasing swipe that has me pressing closer to him, not caring about the setting at all.

Only when he draws away does he answer my question. "Kissing my wife, obviously."

His eyes are bright, sparking with life. He's panting, and since he kissed me breathless, so am I.

People talk and move around us, but it all fades away when his next words hit my ears. "Take my mask off, baby."

"*What?*"

"You heard me."

"But, Rhys…" My eyes bounce between his, my heart suddenly lodged in my throat. "You—"

"Tabby, I'm tired of hiding. I don't need to anymore, thanks to you. This is my choice. You and me. Together."

My eyes well with tears, and for a girl who couldn't cry for months, I feel precariously close to crying. "You're sure?"

He nods, hands cupping my jaw. "Very sure."

I lift one trembling hand to the back of his head and fumble with the snaps on each of the two straps as the arena goes eerily quiet. Without even realizing, my left hand has been holding the mask in place, keeping it from falling away.

My eyes meet his again, searching for one last confirmation that he wants this. My lungs are tight, and it feels as though all the oxygen has been sucked out of the arena.

His lips tip up in the smirk that used to infuriate me. Now, it makes my core hum with excitement. "What are you waiting for, Mrs. Wild Side?"

With a tearful giggle, I shake my head at him and pull the mask away to an incredible surge of raucous cheering.

He kisses me again before pressing his forehead against mine and whispering, "I love you, Tabitha."

Then he's gone.

Facing the cameras, heaving the belt above his head, looking smug as hell.

He makes his way back into the ring to address the audience.

Every eye in the stadium is on him.

But his eyes are on mine the whole time.

CHAPTER 43

Rhys

"I CAN'T EVEN LOOK AT YOU," ANTHONY SCOFFS AS HE STORMS past me on my way out of the stadium. Elle was pissed too. She'd muttered something about respect for the business before walking in the opposite direction.

But I've spent over a decade respecting this business. Tonight, I respected my marriage instead.

The door slams behind Anthony, and I smirk because I know he can't afford to get rid of me. No one has the crowd the way I do. No one sells the merch I do.

With my bag hiked over my shoulder, I head straight to Tabitha's hotel.

After a single knock, she swings the door open, wearing only a pair of skimpy fucking underwear, and then she's on me—arms around my neck, legs around my waist, lips on mine. She told me once that she'd climb me like a tree, and she does. I walk into the room and kick the door closed behind me, drop my bag, and carry her back toward the bed.

"I'm so fucking proud of you," she murmurs between kisses. "I could burst." Again, she kisses me. My lips. My cheeks. My neck. "How are you?"

I lay us down, pulling back to look her in the eye. "Beyond exhausted but also horny as hell because my hot-as-fuck wife answered the door wearing strings for underwear."

"Nothing less for a universal champion," she teases, combing her fingers through my freshly washed hair.

"Thank you, Tabitha."

"For what?"

I search her face, hoping to memorize every detail. The slope of her nose, the angle of her eyebrows, the swoop of the bow shape on her top lip. How can I encompass all the things she's done for me in a thank-you? Especially when there's still a tiny voice in my head that tells me I don't deserve her. Or this happiness.

The troubled little boy in me rears his head now and then, wanting me to question everything I've earned. He reminds me that good things don't usually last. But with Tabitha, it's just a little bit easier to move past that voice.

"Turning my life from black and white to full color."

She blinks back at me, lips tipping up into a sad smile. "You did the same for me. I help you find your color, and you help me find mine."

I swallow, letting her words seep into me. I don't know what to say back to that, so I just drop my head and kiss her.

Then I spend the entire night making love to my wife.

Tabby: Tell Will he's charming, but I still hate him. See you tomorrow. I love you.

Rhys: Love you too.

I chuckle as I toss my phone into the dressing room locker. We're in Anaheim tonight, a new market, but an easy trip from LA, since Saturday to Monday doesn't give us much time to recover.

"Hey, Little Willy, my wife says you're charming, but she still hates you."

He just laughs. Will has his back to me, and I see the bruises from our match have slightly yellowed. "I'll win her over yet."

I cross my arms and quirk a brow at him, somehow doubting that's the case. I know better than anyone that if Tabitha dislikes you, she isn't easy to win over. "What did you say to her on Saturday?"

He turns to grin at me, tossing out a little wink. "Why? You worried?"

I just continue glaring. I know I can look imposing whenever I try, and I fall back on it often.

He throws a towel at me. "Dude. You are terrifying when you do that. All I said was it was nice to meet her, even though she hates me."

I sigh and roll my eyes at him. This fucking kid. "Only you would think that was the moment for that conversation."

A roadie pops their head into the dressing room. "Wild Side, you're up. Show starts in two. Will, wouldn't hurt for you to follow."

"Thanks." I tip my chin at Will. "You ready?"

"To ambush you and get my ass beat publicly again? Yeah, I love it so much."

I clap his shoulder on the way past. "You'll get it back. Or another belt. You're not a flash in the pan, kid. Up and down, we ride it out. Just keep working hard, and I know you'll have a hell of a career."

He blinks at me, face blank. "My god, marriage has made you so soft."

This time, I punch him in the shoulder, and he laughs as I depart and make my way down to the ring.

My entrance is sweeter than usual with a shiny new belt slung over my shoulder. I've got my mask on because I still feel more confident with it. More like Wild Side and less like Rhys Dupris. The reveal was exciting in some ways, but I still feel my best in the ring with it on.

I usually take my time entering, but tonight I really soak it up. I've got my freshly branded tee on, and all I have to do is chat a bit and then fend off a bitter ex-champion who just can't let go of the spotlight.

Overall, an easy night.

Mic in hand, I press the middle rope down to step into the ring.

When the crowd finally quiets, I hold the mic up to my mouth. "Anaheim! Welcome! To the Wild Siiide!"

A few chants of *take it off* start up, but I wave them away, the gold on my left ring finger glinting under the arena lights.

"It feels good to be back here, especially with what has always been and will always be... *mine*." I point to the belt. "That's right. I know it. You know it. Santa Claus knows it. Hell, even Little Willy's mom knows it."

I smirk, pushing my tongue into my cheek as the crowd laughs and cheers. The mom jokes just never get old.

"This belt is back where it belongs. Willy isn't here tonight to see me wearing it, but when he's done licking his wounds in whatever hole he crawled back into"—the crowd shouts, and I know he's creeping up behind me—"you better believe I'm going to rub his smug little face in—"

A chair cracks me against the back, and I stagger forward, pitching the mic from my palm as I reach for my lower back with a look of agony on my face. The crowd noise reaches me on a delay, but I can hear their shouts. It never fails to drive me onward. "Came back for seconds, did ya?" I shout at Will, right before he clocks me with a high kick of his own.

Eager little fucker has been practicing.

I swipe a hand over my cheek before dropping and rolling under the bottom rope, seeking a reprieve at the side of the ring. I double over, which fans in the crowd shout at me not to do. But this is the plan. This is what we walked through.

I stand up just in time to see Will has left the ring and

is standing on the banister next to the announcer's booth. From a standstill, he backflips toward me. He's supposed to twist in the air so he's horizontal, and I'm going to catch him and turn the stunt on him.

I can tell midair that he's misjudged the jump and taken off too early. I move back, trying to cover for it, to give him more time. But we collide harder than necessary, and when I fall back, I hit the edge of the metal stairs at an awkward angle. My mid-back takes the full brunt of his two-hundred-twenty-pound body.

A hot blaze of pain hits me hard and fast, and then it's gone. Lights flash in my eyes when my head follows, hitting the ledge on the way down.

I crumple with him on top of me. I try to roll away... but my legs don't seem to respond.

Will whispers, "Fuck, sorry. You okay?" as he gets up.

Dread chokes me, and words don't come.

But I do manage to wiggle my pinky finger.

CHAPTER 44

Tabitha

The TV cuts to a commercial break—one that lasts *far* too long—and I'm left staring at the screen, slack-jawed. An invisible fist clenches around my throat and won't let go. To the average viewer, this is your average commercial break.

But the way Will rolled to his knees over Rhys and dropped his head low to talk to him was…not for show.

I reach for my phone and pull up our messages. His *I love you too* hits me like a ton of bricks, and I force myself to suck in a deep breath. He's fine. Probably concussed or something. I feel myself slipping into a familiar mode—survival mode—where I convince myself that everything is not as bad as it seems.

A call from Erika in the middle of the night? Most likely a butt dial. But I'd still get out of bed and search for her around town.

That eerie sense of calm settles over me. It's a defense

mechanism, but it hasn't failed me yet. Except to make me a completely unemotional automaton who gets shit done.

I fire off a text.

Tabby: Checking on you.

Then I wait. Ten minutes pass, and I stare at my phone the entire time. I tell myself it hasn't been that long. He could be showering. One of their medical staff could be checking him out. Then I give in to the brewing panic.

Tabby: Can you drop me a line when you get a sec? I would settle for an eye roll emoji.

Ten minutes turn into twenty, and I stand. Twenty turns into thirty, and I pace. And then the forty-minute mark hits, and a growing sense of nausea takes over. I clutch my phone in one hand and keep the other slapped over my mouth.

Finally, the phone rings, and a photo I snapped of him wearing only a towel lights up the screen. His head is tilted, and he looks irritated, but the subtle tilt of his lips tells another story.

I answer in a heavy rush of breath. "You scared the shit out of me."

The line is silent, and I pull it away from my ear to check that there's still a connection.

"Rhys?"

Then I hear a voice. But it isn't Rhys.

"Tabitha? This is Will."

Everything in me goes cold. I *know* in my bones that something is wrong, but I ask anyway. "Will? Why?"

"Rhys—" His voice breaks, and all the cocky surety I see in the ring isn't here right now. He sounds young and terrified. "I think you should get to Anaheim. He's on his way to the hospital. I'm going to follow. I'll keep his phone on me."

Everything feels numb, but I move anyway.

"What's wrong?" I ask simply, as I march up the stairs.

"I..." He sighs, and his voice shakes. "I don't know. He...he said he couldn't move his legs."

I freeze on the steps and feel as though I've been sucker punched in the stomach. Winded. "So I don't know. They strapped him down right away. All he kept saying to me was *Call Tabby*."

Fuck me. This poor guy sounds like he's crying. I spring into action, hustling up the stairs and rifling through my closet.

"Okay, Will. You did good." I toss clothes into a backpack, wondering if I should pack for Milo and then wake him up too. "I will be there. Can you please text me which hospital?"

"Yeah. Okay..." He trails off, sounding distraught.

"Hey! Will!" I snap at him. "Zone in. Okay? I can't be there right away, so I need you to be. Rhys likes you—"

"It doesn't seem like he—"

"Will, shut up. I'm telling you that he likes you. He trusts you." I continue shoving random clothes into a bag. "For a man who has no friends, you might be the closest thing to it. So get there, and do not leave. Be annoying. Ask for updates. I don't know if Will is your real name, but throw that cocky, obnoxious Million Dollar energy around, 'kay?"

"But I'm not family."

"Then lie!" My voice comes out shrill.

"Okay. Okay."

"Okay, text me. Bye." I hang up on a clearly spiraling Will and pull up a browser to check for flights, cursing as I scroll through them. They are all tomorrow, and I'll need to drive three plus hours to get to the Calgary airport—which is right now since there's no way I'm sleeping. It's all just... too fucking slow. I want to be there *now*.

I groan, but it edges on a sob. Living in a small town is all fine and dandy until you need to be somewhere fast. What I really need is—*Rosie*.

I dial her, and she picks up with a singsong, "Hellooo," on the third ring.

"Rosie, I need help."

"What's wrong?"

"Rhys is seriously injured, and I need to get back to California. You're the only person I know who is married to—"

"A billionaire with a private jet? Say less. Ford!" she shouts, and I hear her footsteps rushing through their house. Murmurs filter through the phone, and I can hear her relaying the story.

"I'll call my guy. It's not that late. Tell Tabitha I'll come pick her up." I let out the breath I'd been holding when I hear Ford's voice. He's so matter-of-fact, and that authoritative vibe he has does nothing but bring me comfort in this moment.

"Okay, Tabby. Ford is on it. What can I do? Tell me what you need."

I look around and let out a whimper when I think of Milo sleeping peacefully down the hall. It all seems so unfair. Have we not been through enough?

But I shake off the sentiment and put even more energy into the belief that everything will be okay.

"Milo is here. And our cat, Cleo. Is there any—"

"I'll be right over."

Then she hangs up on me, and I finish getting ready, doing my best to ignore the tears in my eyes.

I blast into the hospital with Ford hot on my heels. He might be the least annoying moral support I've ever received. He's just *there*. Getting shit done. Not asking me about my feelings. He got us a retired pilot he uses who lives in Rose Hill. He booked us a car on the landing side. He called ahead to the hospital to make sure Rhys was in the best room money could buy.

One day, I'll weep over his steady, supportive brand of kindness. But right now, I just feed off his big-swinging-dick energy and cool, collected demeanor.

He makes it easy to hold it together.

I jam my finger against the button in the elevator and tap my foot as it ascends. My eyes stay locked on the numbers above the door.

"You don't need to be here, you know." I don't look at Ford as I say it to him, but from the corner of my eye, I can see him shrug.

"I know."

"You can go back home."

A nod. "I can."

I turn to face him. "Honestly, Ford. You've done enough."

He regards me carefully. "You know what you and I have in common, Tabitha?"

My head tilts. "Aside from our good looks?"

Ford rolls his eyes.

"Sorry, I fall back on dumb humor when I'm stressed."

He breezes past the discomfort. "We're both willing to do anything for the people we love. For family."

I swallow roughly. "You love Rhys?"

He chuckles now, one hand tugging at the ends of his hair as he messes it up. "I mean, we're on the same bowling team." He says it like *Duh, obviously*. "Bonded by humiliation of having to wear those shirts West designed and a mutual hatred for that fucker, Stretch."

A watery laugh leaps from my throat.

"And you. Rosie loves you, and I love Rosie."

"So you love me by one degree of separation? I guess that means I love you back."

We both chuckle, because what the fuck else do we do in this situation? And when those elevator doors open, we spring into action. I stride out into the ICU waiting room, bolstered by the feeling of Ford at my side.

Will is sitting in a green vinyl chair that is just a darker shade of the mint color on the walls. The walls are just a more concentrated shade of the color on Will's face.

He's slumped over, hands on his chin, elbows propped

on his knees. Watery, red-rimmed eyes land on mine. "Oh good, you're here." The words spill from Will's mouth on a relieved sigh.

But the middle-aged man beside him stands up. He's wearing a lanyard that says *training staff*, and he starts talking to me like I'm some sort of interloper or trespassing fan. I see his lips moving, but the words don't register until he tries to tell me the WPW isn't allowing any visitors.

I cut him off before he can go any further.

"I'm not asking permission! Where the hell is my husband?"

The trainer stops and draws back, looking offended by my biting tone, but Will pulls my attention away. He speaks as he pushes to stand. "I'm so sorry, Tabby. This is all my fault. I misjudged—"

"Will, I don't care about that right now. Where is he? Just tell me where he is."

"Getting a scan. They'll come get me when he's back. They think I'm his brother."

I walk forward, effectively blocking out the man who thinks he's going to keep me from Rhys, and squeeze Will's shoulder. He looks so fucking stricken, I can barely handle it. "You did good."

He turns his head down, the heels of his hands pressed against his forehead. "I didn't. I did this. If I had been more accurate, he wouldn't have adjusted his position to make it work, and…and I—"

I crouch down, squeezing his forearms. "Hey, hey. Stop." I give him a shake. "Fucking stop it. Don't do that." His big baby blues, swimming in tears, leap up to mine. "Believe it or not, I know a thing or two about blaming yourself for someone else's health. And guess what? It will eat you alive and not change a thing. A million little things happened last night that could have had a million different outcomes. Maybe if he hadn't moved, he'd have hit his head. Maybe if you had landed differently, it would have been your back."

I shake him once again for emphasis. "Do not, under any circumstance, do this to yourself. It solves nothing. Now pull yourself up by the bootstraps. He'll need his friend. Go and get some sleep. I'll stay now."

He gives me a nod on a shaky exhale. "Okay. But I'm not leaving."

It's then that a door opens, and a nurse pops her head in. "For Dupris?"

Will wipes at his face, nods in my direction, and does me a solid when he announces, "Yeah, his wife is here now."

The woman smiles kindly at me. "Okay, Mrs. Dupris, you can come with me."

I turn and give Ford a pointed look. He's not an emotional person, but I want him to stick with Will and keep the WPW police off my ass. He picks up on my intention immediately and moves to sit one chair down from the other wrestler.

Then I turn and follow the woman back into the eerily silent ward. The only sound aside from my footsteps is the insistent beeping of monitors.

When she turns, I quicken my pace, that invisible pull I've always felt toward Rhys stronger than ever. I may not have all the answers, but I'm certain of one thing—if I can be with him, we'll be okay. Together, we can get through anything. This much I know about us.

If everything life has thrown at us hasn't been able to pull us apart, this won't either.

I let out a whimper when I see him and rush toward the bed. His tan skin looks pale against the sterile white hospital sheets. His tall frame overwhelms the bed, and he belongs in something bigger, something plusher—something where I can bring him home-cooked food.

"Gentle, hon." The woman's warning has me drawing up. "We need to keep him still. Doctor will be right in."

Rhys avoids making eye contact with me as the nurse heads out. His lips are pressed together tightly.

I take the last couple of steps slowly and wrap both my shaky hands around his large one. "Hi, baby." I turn the term of endearment back on him, his eyes flitting to the side to see me. "I got here as fast as I could."

I fold at the waist and press a kiss to his upturned wrist. "God, it's so good to see you." I look him over. Jaw clenched, throat working.

"How—" He sounds choked up and covers the emotion with a cough. "How did you get here so fast?"

I lift a shoulder in a casual shrug. "Ford and his toys."

His lips twitch, but I'd never call his expression a smile.

With that, the door opens, and the doctor breezes in, nose to the clipboard in her hands as she announces, "Well, Mr. Dupris, we've got good news, and we've got bad news."

CHAPTER 45

Rhys

GOOD NEWS AND BAD NEWS.

That's the thing with me. They always go hand in hand.

When the doctor finally looks up, her eyes land on Tabitha, who is holding my hand. She rubs her thumb in soothing circles like that might magically make me feel my feet again.

The silver lining is that I'm pretty sure I feel blood rush to my dick.

"You must be Mrs. Dupris."

The name stings. I'd never put this name on Tabitha, not now that I know the pride that comes with being a Garrison. She deserves *that* kind of legacy.

But she doesn't correct the doctor. She smiles and replies with a soft, "Hi."

"I'm Doctor Osei, a neurosurgeon here at the hospital. Rhys, hello again. So I'm just going to cut straight to the chase. The good news is that with imaging, I can see clearly that there was an impact to your T10." She fires up a computer in the corner and turns it to face us, pointing at the spot.

"There are a couple of small floating bone chips, but aside from that, the spinal cord has not been directly injured. I believe what you're experiencing is spinal shock, which is your body's way of forcing you to stay still while it puts energy into healing. Feeling should come back in anywhere from a couple days to a few weeks. Recovery will require rehab."

I watch Tabitha let out a deep sigh, her shoulders dropping with relief. Me? I still feel sick.

"What's the bad news?" I grumble, drawing a raised eyebrow from the woman.

She spins on the small stool to face us. "You have a concussion, and I am not a fan of leaving those chips in there to wreak havoc on your spinal cord. You are young and fit and a good candidate for surgery to remove them."

Tabitha bites at her lip, her thumb still swirling. "And the risks associated with that are?"

I can't tear my eyes from my wife as she listens intently, soaking up every word the doctor gives her. All I can hear is that voice in my head telling me I don't deserve her. This loyalty and dedication feels...uncomfortable somehow. Intensely personal.

No one was with me when I had surgery for my ACL. Somehow, I didn't expect her to actually come here. Not for me. Not with everything she has going on at home. A business, a child, a *life*.

Eventually, I cut in, "And if this isn't spinal shock? Then what?"

The doctor looks borderline offended that I'd question her diagnosis.

"Like if my ability to move my legs doesn't come back, then what?" I'm being snippy, but I've barely slept, and underneath my stoic exterior, I am fucking crumbling.

All I can think is that I might never wrestle again. Might never chase Milo at the park again. Might never stand up tall while my wife climbs me like a tree.

All I see is everything I've been gifted these last few months slipping away.

"Well, Mr. Dupris, if you never regain movement, then you would be a paraplegic." My brows furrow. This woman is direct as hell. If I wasn't already feeling surly, I'd appreciate it a lot more. "But that is not what the imaging shows. And if I get those bone chips out, there will be nothing left to injure the spinal cord."

"We're not going to think that way, yeah?" Tabitha squeezes my hand and looks down at me with empathy in her eyes.

It makes me squirm.

"Listen to your wife. A positive mindset will not hurt you or your recovery."

My tongue presses into my cheek, and I avoid looking at them both. There's something about being injured and laid out that leaves me feeling helpless. If fight or flight are my reaction options when I feel vulnerable, I usually pick fight.

"Let's do it then."

The woman nods, looking sure and satisfied. Her attitude gives me some semblance of peace.

"I will send someone in to go over the paperwork and see how quickly I can book an OR." With that, she spins on one sneakered heel and struts out of the room.

Tabitha squeezes my hand. "Hey, you got this. We got this."

I look away, out the window that faces the water. If Ford was involved, that explains the room upgrade I got. "You don't need to be here, you know." I hate myself the minute the words leave my mouth, which is why I can't meet her eyes.

Annoyingly, she smiles. "I know."

"You have a life, Tabby. Milo. Your restaurant. Your family. You should go be with them. You don't need to see me like this." I attempt to pull my hand away, but she grips me harder.

"I am with my family, Rhys. If I didn't want to be here with you, I wouldn't be."

I groan. "You don't want to be a Dupris, Tabby. I don't even want to be a Dupris. This is going to be weeks of recovery. You didn't sign up for this."

She straightens, the shimmy of her shoulders and the regal way she holds her neck drawing my attention. "I did sign up for this. And I'd do it again."

I scoff as every destructive piece of my personality rears its ugly head. The unwanted kid, the lone-wolf teenager, the intensely private man who trusts no one. They all sit down in the driver's seat, and I'm too fucking fragile right now to stop them. "We both know you married me out of necessity. Go home."

She jerks back, blinking rapidly as though I've slapped her. It's the closest I've come to crying since this injury happened. Even the briefest glimpse of hurt on her face makes me feel nauseous.

Her voice is steely when she responds. "No."

Frustration courses through me. I've never needed help and have never been offered it either. She's stubborn as hell, and it makes me lash out. "I don't want you here!"

Her hands leave mine, and I immediately want the heat of her back on me. Her eyes fill with tears and her mouth opens and closes silently. Once. Twice. Then she shakes her head, the look of defeat on her face telling me everything I need to know.

And when she gets up and walks out without a backward glance, my stomach bottoms out and my self-loathing hits an all-time high. One tear leaks out the side of my eye.

Crying over an injury didn't seem worthwhile. But crying over driving away the best thing that's ever happened to me seems like a worthy cause.

CHAPTER 46

Tabitha

I EXIT THE DOOR, TURN RIGHT, WALK TWENTY FEET, FEELING like I'm going to hurl all over the floor, and immediately press my back against the wall and my hands against my churning stomach. I suck in big, fast breaths, trying to regain my composure because watching Rhys hurt like this is fucking killing me.

I feel helpless. I feel useless. I want nothing more than to crawl into that bed and hold him until he's better.

But he doesn't want me there.

Or so he says.

Fucking dick.

"You all right, hon?" the nurse from earlier asks me.

I give her a feeble nod and a watery smile. "Needed a second to compose myself, that's all."

She nods back, looking at me like she just *knows*. "There is something very vulnerable about being stuck in a hospital bed. Makes people do and say things they usually might not. I see it all the time."

"What about people who aren't in the hospital bed who desperately want to bludgeon their husband for being stupid and stubborn as hell? Is that something you see very often?"

She chuckles. "Actually, it is."

I nod quickly and glance away, feeling mildly embarrassed as I reach up to swipe a tear from my cheek. "Perfect, I'll have company in prison."

"Well, if you need an alibi, you just let me know." The woman winks at me, and it reminds me of Rhys.

It reminds me of what we've been through. It makes my throat ache with how much I love him. And it gives me the boost I need to walk back in there with my composure fully intact.

CHAPTER 47

Rhys

I'M ROLLING AROUND IN MY OWN PUDDLE OF SELF-PITY WHEN Tabitha appears at the door again. Relief hits me like a tidal wave.

She's back.

And she looks fucking furious.

She storms over to me, hands clenched in fists, feet stomping on the linoleum floors. She blows right up to the bed, a look of sheer determination on her pretty face as she peers over me.

"Rhys, I know you want me to leave, but that is just too fucking bad. Because I refuse. But I'll go get a coffee to give you a minute for processing purposes, and then I'm coming back and I'm going to sit in that corner. Feel free to pretend I'm not here if you need to. I don't care."

She points across the room. "And when you're done stewing in whatever feelings you're feeling right now, I will be *there*. Just like you were there for me. This is who we are now." Her eyes are so fierce, she pierces me with them. "This is what you do when you love somebody. And I have every intention of loving you just as thoroughly as I know you love me. You just have to let me." Her voice cracks, and my chest shatters.

Tears well in my eyes, and one slips out, rolling toward my hairline.

She reaches forward, wiping it away with a gentle finger. "Because even at your worst, I still love you, Rhys. Just try not to be an asshole when I get back, 'kay? Because I *am* coming back, and this tantrum is annoying."

She turns and leaves the room, forcing me to lie here with my guilt and turmoil. The ten minutes it takes her to get a coffee and come back are so excruciating that they feel like hours. She really pressed on a sore spot when she mentioned coming back.

But even assuring me doesn't completely convince me. No one has ever come back for me.

She does though.

I let out a rough sigh and close my eyes when her outline graces the doorway. She doesn't address me. She just pads to the corner of the room, where she flops into the chair and starts scrolling her phone, only peeking up from the screen to stare daggers at me.

I finally break the silence. "Why are you mean-mugging me?"

She flattens her lips but doesn't look up. "Sorry, I'll try to gaze at you lovingly from where I've been exiled."

My tongue presses against my cheek. Okay, I deserved that.

She just grunts, then smiles as her eyes zero in on her phone.

I try again. "What are you watching?"

"Raccoon videos that Gwen sent me."

"Raccoons?"

"Yeah. My next pet, I think. Hopefully, you're allergic."

My lips twitch because this feels…familiar. *Normal* in a not-normal situation.

"You can't be mean to someone with a broken back."

Her eyes roll. "Your back isn't broken. At this point, I'm more concerned about the concussion, because you're acting a fool."

I almost laugh. It's so *her* to be both furious with me and supportive in the same breath.

Someone comes in and leaves me with a contract for the procedure, which draws my attention away for a while as I read through it carefully.

I clear my throat and turn my head to look over at her. "Can I put you as my emergency contact?"

"Does a broken back make a person this confused?"

"My back isn't broken."

"Oh good. Maybe the concussion is healing after all."

God, she drives me nuts—in the best way. Calling me on my shit left and right.

"Tabby, can you just answer the question?"

"What do you think?"

I swallow, letting out a thread of my inner turmoil. "I

don't know." It seems obvious that my wife would be my emergency contact, but I just don't know right now.

She drops the phone flat on her leg, blowing out a heavy, exhausted sigh. This woman who moved mountains and traveled all night to get to me without even being asked. The truth is, I wanted her to know I was okay, but I never expected her to come.

Old habits die hard, I guess.

Her head shakes as she makes her way across the floor toward me. Then she kneels at my bedside, dropping the railing down so there's nothing blocking our view of each other. "Rhys." She props her elbow on my mattress and holds her pinky up. "I pinky promise to always come back."

My throat feels tight. It hurts to swallow. Seconds pass as I regard her. Then I wrap my pinky around hers and squeeze as I nod firmly. "I pinky promise to always come back."

"You fucking better." She laughs as she returns my nod.

And then she drapes herself over my torso, hugging me as gently as possible.

A strangled laugh bubbles up out of me as I wrap my arm around her narrow back. And *fuck*, holding her might be the best feeling in the world.

Ending up here is almost funny if I think about it. It reminds me of her marching into my house all those years ago, forcing her pinky swear on me.

I remember thinking she was fierce and loyal and fucking incredible. I remember wondering what it would feel like to have someone like Tabitha love you.

And now I know.

Surgery is a success, and five days after that, I wiggle my toes.

Tabitha is like a barnacle, stuck to my side, questioning every doctor and therapist. She refuses to leave the hospital, and our next disagreement is about her sleeping slumped in a chair. I don't like it, and she doesn't give a flying fuck. Luckily, she hits it off with one of the nurses, who takes pity on her and hides an extra rolling cot in the room.

One she pushes right next to mine. And just like before, I spend many a night watching her sleep, reveling in her nearness.

And once I'm moved out of the ICU, she makes it her mission to bring me extra meals. She's firm when she needs to be, and kind when she wants to be. I'm pretty sure she drives my therapists up the damn wall.

The only person she swaps out with is Will. He doesn't talk much, except to apologize. He looks tired and disheveled, but he never stops showing up.

He's here at physical therapy with me today because Tabitha went to a local gym to have a workout and a shower. I hate thinking that she doesn't get any downtime, that she's living out of a bag and sleeping on a shitty bed because of *me*. But she never complains, so I've decided to just surrender and let her take care of me.

She's taken time away from the restaurant, but everyone has pitched in to help. Cleo and Milo are both cared for. The walks are getting shoveled since snow has finally fallen. It's a team effort. A family effort. It's a foreign experience. But

Tabitha has shown me it's okay to lean on people. That I'm not a burden. That indeed, they will come back even when it seems inconvenient.

The guys from bowling even took a trip on Ford Grant's fancy-ass private jet to visit. It was the surprise I never expected. *Friends.*

Plus, Crazy Clyde was the absurd entertainment I never knew I needed. The man himself showed up in a wheelchair, looking sicklier than I do, while spouting off about how he knows a guy who has a medical blog that could give me a second opinion. All I need to do is send him my scans.

West laughed, and Bash and Ford groaned. It all felt... familiar somehow. A good reminder that I have so much back in Rose Hill. Even if one of those things is an old man who believes every conspiracy theory ever recorded.

Gripping the bar, I repeat sitting and standing, still experiencing lingering traces of numbness but feeling significantly better. For a while, I wasn't sure I would. But every day is an improvement.

"Kid, aren't you supposed to be back on the road?" I ask Will.

He props against the wall. "No."

"I don't need you to babysit me."

"I'm taking a break."

I look up at him as the therapist says something to me about focusing on pushing through my heel. I ignore him, glaring at Will instead. "A break?"

He shrugs. "Gotta get my head right before I step back in the ring. Maybe get more practice under my belt."

"Will, you're on track to be a company superstar. Don't do this. Don't blame yourself. Shit happens in this business sometimes. We gotta pick up and move on. I fully intend to be back in that ring, kicking your ass."

He smiles, but it's forced—flat. "Okay."

"Honey, I'm home!" Tabitha calls from the door, her hair still damp like she rushed to get back here.

"All right." Will ducks his head like he can barely face Tabitha. "I'm out."

He breezes past her, but she follows him into the hallway, where I see her wrap him in a firm hug that he barely returns. It chokes me up a little to see him suffering like this, and I don't know what to tell him to make it better.

I hope Tabitha does. I watch her lips move as she holds him by the shoulders. Tiny little spitfire manhandling a huge professional wrestler. She gives him a little shake, no doubt doling out her own special brand of tough love.

He said he was going to win her over, but I doubt he realizes that he already has.

When she walks back in, she seems distracted. I can see the wheels turning as her teeth strum at her bottom lip, but that faraway look disappears when my physio announces, "Honestly, I think you can go home."

CHAPTER 48

Rhys

"I THINK BREAKING YOUR BACK MADE YOU A BETTER BOWLER," West exclaims as I throw my first ever strike.

Although I still feel a slight unsteadiness, I am officially healed enough to bowl—which I am unexpectedly excited about.

Bash groans and scrubs a hand over his face. "Do you ever think before you open your mouth?"

Ford's dry "No" makes me laugh.

West just chuckles, rolling with the punches. "What fun would that be? You smile so pretty when I say shit like that."

That gets chuckles from Ford and me, but not Bash. He stares at West with his best resting bitch face. He's always been friendly enough with me. I can't tell if his humor is just really dry or if he's genuinely in this bad of a mood all the time.

"Ooh. You're hitting me with the Gwen smolder. I like it!"

Now it's Ford's and my turn to groan. We all know there's something weird between them, but usually we tiptoe around it. Bash isn't exactly forthcoming.

"There is no Gwen smolder."

Ford scoffs. "There is *definitely* a smolder."

Bash turns to me, clearly searching for backup since the two of us have forged a tentative sort of friendship.

I take a long pull of my beer and tip my head from side to side as though I'm considering. "Sorry, man. I gotta say, there is a smolder."

"See? Everyone knows. It's just… There's an *energy*." West is teasing, but Bash does not look amused.

"Don't mock her. You can mock me, but not her." The words come out snippy, and I quirk a brow at him. "Don't give me that look. She's my son's ex-girlfriend. That suggestive eyebrow lift is not necessary."

I still. We've talked about security systems. We've talked about bowling. But never once have we talked about his family.

"Wait, how old is your son?" One thing I've appreciated about Bash is that he doesn't pry. So I have never pried back.

"Twenty-four."

"Huh." I wasn't expecting that. "How old are you?"

West gets the giggles, and Bash rolls his eyes. "Forty. Young enough to give Clyde a kidney."

We all freeze, and I marvel at the way he managed to shock us all into a brand-new conversation.

"Crazy Clyde?" Ford asks with a furrowed brow.

"Yep."

"Does Clyde know about this?" West asks, all of us nodding, because there is no one who spews more conspiracy theories than Clyde. "He seems like an…unlikely candidate?"

Bash shrugs. "He has come to terms with the *fact* that he will be getting a new kidney along with a government tracking device."

"*Wild*," Ford mumbles, shaking his head.

Bash shrugs again. "I've got two. We're a match. And I can take the winter off to recover, be back in action for fire season."

"You're a lot nicer than you look, Bash." West slaps the older man's shoulder appreciatively, which only gets him a glare that looks like it might kill him.

The night carries on in good spirits. Teasing and camaraderie and a mutual distaste for Stretch, who pitches an absolute fucking fit when we *finally* beat him.

It feels surprisingly similar to becoming a universal champion.

When Stretch walks over and runs his mouth, I stare him down with my best Wild Side glare, lifting my hands up and miming a twisting motion like I'm wringing out a dish rag.

As expected, he skulks away and avoids eye contact when I pass him on my way out. News of my profession has spread through town, and I can't help but wonder if he's a bit scared of me.

I hope he is.

I cruise down the highway, feeling happier than I can ever remember. I'm headed *home*. To a house where a woman

I love lives. Where a little boy I love lives. Some days, I pinch myself with how fortunate I am.

Every day I spend married to Tabitha Garrison, I feel more whole and settle into this being real, and not some fever dream. I fall asleep next to her every night, and I wake with her in my arms every morning.

I itch to get back in the ring—which some people have opinions on. But not Tabitha. She knows that having a purpose is important. She knows hard work. She knows I'll be happiest pursuing my passion.

And the same goes for her. Her restaurant is thriving—especially since I paid off the loans she took out against it to put Erika through rehab. She had her own moment over that but eventually relented when I brought her sentiments full circle.

We're a team. Let me help you.

The more time we spend together, the more all the lines in the sand between us blow away. What was hers and mine became ours. And for the first time in my life, I don't feel the need to hoard and hide and protect.

I let her in, and I think it healed me in a way. My therapist thinks so too.

When I enter the house, I know she's up because the patio lights are glowing through the windows. Spring has sprung, and she's back to sitting outside every chance she gets.

I trudge through the house, going straight to her. But not before Cleo intercepts me with her signature *prow prow prow* as she comes trotting out of thin air.

"Hello, sweet girl," I murmur, lifting her up and holding

her like a baby. She purrs instantly, nuzzling against me. And I don't even pretend I don't enjoy it. I carry her out onto the back patio. Tabitha is there, under the heater I bought her, waiting for me.

"I thought I was your sweet girl?" Tabitha asks from where she's seated with crossed arms and one quirked brow.

I chuckle and place Cleo on one of the chairs before striding straight to the love seat and lifting Tabitha onto my lap. My hands fall to her hips as she straddles me and grips my shirt. I kiss her soundly, sighing the moment her tongue tangles with mine.

Home.

I pull away only to tease her. "No. My Tabby Cat isn't sweet. She's spicy. Sometimes even salty."

Her arms wrap around my neck, and she sticks her bottom lip out dramatically. "The only thing I'm salty about is that Cleo loves you so much more than me when you"—her fingers lift in air quotes—"hate cats."

I shift to look over Tabitha's shoulder. "Don't listen to her, Cleo. I *love* cats."

I hear Tabitha let out an amused scoff, but something on the table catches my eye. Milo's monitor sits dead center, along with a legal-size manila envelope beside it.

"What's in the envelope?" I ask, leaning back to meet her gaze.

Her head joggles as though she's searching for an explanation. "An idea."

My forehead scrunches as I hug her close and reach forward for it, curiosity getting the best of me.

She doesn't stop me when I open the envelope right between us and reach inside.

"If you don't like the idea, that's okay."

All I feel is paper.

"Like, I don't want to offend you in any way. I just..."

She rambles on as I pull the sheets out. Her voice fades away as I soak up the words on the page. Terms like *legal name change* and *name of a spouse* pop out.

"What is this?" My hands shake.

"I thought maybe you'd want to be a Garrison. You, me, and Milo? *So* presumptuous of me. I just hate knowing you don't like your last name. Feeling like we're all together might be nice? I don't know. Maybe I'm out to lunch. If you don't want—"

Rhys Garrison.

I don't let her say anything more. With the papers crinkling between us, I lean forward and kiss her, my hand at the back of her head. It's firm and desperate. It ends with our foreheads resting together and my whispered words lingering between us.

"Yes, please."

CHAPTER 49

Tabitha

THE ROSEBUSHES ARE BUDDING IN MY FAVORITE SPOT, AND that summer feeling in the mountains makes everything feel warm and hazy. The sun beats down on my skin, and Milo's laughter as he and Rhys run down the hill is music to my ears.

I watch as Rhys scoops him up and twirls him, rubbing his beard against the side of his neck until the little boy squeals. His movements are sure and powerful, his recovery nothing short of a miracle.

He's back in the ring, doing what he loves. He comes home often, also to do what he loves. Which is being with us.

Everything between us is so...easy. That uphill climb has made the flatland stroll an absolute dream. We walk hand in hand, knowing that there isn't much life can throw our way that we won't be able to tackle together.

I've never felt more secure in my life than I do knowing

that Rhys is here now, and that even when he's not, he'll always come back.

I'm propped on my hands, legs outstretched before me, the old sleeping bag laid flat beneath me as I admire them.

My sister's urn is at my side.

"You know what I've learned through this all, sissy?"

She doesn't respond, because why the hell would she?

"Life is all just shades of gray. People are shades of gray. You. Me. Rhys. Mom and Dad. No one is perfect. I think Milo might be pure light. For now, anyway. But I'm sure he'll disappoint me one day." I snort. "After all, he's related to us. And god knows you and I aren't perfect. But you know what? That's okay. That's just…being human. I don't think I've ever known someone more unapologetically *human* than you. You did some bad shit, but you did some really incredible shit too. You left me…"

I turn and lift the brass container, watching the sun spark off the metallic finish. "But look what you left me with." Milo is mauling Rhys. Now that he's more aware of what Rhys does for work, he likes to try his hand at wrestling with him when he's home. There's zero polish to his attacks, but joy lines his every movement. "Look at them." My voice cracks. "I wish you could see them. And maybe you can. I hope you can. I know that for all our complicated feelings about each other…I know seeing this would have made you happy. I only ever wanted you to be happy."

I swipe a tear off my cheek. The ache of missing my sister is no less sharp, but now I can cry happy tears over her rather than just sad ones.

"I don't think you'd be pleased about sitting on my shelf in a jar. It just doesn't feel very… you. I think here—on the wild side of the mountain—might be where you belong."

I twist the lid, swallowing as it loosens. I reach in, feeling the fine ash slip through my fingers. And I smile as I watch my sister's ashes dance across the wind.

When I inhale, it feels like my lungs are filling with more air than I've breathed in years. It feels like here, Erika can be safe and free and with us all at once. I do it alone, because it feels like I need to. And when the urn is empty, all I want are my boys.

When I look down toward them, Rhys is already watching me. Because of course he is. His eyes are always on me. He's always supporting me—quietly, gently. In that way of his that feels like a warm blanket wrapped around me on a cold day.

When I hit him with a watery smile, his head tilts. I can see the question in his eyes. He knows I needed that moment with my sister. I needed that closure. I didn't need an audience, but he still managed to be here for me. Like he always is.

But now I want them both closer. I want to hold them. I want to be all together. And like they just *know*, both of them walk up the hill toward me. Hand in hand.

"I wanna pick out shapes in the clouds," Milo declares with pink cheeks and a wide smile.

All I can do is nod and stare back at him, marveling over how much I love him. I think I'd do absolutely anything for this little boy.

Rhys must see the emotion on my face, because he ushers Milo to one side of me before he takes a position on the other. My boys flank me and we watch the sky together, picking out shapes until we all fall into a companionable silence. Their warmth heats me to my marrow. Nothing has ever felt more perfect. I let my eyes flutter shut to soak up the moment, only made sweeter by Milo's soft voice cutting through the hush of the mountain.

"That one kind of looks like fingers. Hooked together."

I smile and turn to my side, drawing Milo into me. Slotting him right against my front. He smells a little bit like Erika and feels a lot like home. As does the man who presses closer behind me. Spooning me just like I'm spooning Milo.

When he wraps his arm over us, his pinky links with mine.

And we drift off like that, under a bluebird sky with big puffy clouds floating above us.

Together.

EPILOGUE

Rhys

FOUR YEARS LATER...

THE ROPES SLAP AGAINST MY BACK AS I GO FLYING STRAIGHT at Will, sending him down hard with an outstretched arm. He flies backward in a perfect arc before rolling over on his side, gripping his lower back dramatically.

I try not to smile, but this is my last match. And I'm having a hell of a time.

The crowd has fallen into their usual *This is awesome* chant that almost always gets pulled out when Wild Side and Million Dollar Bill wrestle. After years of practice, it feels like the two of us could do this with our eyes closed. I refused to have it against anyone other than Will. It's taken him a long time to come back from my accident. But he's been one of my longest-standing friends, and he's a wrestler I respect immensely.

There's no other way I'd rather go out.

Turning away, I place a foot on the rope and look into the crowd, soaking up the view of green merchandise as far as the eye can see.

It's been four years since I thought I might never get to stand in the ring and look out over this view again. And now I'm back at Pure Pandemonium for one last match.

It's the last time I'll look out over a sea of people this way. The last time I'll climb the ropes and hear people chanting my name.

And oddly, I'm not sad about it at all. I'm ready.

My eyes drop lower, to the front row of floor seats where my wife sits.

Milo, now seven years old, sits on one side of her waving a sign that reads *Wild Side is my dad* in the messy scrawl of a small child.

Our daughter, Minka Garrison, is wrapped against her chest with a pair of lime-green earmuffs covering her shock of dark hair.

My in-laws, Lisa and Paul, are here too—decked out in every piece of Wild Side gear that money can buy.

I get lost for a moment, staring at them all. My family. My home. Seeing all these people who've cheered me on for so many years, I'm overcome with gratitude.

For this life. For this adventure. For all this love.

I shake my head and let my lips tip up as I gaze out over the culmination of everything I've been through.

It took me a long time to get to this place, but I've finally made peace with feeling like I deserve all the happiness I have. I've worked hard for it, and now I plan to spend the rest of my days enjoying everything I've been given.

Tabitha winks at me and gives her chin a nudge in my direction, knocking me out of my stupor.

Poor Will. I almost chuckle. He's going to kill me for making him play up that back pain for this long.

I wink back at my wife and continue my climb to the top rope. The roar of the crowd's cheers buzzes across my skin and blocks out any other sounds or thoughts.

Only as I look down over my friend—who is still writhing in "pain"—do I make one final symbolic gesture. Slowly and with intention, I peel my mask back and off my face. The noise in the arena hits a deafening decibel, and I finally grin.

Then I turn and toss the mask toward my girl. She catches it and, without hesitation, pulls it over her face before standing up, clapping in time, and joining the crowd in their cheers.

I laugh, because suddenly, I'm back in that unfinished basement chasing Tabitha around. She's laughing, wearing *my* mask and *my* ring. And it feels just as thrilling. I'm even more obsessed with her now than I was then.

As I take my last leap from the top rope, an entire lifetime of adventures flashes before my eyes.

I've been a lot of things in my life. Traveled a lot of places too.

But now I'm not just a wrestler. I'm a dad, I'm a friend, and I'm a husband to Tabitha Garrison, the mega-hot brunette who makes the best carbonara in the world.

And it strikes me that *this* is my favorite thing I've ever been.

READ ON FOR A SNEAK PEEK AT THE NEXT BOOK IN THE ROSE HILL SERIES, *WILD CARD*

Bash

ONE YEAR AGO...

I'M STUCK IN AN AIRPORT, AND EVERYONE IS ANNOYING ME.

"We're delayed again, but it's so beautiful outside that I don't even mind," a voice singsongs from the row of blue pleather chairs behind me. It's a nice voice. Rich and calm and not at all frustrated by being stranded in a snowstorm. "I feel like I'm living in a snow globe or something."

I scoff, flexing my fists beneath my crossed arms. We've been waiting to board for three hours and this woman *doesn't even mind*.

And I believe her. I don't bother looking in her direction, but I can tell by her tone, the awe seeping into every word, that she's probably never seen snow and would describe this nightmare as *cozy*.

"Yeah, honestly...it's cozy."

Yep. There it is. Whoever she is, she's enjoying this.

Must be fucking nice, because I'm ready to crawl right out of my skin. People sneezing without covering their faces, babies crying, the smell of stale bagels. I've walked laps like a tiger pacing his cage and even that isn't taking the edge off anymore.

Leave it to Vancouver to be the only place in Canada that doesn't know how to handle a snowstorm. And it's not even *that* bad.

The crackle of the speakers filters through the low hum of Gate 82's waiting area. "Attention all passengers awaiting boarding for Air Acadia Flight 2375 with service to Calgary. We regret to inform you that your flight has been canceled and rescheduled for tomorrow morning. You should receive an email shortly with updated flight information. Please see a booking agent if you require further assistance. We appreciate your patience and understanding and look forward to serving you tomorrow."

A communal groan rolls through the space.

My head drops back against the metal top of the chair, and I let out an exhausted sigh. It's been a crappy week, and this is just the bread that makes the whole thing a shit sandwich.

I'd empty my entire bank account just to sleep in my own bed tonight. To be alone with some fucking peace and quiet. To *decompress*.

Instead, I am being fully compressed. Every muscle feels tight, and my jaw hurts from clenching it. Even my lungs feel constricted.

This was the last thing I needed after having my entire world turned upside down.

"Yeah, canceled." That too-happy voice floats through the air toward me. "It's okay. It is what it is. I'm going to make the most of it! When life gives you lemons..."

It squeezes the acid right into your fucking eyes. I push to my feet.

A peek over my shoulder reveals a shock of wavy platinum hair draped over the woman's face as she riffles through an oversized bag, her phone pressed to her ear. I can see the dainty lines of a tattoo wrapping around her forearm—a vine with small leaves that disappear beneath the sleeve of her cream-colored sweater.

My brows scrunch low as she *laughs* at whatever the person on the other end of the line has said. I shake my head as I turn away and heft my bags onto my shoulder, deciding she's altogether too happy. It's not normal.

For some reason, her cheerfulness sours my mood even further. So, with my heavy footfalls echoing on the polished concrete floors, I head toward the booking agent's desk to see if there's a way I can get the hell out of here.

Waiting in line doesn't ease my annoyance. As it turns out, I'm not the only one in a foul mood. An angry middle-aged man ahead of me has gone from agitated to a full-blown meltdown. I watch him wind up right before my eyes. He points his index finger at the frazzled customer service representative, demanding she fix this—as if she personally created the snowstorm.

He's mad about his bags. He's mad about the lack of

available accommodations. He's mad about the new early flight time.

I'm mad too, but I'm not punching down over it. And the longer I watch, the more I'm just mad about what a royal asshole this guy is.

The girl's cheeks darken and her bottom lip wobbles. When her eyes fill as she shrinks back from his tirade, I've had it.

"My man." I project my deep voice toward the desk. "Shit happens. No need to speak to her that way."

Heads swivel in my direction, including the one belonging to the red-faced man. "Excuse me?" His jowls vibrate with fury, his lip curling beneath his thick mustache as his eyes narrow on me. I get the sense that he's not accustomed to people telling him off.

I shrug. Looking nonchalant is the ultimate affront to someone who wields their power in such a belittling way. "Take a walk," I say in a low rumble. "It is what it is."

"It is what it is?" His eyes bug out, his pie-face turning an even deeper shade of red.

I can't believe I just used that woman's line on this guy, but I'm getting a kick out of confronting him, so I borrow another sentiment from Mrs. Happy.

"Yeah, it's like, when life gives you lemons…don't be an asshole to the service staff. Or something like that."

The man stares at me, and I stare back. His gaze sweeps over my favorite plaid flannel shirt, then down over my black jeans and leather boots. I'm bigger than him, and while it's been a few years since I threw a punch, I'm not above it. I may be pushing forty, but I'm in great shape, and it might feel good to release this tension.

His beady eyes skitter across the quiet crowd, as though assessing how embarrassed he should be (the answer is very embarrassed). He must realize I'm not an easy target, because he turns back to the woman behind the desk—who looks suitably shocked—and swipes his paper ticket off the counter before storming away as fast as his furious little legs will carry him.

Watching him waddle away in a huff makes my lips twitch.

And here I thought nothing could make me smile tonight.

Though her shy *thank you* pulls on my heartstrings a bit, my polite exchange with the agent behind the desk doesn't make anything any better—the closest hotels have no availability because of other cancellations, and our flight has been rescheduled for a 6 a.m. departure.

It's currently 11:08, which means by the time I get through the hellish traffic in and around the city to a place with a vacancy, I might as well turn right back around since I'll need to clear security all over again. The only reasonable solution is to sleep on a bench in the terminal.

Everything about tonight sucks, but I swallow my frustration like a real man and thank her for her help before leaving to find a place to hunker down for the night.

Tired legs carry me through the airport as I scan for a spot where I can go horizontal for a few hours. Years of battling active forest fires has left me with the uncanny ability to doze off almost anywhere and function with little sleep. Wildfires don't care about your bedtime and often like to do their worst after dark, so I'm no stranger to catching some shut eye in uncomfortable places.

Except, I'm not the only person who seems to have resigned themself to sleeping at the airport tonight.

I stand in place, hands on my hips, searching for even a free corner, but the place is like a fucking hostel, people and bags splayed all over the place.

The only place my eyes land on that has a free spot is the bar. One lone table for two at the edge of the seating area, tucked right next to the walkway that leads to the bathroom. It's not glamorous, but it's something. And a drink sounds pretty damn good right now.

ACKNOWLEDGMENTS

Obviously, I first and foremost have to acknowledge the one and only Tribal Chief, Roman Reigns. Just kidding (sort of—only the wrestling girlies will get that joke), but if you aren't familiar, you should probably Google him for a little bit of my Rhys inspiration.

Honestly, writing a book that involves a sport I enjoyed watching as a kid (and have recently gotten back into with my own child) was a freaking riot. From attending live events, doing a deep dive on the inner workings of the business, and listening to autobiographies read by actual wrestlers, the research for this book was just plain FUN.

If any of you are looking for a great read (or audiobook, because there's something so heartwarming about listening to her read the book) set in the world of professional wrestling, check out *Becky Lynch: The Man: Not Your Average Average Girl* by Rebecca Quinn. It's a fabulous story that I know I will continue to reflect on often.

So aside from The Rock (one of my first crushes), Roman Reigns, and Becky Lynch, I do have some people to thank for helping me publish yet another book.

First, my husband. My actual rock (lol). This was a big year for us. A lot of incredible highs and a few pretty heartbreaking lows. Basically, it was another year of me realizing there's no one I'd rather have at my side through it all. I love you.

My son, my sunshine. My happy boy who makes even the worst days feel so much better. I love you to the moon and back.

My assistant, Krista. It's been three years now and you are still the most incredible support. A safe space to laugh, bitch, and cry. Thank you not only for your hard work but also for your friendship.

My editor, Paula Dawn. This is our TWELFTH book together. You make me laugh, you make me think, you make me a better writer. Here's to twelve more!

My beta reader/proofreader, Leticia Teixeira. Your dedication to me and these characters is unrivaled. Thank you, thank you for your tireless support. I love the way you read a love story, and I especially love that the universe brought us together.

Aimee Ashcraft, I have quickly become incredibly attached to your feedback. Thank you for whipping this manuscript into shape. I know you loved this book the way that I do, which means that not only are great at your job, but you have exceptional taste.

My agent, Kimberly Brower, who has been my biggest champion and confidante this year. My career would not be what it is without you. Thank you, a million times, for believing in me and for always having my back. And a special shoutout to everyone at Brower Literary who works so hard to make every publication possible.

My editor, Christa Désir—working with you is always a highlight. Thank you for reading one of my books once upon a time and thinking there was something there. I wholeheartedly believe I am where I am today because of you.

My publicist, Katie Stutz. I just…adore you. This year I've gotten to travel with you, meet you at Disneyland, and advise you on which Crocs you should and should not buy. I wouldn't have it any other way.

And to the entire team at Bloom Books, I am forever grateful for the love you all put into publishing. I am honored to be part of the team.

My editors, Rebekah West and Anna Boatman, and the entire team at Piatkus and Hachette. Thank you for your endless hard work and thank you for sharing my books with the world. Seeing them in the hands of readers from so many places is such a thrill.

Finally, to my readers. You blow me away every day. Your love. Your support. Your excitement. I'm so lucky to have every last one of you. Thank you for trusting me and following me to Rose Hill. I hope you love it here as much as I do.

I say it pretty much every book, but I'll say it again: Elsie readers are the best readers.

xo,
Elsie

ABOUT THE AUTHOR

Elsie Silver is a *New York Times* bestselling author of sassy, sexy, small town romance. She's a born and raised Canadian girl who loves a good book boyfriend and the strong heroines who bring them to their knees. Her books promise banter, tension, and a slow burn that comes to a screeching halt.

Website: elsiesilver.com
Facebook: authorelsiesilver
Instagram: @authorelsiesilver